SHOT IN THE DARK

MARY DUBLIN
ANNE KENDSLEY

Book Cover by Mary Dublin

First edition 2024.

PRONUNCIATION GUIDE

Nowak – [n-OH-v-ack]

Elysia – [eh-LIHZ-iy-ah]

Laelithar – [lay-LIH-thar]

Daeharice – [day-HARE-is]

Caerthynna – [kay-er-THIN-uh]

Aelthorin – [AL-thor-in]

Cliff – ~~[KLIF]~~ *a damn delight*

SHOT IN THE DARK

MARY DUBLIN
ANNE KENDSLEY

"The banter between the characters had me laughing out loud at some points and gasping and close to tears at others."
-Kendra, Goodreads

"It has to be one of the best fantasy books I've ever read. The banter among them is refreshing in a story that combines the ethereal beauty of the fairy fantasy world with the threat of real monsters. It's like the perfect combination of murder, mystery, romance and magic."
-Julia, Goodreads

"Kendsley and Dublin weave a narrative as magical as the protagonist herself – a spell-binding tale of trust, danger, and kinship beyond boundaries."
-Fabian, Goodreads

"It's a world you will want to stay in forever... To anyone missing Sam and Dean Winchester, feels the pull of old magic on their fairy souls, feels their blood pounding at the thought of hunting evil with a shotgun and a knife, or even just longs to fall in love... pick this book up."
-Cortnie, Goodreads

"You will be left wanting more."
-Jenn, Goodreads

CONTENT WARNING

This fantasy story includes some content that may be troubling for some readers, including:

Profanity, kidnapping/captivity, loss of a parent, violence, and blood.

"There is a charm about the forbidden that makes it unspeakably desirable."

-Mark Twain

DEDICATION

For everyone who grew up building fairy houses,

and for those spirited girls still looking for their place in this world.

1

SYLVIA

From what I understood, Alice had died slowly and painfully over a hundred years ago. Luckily, ghosts appeared to have a selective memory. Alice didn't recall her final days unless prompted. So, I did my best not to prompt.

I entered the decrepit Dottage mansion through the shattered attic window. The building was massive, even by human standards. The attic alone could hold the entirety of Elysia and then some. Alice seemed to be the only restless spirit who wandered the countless rooms. Still, her presence could make me jump out of my skin if I wasn't prepared, so I perched on the dusty dresser to get her ominous arrival over with.

"Hello?" I called. "Are you here? Don't you dare sneak up on me this time."

Sure enough, the music box sitting beside me slowly creaked open on its own. A familiar, out-of-tune melody tinkled through the attic. The tiny likeness of a human man and woman steadily spun together in the middle of the velvet-lined box.

My skin and wings prickled with vicious cold, and my breath puffed visibly through my lips. A warning pang in my gut accompanied the crescendo of my heartbeat. I muscled down the overload of sensations and managed to smile as Alice materialized in the corner of the attic.

Emerging from the shadows, she looked the same as ever: soft strawberry blonde curls tumbling over one shoulder, a slim dress cinched at the waist, and pouty lips untouched by color.

I had shrieked myself hoarse the first time I saw her several months ago. Her response to my panic had been a mere tilt of her head before she went about her business—a melancholy beauty trapped in a loop. She hadn't lunged or tried to devour me, as I had always been warned humans were inclined to do. She had never once commented that she and I were wholly different. Maybe dead humans were less ornery than living ones.

A soft smile graced her delicate features when she spotted me tonight. "Sasha!"

"Sylvia," I corrected flatly. At least she got the first letter of my name right this time.

"Sylvia! You're back again." Lately, she had been looking at me with more recognition. Her milky gaze drifted to the broken window and became distant. "Is he here too?" she asked with a dampened tone.

"I'm sorry. He's not. You'll have to suffer through my company for now." If only Alice could remember her own tragedy, I wouldn't have to routinely disappoint her. Reminders that her lover was long dead never went over well.

Alice brushed a hand over the music box, her ghostly fingertips lingering on the lid's engraving. *To My Beloved*. I had traced my fingers through the grooves more than once, wondering how a human artisan could carve such steady, elegant letters.

"He'll come for me soon," Alice said wistfully. "I'd better make myself presentable. Can't have him see me in such a state."

The same words every time. She began to mime rifling through her wardrobe and makeup, preparing for a dance she would never attend. She hummed in time with the music box's off-kilter melody, though her haunting voice hit the precise notes of the lullaby.

I couldn't bear to look at her when she was like this, so I observed the little dancing couple instead. Before exploring this mansion, I never thought humans would understand anything as refined as dancing. The couple's embrace didn't look all that different from the moonlit revels that took place outside the village—only this was a much softer, slower version. Maybe only humans of the past danced like this.

From the attic window, the nearby human city lights blazed like a line of wildfire cutting through the forest. For all I knew, humans were dancing among those angular towers at that very moment. If I had any talent with glamour, I would have sought the answer long ago, like nomads of past generations.

Alice continued to carry out her routine like a dutiful prisoner within the walls of her crumbling house. I could sympathize—being trapped, unable to roam as she pleased. Perhaps her lack of lucidity was a blessing that spared her this pain. I often wished I could help her, but I had learned to muscle down the fruitless instinct to make her see reality. There was nothing that could be done—much less by the fairy pilfering from her belongings.

I folded my wings to my back and wandered around the music box. The dresser was scattered with personal effects, frozen in time. I padded across a stack of yellowed letters bound by a ribbon. Scrawls of elegant ink stretched across the pages, but the writing was too faded to make out. In any case, I was more interested in the jewelry.

Alice must've been quite the socialite back in her day. A string of pearls beckoned to me from within a cushioned velvet box, their luster slightly dulled by time. Next to them was a pair of ornate earrings with rubies so large that I could barely heft one into my arms. The silver locket was small enough to carry, but after considering the sullen black-and-white image encased inside, I decided it was too precious to take. This could have very well been another gift from Alice's lost lover. Even if she didn't remember, I couldn't do that to her.

The stars smiled on me when I found a charm bracelet. I knelt, sorting through the various charms: a horse's head, a coin, a violin, a skull with diamonds in its eye sockets. I shivered at this last one, seeing as it was nearly the size of my own skull.

I held a charm shaped like a working bell, grinning at the dangling piece inside. Hazel would love this. After glancing over my shoulder at Alice, still humming her endless melody, I decided this prize was safe enough. She wouldn't notice a stray charm missing any more than the other trinkets I had nicked away over the past months.

After carefully prying open the bell's attachment ring, I marveled at the little emerald inlaid at the top of the charm. The dagger strapped to my thigh had a similar gemstone fused to the hilt.

"My father used to bring things like this to me from other forests—even from mountains and human cities," I said loud enough for Alice to hear. "Of course, that was before the council put an end to gem scavenging. Not that I entirely blame them."

Father. My heart ached at the image of him kneeling down with a glowing smile to show me what he'd brought back from his latest venture. Everything felt warmer when you were only nine summers, immortalized in the golden space of memories. I'd felt his spirit in me the very moment I caught a glimpse of this mysterious house months ago: the lurch in me to venture beyond what was familiar and known. *Freedom isn't a privilege; it's a birthright worth fighting for,* he'd told me with fervor.

As much as an idiot he'd been, Father was right about *that.* I felt alive here, outside the forest. And feeling alive was worth breaking every rule for.

I waved the bell charm over my head. Maybe drawing attention to my theft was a tad reckless, but I welcomed a genuine reaction from her nearly as much as I craved an addition to my collection. Alice continued humming obliviously.

"You humans can't tell the difference between a magic-charged gem and an empty one, can you?" I asked. "And yet you love them all the same. You adorn yourselves with them."

"That's wonderful, Sarah," Alice said, rouging her cheeks with an invisible brush.

Sighing, I tucked the bell into my bag. "Well, this is a perfectly ordinary gem, in case you were wondering."

When Alice showed no interest, I turned my attention elsewhere. I doubted she would even notice I was gone. Although many of the doors were shut tight, the wide-open areas on the ground floor held no such barriers.

Despite the distance I put between myself and Alice, the strange sensation of her presence continued to chill my skin as I followed the stairway. Perhaps this meant she was more present in her manifestation tonight, and with any luck, she could be better company later.

I found myself in a room that might have been a parlor once. Furniture was scant or beyond repair, but the fireplace was mostly intact.

Beckoning my skin's glow to brighten, I flitted through the open grate and peeked up the chimney. My cerulean light washed the ashy bricks around me, but darkness ate away overhead. Perhaps I could reach another room if I found an opening through this passage.

My idea disintegrated when a creak came from somewhere below me.

I froze. Another creak followed. And another.

Then, muffled voices.

Holding my breath and lowering my light, I flew out from the fireplace and listened hard. The voices floated from behind the basement door across the room. I had visited that vast space once and found nothing of interest. Now, the basement was by far the most interesting thing I could hope for.

More ghosts?

Cautiously, I approached the ajar door.

"There's nowhere else to go!" A woman's voice, whispery and tearful.

The answering man's voice was harsh enough to make me halt. "We don't have a choice!"

More creaks aggressively approached the other side of the door. Heavy footsteps on the stairs. My throat closed. Ghosts didn't have footsteps.

I darted aside just in time to avoid being whacked by the door as it swung open. The whining squeak of the hinges and the arguing voices overpowered my cry of surprise. I covered my mouth and hid behind the open door. Thudding footsteps entered the room.

Humans.

I was within reach of living, breathing humans with only a rotting wooden door to protect me. If I flew out in search of a hiding place, they'd spot me. If I stayed where I was, they'd hear the hum of my wings. In my panic, I saw no choice but to land on the ground and huddle against the wall behind the door.

"But you don't *know* they're after us," the woman insisted.

The humans idled in front of the open basement. Swallowing hard, I lowered myself to peek beneath the bottom of the door. Shoes stirred the dust and made the floorboards groan.

"I'm telling you, these guys on our tail… I got a look in their trunk, and it's fucking insane. They've got guns. Traps. All sorts of shit, like psycho monster hunters you'd see in a movie."

Hunters.

Images of sharp teeth, bloodshot eyes, and dirty, grabbing hands flashed through my mind's eye. Elysia had no shortage of stories to be shared over the ember nooks that branched off from the dining hall. Over the gentle dance of these perpetual flames, beloved narratives were woven of fairy warriors alongside the chilling tales of hunters—humans driven by insatiable bloodlust and armored in the bones of the monsters that died at their hands. They saw no difference between fairies and vicious creatures of the night—prey was prey. A trail of destruction followed everywhere they went.

As I had grown older, I had often assumed these harrowing stories were nothing more than added fodder to discourage unruly fairies from wandering past the perimeter. Elysia was so wrapped in protective glamour that even the most bloodthirsty human would likely walk in circles until they died of exhaustion if they dared to threaten our village. Now, a fresh thrill of fear rushed through me. Hunters were real, and they were nearby.

The woman sniffled. "B-but maybe they—"

"Stop arguing," the man snapped. "I'll find a place. For now, let's get you home, and you keep your mouth shut. You got it?"

She made another sniffling sound that might have been a confirmation.

The man sighed. "I'm sorry, baby. I'll take care of us. I promise."

A set of creaking footsteps thudded dangerously close. The door flew away from me and swung back into its frame. I held absolutely still against the wall, wishing more desperately than ever that I was skilled at glamour to hide myself. I peeked up, unable to distinguish the humans as any more than overwhelming shadows.

Stars, all they had to do was look down to spot me.

But they didn't. As their footsteps trailed away, I peered a little higher and saw their backs were turned.

Not wasting the opportunity, I bolted into the air and made a beeline for the stairway that led to the upper floors.

"Did you hear something?" the woman gasped.

I was far out of earshot before I could hear the man's response.

Without pausing to say goodbye to Alice, I darted through the attic and out the broken window. I didn't slow until I was safely past the treeline. The air warmed as I left Alice and her music box behind. My breaths came easier.

Perching on a branch, I let my shoulders sag as I caught my breath. My mind raced.

The mansion wasn't always empty. On occasion, there was a car or two outside. Objects were sometimes added to or removed from the vast decaying rooms. But never, *never* had I been within the mansion's walls at the same time as a living human—let alone two. I heard the Elders' constant warnings echo—*nothing but death awaits beyond our boundaries.* For the first time in months, I acknowledged some truth in their words. Tonight's visit could have cost me my life.

Safe, I told myself. *You're safe now.*

As my pounding heart calmed, I was a touch disappointed that my visit had been cut short. At least I'd managed to swipe one treasure. Unlike the bigger objects I stashed under the attic floorboards, I could hide the little charm in my bedroom.

I hoped the two humans wouldn't find my stash. Then again, they seemed concerned with different matters than stolen jewelry.

Hunters. A shudder ran through me. I didn't think they would hunt their own kind, but if the stories were anything to go by, hunters would surely relish spilled blood no matter who it came from.

Pushing the images of sharp teeth and rusted weapons from my mind, I focused on the task of returning to Elysia without getting caught with contraband.

The forest air was pleasantly cool at night, rich with the scent of earth and dew-covered grass. The distant hoot of an owl quashed any temptation to take a more leisurely route. The flight home was best made swiftly and silently. I was intended for better things than being an owl's dinner.

The branches overhead intertwined like a lattice, framing a patchwork of shimmering stars. My heart leaped to my throat, the sight dazzling. Clear nights were for watching the sky with Father, naming the constellations. The String of Sapphires pointed the way home.

The gnarled oaks gave way to a gathering of willow trees. I veered my flight toward the proudest among them, towering with its thick green tresses. I slowed my wing beats, grabbing hold of a frond and peering inside the grove. I let myself sway with the breeze, as pliant as the leaves. Invisible without my glow.

A fellow fairy, fitted with a snug warrior's uniform, glided along the looping tree roots. I watched his path, noting the route he'd been assigned to. If he was on lower patrol, the upper two would be circling the tree's exterior right now. When he was out of sight, I sprang back into motion.

Sneaking past the perimeter guards was second nature to me now. At the risk of sounding conceited, I was probably the stealthiest fairy in the whole village. I had avoided detection dozens of times since I started venturing out to the old human house.

Not that the competition was terribly fierce. Most fairies outgrew the rebellious urge to fly beyond Elysia's boundaries at the age of eighteen. I was twenty-one summers now, and any excuses made on my behalf were growing brittle and strained.

Starlight struggled to pierce through as the foliage became denser with my approach to the willow's base entrance. Glowing orbs and white luminescent flowers took charge of visibility, though I avoided getting too close to them. Hugging the shadows, I paused again, waiting for another patrolling guard to move along.

From there, dropping toward the roots and snaking my way to the entrance was child's play. No one raised the alarm, and before long, I was deep enough underground to pretend I'd never broken curfew. A harmless midnight stroll through my favorite tunnels was no crime.

Light roots crawled along the earthen ceiling. Pathways opened into larger hubs that branched out in all directions. The guards were far more relaxed here.

I silently thanked the stars that Ayden didn't appear to be on duty tonight. Every breath I took was grounds for his suspicion these days. If he caught me with a human treasure, I'd probably be locked in my room for the next few seasons.

However, my perfectly covert outing turned out to be less than perfect when I reached my family's dwelling. I tiptoed through the hearth room without a hitch, breathing a sigh of relief when I entered my bedroom. My sigh tapered into a squeak when I saw a figure sitting at the edge of my bed.

"*Hazel.*" I caught my breath and glanced behind to make sure Mother wasn't preparing to jump me.

My little sister sat with her arms crossed, chin tilted up with all the authority a scrawny girl of ten summers could muster. "Where were you?" she demanded. "I should tell Mother you went out again." A bluff if I ever heard one.

I hushed her. "I just needed to stretch my wings. Go back to bed. You're a living nightmare when you don't get enough sleep."

Her narrowed blue eyes darted to my bag. "What did you bring?" She could speak with that cross tone all she wanted—there was no hiding the note of intrigue.

I fought a grin, turning so she couldn't see the charm as I pulled it out. "Something magnificent," I said breezily. "But tattletales don't get to see magnificent things. Go on, go tell Mother. She'll incinerate this treasure before you ever lay eyes on it."

Hazel pouted and bounced to her feet. Her little wings twitched with agitation. "Let me see!" she whispered, trying to dodge around me and spot what I held behind my back.

I was too light-footed for her, so she resorted to tackling me. We fell into a giggling heap on the bed, shushing each other and throwing fretful glances at the door.

"Alright, alright, you're squishing my wings!" I untangled myself from her and sat up, brandishing the bell charm in both hands.

An awed gleam danced into Hazel's eyes. The charm was heavy in her little hands, but she cradled it with reverent care. The soft light of the luminescent orchids embedded in the earthen walls behind our beds made the facets of the emerald glitter. Flecks of gold and green shimmered over my sister's freckled cheeks.

"It's so pretty," Hazel breathed, much to my pride. While I enjoyed my ventures, the look on her face made the stress of this particular night worthwhile.

"It's from a bracelet," I told her. "The humans that used to live in the house left a lot behind."

Hazel gave the charm a shake, smiling wider when it rang. She stopped the noise short, lest Mother hear.

"You know, you can come with me next time," I said. "You're a strong enough flier. You could pick out the next treasure yourself. There's all kinds of things to see there, Hazel."

"No way. I'd get in trouble."

I raised my eyebrows. "You know I'm too talented to get caught." *Even by humans,* I thought smugly.

"Not always," she corrected. "I think Ayden's still mad about catching you last month."

"Oh, please. He's thrilled to bits to have something to brag about."

Hazel rolled her eyes. She hopped off the mattress to pull out the box I stashed under my bed to house our shared stash of baubles. After pausing to admire the contents, she gingerly set the bell next to a polished white button.

"Come on," I tried again. "I could teach you everything I know. There was a flower charm in the mix. Pretty sure it had an amethyst."

She gave a noticeable pause before pushing the box back under the bed. "I'm not going," she said right in my cajoling face. "But an amethyst flower *does* sound pretty. Maybe I could wear it on my belt."

"Oh, so now you're going to start promoting my adventures? What will you do when Ayden corners you with a million questions about where the charm came from?"

"I'll just say I found it in Father's old stash. No one would know."

I didn't bother hiding my grin. She may have been the *well-behaved* daughter between the two of us, but I swore she got cleverer every day.

With humans milling around the mansion at midnight hours, perhaps it was for the best that she turned down my offer. But the more I thought about my strange encounter, the more I itched to uncover precisely what those humans had been talking about.

2

SYLVIA

I wished I had been born several decades earlier, back when Elysia wasn't so restricted. Back when gem scavengers went out into the world regularly, and the community welcomed nomads by the dozens.

By some miracle, the council hadn't done away with records of the past. Strict as the Elders were, even they couldn't justify barring the community from written accounts and history research.

The entrance to the archives was a deceptively humble archway that opened into a yawning cavern. Light roots crawled outward and upward along the packed earthen walls, illuminating shelves upon shelves of volumes. Looking down over the railing that guarded the steep drop-off, I couldn't help but get a sense of vertigo; the archives winded down four more stories as if sinking right into the center of the earth. The lowest floor was scarcely visible, illuminated only by faintly glowing flora that crept over the old wood shelves. No fairy would bother with casting or maintaining fae lights on a corner of the village that was accessed twice a year.

The archivist didn't bother to ask if I needed help. He barely glanced up from his meticulous work of restoring an old tome when I walked in. He waved me further inside without a word. I no longer required careful instruction on how to handle the materials in the furthermost chamber, where the light roots ended. Hardly anyone touched those shelves besides me. There was no shortage of nomadic journals, but my supply of new material was swiftly dwindling.

I thumbed through one of the carefully bound accounts. The chamber was empty of other visitors—or so I assumed until a hand fell on my shoulder.

Crying out, I whirled to find Ayden's vermillion eyes glowering down at me. I shut my book and pressed a hand to my chest, heaving a sigh.

"For someone who slinks in the shadows," he said, "you lack awareness of your surroundings."

"Is that so? A typical person shouldn't expect an ambush in the archives."

"You're hardly a typical person, are you?"

I rolled my eyes. "What do you want, Ayden? I can't be much of a menace when I'm down here reading, can I?"

"I saw you last night."

He said it so matter-of-factly I thought he was testing me. His stare, however, told a different story. That knowing look in his eyes made me squirm. I considered playing dumb, but if he planned on taking me before the council for punishment, he wouldn't have offered a courtesy warning. Besides, I was too curious about his intentions.

"Do you expect me to thank you for minding your business?" I asked, raising my eyebrows. "I could sing a ballad for you, but then you'd arrest me for sure."

"I could have intercepted you. But I preferred to watch you instead."

"Creepy."

Chewing my lip, I considered telling him about the humans' bizarre exchange in Alice's mansion. But admitting the exact location of my adventures was out of the question. As much as I desired to have someone join me and investigate, Ayden was the last person I would take by the hand and lead toward the house.

He pulled the book from me, inspecting it. Nothing was incriminating there, but I bristled at the way he breezily thumbed through the handwritten pages. He was too harsh with the old paper.

"Despite your childish cries for attention, you show promise," he said. "You might pretend otherwise, but you know it, too. The ice mentors tell me you're talented. Creative. Diligent. And in desperate need of self-discipline."

"Stars, I'm blushing."

He flashed me a stern glance. Guards were to be respected—particularly those who bore a warrior's rune. The mark was inked on the left shoulder of only those fairies who had proven themselves in a valiant effort.

Ayden had earned his rune the night my father died.

"You're twenty-one summers, yet your mother tells me you haven't decided on how you will serve Elysia."

"I don't want to be an artisan. Not that I have much choice." I wrinkled my nose at the image of spending my life crafting frozen archways and glittering embellishments to the construction of the village. Such petty magic compared to the stories of nomadic fairies who froze entire lakes.

Ayden chuckled. "Of course not. But there are alternatives."

"Like what?"

He lowered the journal to fix me with a beseeching look that didn't suit his rugged features. "Sylvia, there is a place for your skills in the Entry Watch."

My mouth dropped open. He hadn't come out of his way to scold me—he was offering me a *position.*

I felt like I'd been dodging the Watch guards all my life. After Father resigned from their ranks in disgrace when I was nine summers, there was little that drew me back toward them—particularly when Ayden was named their captain. I'd rather be shoveling shit in the hummingbird stables than fly by his side, pursuing other fairies that broke curfew for a taste of the world beyond our village.

"You would be outside," Ayden pressed. Somehow, this paternal tone was more unnerving than the lash of his threats. "I know you can't stand being cooped up in the tunnels. I could mentor you. Train you—"

"No. No way, I can't do that."

"Think about it, please."

"I don't need to."

Ayden's nostrils flared. "I know you may struggle to understand, but I care about you. I want what's best for you."

"What you want is to leash me. All you care about is the damn rules!"

A sharp hiss from the archivist—"*Shhh!*"

Ayden and I waved in apology, and he lowered his voice to a firm whisper. "Rules keep us safe, you ignorant child." A vein pulsed in his forehead as he surveyed me. *That* was the Ayden I knew and avoided.

"Give me back my book," I said, making a grab for it.

He moved out of reach and sneered at the cover, lingering on the name scrawled in elegant letters across the front. "You think you're one of these grand nomads?"

"I could be," I said, blushing. "If things were different, maybe."

Ayden dodged me again, and I nearly staggered right into a bookshelf.

"There's nothing out there but death," he snarled. "You might consider actually doing something useful with your life rather than wrapping yourself in delusions. After all, it hardly did your father any good."

Rage rushed through me, hardening into points of magic in my palms. I beckoned the magic into a wordless spell and sent a quilled burst of frost to Ayden's arms. When he jolted, I wrenched the journal back at last and hugged it to my stomach.

I glared up at him, chest heaving. I wouldn't have blamed him if he punished me for the attack: a day confined to our family dormitory or temporary banishment from the archives.

But Ayden said nothing. His expression was both furious and aggrieved as he looked down at me. I ran from the room before he could find the words.

The chill of the ice affinity training caverns bit through the fabric of my favorite jacket. It was thick but breathable, with reinforced panels that cinched around my waist. I shifted into position alongside the dozen other fairies in my training group.

Whispers of anticipation and nervous laughter echoed off the thick frost packed over the jagged stone. Combat training was infrequent for those who weren't inducted into the Entry Watch. My stiff hands tingled with excitement as we watched the ongoing duel. My pent-up energy begged for an outlet. What better release than a good fight?

The third pair to spar in front of the cohort didn't appear evenly matched. Amali always put on a good show, but I nearly rolled my eyes when Ethan was chosen instead of me. He would clean the hummingbird stables for a week if it got him out of combat training. His protests were silenced by a single look from Karis, our silver-haired mentor.

As it was, Ethan looked like he only had a minute or so before he was put out of his misery. Amali had taken an offensive position in the air, hovering with her right foot braced on a rocky outcrop for support. Ice magic swam in Ethan's hands, but he hadn't finished an incantation to give it form. He was too concerned with trying to read Amali's next move, his boots shifting nervously on the ground.

Amali moved with a grace that I envied, conjuring a serpent out of the crystalline mist that sank into every corner of the caverns. The beast's unseeing eyes fixed on Ethan, plunging toward him at a flex of Amali's hands. Her beautiful display earned murmurs of admiration as her icy spellwork shimmered under the scattered illumination of fae lights.

Seconds before the serpent's frozen jaws wiped him off his feet, Ethan shouted a spell verse, throwing up a thick shield of ice that seemed to erupt from the ground itself. Amali had drifted down from her perch—and Ethan spotted his opening.

My jaw slackened when he threw his hands forward and unleashed a blast of power. His shield smacked into Amali's front with an audible *clap* of ice to leather, knocking her out of the air. She landed on her back, eliciting a flinch of sympathy from the rest of us. My own wings tensed a bit, imagining the unforgiving bite of the puckered stone she'd landed on.

"Excellent reflexes, Ethan," Karis commended, stepping in and putting a hand on his shoulder. He breathed heavily, sweat dotting his brow despite the frost clinging to his hands. "Though you might try to wipe that *pissing-your-pants* look off your face beforehand. It emboldens your opponent." Ethan flushed crimson as several fairies snickered, and Karis's eyes softened slightly. "Go on, help her up."

While Ethan hurriedly obeyed, my concentration wandered the cavern to strategize. There were massive, icy creations and archways sculpted to perfection. Blue and amber fae lights danced over their glittering surfaces. Deeper in, there was a frozen waterfall. Freshwater still rippled beneath the ice, giving way to a thin stream. Father would tell me to utilize my environment however I could.

And what would he tell me about Ayden's offer? Utilize the opportunity, or tell him to shove it?

Entry Watch guards did have more freedom than most fairies in the village. I would get to be outside and treated with esteem and purpose to boot. But I'd always have Ayden's eyes on me, ensuring my freedom met his standards.

I would be kissing the Dottage mansion and everything beyond it goodbye.

"Move it, Sylvia." Brigid nudged me to allow Ethan and Amali to pass through.

"Sorry." I stepped aside, wincing at the textured scratches on Amali's wings. "I think I'll be keeping my feet on the ground," I whispered to Brigid.

"She'll be flying crooked all day," Brigid whispered back. Amali brushed off the others' concern—though she pointedly grimaced when she was clapped on the shoulder.

"Cassius and Sylvia." Karis motioned for me and a boy of eighteen summers to step forward.

We had Cassius to thank for the most elaborate ice structures in the training cavern. I had no doubt he'd be selected as the lead architect for Winter Solstice decorations within a few years. Fresh adrenaline hummed in my veins. I couldn't recall seeing him spar before, but clearly, he was a force to be reckoned with.

Chewing my lip, I considered the sweeping ice of the waterfall.

"Don't even think about it, Sylvia," Karis said, raptly following my gaze. "There is no need to destroy an entire structure during a sparring session. No one's been killed on my watch, and I won't have you breaking that streak." She raised a severe eyebrow at me, then nodded for us to proceed.

Cassius, for his part, looked slightly terrified of me after Karis's comment. Nonetheless, he murmured two short verses and summoned chips of ice from thin air—perhaps to show off that he didn't need to borrow from the structures around him. I braced myself and observed his hands, waiting for the precise moment he would send the stinging gale at me. With a grunt, he followed through.

Ice darted toward me, closing the distance in the blink of an eye, but I was ready. With a whisper, I took control of his spell and made the icicles pause in mid-air. Stars, he must have been nervous—I sensed how brittle the chips were, how easily they would melt away.

Breakable ice offered little threat. I reinforced the spell and shot it back in his direction. My range exploded further than intended. Shouts from behind as my cohort dodged stray bits of razor-sharp ice.

"Sylvia!" Karis snapped. "Control!"

But now was not the time to rein it in. Cassius was on the move, having blocked my counterattack. His feet left the ground, wings hurrying to carry him behind a short wall of solid ice to recuperate safely.

I didn't allow him the luxury of time to restrategize. With a guttural cry, I reduced the barrier into a thick, frozen mist and left him exposed.

Karis had warned me off destroying the waterfall but said nothing about using the trickling stream that cut across the ground.

I raced toward Cassius and summoned a bolt of stream water to fuel a single, snaking blade. My spell flew ahead of me to meet Cassius, who fell to a seat in alarm.

The razor-sharp point of the ice stopped at his throat. He flinched, causing a nick that drew a thin line of blood.

"What the fuck!" he cried, scrambling back.

Gasps chorused behind me, and I hurriedly undid the spell. A harmless burst of water rained to the ground in front of Cassius. He hissed, pressing his fingers to his throat. The cut was hardly life-threatening, but I winced nonetheless.

"Here," Karis told Cassius, beckoning him. Her palm glowed with the gentle promise of a healing spell. He was certainly too harried to do it himself.

I blocked his path to Karis. "I'll do it," I said. "I'm so sorry. I can—"

"Get off me," he hissed, sidestepping and shooting me a dirty look. "Haven't you shown off enough?"

I pursed my lips and didn't insist on my offer. Healing may have been only my secondary affinity, but I'd gotten plenty of practice from splinters I'd given myself while searching the Dottage mansion.

Karis made short work of healing the cut. I avoided Cassius's glare as he went to stand by Brigid and Ethan, whose disturbed stares remained fixed on me as well.

There were murmurs from the other dozen ice affinities in the hall, but Karis swiftly set them to work on basic drills before approaching me. She didn't seem livid—only exhausted. And somehow, that was more insulting. As though I was a child she couldn't keep a handle on.

For a moment, I hoped she would order me to spar with her instead, but she heaved a sigh. "You're dismissed for the day. Go on."

My heart jolted. Karis was strict and unmovable, wielding a dark sense of humor that I almost envied. But this was not a joke. Never once had she dismissed me early from a training session.

I took a step closer to her, pleading. "But…"

"You know very well that our aim isn't to draw blood."

"I wasn't planning to hurt him! I was only preparing for what I would do in the circumstance—"

"*What* circumstance?" Karis fired back. "When will you ever have to hold a weapon to another fairy's throat so savagely?"

I clenched my jaw. "Ethan knocked Amali down, and you said nothing!"

"Ethan knows when enough is enough. He has control. You're the only one who doesn't."

"In a *real* fight, wit and power will outmatch control."

She scoffed, raking me up and down. "If you have no interest in heeding my advice, then I have no interest in training you today. Reflect on what you can do to get it through your head, Sylvia—control comes before all else. Come back tomorrow if you're prepared to listen."

Perhaps if we could train outside, like the fire affinities, we wouldn't have to worry so much about control. If I were allowed to experience the full nature of my abilities, perhaps I wouldn't be so careless about boundaries. Father had trained me outside. He never had suggested I was too extreme.

Each one of these arguments had fallen on deaf ears long before today, so I didn't bother. This was *tradition.*

I gave a little bow of my head and retreated instead of igniting the argument I so fiercely wanted to have.

How's that for control?

On my path outside the ice hall, I passed the other affinity training caverns. Faint sunlight came from the direction of the fire and lightning fairies' outdoor grounds. The small number of animal affinities started later in the day and were likely beginning their sessions by the lake or in a clearing with field mice.

Lucky bastards.

At one of the crossways, I found an earth affinity and a fire affinity playfully sending bursts of magic back and forth in a low-stakes duel. In places where their spells combined, the soil became molten.

"Stop!" An instructor's voice bellowed from the earth affinity hallway. "You know that sparring isn't permitted outside the training grounds!"

At least I wasn't the only one pushing the boundaries of what was permitted today.

The willow was basking in warm sunlight when I stepped outside. Although I still simmered over Karis's rigidity, I was lucky to have her as a mentor. Many of the fire affinities often sprinted away from their sessions toward the healers' ward, nursing ugly burns. With any luck, Cassius would see some of *those* poor souls after this afternoon's session and not be so angry about his shallow cut.

Due to my dismissal, I was free for the rest of the day—which would certainly make Mother ask questions. I played around with different lies as my flats sank into the soft soil. Lifting my gaze beyond the willow roots, I glimpsed a number of fairies in the air. The vibrant, drooping willow fronds were so full of life and movement outside of curfew. Fairies not confined by duties sat in the branches, chatting leisurely. Others were returning from foraging, sacks brimming with ripe blackberries. The air smelled sweet and clean, and I breathed it in greedily. Aggravated thoughts of the training caverns were swiftly replaced with the promise of a gorgeous afternoon.

A burst of feathered wings exploded in the corner of my eye. My lips quirked into a grin when I saw a group of toddlers practicing flight riding their hummingbird mounts. I remembered my first mount. I'd loved the sweet bird so dearly that I'd cried when I found out later that I wasn't an animal affinity after all.

I watched the hummingbirds zip through the leafy fronds and circle the trunk of the tree. Younger fairies were awfully cute at that age, squealing in delight at their first taste of the air rushing past them. Their joy was infectious. Once their wings stiffened, they would no longer require the mounts, but they would be familiar with the sensation of flying.

Of course, that didn't stop my sister.

Hazel soared overhead on her favorite hummingbird. If they weren't so adorable together, they could have made a formidable sight—a determined warrior on a steed. She expertly nosedived to the ground when she spotted me, coaxing the bird to slow just before touching down.

"Fancy moves," I said as she dismounted.

"He does all the work." Hazel nuzzled cheek-to-cheek with the hummingbird's vibrant green feathers.

"Careful—pretty soon, they'll tell you're too old to borrow a mount. You're technically already breaking the rule, you know."

Hazel gave me a sour look. "There's worse rules I could be breaking."

I clutched my heart. "Now that's uncalled for."

"Besides, they won't kick me out—not with all the help I give at the stables. Have you been inside lately? There are so many new chicks! They're so sweet when they're sleeping or drinking nectar."

I supposed I should fear the day she took a liking to crows.

A cluster of buzzing wings approached from behind, interrupting us. Before I could turn fully, someone dropped a hand on my shoulder.

"Revel," Kyra whispered in my ear. "Tonight, just after curfew."

I swiftly shooed Hazel back to the stables, and she didn't argue—not when there were hummingbird chicks to fawn over. Once my sister was out of earshot, I squeezed Kyra's hand and grinned. "I swear, you only ever bring good news. It's been *weeks*."

Revel nights were the one type of outing the guards didn't fuss about, but harsh autumn storms hadn't allowed outdoor gatherings lately. The council certainly wouldn't approve a weather alteration—not even a tightly contained one. Tonight would be perfect. There wasn't a cloud in the late afternoon sky.

Several of my peers, free from their training sessions and chores, darted about to spread the news. A rush of fellowship swelled in my chest, knowing that I wasn't alone in my restlessness.

One of the figures paused when he spotted me—Damian. He swooped in closer to land, stumbling a few steps and nearly taking me and Kyra down with him. We all steadied each other, laughing. Damian's hand lingered on my arm.

"Shouldn't you be in a session?" he asked me.

"Is there a reason why you're so familiar with my routine?" I raised my eyebrows at him.

He rubbed the back of his neck and laughed, suddenly unable to make eye contact. "Since you've obviously mastered your affinity and have some free time, why don't you come with us? We're on the final shift for berries."

Because his offer meant getting further away from the village entrance, I accepted without hesitation.

As far as berry-gatherers went, we weren't the most efficient. What started as a challenge to collect the biggest haul morphed into a game of dodging each other's berry-throwing skills. Before we knew it, our hands and clothes were smeared with violet evidence of our dawdling.

Once we were too breathless to perform our assigned task, we settled onto a craggy branch. The sun hadn't quite started to set, but the light was already changing, deepening.

"I was thinking," I said casually.

"Always a risky move," Damian chimed in.

I elbowed him. "I was *thinking*. The weather may be perfect for some exploring after the revel. We'll be out and about anyway, right? The guards won't think to go searching for us. They'll assume we've fallen asleep under the stars."

There was a tense silence, then an uncomfortable chuckle from Kyra. "Seems like you *have* put a lot of thought into it."

My answered laugh was strained. That wasn't a *no*. I pushed further. "It would be like old times. Maybe… maybe we could go further than we ever have. The human house? The crumbling one on the hill."

Their stunned stares made me wish I had kept my big mouth shut.

"You're kidding, right? Please tell me you wouldn't really do something that stupid," Kyra said, voice tight.

Damian was squeezing a berry so hard that juice leaked over his knuckles. I dodged his eyes, knowing he would instantly read the bitter disappointment in my own. We used to be fearless *together.*

"Stars, you should see the look on your faces," I scoffed. "Of course I'm not serious. It's just a dusty old house. What could possibly be interesting in some rotting place like that?"

Embarrassment roiled in me. My closest friends thought my adventures were outlandish. If they had agreed to come, I might have been able to ease them into the secret about the strange human conversation the night before. But even the suggestion of going near the mansion made them bristle. I remembered the look on Hazel's face last night—my own baby sister thought I was crazy.

How could I not entertain the theory that something was innately broken in me? Something that needed to be fixed. But flawed or not, I ached to share this part of myself with someone—*anyone*—who understood.

Father used to go out into the world. He would have understood.

But he was gone.

Judging by the looks on Damian and Kyra's faces, they were still trying to puzzle out whether I had really been teasing or not. An angry buzz of wings approached, killing the hope for any further conversation on the matter.

"You three." Ayden pulled a hover, his glare resting on me in particular. His hand was still pink from my outburst. His tone was more clipped than usual. "Time to head back. Hurry up."

"What?" My grip tightened on my satchel. "Curfew isn't for another hour!"

"Well, *I'm* telling you it's now," Ayden snapped.

"Why?" Damian asked, earning a grateful glance from me.

Sighing, Ayden nodded to the south. "The outer patrol sensed something unusual in that direction."

My breath caught at the fear that he knew what I'd been up to, but he wasn't focused on me anymore. I could only assume that he was telling the truth. Alice must have been manifesting brighter and earlier than usual. Or perhaps the anxious humans had returned. Whatever the case, I didn't push my luck by questioning further.

As Ayden escorted us toward the home willow, I snuck a glance at my friends. We shared a knowing look that somewhat put my upset heart at ease. They may have outgrown their curiosity, but we could all silently agree that the revel was still on.

Even knowing that I would return outside in a matter of hours, I still felt like the tree was swallowing me up as we were ushered underground.

3
SYLVIA

The lively hum of conversation and clinking of utensils already enveloped the dining hall when I entered with my family an hour later. The warm sounds reverberated against the packed earthen walls, reinforced by intricate icy pillars that gracefully mirrored the contours of the domed ceiling overhead.

An eclectic assortment of tables was arranged across the vast chamber; some were long banquet-style benches able to seat upward of ten fairies side by side, while others were cozy four-stool offerings. I followed Mother to a table that would fit just the three of us. An explosion of laughter from the right of the room made me bristle. Off-duty Entry Watch guards sat shoulder-to-shoulder and nursed a pitcher of berry wine. I scanned their faces as I dropped my tray onto our table, more certain than ever that I did not belong in their ranks.

"The early curfew is ridiculous," I grumbled, not for the first time that evening. "It wasn't even close to sunset. I'm going to complain to the Elders."

When all of us were seated at the table, the golden fae lights hovering closest to us brightened automatically to provide more illumination over our meal.

"You'll do no such thing," Mother said. She knew my threats were usually full of shit, but there was an edge of warning to her voice all the same.

"We were in the middle of foraging!"

Mother's eyes narrowed at me over her glass mug of rose tea. "Seems that you should have enjoyed plenty of free time earlier this afternoon."

I knew that look—when I was younger, it used to land me with scullery duties for misbehaving. I found myself engrossed with the serving of herbed brown bread on my plate. "What makes you say that?"

"Karis stopped me in the corridor to inform me you were dismissed early."

Shit. "Would you believe me if I said she was so proud of my excellent spellwork that she gave me the day off?"

The daggers of Mother's stare cut deeper. "You frightened your entire cohort. You mustn't put your practice sessions at risk—or yourself, for that matter."

Guilt burrowed into me. I needed no reminder of my friends' hollow stares. And now Hazel was peeking at me from across the table with trepid curiosity, too.

"It was an accident," I mumbled. Chancing a half-hearted smirk, I peeked up from my plate. "I did get in a bit of extra practice on Ayden's arms in the archives. Scarcely had to move my lips to summon the ice, either. I think that should count as extracurricular training."

Hazel giggled, to which Mother gave a stern look.

"Ayden's not very nice," Hazel said, her grin dropping apologetically.

"See? Even she knows," I said around a mouthful of bread. "And she likes *everyone*."

"Hush, the both of you," Mother tutted, glancing at the other benches. "I've raised you smarter than to agitate the captain of the Entry Watch. As though he needs any more excuse to scrutinize our family. And *you*—" Her eyebrows lifted at me. "I don't want to hear again about you ignoring your mentor's orders so childishly."

"You're just worried I'm turning into *him*," I snapped—immediately wishing I could swallow back the words when Mother stiffened, pain flashing across her face.

"Can you blame me if I was? You refuse to be content with restraint," Mother said. "Your father did much the same."

I hated that she wasn't wrong. Softening, I flexed my fingers, murmuring a spell to freeze Mother's cup of tea—a gentle, delicate crawl of frost that began from the bottom of the glass. Hazel crooned with intrigue at the fractals turning the tea into a solid block of amber, but Mother was entirely nonplussed.

"I've got plenty of control. See?" I offered my smile as a balm.

Mother's hand glowed as though embers lived beneath her skin. Steam hissed from her cup, the tea unfreezing. The lines on her forehead became more pronounced as she regarded me wearily. I knew I'd been the cause of them deepening, seeing as she had to raise her wildest child without a partner to support her efforts. Sometimes, she even used to laugh at my antics when Father was around.

"You don't need to worry about me like you used to," I went on gently. "I'll be living on my own soon."

Mother set aside her tea, tucking into the glazed parsnips on her plate. Some of the tension at the table unraveled, and I felt hopeful that her anxiety had been set to bed for now.

"You could have your own dwelling now if you were to marry," Mother said. "I was about your age when I married."

Great. This again.

"There's still no one in the village turning my head, but thanks for the reminder," I drawled.

"What about Damian?" She searched my face. I wondered if she could sense how my heart stuttered at his name. Perhaps someone had whispered to her about our intimate meetings every few weeks.

"What about him?" I asked.

"He's grown up nicely. He obviously cares for you." Mother shot me a rare, cat-like grin. "I see the way you two talk with each other. The long afternoons you've spent together in the last months. His mother and aunts have noticed, too. He makes you happy."

"Sorry to disappoint our expectant fans, but we're just friends." As I chewed on my next bite, I hesitated. I had already stung her with old memories this evening, but the burn of curiosity urged me past trepidation. "Mother… How did you know about Father? When did you know that you *loved* him?"

"I've told you that story before."

I didn't miss the pain that flickered over her face. Hazel watched her raptly, her spoon hovering over her stew. It was unfair that she only had dim memories of Father. She'd been two summers when he passed.

"You said he infuriated you," I pressed, smiling toothily at Mother. "That he always found himself wandering out to the fire affinity sessions when he had no business there."

Mother rolled her eyes. "He could never follow a simple direction."

"But he was there to see *you*."

The ghost of a smile flickered on her lips. "There was quite a rivalry between the fire and ice cohorts at the time," she said. "He and I were the most skilled, treated as unofficial leaders. He insisted on a friendly competition during a revel. It was nonsense, but I didn't want to be labeled a coward—not by *him*, of all people. Healers in training were on standby, of course."

"The duel ended in a draw," I said dramatically, raising my eyebrows at Hazel, who hung onto every word. "Mother was furious, but he was all smiles, going on about how much fun the challenge was. And against all odds, that's when she started to soften for him."

Taking another sip, Mother averted her gaze. "See? You can tell the story yourself."

"But how did it *feel*, though?" I gestured vaguely at myself. "In here?"

She pursed her lips, emotion churning behind her green eyes. "It's difficult to put into words. Falling for someone is… It's terrifying and wonderful. It's a wildfire that razes everything you know but makes way for something new and divine. It's the cavernous emptiness of a room full of people when he's not there."

A heavy silence unspooled, and I regretted pushing the topic. Maybe I was better off never falling in love if it would spare me the kind of pain that ate away at Mother. She was beautiful, but years of Father's absence had withered her spirit like a flower removed from sunlight. Anyone could see that. I cast a dulled look at my plate, prodding potatoes into the herbed gravy.

"I wish he'd never touched gemstones," I mumbled.

"So do I, my love. Gem magic served Elysia well once," Mother replied after a beat. "But in the hands of fools, it's ruinous."

The last word was hissed with a buried bitterness I knew well. Directing anger toward a dead man was pointless, but resentment rose all the same. Father had been so obsessed with his next gem target toward the end that he'd scarcely joined us for suppers like this. He'd left us—whether he meant to or not.

Contemplative, I threw a glance across the room at Damian. He was with his own family, laughing heartily at something one of his brothers was saying. He was sweet, and I was fond of him, but surely this couldn't be that fierce pull Mother had once felt toward Father. This was no wildfire.

"Maybe the one for me isn't here," I said. "Maybe it'd be better to hold off on getting my own dwelling while I decide what I want to do with myself."

Silence enveloped our table for all of three seconds before they both snapped at me.

"You mean you're *leaving*?" Hazel cried.

"That isn't an option," Mother said coldly.

"Not for you, maybe." I leveled my gaze with Mother's. "But I'd give anything—*anything*—to explore out there instead of flying a patrol circle around the same damn tree for the rest of my life."

"Sylvia!" Mother raised her voice loud enough to turn several heads, who swiftly pretended to go back to their own business. She spoke through gritted teeth, heat radiating off her. "Never, ever speak a plea like that aloud."

I scoffed. "What, will Ayden appear from thin air and arrest me for simply saying I want to travel?"

"That isn't what I mean. You said you would give *anything.* A careless offering like that has power. Ancient magic is around us, in the very air you breathe. If your heart had been in that phrasing, you don't know what might have answered. You know better."

More arguments wavered at the tip of my tongue, but Mother was the one person I could never win with. So I let my shoulders slump and murmured an apology.

I didn't dare tell her that my heart *was* in my plea. My heart was always in it. Nothing had ever answered.

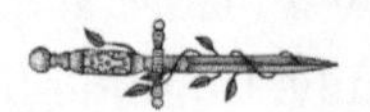

Maybe I would never find love, but passion was a delightful consolation. By nightfall, I was burning to join my friends under the stars.

I wrapped my knife with my favorite satchel bag and stashed them both in a tree hollow on my way to the lake that neighbored our home willow. Fewer guards patrolled the perimeter tonight. Most of the younger ones were partaking in the revel.

The ritual wasn't anything new to me, but the radiance of these gatherings always ignited glee in my chest. I never understood why fairies seemed to age out of it, as though something so beautiful could ever lose its charm.

I slowed my flight to a hover as I neared the lake, drinking in the sight, enjoying every happy skip of my heart.

The soft murmur of water lapping against the grassy bank intertwined with music: fiddles and harps and voices like silk. Laughter and enchanted grins were everywhere I looked. Fairies were painting each others' wings with their fingers, speaking nose-to-nose, showing off their magic in playful bursts of light and heat. A circle of my peers had their hands intertwined, dancing in the air. The moonlight glowed on their bare skin. They sang together to the stars overhead.

"Come," a sweet voice purred to me. Eva, an earth affinity two summers older than me, folded her hand into mine and tugged me away from the tree line. She had the prettiest green eyes—a hue deeper than mine, like moss that grew in secret.

I undressed swiftly to match her. She pressed a polished wood goblet of berry wine into my hands. Her inhibitions were already lowered, and I was eager to catch up, lifting the sweet drink to my lips.

The effects floated to my head before I finished the last gulp. The edges of my vision blurred with brilliant color. I raised the goblet with a grin, throwing my head back to cheer with Eva.

She led me by the hand to the water's edge, where earth and water affinities worked in tandem to create paint from a variety of berries and flowers. A couple of other fairies sat me down. I spread my wings, eager to be their canvas. While they stained my wings with intricate designs, I beckoned another fairy's head onto my lap and wove a crown of leaves into his hair.

Before long, my wings were stunning—hues of purple, blue, and green splashed across the membrane. I thanked my artists with kisses that teemed with giggles.

The dance continued over the water, the music picking up a fervent tempo with each passing minute. I flew up to join the circle, creating a grand entrance along the way. With a wave of my arms, I summoned water from the lake and made it arc high overhead. The droplets came down as delicate snowflakes and glittering bits of ice.

If any of them knew about my blunder during training, they either didn't show it or didn't care. Amid the cries of delight, I found my place in the circle. By now, the cues to break off into groups or pairs were second nature, but it wasn't always graceful—especially with the amount of berry wine that went around. Accidental bumps and collisions were met with good-natured laughter.

I had several partners that night, but soon enough, I found myself in Damian's arms.

"Show off," he murmured affectionately in my ear. The air was still cool from the display of my affinity.

"As if you'd have me any other way." I slowed our movements into a calm hover. All it took was a nod toward our usual tree for him to follow.

The grass was waxy and soft. We shared hushed giggles at the sharp chill of the dew against our skin as we landed on the ground. My lips parted at the first brush of his mouth over mine. Flexing my wings wide, I admired the painted colors glinting in the pale light. I reclined slowly enough to make Damian groan with impatience. He all but tackled me.

I kept my fingers wrapped tightly around his shoulders, the ardor of our union making the music in the clearing seem all the more ethereal. The songs, Damian's soft kisses, the colorful magic of every affinity—it was so beautiful, tears welled in my eyes.

When Damian and I were finished, we didn't return to the revel right away. He folded his wings and rolled onto his back so that I could curl into his side and lay my head on his chest. We caught our breath under the quiet of our favorite tree and watched the dancing continue in the distance.

"Every night should be a revel," I said, tracing my fingers over his abdomen.

Though his affinity was wind and air, Damian had the strong, lean physique of a builder. I loved how his earth-colored skin contrasted with the runes I doodled over him. The marks glowed a muted teal for a few seconds, burning brightest where my fingertip instructed the line. The designs faded after a few seconds like my messages of affection were absorbed right into Damian's body. The magic was playful—mostly done by teenagers to mark their first loves. Still, I grinned when I felt Damian's hand tracing similar runes over my hip.

"Do you want more wine?" I asked, glancing up at his face.

"I think I love you, Sylvia."

The words left him so suddenly, I wondered if it might be the revel affecting him. But his gaze was sober, tender from years of memories shared together. His words hung in the air, suffocating me as I fumbled for a response.

My sweet friend smiled at me, brushing stray locks of my reddish hair off my face. "You like this, don't you? We fit well together."

"We do," I admitted. I was damn comfortable, folded against him. He was kind and patient, laughed genuinely at my terrible jokes…

But could he accept all of me?

I sat up and looked down at him, my heart hammering. His gaze was so full of hope, begging me to return his sentiments. "Damian, I've been sneaking out after curfew."

One of his thick eyebrows rose lazily. "I wish you would sneak into my chambers instead sometime. Where've you been off to that late? The oak groves?"

A lump swelled in my throat. "I've been going to the human house on the hill. For months now."

"What?" Abruptly, he sat up. "Earlier, you said—"

"I lied," I interrupted like it was obvious. "I had to. Kyra would've told everyone in earshot before dinner. You saw the way she looked at me."

The same way he was looking at me now, I noticed with a sinking heart.

I clasped his hand and pressed it to my heart in a desperate plea. "Come with me tonight."

"To the human house?" Damian stammered.

"Yes! There's so much to see. You can't imagine! There's a box of metal and wood that plays music. There are portraits everywhere, bigger than a bedroom. And that's just in one room! There's at least ten in there."

A breathless grin took hold of me as I allowed myself to picture Damian using wind magic to break down one of the ivy-covered doors, unveiling a new room full of human treasures. He'd watch me proudly as we ventured inside. He'd find me a new treasure—a jeweled ring or a flower pressed in a book.

"We could be some of the first fairies ever to see all of this," I said wistfully.

His hand slipped out of mine.

"I can't do that." Damian's crestfallen gaze dipped away from me.

"I know this is a lot to take in," I said softer. "But it's safe. Humans rarely come around, especially at this hour."

"You've been *near* them?"

"I… Not until last night."

Damian shuddered, leaning away like he might catch an illness.

"I didn't know they were there! They didn't see me. Promise. It was quite an adventure, actually." I chuckled weakly, trying in vain to catch his gaze again. "Something was odd about those humans. I almost wish I stayed to learn more."

His eyes were wide, still pointed down. "We need to tell the guards."

"No! That's too rash. Chances are, the humans have moved on. They were arguing about leaving. We can go check together. We'll stay out of sight. Then, if we know something is endangering Elysia, we'll tell the guards. But if it's safe—just think, we could have the whole mansion to explore."

"That's it, then? Humans are milling outside our home, but your priority is to continue to sneak away without the guards knowing? Sylvia, that's..."

"I'm not crazy." My voice cracked. "If you would trust me and see it for yourself—"

"*Stop.* Enough." He finally looked at me, huffing out a panicky breath. "You can't go back there. I don't care how many times you've made it out. Why would you put yourself at risk like that? *All of us*, at risk?"

I wound chains around my heart to keep it from tearing like paper. "Freedom is not a privilege," I snarled. "It's not stupid or foolish to want more. We deserve to know the world outside these woods if we want—*I* deserve that! I don't want to leave my life in the hands of anyone else."

When he reached for my hand to implore further, I was the one to pull away. For a few painful seconds, we both froze and stared, knowing that words would sway neither of us.

I snatched up my clothes and began dressing. Damian followed suit, neither of us saying another word.

"Sylvia, wait!"

His wings hummed after me, but I didn't look back. By the time I reached the tree hollow where I'd stashed my supplies, he had given up on following. I cleared my throat and blinked away tears, hating how much I'd hoped he would chase me all the way to the hill.

As I flew off toward Dottage house, I was glad I'd had the sense not to mention Alice. Then Damian would've *really* thought I was crazy.

4

SYLVIA

I was plagued by the absurd idea that if I found a treasure fantastic enough for Hazel, she would finally join me. And on the chance that the humans were still lingering and posing a threat, I had the even more absurd idea that the council would be grateful that I uncovered the truth behind it. Focusing on a worthy task was better than moping around like Alice.

Seconds after I flew through the broken attic window, shadows danced along the walls. Whirling around, I caught sight of car lights shining in the distance. I dropped onto the window sill and held my breath, listening to the grumble of the monstrous machine. I didn't move until the lights and sounds had faded into nothing.

That would have been an exciting introduction for Damian, I thought sourly.

Promptly pushing him out of my head, I regarded the charms I'd left scattered on the dresser. Truth be told, I was skittish about inspecting the lower levels of the mansion. All seemed quiet, though.

At the very least, I could get Hazel her amethyst flower while I worked up the nerve to venture down. Frustration and envy roiled through me like never before as I inspected the jewelry box. Humans didn't need to live in hiding. They didn't need to scavenge for treasures and tuck them away from judgmental stares. I dug through the box with a scowl, yearning to experience the world freely and properly.

The moment I pulled the treasure out of the pile, a vicious chill settled in my bones and made goosebumps rise along my skin.

"Come for another one, I see."

Breath catching, I turned. Alice stood behind me, observing my theft with rare lucidity.

"I'm sorry." My voice came out in a whisper. "These are so coated in dust, I thought you wouldn't—"

"It's yours," she said, a gentle smile gracing her pretty features. "A gift for keeping me company."

My grip tightened on the silver flower. "It's for my sister, actually. I know she'll love it. But I promise, that's the last I'll take from your bracelet."

Alice looked off wistfully. "No matter, Stella. He'll have another made for me, even more splendid than this one."

I sighed, desperate to hold onto any bit of clarity she had to offer. "Alice, listen closely. Have you seen anyone here tonight?"

Her head tilted. "Is *he* here?" she whispered.

My wings drooped. She was already lost again. Alice hurried away, her ethereal form receding with unnatural grace down the winding stairs. I'd inadvertently set her on one of her fixed paths; rather than prettying herself for a dance, she was off to search room after room for her beloved. There was no holding her attention now.

I watched her until she was out of sight. Her loneliness was aching. Sometimes, it felt contagious. With the new charm safely stashed in my bag, I rose to my feet and took to the air.

Properly exploring every inch of this building would take me years. I had spent much of these past months in the attic and in the dining room on the first floor. The three spacious bedrooms on the second floor must've once been a luxury. Now, almost all the furniture had been reclaimed by other humans. The empty bed frames that remained were made of iron, so I didn't stay in those rooms for more than a cursory glance. Any longer, and my flesh might crawl right off my bones.

I couldn't deny that there was a kernel of truth to Damian's accusation of my selfishness. Although this place teemed with peril, the thought of losing it brought a brutal pang to my heart.

When I flew down to the first floor, Alice had vanished. Despite that, the air was still freezing in her wake—why did ghosts have to be so *cold*?

Although I intended to stealthily search the basement for any sign of the humans, the hanging pictures along the way drew my attention.

There were at least seven frames, varying in size. The one before me was a portrait of several humans—and claw marks marred the canvas. I couldn't decide if the damage was fresh or if I simply hadn't paid close enough attention before. I conjured a soft, cerulean light to my skin, holding my hand out to illuminate the surface. Narrowing my eyes, I recognized the Dottage house in the background, scarcely recognizable with its fresh paint. There were six humans in the image, standing proudly in the front yard. A family, though half were slashed beyond recognition. Alice stood on the far left, smiling brighter than I had ever seen.

Alice was in the photograph beneath, too. There was a young man with combed hair seated next to her on the front steps, both of them unsmiling. That seemed to be the style in many of these portraits, though, for the life of me, I didn't understand why. Perhaps it had been unfashionable for humans to smile many years ago. Maybe I could try to get a lucid answer from Alice on that soon.

Flying higher, I considered a gilded bronze frame that was hung horizontally. I reached out, brushing away years of neglect and grime. As dust came away on my fingertips, a glimmer of sudden movement came from beneath.

"Stars!" I hissed, yanking my arm back.

The surface was reflective, and the stirring in the glass mirrored my own twitchy movements. It was… *me.*

I swallowed, inching closer. On calm days, I could use the lake to survey my appearance. I had a general idea of how I looked, of course. I had my mother's fiery hair, emerald eyes, and a smattering of freckles on my arms. But I had never been confronted with my reflection in such breathtaking clarity.

I touched my cheek, letting out a shuddering breath. My reflection gaped back at me with pouty lips and strong, arched eyebrows. Auburn locks swept against my shoulders and framed silken skin. My neck was slender, still peppered in red marks from Damian's fervent kisses.

I was beautiful. I was a revelation.

Turning slightly, I looked over my shoulder to see how my sapphire top wrapped under my wings. The layered chiffon sleeves rested over my arms gracefully, a deep blue that melted into the forest shadows.

A low, stretching creak made me jolt.

Alice's chilly presence was still somewhere on the second floor above me; any closer, and the pang would be far more aggressive.

I listened, heart hammering in my ears, and the groan came again. A rhythmic pattern—footsteps upon the aging wood floors. Someone was in the house with me.

Humans.

In my triumphant daydreams after last night, I had been fully confident about my ability to evade humans a second time if needed. The pathetic reality was that I froze.

Two male voices carried from the kitchen, low and indistinct like thunder on the horizon. Neither of them sounded like the male from last night. My eyes flitted to the glass doors. Only the dining room separated us now. The voices were covering ground too quickly—I needed time to breathe, to think, to figure out *what the hell am I going to do.*

I wasn't given the luxury of time.

Beams of light danced behind the glass. Before I could make sense of where those lights emitted from, one door creaked open. Dust stirred in the miraculous glow, but my petrified stare was drawn to the harrowing silhouette that filled the threshold.

And all I could do was gape like an idiot, wondering how something so monstrous had snuck up on me.

The figure entered the room slowly. Another, even taller human followed. This one went rigid, head jerking in my direction at once.

"Cliff! Over there!"

I looked down at my hands in horror—*my glow!* The snap of his voice almost made me crumple, but my senses finally caught up. I put out my cerulean glow and bolted toward the darkest shadows of the room.

"What the hell was that?" the other human asked, his voice rough.

Twin beams of light swiveled around the room in chaotic arcs, pursuing me like starving owls. I flew frantically to evade them as the light skimmed my ankles. Most of the windows were sealed. The only guaranteed exit I knew of was in the attic, which would mean crossing the humans to reach it.

With blood pounding in my ears, I became aware of my wings' hum. In a split-second effort to silence myself, I landed on a table scattered with decaying picture frames—a piece of furniture so damaged that it had been left alone. I crouched and covered my mouth to muffle the whimpers that begged to come out.

Calm down. Calm down.

I could get away. If the humans walked just a bit further, I'd fly off faster than they could hear or spot me. It would be easy.

"Maybe it was just a firefly," the taller human said dubiously.

"You're kidding me. You ever seen a blue firefly? There's no way that thing was natural."

"What kind of monster looks like *that*?"

"It's gotta be a trick. A lure, or something, like an anglerfish. Remember that siren we hunted a couple months ago?"

Hunted.

My dinner threatened to make a reappearance. The stars had seen it fit to drop me in the path of the worst type of humans—*hunters*. Bloodthirsty killers who wouldn't hesitate to carve me up if they got their hands on me.

The stars aren't to blame. A voice taunted at the back of my mind. I'd heard the male human last night mention hunters and hadn't considered that they would show up at the mansion so soon—if at all. The stories were real.

The room grew frigid, and for a moment, I fretted that my terror was to blame. Both humans paused. Their breaths pooled in the chill.

"Feel that?" the taller one said, his profile caught by moonlight as he cast a hard look over the entryway.

"Stella?" a new voice chimed in.

I twisted around. Alice stood in the shadows beneath the staircase, eyes fixed on me. She had a pinch between her glossy eyes, halfway between reality and the past. The hunters didn't react, looking right through her.

"Are you alright? You screamed." Alice blinked from me to the rest of the room. She frowned like she couldn't make sense of what she was seeing. She took a step closer to the hunters, seeming drawn to them. "Hello?"

I bit down on my hand to keep from screaming at her to stop. My frantic attempts to wave her off went unnoticed.

"Who are you? What are you doing here?" Alice stopped near one of the hunters and tried to look at his face, her hand outstretched. He walked through her and shivered. She scowled, tears filling her eyes as she stormed after him. Her dressing gown fluttered in an invisible breeze. "Answer me!"

I wanted to scream at her to *shut up*. She was going to get me killed, and perhaps her too, if ghosts could die twice.

The men moved methodically. While one inspected the stairwell, the other traced his light over the picture frames on the wall above me. He brushed a hand over the shredded canvas, muttering something in a language I didn't understand. His search lowered to the table—*my* table. I held perfectly still in the shadow of a gilded frame, scarcely breathing as he set down his light to pick up one of the other pictures. He wiped the glass with his sleeve, considering the faded image within.

Sweat beaded on my brow as I looked down the line of the dust-caked frames. There was nothing to stop him from inspecting them one by one until my hiding place was seized. I lifted a trembling hand, finding it almost impossible to hold my target. If I could knock the last frame on the end to the floor, his attention might be diverted just long enough to—

"Why can't he see me?"

I jerked my head up, rescinding the spellwork. Across from me, Alice's visage appeared in a large, grimy mirror hung on the wall. Had she been human, her body would have to hover ten feet off the ground to reflect her face so high up.

"Alice," I mouthed, glancing toward the nearby hunter. "Help me!"

Anger and confusion battled in her expression. I imagined it had been some time since she had felt any emotion with particular vigor. I had never seen her like this. Her normally placid face didn't contort naturally, and it was all I could do not to look away. The room steeped deeper into a chill. The hunters still couldn't see her, but I knew they noticed *that.* The table rattled as the nearby hunter set the picture down and stepped back to observe the room. His gaze passed right over Alice once more.

"He was supposed to come back for me," Alice moaned. "All I wanted was his heart. And now… he can't hear me. He won't listen!"

I so desperately wanted to shriek. *Alice, these men aren't who you're looking for! They are here to hurt you!*

Her pale mouth opened as though to answer my thoughts—and slowly began to *stretch* as her eyes rolled back. Her pristine features decayed before my eyes.

A wail of horror caught in my throat as my harbored spell shot from my palm—directly into the mirror. The glass splintered, shattering the nightmarish image.

Blinding light spilled over me. I couldn't see, and as I staggered back, the beam mercilessly followed. Alice seemed to have dematerialized, and the room had fallen into a stark silence. Both hunters were angled toward me, edging closer.

"What the fuck is that?"

The weight of their stares bore down on me like a physical force, crushing the air from my lungs. I thought I might pass out where I was. But something else stirred in me, too—a primal instinct to *survive* surfacing, channeling my fear into a single point of determination.

I wasn't going to die tonight.

As one of the humans stepped closer, cautiously outstretching a hand, I burst into flight with a desperate cry. I flew into the space between the looming figures, flinching at the hiss of surprise they both gave. The stairs were *right there*—my path to freedom.

I zagged through the air, but to my horror, they quickly caught onto my pattern. And I was getting tired. I flew through the banister on the stairs, only to have the taller human step into my path. How could they move so fast?

Skirting away from his reach, I landed on a lamp to gather my bearings. Their steps thundered closer, searching. I murmured a spell while I fumbled for my knife. My heart kept drumming in my ears, making it difficult to string together a coherent thought, let alone an incantation.

One human moved from the stairs; the other was lifting his light at me with something else in his hands. A sinister glint of metal.

A strong attack might be my last hope. I could wield my dagger like a conduit, amplifying my power to send invisible, icy stabs of pain to my chosen target. Such lethal magic was forbidden on the training grounds, but Father had shown me how. It had been so long ago. If I could just remember the spell—

An explosion cut through the chaos. After that, time fractured, and I realized three things.

One, I was in agony. I'd never felt pain like this before. It made my breath seize and the fight leave my body. I felt myself rock forward, plummeting like a fallen leaf.

Two, the hunters had stopped advancing as though they knew their pursuit was finished. I watched their shapes distort as I flapped hard and managed to slow my fall. Something was wrong. I wasn't gaining altitude. I craned my head to the side and glimpsed my beating wings seconds before I made contact with the ground.

Three, there was a hole in my wing.

5

JON

What in the Disney hell am I looking at?

The little figure lay on the floor like a broken doll—unmoving other than a disturbing twitch of its dragonfly wings. I shared a glance with Cliff, who gave a terse nod. We inched closer, flashlights and guns still trained on the creature.

"You think it's dead?" Cliff asked.

"Could be in shock."

The creature's twitching stopped, drawing my eyes to the damage.

Cliff's aim never ceased to amaze me; he had pierced one of the gauzy wings directly through the center. If he had shot the creature's body, there wouldn't be much body left to stare at.

"Or it's faking." Cliff cocked his head, eyes narrowing. "Could be playing possum like that basilisk outside of Portland."

Easing forward, I dropped to one knee and nudged the limp figure with the barrel of my gun. As the creature was turned onto its side, its head lolled upward. Short auburn hair spilled away from its face—the face of a young woman.

"I think you shot a fairy," I murmured.

"Should we watch our backs for a unicorn next?" Cliff dead-panned. "Fairies aren't real."

"Then what is it?" I didn't dare tear my eyes away from the woman's prone form. "Haven't we heard about them before? I feel like we have."

"Yeah, from assholes who like to exaggerate and cheat at poker."

"Maybe they weren't exaggerating."

"I still say this is some kind of distraction—"

Cliff stopped short as the fairy stirred. Grimacing, she lifted her head and blinked hard. With shaky movements, she sat up halfway and looked over her shoulder at her wing. The second she spotted the hole in the colorful membrane, she gave a choked cry. Her wings buzzed in a short burst. Her whimpers morphed into an unnerving howl of agony.

Chest heaving, the fairy craned her neck and squinted through the flashlight beams. Her lips moved with half-formed sentences. I couldn't catch more than a few words—something about *"stars"* and *"please don't kill me."* With a pained grunt, she shifted to hands and knees.

"Stay where you are," I snapped, immediately wary of an attack. "Don't move!"

She flinched at the order but didn't stop her mad crawl toward a metallic glint on the floorboard beside her. A small knife.

"I said *don't move*!"

She was on top of the knife when Cliff stowed his gun and reached for her. The fairy snapped onto her feet with a snarl. She brandished the weapon and made a vicious swipe at his fingers. Her aim was off by a wide margin. I stifled a wince at her pathetic attempt.

That didn't stop her from stabbing at Cliff a second time.

"Ow!" Cliff seized his hand back, glaring at the bead of blood that welled from a small cut on his finger. He wrenched the weapon out of her hands with a muttered, *"Bitch."*

Cliff pulled the fairy into a tight fist and inspected the blade in the light—it looked like it was made of silver with some intricate detailing on the hilt.

"Don't fucking touch me!" she shrieked.

"Come on, enough. Know when to fold 'em," Cliff grunted as he shoved her knife into his jacket pocket.

Angling my light, I leaned in for a closer look. Her arms and legs were pinned to her sides, but her torso and wings were visible. The hole in the membrane of her wing was clean—not a drop of blood. Interesting.

"What are you?" I asked her. "What are you doing here?"

She snapped her head toward me, eyes wild. Cliff's brows pinched, and I leaned forward with him to listen as she moistened her lips to speak.

"Let me go," she rasped.

I clenched my jaw. Fat fucking chance of that.

"What happened to the missing people?" I persisted. "Are they still here somewhere?"

I glanced around the shadowy interior of the house. There were nearly a dozen rooms and a steep basement if the cellar doors adjoined to the wrap-around porch were any indication. If we couldn't save those poor people, we could at least lay their bodies to rest.

The fairy ducked and began to shake. She stayed like that for a few moments. I tensed, ready to wrench her away from Cliff. She could be summoning a curse, priming herself to sear the skin right off his hand—

Tears were streaming down her cheeks when she finally lifted her head.

"I have no idea what you're talking about," she said through gasping breaths. "I stay away from humans. I didn't do anything. Please… *please*."

I recoiled slightly. Her desperation was hard to watch. Her face was convincingly innocent—so much like the frightened victims Cliff and I had managed to save over the years. But she *wasn't* human. So, chances were, she wasn't innocent.

Headlights swung into view through the window, illuminating the room.

"Cliff," I hissed, motioning for him to follow.

The two of us scrambled out of view from the window. A car door slammed, accompanied by a harried voice I recognized as the groundskeeper. We'd tried to get some info out of him earlier, but he ran us off the property, assuming we were true-crime fanatics.

"That's right, a gunshot!" The groundskeeper's shadow slunk past the headlights, heading for the front door. "See, I told them down at the station that we need an officer here! They looked at me like I was crazy!"

"Out the back," Cliff said, nodding the way we had come.

I froze for a moment—if only to appreciate how fucking *weird* this find was. A brief look exchanged with Cliff told me we were in agreement—no matter how bizarre, we couldn't leave behind the only lead we'd found on this hunt so far. People were dying, and we were running out of time. If the pattern continued, the next victims would be mere days away. Maybe less.

As we made our way to the back door as silently as possible, a fresh wave of fight gripped the fairy. Cliff stowed his flashlight and covered her mouth with his thumb. That did the trick of silencing her renewed screams, but I could still hear her muffled attempts as we crept outside.

We had hidden the car in the nearby underbrush. While I got situated behind the wheel, Cliff peered back out toward the Dottage mansion.

"Hang on a minute before pulling out," Cliff warned, jerking his chin toward the flashlight beam that bobbed through the windows. "Wait till he gets to the second floor on the other side, at least. He won't be able to make out the car if he sees it."

"You're sick—both of you!" Having wrenched herself back in Cliff's grip, the fairy's voice drew my eyes down. She twisted so violently back and forth that she'd snap her neck if she weren't restrained. "I haven't done anything!"

"Can you fucking hold still?" Cliff grimaced like he wanted nothing more than to drop her on the car floor. He glanced at me, looking for sympathy. "She's squirming like a coked-up hamster."

She turned her face away from Cliff. Her gaze met mine for half a second before she regarded her wings. Fresh tears welled in her eyes as she stared at the ragged hole.

Cautiously, Cliff reached toward her wings with his free hand to inspect his handiwork, inspiring something between a snarl and a whimper from her.

"Don't!" She tucked her chin down and wept, shoulders hunched to brace herself.

Her cries weren't loud anymore, but they were raw. Pained. I gave Cliff a silent nudge to back off, and he did.

We needed her conscious to get answers out of her.

"Is it going to kill you?" I asked after a beat. "That wound?"

"What does it matter?" Shuddering, she wouldn't look up. "You're going to kill me anyway."

Something flickered over Cliff's expression. I felt it, too—the uncertainty. But there was no room for leniency when she might very well be the thing that had caused two ravaged bodies to turn up in the last month alone.

"At the moment, you're more useful alive," Cliff said.

The groundskeeper's flashlight beam bobbed through one of the upper windows. I took that as my cue to start the car—headlights off.

I tore my attention away from the passenger's seat and focused on getting us the hell out of there.

Finally, we had a lead.

6

JON

Most monsters didn't have the intelligence to beg for their life. Banshees, prowlers, and kelpies were driven by animal urges, the basest of which was simply to survive.

If only every non-human were like that. Unfortunately, some creatures that drained human beings like Capri Suns also had brains. Whatever higher power allowed *that* had to be a sick fuck.

Killing monsters was more complicated when they were intelligent. Vampires tried to outsmart you or reason with you, having invented some demented ethical mantra for preying on innocent people. Held at gunpoint, werewolves begged for their lives, promising to only feed on animals if they were spared.

I'd never once met a monster who could keep their word.

Following Cliff into the motel room, I bolted the door behind us. The curtains were already drawn tightly, leaving the room in near-pitch darkness until I elbowed the light switch. He'd been hiding the fairy under his jacket as we made our way through the packed parking lot, and she looked disoriented as she blinked in the light.

My gut twisted as I watched her cautiously. She was *very* intelligent. Harmless as she looked, we had to keep our guard up.

She started up again, glaring at Cliff with bloodshot eyes. "Get your sweaty hand off me! Let me go!"

"My hand's not sweaty," Cliff scoffed. "And if I set you down, you'll attack us with hellfire or whatever it is fairies do. So, no deal."

"Don't you think I would've done that already if I could?"

"You tell me."

A feminine growl escaped her. Then, to my surprise, her voice softened. She'd been fighting to free herself for half an hour. She had to be exhausted.

"I don't have any magic to attack you with," the fairy said like it was a shameful confession. "And my wing is damaged. I can't fly. I can't fight. If you put me down, I promise there's nothing I can do but stand there. Terrifying, right?"

Cliff's expression flickered as he considered her claim. He caught my gaze, assessing me. I offered a small tilt of my head. Her dagger was confusing, I'd admit. In the few stories I'd heard of fairies, none of them had mentioned melee weapons in place of magic. But if she was telling the truth, the risk was minor.

Her little sneer cut through my thoughts. "Are you really that scared of me?"

I shot her a flat look. She blanched and lowered her gaze.

Cliff took a seat at the small table the room offered and slowly unfurled his hand against the wood.

"If you try anything, this night is gonna get a helluva lot worse for you. Capiche?" Cliff told her.

I sat across from him. Now that her body was fully visible again, I had to fight the instinct to lean in closely to get a better look. There were so many details on her clothes and wings I could barely make out even when I squinted. Judging from the way she hugged herself and sulked toward the wall with her head down, my curiosity was entirely unwelcome.

Still, I couldn't help but stare. The lamplight offered a better view. She had reddish hair swept back in a messy half-ponytail. Her wings held a patchwork of colors across the swirling iridescent membrane. She wore earth-colored clothes and a lean thigh holster with an empty sheath. I couldn't tell for sure, but her eyes looked a vibrant green when they caught the light.

Though her face was blotchy from crying, she was pretty—which further convinced me to keep wary. Last summer, we'd ambushed a vampire coven and found a sobbing young woman hidden in a cupboard. She'd thrown her arms around Cliff in gratitude and promptly attempted to sink her teeth into his neck. She'd been their queen.

Leaning back, Cliff grabbed a water bottle from the stash beside the wall. He gulped at it before offering some to the fairy—a veneer of charm.

She shook her head and dropped to a seat, unblinking. "So you can poison me?"

"Sweetheart, why would we bother with poison when there are a million quicker ways to kill you?" Cliff asked.

"Hunters thrive on suffering."

Her tone was sharp, but it quivered at the edges. Dangerous or not, she was afraid—and fear was a potent stimulant to coax information out of anyone. Folding my arms on the table, I leaned to where she'd rooted herself by the wall.

"Those two victims aren't the first to go missing near the Dottage house," I said. "Do you live there?"

She peeked up from her knees, glaring between the two of us. "I'd never been inside before tonight." She was trying too hard to sound matter-of-fact. "A shame, since I was clearly missing out on this warm, human welcome."

My skin prickled at the venomous dip in her voice when she said *human*. Other monsters said it the exact same way.

"You know, this'll all go a lot easier if you agree to be honest," I said. The darting eyes, the hesitation behind every word; she was lying about *something*. It was a matter of figuring out which parts. "You had a reason for being there. Hoping for more victims, but you got us instead?"

"For someone who hasn't seen a fairy before, you're certainly eager to accuse me of murder," she said.

Cliff lifted an eyebrow. "In our experience, things that look sort of human enjoy killing humans. So you can drop the innocent act."

"It's not an act!" Frustration brimmed in her misty eyes. As she looked between us, her brow furrowed. For half a second, she looked more puzzled than terrified. "Your teeth..."

Cliff reached for his mouth. "What, first you accuse me of being sweaty, now there's something wrong with my teeth?"

Her gaze drifted back to me. "They aren't sharp?"

"What the hell are you talking about?" I frowned, driving her flighty attention back to the tabletop.

"I just. I always heard that hunters had..." She shook her head. "Never mind."

"So, you know about hunters, then," I noted.

She folded her arms tightly over her chest. "Obviously. Why do you think I've been so friendly?"

Bad liar. Decent sarcasm. Every word she spoke got further under my skin with how human-like she was.

"Look at these pictures. You recognize their faces?" I pulled out my cell phone, pulling up the screenshots of the four missing persons posters the police department had circulated.

Leaning away, she wrinkled her nose. "Friends of yours?"

"Innocents," Cliff said. "Just regular people going about their day."

"First two were found last month outside city limits," I said. "Torn to shreds, half-eaten. The next two, Rick and Charlie, just vanished a week ago. Car was found, but not them. Dottage is the only building for miles out there." I set my jaw, watching her face for any twitch of a bluff.

"It's just wood and dust in that place," the fairy said. "You've made a mistake."

I stifled a laugh, muttering, "Where have I heard that before?"

After a few tense moments, she shifted and reached for the satchel at her hip. I tensed, whipping my hand out of reach—but she didn't withdraw a weapon.

"Look–" she started.

Cliff snapped the dime-sized object out of her grasp, eliciting a yelp from her.

"It's a flower," he announced, pulling a face at the tiny glint of metal and gemstone pinched before his eyes. "Like a charm, I think."

"There's a lot of them at the old house. That's all I wanted," she said, peeking through her fingers and talking with more fervor as if this was the key to her freedom. "I didn't think anyone would miss a few dusty bits of jewelry."

Cliff quirked a brow at the fairy and tossed the trinket to me. I turned it over in the light. It looked human-made and harmless. The metal was dirty and tinged with age, but its simplicity reminded me of the ones advertised at the mall for teens. This kept getting weirder.

"Wouldn't a charm bracelet be a little loose on you?" Cliff asked. "What, are you like a crow or something? You like shiny things?"

"I just thought it was pretty," she said softly.

I pushed the charm to the other side of the table, eyeing the way her little shoulders rose and fell with labored breaths. As she cradled her head, her wings drooped together—apart from the one with the hole. That one remained stiff and twitchy.

"Does that still hurt?" I asked.

"Take a guess," she muttered.

"I have something that might help with the pain," I said. "I promise, it's not poison."

She didn't even look up. "A hunter's word means nothing to me."

"Fine, then you can sleep without it." I stood, and she flinched hard. As I pocketed my phone, she studied me with mounting desperation.

"Wait!" She staggered to her feet toward me. "Can I see it first?"

I went for my bag and dug out my salve. I was down to one jar—I'd have to make more soon. When I returned to the table, I beckoned the fairy closer. Wringing her hands, she inched toward me like we had all night. Once she was close enough, I scooped a bit of salve onto my fingertip and held it out for her inspection.

She wrinkled her nose. "It smells foul."

"I make it myself from aloe vera and different oils and vitamins. Turn around."

Her face screwed up with hesitation. "What kind of oils—"

"You want it or not?"

With a huff, she crossed her arms and turned around. "You're an awful healer."

"Just hold still," I said.

Seeing how she flinched at every turn, I brought my other hand close to steady her. My fingers jumped a little at the first contact with her waist. She was soft to the touch but shaking hard enough for me to feel the tremors rattling her body. The moment I grazed her wing, any semblance of bravado fled. She began breathing so hard, her satchel rustled against her hip. Against my better judgment, I hesitated.

"Hey," I said, softening my voice. "It won't hurt. It'll just tingle for a bit. I can't tell you how many times this stuff has saved me from infection."

Shuddering, she gave a quick nod—*get it over with.* As I began applying the ointment, the vibrant color of her wing rubbed away where I touched it.

"The hell?" I frowned, leaning in closer. The membrane was actually a soft, translucent blue underneath. "What's this on your wing?"

"A hole?" She peeked back and jumped at how close I had gotten. "Oh. It's paint."

"Why do you have paint on your wings?"

She shrugged. "Why do you wear a green shirt? Colors are *nice.*"

I exhaled sharply to keep from chuckling.

With the ointment fully coating around the hole, I pulled my hands away from her. Whatever sense of humor she had quickly faded the longer she looked at her damaged wing.

"How did you do this to me?" Her voice was so soft, I couldn't even be sure she meant to be heard. But then she glanced up questioningly. "You… you were both across the room when it happened. How?"

"A really good shot," I said, looking pointedly at Cliff.

The fairy gripped the strap of her satchel for dear life as she regarded him. "You nearly killed me, and for what? A little game of questions I can't answer?" She spat on the table, eyes blazing toward Cliff. "Our stories were right. You're a savage. Both of you are."

The *cajones* on her. I didn't envy being on the receiving end of Cliff's scrutiny.

"I don't give a shit about your campfire stories," Cliff said, his voice sharpening to a point. "Blink those little doe eyes all you want, sister—you're keeping something from us. If you think we won't find out what that is, you have another thing coming."

He reached past the bottled waters for the twenty-dollar bottle of bourbon we'd been nursing since we checked in the other day and helped himself to a two-finger pour. He offered the bottle to me. I nodded, and he prepared an identical glass.

Cliff tipped back half of his drink, then rose from his chair and headed for the door without a word. I could see how the fairy's wings flickered yearningly as she looked through the open door before Cliff slammed it shut.

"Now what?" she asked without facing me. "What are you going to do to me?"

I eyed her earth and jewel-toned clothing. She would blend right in among trees and foliage, and there was a massive stretch of woodland near Dottage. The back of my mind stirred with fragments of folklore my mom used to share about nature spirits.

Respeta la naturaleza, mijo, y los espíritus te bendecirán.

Respect nature, and you will be blessed.

Spirits were benevolent in those stories—usually. But the reality behind lighthearted myths was never accurate.

"We still don't really know what you are," I said. "We can't just turn you loose when we don't know what you're capable of. People are getting hurt." I chewed my lip before casually tacking on, "How many more of you are near that house?"

She stiffened. "None."

"*Our stories*. That's what you just said. Unless you're talking to squirrels and rabbits about hunters."

"I heard those stories when I was a child," she said, then squared her shoulders with a touch of bravery. "I'm alone now. I'm... *nomadic*."

"Really? So you expect me to believe you have the reach to paint your own wings?"

The fairy whirled to face me, folding her wings as though I might forget the paint if I couldn't see it. Her mouth opened and closed with half-formed lies.

The door swung open. Cliff returned with a sturdy shoe box tucked under one arm—one of several we kept in the trunk of the car to hide bullet boxes inconspicuously. After all these years together, we could read each other pretty damn well. I knew exactly what he was doing, and while it made me uneasy, I knew he was right.

What other choice did we have?

"What is that?" the fairy asked as Cliff set the box on the table and removed the lid. It was empty.

Despite the questioning looks she threw my way, I let her flounder in her confusion while Cliff added a cap of water to the shoebox. When he crumbled a cracker into bits and laid those down, too, she finally pieced his actions together. I snapped out a hand, grabbing her by her waist before she could bolt.

She clawed and kicked. "You can't just contain me like some rabid animal!"

"I'm sorry," I murmured, and I actually meant it. "Lives are at stake. We can't risk it."

The box was taller than her. She ran at the sides the moment I released her inside, but she couldn't escape without her wings in working order. She thrashed against the thick cardboard, eyes wide as Cliff reached for the lid.

He paused to give her a small, humorless smile. "Maybe you'll be up to talking more tomorrow. Sweet dreams."

He fitted the lid on and placed his journal on top. We stood back to observe the box's security for a few minutes. The thick cardboard juddered slightly as the fairy pounded on every side, but the lid didn't budge. It would hold her until we figured out what the hell to do next.

7

SYLVIA

I should have stayed with Damian.

I screamed myself hoarse before realizing the hunters, in all their cruelty, could completely block me out. Of course they could. They probably had someone tied up and begging for mercy twice a week.

My foot sank into the cap of cold water. Snarling in a voice I hardly recognized, I kicked the cap as far as I could in the darkness. I felt around for the pathetic food offering and crumbled it between my hands. After tossing the crumbs aside, I sank with my knees to my chest.

Hours ago, I'd been drinking berry wine under the night sky. Now, I was caged like an animal. Or a monster. At the moment, I wasn't sure which option was worse.

Burying my face in my hands, I tried to steady my breath and *think*. My options weren't great.

An ice spell could tear through the box, but then what? As talented as the hunters were at ignoring me, they were bound to notice that I wasn't as harmless as I claimed. Besides that, I couldn't fly. They'd tear me to pieces before I could get away. Even if I escaped the box, I'd have to evade them on foot.

Healing the hole in my wing was tempting to try, but I had the horrible feeling that these hunters could sniff magic out like hounds. My pulse quickened at the image of the men holding their breath out there, waiting for me to summon magic so that they could pounce. I wasn't even sure I could heal such a serious injury. I'd soothed a few scrapes on the membrane after flights through brambles, but nothing like this.

I took a deep breath and released it, urging my racing heart to slow. If they continued to think I was entirely powerless, maybe I could survive.

As that resolve settled in, my nerves revolted at the thought of sitting complacently in the darkness. I couldn't wait around for them to torture me when it suited them. Putting my hands to the walls, I felt around for weaknesses in the box. The walls had some give, constructed out of a strange texture that I might be able to claw through, but that would take ages. Days, maybe.

I lifted my eyes to the lid—out of reach but not by much. I selected a spot near the center. I jumped with my arms overhead and missed contact by a whisper. Gritting my teeth, I tried again—this time, giving my wings a brief buzz. My injury screamed in agony, but the burst provided an extra boost. My palms hit the top. The lid jolted a little. There was something weighing it down. *Dammit.*

"Assholes," I muttered, falling back to a seat. I was out of breath, all for nothing.

Reluctantly, I considered the textured walls surrounding me. A slow plan was better than no plan at all.

I scooted to the nearest corner of the box and started clawing.

They didn't torture me. Not how I expected, at least.

After the hunters' endless stream of questions last night, I was surprised to be left alone for most of the following day. Time seemed to stretch in the darkness, stewing me in my own panicked thoughts.

Nightmares had stolen any relief sleep might've offered when I finally succumbed last night. I dreamed of hunters tearing my wings apart piece by piece. My throat felt raw. I must've screamed in the night—symptoms of night terrors I hadn't had since I was a child.

As the hours passed, thoughts of monsters occupied my mind when I had run through every self-pitying mantra. Such beasts had never troubled Elysia in my lifetime beyond pages in the archives. The thought of one being so close to home made me all the more petrified to be separated from my family. The pictures the men had shown me last night… I shivered to think of those faces torn to shreds. If the hunters had simply killed whatever monster was loose without dragging me into their hunt, I might've been grateful.

They gave me more water and something to eat. *Meat* this time. It smelled no better than scorched rabbit. The hunters, in all their wisdom, picked up on my revulsion when I gagged violently, and a nutty cracker replaced the meat. I should have been dizzy with hunger, but my appetite was dulled. Instead, I used the cracker to hide what little progress I made in clawing away at the wall.

From what I could garner, both hunters were usually in the room, but occasionally, one of them left for one reason or another. To my disappointment, they weren't arrogant enough to leave my prison unattended.

They spoke to each other sometimes—two living thunderstorms conversing. Most of it was indistinct crumbs of information: grumbles about *management* and how the water pressure in the shower was even worse than in the last place. Before long, I realized the hunters didn't dwell here permanently. They were like nomadic fairies, finding different destinations as they made their way around. But instead of living for the joy of freedom, they lived for blood and death.

My ears perked when Cliff seemed to be talking to himself for a long stretch of time, pacing up and down the length of the room. The Other was silent, yet Cliff was clearly responding to *someone.* I leaned against the wall and listened with a frown when it became obvious his one-sided conversation was about *me.*

"That's right, man, a fairy. Wings like a dragonfly, attitude like you wouldn't believe." Cliff paused, then chuckled humorlessly. "Then this is one hell of a long drug trip. Help me out here. You sure you haven't seen one before? Or know anyone else who has?"

I held my breath and listened hard, but I couldn't hear the answer.

"Yeah… yeah." Cliff huffed. "Thanks for nothing, asshole."

The Other spoke up. "Did he laugh?"

"Of course he laughed, the bastard."

A weighted pause followed before the Other asked, "What about Tammy?"

"Already tried. Line's disconnected. You know how it goes—she'll be calling us from a different number weeks after we're done with the case."

A fresh chill crawled down my spine. Somehow, they were able to get in contact with other hunters who weren't in the room. This place was filled with all manner of strange devices that I hadn't gotten a good look at.

The Other had several more one-sided conversations that went more or less the same way as the one I'd heard. A small measure of relief coursed through me, knowing that, apparently, fairies didn't end up as hunters' prey often enough to be common knowledge.

I was the one who had to go and screw that up.

Dry crumbs stuck to the inside of my throat when I forced a nibble of food. I shoved the cracker aside, longing for the dining hall. Chances were, I would have sighed with discontent at the routine breakfast set before me. I couldn't begin to count the number of times Damian had snuck me a second helping of dessert when the main course was lackluster.

Damian.

I pressed my lips tightly together to hold a sob at bay. For a blissful moment, I allowed myself to escape. His eyes had been so bright, so hopeful the night of the revel—but I couldn't bring myself to think about that now. I thought further back to the first time we kissed.

Six, maybe seven springtimes ago, I had displayed a decent aptitude for healing. I was encouraged to spend mornings in the healing ward to train my secondary affinity. Damian had shown up in a bloodstained shirt, having gashed his shoulder on a thorn while flying. The wound was too deep to mend with the base-level healing most fairies were capable of.

I'd teased him, of course, pointing out how he always accused *me* of being a reckless flier. A proper healer took care of the deepest part of the gash and instructed me to close the rest.

"*Promise not to make it worse,*" he'd said playfully.

"*Hush. I only make things better.*" But when the healer left us alone to tend to another fairy, my nervousness must have been palpable.

When I began the spell, he hissed in mock pain and made me flinch. Normally, such taunting would have inspired my temper. I'd peeked up to find our faces a breath away from each other. His grin had been so warm, so good-natured. He'd only wanted to make me laugh. My face had heated, stomach stirring with butterflies.

My intention had been to fluster him in retaliation, so I did the only thing I could think of—closed the space between our lips.

And flustered he'd been, but not upset. Damian pulled back and beheld me like I had given him a gift.

Heavy footsteps approached, jolting me from the pleasant image of Damian's enamored expression. *Cliff*. After a mere day as their captive, I could tell the difference between him and the Other by gait alone. When the lid vanished, I backed against the wall as though I could melt into the box.

"Good, you're still awake." Cliff's deep voice made my body tense of its own accord—more so when his mossy eyes traced over me studiously. "Comfortable?"

A dark laugh spilled out of me as I cast my gaze around my barren surroundings. "Nothing says *homey* like a dusty old box."

The corners of his mouth twitched upward. "Come into the light."

The command was effortless—a man used to barking orders and having them followed. When I refused, he plucked me up by the back of my blouse and deposited me unceremoniously on the table before him. I scrambled to right myself on my hands and knees, torn between terror and indignation, as I glared at him.

"Hey, don't look at me like that," Cliff said. "I told you to move. This would've been easier if you weren't so stubborn."

"Choke," I muttered.

A quick scan of the room from my exposed vantage point brought *some* good news. The Other wasn't here.

That little smirk played on Cliff's lips again. He nudged an overturned bottle cap toward me, brimming with an amber liquid. He jutted his chin at me in an unspoken command—*drink.* Lifting it in both hands, I sipped tentatively. The liquid seared my tongue. *Not water*, I realized with a flinch. It burned stronger than the juniper liqueur mother snuck into her tea sometimes when she thought Hazel and I weren't looking. And it lacked all the heady sweetness of last night's berry wine.

"Swallow," Cliff said, watching me until I did. "It'll help with the pain—maybe your memory, too. You'll thank me later."

I coughed into my sleeve. "I doubt that."

"Just relax. This won't hurt."

All but shoving the half-emptied cap down beside me, I then froze as my gaze snagged on the weathered book Cliff had spread before him. The book's cover was an earthen color, worn thin. It was not entirely dissimilar to the nomadic journal I'd last been reading in the archives.

I noted the pencil in Cliff's right hand. As I stared openly, his intense gaze alternated between me and the spread pages. I stayed rooted, too dumbfounded to protest. Was he… *drawing me*?

With each stroke of graphite, my form took shape upon the paper. Even in the initial sketch, the meticulous attention to detail awoke a begrudging admiration in me. I recognized my tousled chin-length hair and the gentle sway of the deep blue fabric hugging my waist, revealing a wide swath of my navel. He was talented, and it left me feeling both captivated and unnerved.

"Spread your wings," Cliff said. His voice cut through my train of thought, startling me into momentary obedience like a child caught with a wandering gaze during affinity training.

He continued his work, and I studied the finished page beside my own: a dark, detailed drawing of a creature with elongated limbs and a distorted, humanoid face. Even upside-down, the image made goosebumps rise. Scrawled notes crammed the remainder of the page. *Known names. Location. Weaknesses. Feeding habits.*

My stomach dropped to my feet. Panicked magic rose up in my blood, the unearthly chill rushing through my skin and bone. This was why they were prolonging my death. Cliff was immortalizing his latest kill.

It took all my strength to muscle my magic back down before Cliff saw because—*fucking stars, my life is going to be reduced to mere entry in a journal, and no living fairy will know but me.* Spellwork flowered easily under strong emotion. If I wanted to maintain my claim to docility, blossoming ice all over the table would royally fuck me over.

As much as I enjoyed my dark, frozen fantasies of skewering blades of ice into the hunters' hearts, I knew I was outmatched.

"I'm guessing that silver's not your weakness since you're still breathing," Cliff remarked as he sketched the veining on my wings. He paid careful attention to the details of the tattered hole he'd created.

His searing gaze steadied on my face for a moment. I gave a slight shake of my head, gritting my teeth as I willed my skin to warm.

"The bullet I hit you with was silver," he went on. "Would you have been worse off if I had hit you with steel or copper?"

I focused resolutely on the gentle flicker of the light at the far side of the room. He was leaving out one important substance: iron.

No metals burned humans. Iron, copper, silver, none of it. The hunters handled it all without worry. But me… I shared the same iron vulnerability as many of the beasts these hunters must have encountered.

The meager food in my stomach churned at the thought of the hunters testing all of their metals on me until they found one that made me scream. My own skin would betray me. I didn't sense any iron in the room now, but that didn't rule it out from their arsenal.

"I do have a weakness, actually," I said, peeking up to watch his stare sharpen with interest. I leaned forward conspiratorially, bracing my hands on my folded legs. "Strawberries. Don't give me any, and *definitely* don't soak them in honey and coat them with sugar."

Cliff exhaled a laugh and ran a hand through his hair—shorter and lighter than the Other's. It was still a shock to register his disarming smile—teeth white and not sharpened to fangs in the least.

"But wait," I interjected, holding his gaze. "The cruelest thing you could do is give me fresh air. I'd suffocate in seconds. Thank you so much for keeping me in that little box. I've never felt more alive." I imagined my growing grin was a touch demented—but I needed to smile, or I'd break down in tears again.

"You've got jokes, I'll give you that," Cliff said with a soft chuckle. His eyes flickered down to his journal. "Listen. If you cooperate and let me finish these sketches, you get to stay out here for a little instead of being in there." He nodded at the box. "Capiche?"

That word again. "I still don't know what that means," I admitted.

"You just say it back. Capiche."

I hesitated. "Capiche." Hopefully, I hadn't just signed myself away to an oath-like contract. With the hunters' aversion to magic, I supposed I was safe.

However, I soon found myself questioning whether humans *did* have some form of magic after all, given the odd furnishings they had at their disposal. After following Cliff's instructions to turn my back to him and spread my wings, my gaze wandered, trying to make sense of my surroundings. The only time I'd caught a glimpse was when Cliff carried me to and from the washroom for two minutes of hygiene.

This room was not at all how I pictured a hunter's lodgings. The walls weren't splattered with blood or adorned by gruesome trophies of past kills. Green and white motifs danced across the wallpaper, peeling at the edges like old wounds. Two beds dominated the space. Nightstands stood on either side, their surfaces marred by scratches and stains. Slivers of muted sunlight struggled to penetrate through the curtains, casting shadows across the worn carpet that stretched across the floor.

"What's that?" I breathed, eyeing a large black box mounted to the wall.

"TV," Cliff grunted. The scratch of pencil on paper didn't slow.

The device noiselessly flickered with vivid images—*humans.* Talking, laughing, sorting through papers.

"Those people can't see us, can they?" I asked.

"Nope."

"What are they doing?"

He cast a quick glance over his shoulder. "Giving the news."

"About what?"

"I dunno, I'm not paying attention to it. You're closing your wings. Keep them open."

I fanned my wings and peered at the TV again. "What happened? Where did they go? Who are *those* people?"

"It's a commercial." Although he was beginning to sound exasperated, I could hear a note of amusement underneath.

"What's a—" My words broke off in a cry as the picture suddenly turned black. I turned to look at Cliff for an explanation and found him pointing a handheld device at the TV. I cocked my head.

"TV remote," he said before I could ask. "Turn toward me now. Ah-ah—" The end of the pen tapped under my lowered chin. "I need to see your face."

I swallowed hard, complying. It was worse, watching him watch me. A self-conscious flush spread across my cheeks despite my best efforts to maintain a semblance of dignity.

While I didn't appreciate posing like a doll, *anything* was better than being imprisoned in the dark. There were plenty of distractions around the room to keep me occupied. My burning curiosity felt like a betrayal. It was the reason I was in this mess, but I couldn't keep my mouth shut.

I bubbled with questions again and again, pointing as best I could without breaking my pose. A majority of Cliff's answers were clipped, but he went into brief explanations on a few. The TV remote controlled the TV. The lamp brought light when it was dark. The air conditioner kept the room cool. All of them worked due to something called *electricity.*

"How have you survived this long if you're so vulnerable?" he asked.

My wings gave an involuntary twitch of annoyance. *What an asshole.* "Do you flatter all of your prisoners this much?"

"You've been asking enough questions to make someone wanna take a bath with a toaster. Can't I ask a few without you freaking out?"

"Was that a question or just an insult?" I replied, narrowing my eyes.

"Don't get your panties in a twist. We can't be the first ones to come across you."

"Guess I've just never encountered a threat as incredible as you."

He chuckled. "Easy, tiger. I found your stash, by the way. Gotta say, your taste is questionable."

"What are you—" I stopped short when he set his pencil aside and reached into his jeans pocket. Soft metallic jingling caught my ear. Cliff held up a broken string of freshwater pearls and a rusted skeleton key. *My treasures.*

My mind raced, cataloging every time he'd been out of the room today. He had gone back to the Dottage mansion. I silently thanked the stars above that Damian and my family had possessed the wisdom to stay away, lest they, too, fall prey to this fate.

Cliff's eyes glimmered with a self-satisfied gleam as he observed my dismayed expression. He deftly spun the key in the light, a simple action that sent a pang through my heart, recalling how I had carefully concealed it between the floorboards of the mansion long ago.

"Looks like you built up quite a collection," he drawled. "Are these the original keys to the Dottage house?"

"No, they're tiny saws," I said, fighting the urge to fly up and snatch it out of his hand.

His smile widened by a degree.

"This obviously wasn't your first time up at Dottage. What else were you lying about?" The demand came without a shout. He was smooth and collected, utterly confident in his ability to pry this information from me. I hated to admit my resolve was weakening. He leaned closer, casting his rugged features into shadow. "Did you lure those victims into the house?"

I lifted my gaze, willing hatred to ascend the exhaustion in my eyes. "No."

"Did a monster have something on you? Force you into a Bonnie and Clyde situation or something?"

"No!"

"If I toss your collection in the garbage, will your answer change?"

"Be my guest," I snapped.

Cliff's expression didn't twitch as he tucked my delicate treasures back into his pocket. "Suit yourself."

I moistened my lips, my resolve wavering at the muffled clink of the pilfered jewelry.

There was a man and a woman there the other night. They were afraid of you.

No. These hunters were eager to spin their own stories about me. Admitting to anything could very well lead to iron being dragged across my skin to pry out even more—especially if it meant they'd catch their *prey*.

I pushed myself to my feet, ignoring Cliff's command to stay in position. Smugness flickered beneath my misery when I noted a subtle tick in his square jaw.

"What's the matter?" I asked. "Out of questions and lost without something to brutalize?" The purred words were surely my death sentence as they slipped out of me, but I wondered if it wasn't a more honorable death to go down fighting—*a warrior's death.* I mustered a crooked smile—the finishing blow. "How pitiful."

Cliff's expression darkened, a ripple of tension making his powerful frame go taut against the wooden chair.

"Look at me," he murmured. "Do I look like the kind of person you want to fuck with? Keep it up, and this is gonna get a lot less friendly."

My hands flew to my hips, wings snapping shut. "This is your idea of *friendly*?"

The corner of his mouth lifted in a humorless smile. "Sweetheart, you haven't begun to see me pissed off."

The door unlocked, and we drew apart, tension severed as the Other strode inside. The sight of his warm skin and wavy brown hair didn't feel real after facing his shadowy form last night. His muscular arms gleamed with perspiration beneath the crisp white undershirt he wore as he bolted the door.

My focus slid to his hands, my eyes widening in alarm as I sensed the unmistakable, sickening aura that had entered the room with him—iron. He was wielding iron.

"How's she doing?" Cliff called over, straightening in his seat.

"It's still making that weird noise," the Other replied, and I realized they were talking about an object, not *me*. "But I think it'll run. It might be the serpentine belt. Pretty cheap fix."

"I'll just be happy if we get another fifty thousand miles out of her," Cliff said. "This car's too young to crap out on us now."

"If we can at least get it through this case, we'll take a breather and have a shop look at it."

Cliff sighed, snatching up his pencil callously. "Wish we could've gotten to the morgue before they cremated the bodies. A good look at the teeth marks would've narrowed it down."

"Hey, maybe we'll get lucky. I called the station again." The Other wiped grease from his hands on his dark jeans. He walked between the beds, dabbing his face with a towel tucked near the headboard. "The cops are still convinced it's a coyote."

Goosebumps rose along my arms as they shared a laugh.

"If it's a coyote, I'll eat my belt," Cliff muttered. "Place is definitely haunted with that chill, but that's gotta be circumstantial. Ghosts can't take a corpse that far out from where they're bound. What've we got it down to now? Ghoul, werewolf, psoglav, banshee…"

"And at least a half dozen more."

"Does *every* monster in the book have to ravage people's insides like silly string?"

Their voices dulled in my ears as I raptly watched every flex of the Other's hands. The rod he held was thin and small in comparison to him—not even the length of his forearm. The ends were blunt—*not a skinning knife, thank the stars.* It had to be a tool of some sort, perhaps for their vehicle, judging by the oily residue that matched the smudges on the hunter's shirt and hands. But it was cold iron nonetheless, pure enough to sear me to the bone—my skin prickled with a thousand invisible needles at its proximity.

My gaze locked with the Other's—I couldn't help it. A new heaviness crushed my lungs as the Other looked from me to the iron, a slight furrow in his brow.

Cliff took notice of my abrupt, slack-jawed silence. "The hell's wrong with you?"

A burst of courage swelled alongside my curdling fear. I lifted my chin and held Cliff's stare without faltering. My father used to say you could only prove your fortitude when you were most afraid.

"Draw your damn picture," I said in a low voice.

His lips parted slightly in surprise, frustrated green eyes burrowing into mine like talons.

I found myself thinking of Mother's ever-unshakable posture and calm poise when challenged. She had always seemed unbreakable. I straightened my spine like hers as Cliff resumed his work in silence.

I tried to tell myself that I was surviving, but it didn't feel like that. I felt pathetic and dirty. Hot tears slipped down my cheeks.

"For what it's worth," the Other said from across the room. He still studied me with an inscrutable intensity. "Once we know you're not a threat, we don't need you anymore."

He didn't bother specifying if the end of my usefulness meant freedom or death, and I was too afraid to ask.

8

SYLVIA

My cupped hands trembled under the stream of water in the washroom. There was a mirror over the sink, but I was positioned too low to make any use of it. I doubted that looking at myself after a day of captivity would have the same charm as the Dottage mansion.

The ceramic walls containing me were too smooth and steep for escape—I'd tried that morning. My energy was spent from ripping up the box corner, surviving one hour to the next, and praying I would feel the sun on my skin again. I envied the water as it found freedom through the dark opening at the bottom of the basin. I would have followed it if I could fit.

A single, hard knock of warning at the door threatened to make me lose my footing. I hurriedly washed my face and finger-combed water through my hair.

Exactly thirty seconds later, my privacy was up.

"This'll be the last time for the day," the Other said, filling the doorframe. "Are you sure you're finished?"

More than anything, I wanted my interaction with him to be over. I nodded.

I had nearly turned down this washroom visit when *he* was the one who offered it. His recent contact with iron made me worry that residue alone could fry my skin. Although I now knew that wasn't the case, I still held my breath when he took me out of the basin.

As the room flew by on the way back to the box, I didn't bother peering around at the oddities that filled it. I only had eyes for the window, where orange sunset light spilled past the curtains.

Curfew was around the corner. My eyes, already sore from crying all afternoon, had the capacity to form more tears.

What must my family think? *Lost, run away, killed.* I would become Elysia's first cautionary tale in decades. Meanwhile, the council and guards might be interrogating Mother for my whereabouts. I wouldn't put it past Ayden to demand information from Hazel, too. The thought of her weeping in admission to my Dottage visits made bile rise to my throat. She would blame herself, my sweet sister.

And then, I pictured what would have happened if she agreed to come with me on an adventure. Against my will, images flashed through my mind: Hazel shut away in a box, forced to pose for sketches, touched by iron, bones broken by a hunter's uncaring fist.

A low whine escaped me.

"What's wrong?" The Other paused and frowned, holding me over the box.

"My wing," I said hollowly. "You may not have noticed the subtle, gaping hole."

His lips twitched, but he didn't taunt me. "The salve lasts about a day. I could give you more."

It meant longer exposure to his touch. But it also meant the company of the sun's dying rays.

I nodded.

When he retrieved the salve and shuffled me to the tabletop, I merely turned myself around to face the window and crossed my arms. Primal fear shot through me when his fingertips brushed against my wings, every nerve in my body aching to *run, hide, attack, attack, attack.* I envisioned a cold mist gathering in my hands, ice sharpening into deadly spears to plunge through his vile heart.

I'd never killed anything before. If I wasn't quick enough to follow through on such a spell, I had no doubt he would kill me so fast, I wouldn't even realize I was dying.

There was something morbidly tempting about that gamble.

"You were screaming last night," the Other said, as though this was a normal way to begin a conversation. "Bad dream?"

"I was screaming for you to release me."

"After that."

"Of course. You must be well-versed in all manner of screams. Which is your favorite? The one that comes at the beginning of torture, or the one that comes shortly before death?"

The Other's voice remained low and calm, ignoring my jabs. "I've had nightmares before. Brutal ones. What were you dreaming about?"

"Are you disappointed that you couldn't *watch*?" I sneered.

He stayed quiet, not rising to the bait like Cliff.

"You tore off my wings one by one," I said after a beat. "Then you put me back together with your salve so you could do it again." I tried to sound angry, but my voice caught at the end. *No*—I would *not* cry again.

His fingertip paused, resting on the base of my right wing. I shivered at the pressure—every touch was amplified on that sensitive patch of skin.

Strange caution filled his voice. "You think I'd do that?"

"If I did something crazy like bit you, maybe. I'm not keen on testing that theory. I've heard enough stories about hunters."

"What kind of stories?"

Squaring my jaw, I tore my attention from the window to glare daggers into his studious brown eyes. "The kind about creatures fighting back against men like you and winding up dead."

He made a slight noise that might have been a chuckle, sending a chill down my spine that rivaled the warmth of his touch. "That one may be true. But I wouldn't kill you for biting me—assuming you're not venomous, that is."

"I'm not."

"I didn't think so." One side of my wing was coated with the strange-smelling balm. The Other dipped his finger in the jar, gathering enough ointment for the reverse side. "I've been wrong before… but you don't seem bloodthirsty. Which is—" He hesitated, stumbling over his words. "It's confusing."

Admittedly, I was confused, too. His touch was far gentler than I expected. His fingertips grazed over the hole in my wing with astonishing, feather-light pressure. Hunters tore and raved and skinned. They weren't supposed to be capable of such delicate actions.

"I don't know what other rumors you've heard about people like me and Cliff, but we help people," he said. "Most humans don't know how to defend themselves from monsters. We're trying to save lives."

"*Humans*," I snarled. "You're trying to save humans. My life has a very different value to you, doesn't it?" I wet my lips, my boldness finding a second wind. "What is a monster, in your opinion?"

A dark shadow crossed his gaze as if he was seeing something beyond the dingy room. "A monster preys on, hurts, and kills the innocent."

"I am innocent," I said, trying once again to sound brave through a fractured voice. "You preyed on me. You hurt me." *And you soon may kill me.* "By your own definition, *you* are a monster."

The Other was quiet for a full minute—the amount of time it took him to finish up and screw the lid on the little glass jar. The air crackled with a new tension that set me on edge.

"For someone scared for their life, you have no problem running your mouth," he said, arching a brow as he set his gaze back on me.

"Says the man with the savior complex."

A disbelieving smirk tugged on his lips, but it didn't meet his eyes. Perhaps I'd struck a nerve. *Good.*

"Keep it up, maybe I'll wipe that salve right off. You want to be set free, but I know when someone's lying to my face. You're hiding something."

"You're right," I said, squaring my shoulders. "I've been withholding how much I'd like to stab you in the eye."

"Come on, with that little knife you had?" He scoffed skeptically.

"Any sharp object will do. I'm not picky."

The look on his face became utterly unreadable—though I got the sickening feeling the Other could see right through my bluff. I averted my gaze out of habit and stared at the glint of gold that hung off his wrist. At first, I thought he might have been cruel enough to claim a trophy from my stash, but I'd never seen this piece before. The chain held black and blue beads, unlike anything I'd found in Alice's home.

"Look, I want to believe you're innocent," he said, drawing my attention back up. "You can go on about torture all you like, but we don't normally keep prisoners. The problem is, you're not giving us much to run with. So we do what we have to."

He was talking about *my life* like it was a matter of business. As though it was my fault they were inconvenienced with the task of holding me against my will. Anger churned with my fear, surfacing magic in my blood—the kind of simple, raw power that didn't require a single spell to touch my lips. My skin went ice-cold. Unlike earlier, the Other was too close to give me time to oust the ice magic. A frown registered on the hunter's face as his fingers brushed my side.

"You're freezing," he said.

For a moment, I couldn't breathe. His intense expression was concerned, confused… but not furious. No shout of alarm followed.

"Well, you didn't give me a chance to bring a quilt and cloak along, did you?" I tried to keep the quaver from my voice. I desperately buried the magic and warmed my skin—hoping it wasn't too little, too late.

Frown still etched, the Other nodded slowly and put me back into the box. Apparently, hunters couldn't smell magic as some legends claimed, *thank the stars*.

"Your wings are still intact," he said. "Better than your nightmare, right?"

I folded my wings, heavy from the balm. I wouldn't admit that the ache of the injury was dulled.

"That remains to be seen," I answered.

I swore there was something resigned about him as he shut me into darkness.

Only a minute passed before the lid opened briefly, and the Other set down a folded cloth next to me without a word. When his steps trailed away, I touched the fabric. It was soft from wear but large enough to be—

A blanket. He was offering me a blanket. To him, it had to be a handkerchief.

In the darkness, I didn't have to hide my bewilderment. Kyra used to tell the most horrific stories about hunters over late-night mugs of berry wine. Legends about hunters cloaked in furs and monster skins, proudly wearing vampire fangs like jewels on rings and medallions. She painted a vivid picture of how the bloodlust would gleam in their stare, much like an owl's eyes caught moonlight in the dead of the woods. How their teeth went sharp from years of living savage lives—the mark of their chosen path.

Cliff and the Other didn't look at all like that, but the legends failed to accentuate how intelligent hunters could be. More intelligent than any predator I'd ever known. Dealing with a brute would be more straightforward than a man who knew manipulation worked wonders where threats lacked.

I pointedly stalked away from the handkerchief even as the chill of the air began to bite at my exposed shoulders and navel. The Other was trying to wheedle information from me by making a show of kindness.

I wouldn't fall for his games.

Sometime after sunfall, I heard the hunters discussing a human body found in pieces in the neighboring town. They assumed that the same monster they were tracking here was responsible. The car was running well enough, and they debated who would make the journey. My heart leaped when they considered both going; they would undoubtedly drag their prisoner along for the ride, separating me even further from home.

Relief crashed into me when I heard Cliff grumble that he didn't want to deal with the headache of transporting me. It was settled between them that the Other would stay behind.

"Whatever it is obviously fed already," Cliff went on in a gruff voice. "Safe enough for a one-man sweep. I doubt it stuck around, but there's gotta be a thread there we can pull on."

I heard a jacket grabbed off the chair. Supplies were taken from a bag. A sinister, metallic *click* came from the awful thing he'd shot me with. I could imagine them taking note of my nosy silence. After a beat, their voices lowered further. I had to hold my breath to make out the next part.

"Cliff… We have to dump her soon," the Other said.

"I know."

Dump her. I didn't need to guess at that implication. The Other could stuff a hundred handkerchiefs into the box to keep me warm—that wouldn't change the fact that the hunters would do away with me in the end. Perhaps it was starting to dawn on him that the cold he'd felt on me this evening was *unnatural.*

I should have been paralyzed with panic at the certainty of my demise, but for the first time since my nightmarish meeting, I felt true, maddening hope.

There was only going to be one hunter in the room with me tonight.

I moved the stale cracker away from my chosen corner and pried at the papery material for what felt like the thousandth time. The box had once been unwavering against my beating fists, my bleeding fingers seeming like a waste against its structure. But my work had not been for nothing—there was a hole as large as my head in the corner. When I pushed at the surrounding material, it bent.

If the stars determined our fate, I had been certain they despised me. But maybe I was wrong. In the dark, a grin spread over my face. I could have a hole big enough to crawl through *tonight.*

I would not be a victim. I was a survivor—a triumphant warrior rather than a noble dead one.

I endured an excruciating hour waiting for the Other to fall asleep. Then, to be safe, I waited another few minutes, listening to his slow, measured breathing. I wasn't going to spit on my chance of freedom by being hasty.

But I didn't know when Cliff would return, either.

I took a steeling breath before tearing through the final layer of the box's coarse material, my fingernails throbbing. And then, there it was—*freedom.*

The corner faced the wall. I climbed through and steadied myself on shaking legs. *Pull it together.* I wasn't getting out of here if I was as twitchy as a child learning to fly. My first breath outside the box was electrifying and pure.

I peered around the side of the box toward the Other's bed. Still breathing evenly.

My gaze moved to the main door. I had played this moment out in my head dozens of times. If there was no gap or crack in the door I could worm through—which seemed unlikely given how unloved the rest of the room was—I would wait crouched by the entry until Cliff returned from the other town. In the time it took him to realize I was gone, I would have slipped right past his ankles. I'd be outside, and my captivity would begin to fade into a bad dream that would pass away in time.

I ran faster than I'd ever run, faster than I thought I could. Flying came more easily to me than running, and I considered pausing to conjure a round of healing for my wing. But it would take at least five passes to fully heal the gaping hole in my membrane. I didn't have the time and energy right now.

I didn't risk even a moment of flight. The Other would hear, or I would fall.

By the time I had scaled down the table leg, I was panting for air. I made a mental note to suggest to Karis more running at our next training session. I was one of her best students, regardless of how tough she was on me. How could I possibly be so out of breath?

From the carpet, the human room loomed around me. The alarm clock cast an eerie red glow over objects that otherwise towered in shadow.

I bolted again. Running on the carpet was challenging. My shoe caught on one of the coarse strands almost immediately and brought me crashing to my knees. Cursing, I brushed myself off and resumed pace.

The bed creaked.

I should have kept running. I shouldn't have hesitated or turned to look my nightmare in the eye as every hair on my arms stood on end. Maybe then, I would have had a real chance.

The Other was sitting up in bed.

9

JON

I couldn't remember the last time I'd slept for longer than a couple of hours at a time. Tonight was no different. After a few years on the road, waking up to take note of my surroundings became second nature. With Cliff away for the night, I was even more on edge.

Blinking in the darkness, I was fully prepared to turn over and fall back asleep—but then, I saw it. The movement was so small that I thought I imagined it. But I'd looked at the fairy's wings plenty over the past day, and there was no mistaking that shimmer of iridescence.

On the *floor*.

"Shit!" I bolted out of bed and tore open the nightstand drawer to grab the iron bar I'd stowed away.

So much for peace offerings, I told myself, thinking of the handkerchief.

She had started running for the door, but the lack of hiding places sent her doubling back to the table. I relaxed marginally—at least she was still in sight. Gripping the iron tightly, I dropped to my hands and knees and then made a grab. She dodged out of the way faster than expected.

"*No*!" Her shriek pierced the air as I lunged between the chair legs.

I was so focused on her that I misjudged how close I was to the seat. I knocked my head on the edge and reeled back, grimacing.

Embarrassing as hell, but my grab herded her out from under the table. She stumbled into the open on my left, eyes on the dresser.

"Stop!" I pointed the iron rod at her, and she froze.

The chase ended abruptly. The fear in her expression shifted into something manic—eyes on the rod, not on me. The same look she'd given the iron earlier that day. My suspicions were confirmed. I didn't know what the metal did to fairies, but it had to be gnarly to justify how she gaped like the bar was a snarling lion.

"Where did you think you were gonna go?" I barked, not expecting an answer.

I grabbed her with my free hand before she could snap out of her fear and make another break for it. She let loose another scream. I wanted to look away from her face—her expression made my insides twist. She struggled to break free from my grip, but as I stood, she went very still. Tears streamed down her cheeks suddenly. Then, she tucked her chin low, unable to look at me any longer.

"P-please," she gasped out. "Not the iron. Put another hole in m-my wing. Keep me in the box for a week without opening it. Just, please… No iron."

Her refusal to look up gave me time to school my expression. She'd cried and begged before but never while suggesting alternate methods of torture.

"I don't get you," I murmured. "Scared out of your mind all the time about pissing us off, but you won't back down."

"I… I had to try. Am I supposed to wait around until you decide to *dump me*?"

"That's not—" *Not what I meant.* I doubted she would believe me, and I couldn't blame her.

Huffing, I regarded her for another second before heading back to take a seat at the edge of my bed. I turned on the lamp and set the iron aside on the nightstand. Hesitantly, I loosened my grip and let her fall to a seat in my palm.

"W-what are you doing?" She looked wildly in all directions, her chest moving with rapid breaths. "What are you going to do to me? Please..."

"Calm down," I said. "Take a deep breath, and let's talk."

She refused, straightening viciously. "Calm down so you can *kill* me easier? Tell me what you're—"

I put my fingertip over her mouth. "*Shh.* You can't freak out on me and listen at the same time."

She squirmed and gave a pitiful growl, immediately followed by a pinprick of pressure on my finger. She was trying to *bite* me.

"You don't let up," I scoffed in amazement. "What if I told you I'm not planning to kill you?"

Her little hands clawed at my finger until I pulled it away. I expected her to keep fighting, to maybe even try to jump out of my hand. But she didn't. As she caught her breath, all the fight vacated her at once. She pulled her legs close and hugged them, peering up at me from behind her knees like she was waiting for me to hurt her.

"Of course you won't kill me." Her voice was so soft that I had to lean closer to hear. "Then your fun would be over."

Not for the first time in the past two days, a stab of discomfort coursed through me. Looking into her tear-filled eyes worsened the feeling. I'd seen something similar to that look nearly a hundred times when monsters were rendered powerless and waited for me to deliver the killing blow.

I remembered her cold declaration that I was a monster. In her eyes, the assessment was justified. She couldn't fathom the horrors and deceptions we had encountered.

That didn't change the fact that our precautions had to take a higher priority than her feelings. But it was becoming so damn *hard.*

"Do I look like I'm having fun?" I muttered.

She didn't answer.

As I continued to observe her, something caught my eye. When she sniffled and wiped her face, streaks of crimson came away on her cheeks. I frowned, brushing her tousled hair off her face with my other hand for a better look. I ignored her feeble attempt to lean away from me. There was *blood* on her face.

"You're hurt," I said.

I pinched her wrist for a better look. What the hell had she done to turn her fingertips ragged and bleeding? I glanced at the box, noting that the lid was still firmly on with Cliff's journal weighing it down. Cardboard crumbs littered the other side of the table. My jaw went slack with realization.

"You dug through the fucking box," I breathed, unable to mask my astonishment. That had to be the equivalent of a human clawing through plaster or drywall with their bare hands.

And now, she was shaking like a leaf in my hand, her blood all for nothing. I wasn't used to this tug in my chest when dealing with a non-human—the kind of compulsion that had me reaching over to my duffle to find my jar of salve without thinking.

"What are you going to do to me?" the fairy asked again, rubbing her wrist where I had touched it. "What would *he* have you do to me?"

I snorted. "Cliff? What, you think he's in charge around here or something?"

"He's the one who put the hole in my wing… And he's—" She wrestled over the wording. "He's loud."

I fought off a smirk, making a note to share that little tidbit with Cliff when he returned. "I've got this handled," I told her. "Show me your hands."

Immediately, she plunged her hands into her lap. "Why?"

"Just hold them out."

"No."

"*Ay, puñeta*," I huffed in annoyance, reaching with my free hand again.

There was nothing I could say to convince her, so I'd prove my intentions instead. She twisted away, angling toward my fingers and making it difficult to grab her tiny arms without snapping a bone in my haste.

"Hold. Still," I gritted out.

Finally, I had a firm grip on both her arms. I forced them forward and held them there until she understood that she was better off preserving her energy. Lips pursed, she turned her hands palm-up.

Cautious of any sudden movements from her, I released her arms so I could prepare the ointment. She held still, wearing a miserable scowl that quickly scrunched into disgust as I applied the medicine. Her heels scrabbled against my palm like she couldn't contain a full-body reaction.

"It feels like snail mucus," she whined.

"It'll help with the pain like your wing. I'd be worse off with scars if I didn't use it." When the fairy's eyes widened, I added, "What's so shocking about that?"

"It's hard to imagine anything hurting you—not that I haven't tried to picture it." She grimaced and shook out her hands, blowing on them to dry the gel quicker. "Notice how I haven't given you a reason to use this stuff on yourself?"

"That knife looked like it could do some damage," I said.

"Why don't you give it back, and we can find out?"

I shook my head, stunned by her bravado. Clearly, she wanted to survive, but she couldn't seem to stop herself from snaps and sarcasm. "Do you have any idea how many times dead you'd be if you said that to the wrong hunter?"

Tammy wouldn't have hesitated to sear the fairy with iron for information—*all's fair in this brutal business, boys*. Hotheads like those amateurs Jameson and Rhett we'd hunted alongside in Oregon years ago might've obliterated her for any injury to their pride alone.

"You're lucky we're the first ones who found you," I told her, lifting a brow.

"Oh. Yes. Every minute I sit in that box, I can't stop thinking about how *lucky* I am." Razor-sharp words aside, she was still pale as a sheet.

"You're looking at me like I'm about to eat you," I said. "No sharp teeth, remember?"

"True. But after consideration, I don't think sharpness makes much of a difference." For all her deadpan quips, she didn't seem to be entirely joking about this one.

"Why would I want to eat you when I've got this?"

When I set my hand on the nightstand, she hurriedly scooted off. As I pulled a half-eaten chocolate bar from my bag, my head began to clear—thoughts catching up with actions. Fairy lore was too intense and deep to cover in a couple of days, especially when we had an active hunt and a faulty car to worry about. But *glamour* had come up in my research. For a moment, I wondered if she was winning me over that way. Except, she wouldn't be trapped for so long if she was capable of influencing us.

For a non-human, she was scarily… *human.* Intelligent, yes. Bloodthirsty… I wasn't so sure anymore.

"What's that?" the fairy piped up. Sure enough, she had moved to the furthest edge away from me.

"Chocolate. I think you could use some."

She frowned. "More healing?"

"Kinda."

Cliff wouldn't be happy if he saw this. Then again, even Cliff would have to admit that keeping the fairy locked up hadn't done much good in getting answers out of her. Maybe some simple human kindness could win her over.

She made a choked noise when I pulled my pocket knife from beneath my pillow, but she relaxed marginally when I cut off a small piece of the chocolate bar. I dropped it in front of her and nodded encouragingly. She hadn't eaten much lately, but it was worth a shot.

Something lit up in her eyes when she bit into the corner. She dove back for a second bite, bigger than any I'd seen her take. Apparently, we should have been feeding her sweets all this time.

"Now what? Back to the box?" the fairy asked.

"You tore a hole in it," I pointed out. I supposed I could tape it up, but that felt like a sloppy risk.

I glanced at the nightstand drawer. The solid wood could hold her, but I didn't love the idea of harboring a prisoner indefinitely. We weren't those kinds of hunters. The fairy was standing there rigidly by the lamp, trying to read me with a taut expression.

But she wasn't running anymore. She wasn't fighting. She simply looked so exhausted and tormented that I couldn't stomach it anymore.

Nearly every attempt at kindness could be misconstrued as a trap, so I had to make a drastic leap of faith to have any chance at gaining her trust—and learning whatever she was clearly hiding.

"Tell you what," I said, tapping two fingers on my spare pillow. "If you behave, you can sleep here."

"But... That's yours."

I shrugged. "I won't be sleeping much more tonight anyway. You can take it."

Her watery eyes narrowed. "You'll be watching my every toss and turn."

"Beats getting locked up in the microwave, doesn't it?"

"The what?"

"That thing." I pointed across the room. She couldn't possibly know it was used to heat up food, but she looked like she might faint all the same.

She folded her arms, made contact with the salve on her hands, and gruffly unfolded them again. "Won't he be mad?" she asked. She regarded me thoughtfully, then gave a heavy sigh. "I can't tell which of you is worse."

"Well, *I'm* the one who gave you chocolate." I held out my hand to her, lifting an eyebrow. "Come on. No tricks, I promise."

The fairy balked for a full ten seconds before she let me move her to the pillow. Her weight was slight, hardly making a dent in the cotton. I gave her space, noting how her gaze inevitably lifted toward the front door. Her lithe body tensed, muscles coiled.

"Don't," I warned her in a low voice. "Just sleep. No need to hurt yourself worse."

As eager as I was to get through to her, I was taken aback when her demeanor shifted.

"I don't understand," the fairy said, shaking her hair off her face. "Why… Why did you put away the iron?"

Her voice was so fragile. I studied the jar of salve in my hands.

"Guess I noticed that you're more interested in running away from us, not toward us for revenge."

"Then… Why not let me go? Please."

I tightened my grip on the jar before tossing it at my duffle. It missed the opening and rolled onto the bed. I couldn't look at her.

"Every non-human I've ever met only causes pain and death," I said. "They want us to bleed by their very nature. But… you haven't tried anything. You haven't tried to kill us, seduce us into selling our souls, or trap us in an eternal nightmare. I don't understand you."

The fairy's eyes widened, and she scoffed at me. "Well, forgive me for confusing you by not being a murderer. How can someone like *you* be remotely afraid of me?"

"Looks can be deceiving."

"And sometimes, they're exactly what they are," she fired back.

I didn't wrestle off the tired, wry smile that came to my lips. "For someone the size of a mouse, you've got a lot of spirit."

Her green eyes flickered, raking me up and down. Her posture softened like she was slowly seeing less of a snarling animal in me. "If you weren't a hunter," she said. "I might actually accept that as a compliment."

"That's a shame, then."

"It is." She sniffed, looking away pointedly.

The tug in my chest resurfaced—I couldn't let her sleep thinking I might smother her before she awoke. She had to know we were going to release her. Somehow, it mattered to me that I wouldn't stay a complete monstrosity in her eyes.

"I lied to you," she announced, halting my train of thought.

I drew in a sharp breath and leaned away from her slightly. She didn't appear to be priming herself to attack, but I stayed wary all the same. "What is it?" I asked.

"I…" She wet her lips and wrestled with herself. "I was there the night before you caught me. There were two humans. They didn't see me, but I heard them. They… mentioned that hunters might be after them—"

"*What?*" I blurted, crowding toward her.

She cringed away, casting a wild look around the room for an escape.

"Hey." I lowered my voice. "I'm not gonna hurt you. Look at me."

Hesitantly, she did.

"You can tell me," I assured. "It's alright. What did they look like? What'd they say? Any names?"

"I couldn't see their faces, and I don't think I heard any names, but… I'm starting to think one of them was your monster. I've never been near one before, but something felt horribly wrong."

"What does that mean?"

"There's this… *ability* I have. A sort of instinct." Each word fell from her lips hesitantly as though any one of them might set me off. "I can sense non-humans and other beings that you would consider unnatural. It's meant to help my kind steer clear of those things. Maybe I could point you in the right direction if you take me back to that old house. But if I do that, you'll have to let me go. Does that sound like a fair deal?"

Desperate hope painted her face. It was a little heartbreaking. I considered telling her I planned to release her regardless of what she offered, but it *was* a tempting ability to make use of.

"Why didn't you say something about this earlier?" I asked.

Fresh, uncertain tears welled in her eyes. "I thought you'd kill me if I told you everything. You wouldn't have a use for me anymore. And then, I thought if I admitted I lied…"

"You thought we'd kill you for *that*," I finished. "So why admit it now?"

She shrugged, mumbling, "You didn't lock me in the microwave. That counts for something, I suppose."

After pondering her offer, I nodded. "Okay. We have a deal. You help us at the house, and you're free to go."

"Free to go *immediately* after," she said, pointing a finger at me. "Swear that you won't enslave me."

I scoffed. "That didn't even cross my mind."

"Not even for a second?" She frowned suspiciously. "When was the last time you negotiated with a non-human? Stars, when's the last time you *spared* a non-human?" When I couldn't come up with an answer, she made a small noise of contempt.

"Fine," I said. "I promise there's no strings attached after you help us. But we're not going anywhere until Cliff comes back with the car, so we may as well get some rest."

That was easier said than done. Even after I turned out the lamp and laid down to offer the illusion that I planned to sleep, the fairy continued to sit stiffly. As the silence dragged on, she wouldn't stop glancing at each corner of the room and then at me as if she was waiting for the other shoe to drop.

"You can sleep," I told her, a thread of exasperation entering my voice.

"You first."

Sighing, I grabbed my phone and my earbuds, feeling the vigilant prickle of her stare all the while.

"Here." I set one of the earbuds on her lap. "Listening to music helps me relax."

She picked up the earbud and made a face. "What is this, an instrument? Do you expect me to play it for you?"

Stifling a chuckle, I put the other earbud in and settled back down. The fairy jolted when one of my playlists started. Jaw agape, she stared at the earbud as flutes, strumming, and soft vocals began pouring out. The music didn't bring the peace I'd hoped. She shifted to her knees, clutching the earbud close and looking at me with wide eyes.

"What is—how did you make this?" she exclaimed. "It's amazing!"

"I didn't make it. Don't you have music wherever it is you come from?"

"Not like this! I didn't think a hunter would want to listen to something so pretty."

She felt the wire up and down like she might be able to figure out how it worked. There wasn't a trace of fear in her eyes for once. Just wonder and burning curiosity. I'd caught only a glimpse of it when Cliff was drawing her, but now, it was unbridled.

A soft smile tugged at my lips, but with it came a dismayed whisper at the back of my mind: *We fucked up*.

I cleared my throat. "Hey, can I ask you something else?"

She froze, walls rising. "Depends."

"What's your name?" No answer came, so I pressed. "I'm Jon."

"Jon," she murmured. "I'm Sylvia."

A startled laugh shook through me before I could stop it.

"What?" she demanded.

"It's just so… normal. Human. I was expecting something with five *y*'s in it."

Sylvia hugged the earbud, looking offended. "It does have five *y*'s," she said flatly. Then, she laughed at my incredulous expression. A real laugh. Her dimples were barely visible under the tear tracks. "I'm kidding."

As she continued to inspect the wire, I noticed how carefully she was handling it. "Are your hands feeling better?" I asked.

"Your salve works well," she said begrudgingly. Her eyes narrowed, and she leaned away from me. "This better not be a trick—the chocolate and the music. Because it won't work."

"It's not," I assured, deciding not to spotlight the fact that she was willingly sitting on my pillow and not trying to escape. If it was a trick, she'd dived headfirst into it. "Come on, Sylvia with five *y*'s. If I wanted to hurt you, I wouldn't use sugar and ten-dollar earbuds."

Lips pursed, she stared at the earbud on her lap like she was still trying to work out why I chose to share it with her.

"Do you like the song?" I asked. "It's one of my favorites."

"It's decent," she said stiffly. After listening a few seconds more, she relaxed somewhat but still wouldn't lie down.

"Hey, you'll need your energy if you want to keep your end of the deal," I pointed out. "Get some sleep. Seriously."

She gave a harsh laugh. "Haven't you figured it out? I am *not* falling asleep next to a hunter."

10

SYLVIA

Stars, I hadn't been this comfortable in days. I woke up cocooned by warmth and soft fabric. Smiling, I arched my back and stretched into the cushiony surface. There was a pleasant smell in the material beneath me, notes of sharp citrus mingling with something more masculine. My room at home didn't feel like this.

My eyes flew open.

The hunter's bed.

Seizing up on the pillow, I swallowed the urge to shriek. I cursed under my breath and looked around frantically, thinking of the awful things that human could have done to me while I slept. My skin was unburnt by iron, my wings intact. The sheets had even been tugged up to my shoulders.

That didn't matter—I should have been stronger. I should have stayed up all night to keep an eye on the hunter.

Low voices caught my ear, making me glad that I hadn't reacted more dramatically. Both hunters were in the room. I steadied my breath. Rolling over carefully, I peered across the pillow. Cliff was seated at the foot of the other bed. His square jaw was clenched hard as he laced up his boots.

"I can't believe you made a deal with her," Cliff muttered, throwing a dirty look at the Other—*Jon*.

Jon was less frightening now that he had a name, but my stomach twisted anew as he pulled a clean shirt over his head. He was built like the type of warrior we only heard of in legends anymore, scarred and muscular. Built for *violence.* The number of scars was astonishing—evidence of battles fought and won.

"I don't think she's dangerous," Jon said, adjusting the thin gold bracelet on his wrist.

He looked over at me. I shut my eyes and held my breath as the weight of Cliff's stare joined.

"Did you have to test that theory by inviting her into your damn bed?" Cliff snapped. "Look what she did to the fucking box. You're lucky she didn't claw your eyes out in your sleep."

"Give me some credit. Obviously, I would've killed her if she got hostile. I felt out the situation and watched her all night to make sure she didn't try anything."

"Bullshit. You were out cold when I walked in. How am I supposed to sleep knowing you're gonna bend every time a vamp or werewolf has a pretty face?"

I dared to squint my eyes open as I heard Jon's heavy steps move. "Hey, fuck you, it wasn't like that. I… talked with her." He pulled on a navy jacket. "For the record, she said more in that half-hour than in the past day."

My heart sank. Had his kindness last night been another manipulation?

Jon's voice softened. "Look at her. If she's a monster, she's a pretty sorry one. There's nothing else we can get from her."

"She lied to us from the start," Cliff growled low in his throat. "How do we know she's not keeping more from us?"

"You really don't trust me?" Jon's voice rose with—was that *hurt* I sensed?

Cliff shrugged with a poor attempt at stoicism. "Just a bad call."

Jon scoffed. "What, are you gonna leave again? Over *this*?"

A heavy pause settled into the room. Obviously, this had struck a chord. So, the stonelike hunters *did* have a soft spot—each other.

"Sorry," Jon muttered, breaking the tension after a moment. He sighed through his nose before straightening his stance. "Cliff, we have bigger issues to deal with. We should take her up on her offer. Her info's the closest thing we have to a lead. If you've got another idea, I'm listening. Otherwise, the trail's cold."

I supposed that answered how Cliff's investigation had gone last night.

Cliff's green eyes were like chips of cold fire as they rested on me. For a moment, I swore he was fully aware of my eavesdropping. Could hunters *smell* when you were awake or asleep?

"Fine," he muttered, standing. "Just promise not to take any more catnaps with her."

They went about their morning routine with hardly another word. As usual, a dripping sound came from one of the devices I'd asked Cliff about—*a coffee machine*. As its smoky aroma filled the air, I continued to lay in silence, conflicted.

Against all odds, Jon trusted me. As much as a hawk trusted a field mouse, anyway. If I weren't still terrified of revealing my magic, I'd demand that we seal our agreement with a blood oath. That way, I could be sure they would be punished with shooting, white-hot pain if they broke their word to me. The pain was said to be temporary but intense enough to drive fairies mad—or so I'd heard. I'd never known anyone brazen enough to risk it by breaking a sworn blood oath.

Hopefully, Jon and Cliff would show a scrap of decency and keep their word without the threat of agony.

Rattling footfalls approached me, stirring my thoughts back to instinctual self-preservation. I squeezed my eyes shut, burying my fingers into the pillowcase. Before I could relax into a more natural sleeping position, the sheets were ripped off of me.

"Morning, sunshine," Cliff said.

I jolted upright, eyes flying open to find both hunters standing near the bed, fully dressed. A thin rectangle of early morning light cut through the window, etching a severe contour to their profiles. For once, I held back from snapping something to Cliff in return. I couldn't ruin my chances of going home now. Not when I was so close.

"Apparently, you were pretty chatty last night," Cliff said. "For your sake, you better not be lying—*again*."

Jon hid me under his jacket as they exited the room. My nerves curdled at the insult of being tucked away against his person, but it was a means to an end. At the very least, his grip didn't agitate my damaged wing as badly as I'd feared. A hint of citrus clung to the fabric of his ivory shirt—the smell I'd woken up to, I realized with a flushing face.

Outside, the first taste of fresh air whispered around me. Petrichor promised *home.*

My heart fluttered. The best part of this arrangement was that I didn't even have to find the damn monster they were looking for. I would let the hunters wander around the Dottage house's lower floor and then point them urgently in a random direction. If Jon were as amenable as he'd been last night, they'd let me go.

I had to craft a story to tell my family. By the end of today, I'd be in Mother's arms, squeezed so tightly I would barely be able to breathe. I burned to tell her the truth about everything, but Elysia would go into a panic if they knew I'd had direct contact with humans. No one had spoken to humans in decades—perhaps centuries. I racked my brain, realizing I wasn't quite sure. A long fucking time, in any case. The council might keep us all underground for years if I spilled my near-fatal encounter.

No, lying my face off was the responsible thing to do. I had been trapped under rubble at Dottage, maybe. Wounded by an owl. The hole in my wing could serve as evidence.

I'd workshop it.

The hunters climbed into their vehicle, the slam of the car doors making me jump. The car roared after a couple of tries.

Cliff was sitting behind the wheel today. He checked mirrors and fiddled with a stick in between him and Jon. The car moved at his command.

Jon pulled me into the light and relaxed his hand. I scooted toward his fingers, quickly realizing that I had lost a shoe while moving about. Jon fished it out of his jacket, mumbling an apology as he handed it to me. I eyed him warily as I fitted my shoe back on and tugged at the laces that wound around my ankle. Hunters were vicious. They didn't say *sorry*.

In the pale morning sun, I could see Jon more clearly. The shadowy lamplight had been concealing devastating good looks. He had a strong jaw, tousled chestnut hair, and sun-kissed skin. His eyes, no longer flashing at me angrily, were the color of tree bark flushed with morning sun. He couldn't have been more than a handful of summers older than me, at most—unless the stories were true about hunters drinking siren blood to obtain eternal youth.

"Do you live with that many humans?" I asked, pointing toward the window. A group of people were chatting amicably around the other parked cars. Gray clouds streaked past in the sky, tinged by rays of pink and gold as the rest of the world woke.

"We don't know them," Jon said with a chuckle. "This is a motel. We're only crashing here until we get rid of the monster."

In the blink of an eye, the motel was gone, along with the humans milling outside. Other buildings drifted by, though I could scarcely get a look at them before they were out of sight—a headache formed as I struggled to make sense of my surroundings. Exploring Dottage and peering around the motel room at my leisure wasn't this overwhelming. I was now assaulted by new structures and materials faster than I could ask questions.

One consistency was the black path that the car crawled upon. "How do humans get the ground to be so dark and smooth?" I asked.

"It's a road," Jon said. "There's, um... machines involved. It's made of asphalt."

"How far does it go?" I leaned closer to the edge of his hand, peering through the wide window at the front of the car. "Are those lights over the road for decoration? And do humans live in those buildings over there? Are they *motels,* too? Why are those humans walking instead of using a car?"

Cliff groaned. "It's too early for this. Can't you just sit quietly until we get there?"

I flinched as his hand lashed out, but it wasn't toward me. He pressed one of the buttons on the front center panel of the car. Music and voices poured into the car out of thin air, not unlike the miraculous device Jon had lent me last night.

"Are you hungry?" Jon asked.

He didn't wait for my answer, digging into a bag at his feet. I wondered if my desperation was obvious on my face. My stomach was hollow after only chocolate the night before. Withdrawing a colorful box, Jon tore open a metallic wrapper to reveal a frosted pastry dotted with little flecks of vivid color.

Jon broke off a corner of the food, offering some to me before popping a piece in his mouth. "Pop-Tarts. They're sweet. Like the chocolate."

He wasn't kidding. The pastry's sugary taste burst over my tongue, sweeter than any fruit I'd ever had. There was a rich filling like a berry jam sandwiched between the crumbly bread. I dragged my finger through it to taste it in isolation.

Cliff glanced over to us. "Strawberry," he noted. "Your favorite, right?"

"It's fine," I said around a big bite. Another lie. It was *amazing.*

"That's Jon's favorite flavor, too."

Jon's head swiveled. "No, it's not."

"What? Yes, it is. You always buy strawberry."

"Just because they don't stock the more unusual flavors in most stores. Come on, you've known me for like ten years, and you don't know what my favorite flavor is?"

Cliff gave it serious thought. "S'mores."

"No."

"Hot fudge."

Jon's smile was goading. "You're never gonna guess it. I thought you knew me."

"Fine, tell me."

"Wild Berry Extreme."

Cliff took his eyes off the road to glare at Jon, mouth slightly agape like this was treason. "What the hell is wrong with you?"

"What?" Jon demanded.

"Wild Berry? That's basically strawberry! I fucking guessed that!"

"If you tried them, you'd know there's a huge difference."

Cliff waved a hand, muttering under his breath. "I can't stand that sugary crap."

"I'll have more!" I piped up timidly. "If... that's okay."

Jon gave me another piece the size of a dinner plate. I tucked into the pastry ravenously, finding my appetite had returned in the wake of my tentative freedom.

"My sister would love these," I said.

Shit. I shut my mouth. A beat passed in the car, and I knew I wasn't lucky enough to have my slip-up go unnoticed.

"Well, she'd have good taste," Jon said.

To my utter shock, I wasn't interrogated on the subject. I forced myself to stay quiet for the rest of the drive. The less information on me they had to fill in Cliff's journal entry with, the better. I didn't have to wait much longer.

I'd be rid of them soon.

The drive felt agonizingly long after that.

My breath caught as the mansion came into view. For a while, the car had been surrounded by nothing but towering evergreens on either side, lulling me with their familiarity. Now, there was no ignoring the task at hand.

After months of following my set route from Elysia, approaching the building was surreal from this angle—bathed in stark daylight, no less. The once-majestic residence appeared even more unsettling under the unforgiving sun, as if the night had served as a lavish veil to conceal its numerous blemishes. I had never noticed how many shingles were missing or damaged beyond repair. The uppermost window, which Alice frequented, was empty.

Cliff maneuvered the car toward a patch of vegetation in the shadow of the house, where basement windows were overgrown by dead grass. Fresh air rushed around me as Jon opened the door. The moment he stepped outside with me in hand, I looked toward the tree line. I'd never been around Dottage during daylight hours, but the direction of *home* was unmistakable.

I ached, imagining the cool breeze on my face as I flew through the trees, leaving the hunters and their gruesome hunt far, far behind me.

Jon quietly followed my gaze, and my insides churned at the idea that he might be analyzing my behavior—much like with the iron. For all I knew, this was a ploy for me to lead them to my village, and I'd all but marched him in the right direction.

"It's a shame that the house is falling apart," Jon said. "But it's good, in a way. Since it has less attention, the land here stays untouched. It looks beautiful out there."

His expression was sincere, eyes roving the trees instead of scrutinizing me. Maybe bloodlust and destruction weren't the only things on a hunter's mind after all. But he was still a killer. Things died painfully at his hands.

"You see that?" Cliff gestured toward another car that was parked by the house. "Security wasn't here this early before. Either they're off schedule, or…"

"They never left last night," Jon finished.

His words left the air stale. My daydream of giving them a false lead and demanding my release dissolved before me.

"Is it normal for a guard to stay all night?" I asked.

"No," Cliff said, fixing me with a stern look. "It's not."

11
SYLVIA

The mild warmth of the overcast morning vanished as we entered the house.

Cliff insisted on being the one to carry me, suggesting that Jon was too *distracted* by me. Jon had spouted colorful language at Cliff's assessment, but I was more interested in getting things over with than arguing.

"Quit moving," Cliff muttered as I struggled to find a comfortable perch on his shoulder. "It'll be your own damn fault if you fall."

"*You're* the one who's walking too fast!" I scrabbled against his neck. Years of perching on branches should have prepared me, but trees didn't complain when I grabbed them. I clutched his collar in one hand, the other tugging a lock of hair.

He flinched. "Don't do that," he snapped, shooing my grip.

"So sensitive," I said, pretending my heart wasn't in my throat as I steadied myself.

Every cautious step Cliff took made the old floorboards creak. I realized how quiet it was inside. Cheerful bird chatter and the morning breeze were swallowed up by the heaviness in the air. A seed of unease sat in my stomach, growing with every inch we moved inward. The house had always been creepy but never so… hostile.

"Feel anything yet?" Cliff's rumbling voice made me jump.

"N-no," I said.

He passed through the foyer. I could easily pick out the hole in the tattered wallpaper above the lamp where Cliff's weapon had shot through. It was like revisiting an awful dream. Vivid flashes of that night made my throat grow tight. I leaned a little further from Cliff's neck, my wing twitching at the memory.

The hunters cleared the first floor and made their way to the second. Halfway up the staircase, the hairs on my arms rose. The sickening chill that ran through me was familiar.

I straightened, searching expectantly for Alice. But then, I thought of the abandoned car outside, the way Jon and Cliff's faces had darkened at the sight of it.

What if this plummet in temperature *wasn't* Alice? I'd been so sure the human couple were long gone that I hadn't prepared myself for walking into a monster's den. My breaths came in shallow bursts. I looked at Cliff's profile, a part of me possessed by the childish urge to be put back into a pocket so I wouldn't have to see what awaited us at the top of the stairs.

On the last groaning step, Cliff stopped dead in his tracks and nearly rocked me off his shoulder. A slender woman in a long, lacey gown was silhouetted by the massive arched window. Beautiful, but my skin crawled viciously.

"Alice," I gasped, still uneased. She didn't look at me. Her gaze was milky and unfocused. A weapon was in Jon's hand with disturbing speed.

"Wait! What are you doing?" I twisted toward him. He aimed at her head.

"You can see me." Alice's voice was a delicate whisper, trembling with relief.

She lifted a hand as though she wanted to reach across the distance to caress Jon's face like her lost love. Then, she frowned. I glanced about, almost expecting a second spirit to manifest beside her—not that I had seen any others before. Alice's hand shook and changed path, a single finger pointing down at the floor. Her pale lips formed a question.

Jon pulled the trigger. The explosion cut through the air. I saw Alice vanish in a haze as the bullet cut straight through her spectral form.

That awful noise.

The hole in my wing.

My body seized. I buried myself into Cliff's neck, scarcely keeping myself rooted in place as the memory surfaced—plummeting downward. Cornered. *Trapped.*

"She'll be back," Jon muttered. "I knew I felt a spirit last time."

"Why," I breathed. My voice rose furiously. "Why did you do that? She was just standing there—she wasn't trying to hurt you!"

Cliff dragged me off his shoulder. I couldn't look him in the eye as he brought me in front of his face. Both hunters' gazes drilled into me, hostile suspicions rising once again. I wanted to curl into myself, but Cliff's grip wouldn't allow me.

"You know her." Cliff's accusation sliced like a blade. "*Alice.*"

I paled, the truth spilling out. "She's harmless. She's just a lost spirit. A *kind* one." But I couldn't expect the hunters to understand. All they could focus on was the fact that I'd deceived them—*again.*

"I told you she was keeping something," Cliff spat at Jon, who gave me a barbed look of disappointment.

"There's no such thing as a harmless spirit," Jon said, his tone far harsher than it had been all morning. "She could be the thing that's murdering people, and you kept that from us."

"Because she's not dangerous!" I forced myself to meet Jon's gaze, pleading with him to believe me.

"You don't know that. Maybe she's been tricking you into covering for her."

"How stupid do you think I am?" I seethed. "All she does is float around and look sad and talk about her lover. Your hunt has been taking you outside of the house, too, hasn't it? You said it yourself—ghosts can't leave. Obviously, she's not your monster."

Sighing heavily, Jon pinched the bridge of his nose. "You don't know the first thing about hunting. About any of this."

"You were wrong about *me*. You admitted it yourself. I haven't hurt anyone, and neither has she. If you could get it through your thick skull that not every non-human is murderous, maybe you'd be a better hunter."

Jon's face darkened, frustration making him fall silent instead of slipping into further argument.

Cliff scoffed. "Sorry, exactly how many spirits have you dealt with, sweetheart?"

"I-I… That doesn't matter," I snapped. "I've been around Alice for months. You've been here ten minutes!"

"Take it from an expert. Spirits are exclusively dicks." Cliff set me back on his shoulder and started cautiously toward where Alice had stood. "But maybe your friend was trying to tell us something. She was pointing down, wasn't she?"

I ignored the acid simmering beneath the word "friend."

"I saw those two humans come from the basement," I muttered, cheeks still burning.

As the hunters made their way back downstairs, I peered around drearily for Alice. Jon said she would be back, but this was the first time her presence had ever felt so distant. I wondered if the gunshot had hurt her even though she was already dead. I had never thought to question whether silver wounded ghosts the way iron hurt fairies.

The door to the basement was ajar. A single bulb hung from the ceiling, but it looked like it had been years since it last offered light. Cliff produced a flashlight and shined it down the narrow passage. A thin blade of light cut through the dark, illuminating a set of stairs that looked like they might splinter under either man's weight. But *someone* had clearly been here recently. Fresh mud was smeared on several of the steps.

"Hello?" Cliff called. He squinted into the passage. "If you're not dead, shout back."

Nothing answered but the distant, echoing drip of water.

Cliff hung his head, muttering a sobered curse before starting down. Jon followed behind him. The air immediately cloyed with the smell of decay and moisture—something metallic—*blood.* I glanced at Jon and Cliff to see if the humans shared my revulsion. How could they press on without wanting to vomit? The goosebumps on my arms hadn't gone down since Alice had vanished.

"Something's not right." My voice was tight, scarcely recognizable.

Cliff slowed his gait. "Do you sense something?"

His flashlight swept over the basement floor, and the rest of my words dried up in my mouth. Against the wood and stone foundations of the house, a vibrant crimson smear glinted. Cliff's other hand vigilantly trained a gun in front of him as he followed the path to its source. A human male was slumped against the brick wall.

I felt like I forgot how to speak. I had never seen so much blood in my life.

A clean kill would have been a mercy. The human had been *ravaged* by something. Pieces of him were all over the floor, making me wonder if there were multiple bodies. I covered my mouth, nearly heaving my breakfast over the side of Cliff's shoulder.

The chill that snaked through me was like nothing I'd felt before. Despite secondhand accounts from other fairies, I hadn't known I would intuitively know the difference between a monster and a friendly spirit. I wish I hadn't. This was far worse than the discomfort that came with Alice's appearances. Every inch of my skin buzzed with a thousand invisible screams that something hostile was close to me, watching me.

The sensation, I realized, was a harsher version of the one I'd experienced from the human couple.

"Take me back to the car." My shoes scrabbled against Cliff's jacket. I pulled on his collar, his hair, anything to stop him from moving deeper into the shadows. There had to be a shred of compassion in him somewhere. "Take me back, *now.*"

"We had a deal," Cliff said, resolute.

At the landing of the stairs, Jon stepped forward, covering his nose with his sleeve. "This is fresh. It can't have gone far."

He started toward the body to investigate while I looked longingly back toward the first floor—and that's when I saw the pinpricks of light reflecting from beneath the stairs. A pair of eyes.

"Wait, *stop*!" I howled. "Behind you!"

The world spun as the hunters heeded my shout.

Mottled creatures burst into the open, charging. Jon fired off a gunshot. I covered my ears, but my hearing was shattered regardless. The two creatures looked like approximations of dogs, limbs long and backs hunched. Their skin was swollen, marred with scar tissue and ragged patches of fur. Entire chunks of flesh were missing, innards pulsing and festering.

One of the creatures yelped, struck by the shot. The other continued straight for Cliff, muzzle wet and red.

The beast collided with Cliff, throwing me off his shoulder. I flailed, wings buzzing enough to slow my fall. Twisting, I landed hard on my side and coughed in the dust.

My attempts to pick myself up were thwarted by the quakes of Cliff grappling with the monster. Meanwhile, the other creature—the one that had been shot—recovered quickly. It turned its muzzle toward me, sniffing the air. Dim light caught its glistening, yellow teeth.

It charged, and all I could do was gape as death came for me.

But the beast never reached me. Darkness fell across my vision, and it lunged into the monster. *Jon.*

He scrambled to stay on top of the beast, and though it was half his size, those claws and snapping jaws were ferocious enough to keep him occupied.

Each of Jon's shoves pulled the writhing creature further away from me. He pinned the beast onto its back and pressed his gun into its middle. Three shots exploded in rapid succession. The beast wouldn't stop thrashing. A silver knife glinted in Jon's grip, and I wanted so badly to look away, but I couldn't. I watched each blow, positively frozen as blood splattered Jon's shirt and hands.

Finally, the monstrous dog fell still, and Jon removed himself from it.

There was a wildness, a terrifying rage that lingered in his eyes when he searched the ground and found me. With a heavy exhale, he reached for me. I flinched at the sight of him, and he immediately pulled his hand back, shame flickering over his face.

"Are you okay?" he asked breathlessly. Blood soaked his arm. Claw marks shredded the fabric of his jacket.

I couldn't speak. A hunter had saved my life and torn a monster apart right before my eyes. He could have let me die to help Cliff. But he chose me even though he didn't need me anymore.

Jon didn't try to coax an answer out of me. When Cliff grunted from exertion on the other side of the basement, the ground shook again as Jon raced past me. "Find cover!" he called to me. "Don't get in the way!"

A second ago, I would have obeyed and fled to the corner. Now that the shock had worn off, survival instincts surged within me like wildfire. I would have been devoured if Jon hadn't stopped the dog. Pretending to be powerless no longer served me. It didn't matter what the hunters thought of my magic. If I stayed grounded, I was as good as dead.

First, my wing. I unfurled my wings wide and flexed them toward my reach. I extended my right hand over the gunshot wound in my upper left appendage. I shook hard, stumbling over the words of the healing spell. Finally, the magic caught. Cerulean light eased from my palm as cooling, pure magic washed over the wound. I shuddered with relief to use my magic again.

The healed film covering my wing was still paper-thin and could rip through at any moment, but it would hold my weight in the air—hopefully long enough to get me the hell out of here.

Lifting into flight, I hugged the cobwebbed ceiling. The remaining creature tackled Cliff to the stairs. He kept its snapping jaws at bay with a pipe to its neck, baring his teeth in effort.

There were more pipes above me, caked with rust but brimming with more water than the ice training caverns. Power thrummed in my chest, begging to be released. I thrust my palms out and chanted. The water surged at my command, bursting through old pipes and solidifying. I shaped it into a dozen glistening icicles and hurled them downward, but the distance was further than any attack I'd ever had to volley in training. Most of them missed and shattered on the stone floor.

Time slowed for a moment as Jon and Cliff whipped their heads toward me, faces ashen and eyes bugging in shock.

"What the *fuck*?" Cliff snapped in a strained voice.

Crying the chant again, I pulled more of the gushing water and sent another wave. This time, several large shards embedded themselves deeply into the dog's mangy fur. The creature yowled, and Cliff was able to smack it hard enough with the pipe to send it sprawling across the floor.

Frozen magic crackled the air around me in a frenzy. *Control, Sylvia*, Karis snapped at the back of my mind. But this was no time for control.

As Cliff got to his feet, I briefly entertained the idea of plunging ice into both hunters. They would deserve it for what they did to me.

But Jon had saved my life, too, even though I wasn't human. Even though he had caught me in lie after lie.

Shaking itself off, the creature eyed Cliff with unbridled rage. It charged. Jon fired off another shot. I thought he knew by now those bullets seemed to do nothing, but I realized he was orchestrating movement. Creating a distraction. The dog redirected toward him, allowing Cliff to take it from behind with another brutal slam of the pipe to its skull.

I flew closer, staying far out of reach of the fight below. The creature bucked wildly as the men closed in. I could smell its fetid breath as it snarled. Cliff struggled to keep it pinned by its neck with the pipe. Jon knelt swiftly, brandishing his bloodied silver knife.

The creature's eyes rolled with maddened fervor, but I allowed myself to relax somewhat, certain this was all about to be over.

None of us were prepared for the beast's desperation to overpower Cliff. It gave a vicious jerk and broke free, scrambling for Jon.

As the mass of fur and sharp points tackled Jon to the ground, I hastily sent another wave of icicles at it. Some of them sliced through the monster's flesh, but I was certain a few stragglers also nicked Jon's skin. There was too much blood to tell.

I slowed my volley as Jon gave a roar and got the upper hand. He rolled onto the beast, and his knife found its target. Several hair-raising yelps later, the horrible creature stopped moving.

Jon slumped back and tilted his head up. His choked gasps replaced the chaos of the fight.

Blood leaked from the teeth marks across his neck.

12

SYLVIA

Cliff bellowed a curse and removed his outer shirt. He knelt beside Jon and pressed the fabric to his neck to slow the bleeding.

As adrenaline continued to pound through my heart, I could only watch in shock. Jon was shaking, and Cliff wore a look of panic that I never would have expected from him. Although Jon was bleeding buckets compared to me, it hardly seemed like enough to kill him. I couldn't understand why they both looked so hysterical.

Jon wrenched himself back and shoved Cliff.

"Don't touch me!" Jon felt his neck, grimacing. "It's spreading. I-I can feel it. It's *hot*." He lifted his gaze to Cliff, who was frozen in a kneeling position. "You know what you have to do," Jon breathed.

Cliff leaned away. "No."

"*Please*." Jon wrested the knife from the monster's corpse and slid it across the ground to Cliff. "I can't do it myself. I *c-can't*. Please. I don't want to hurt anyone. You have to."

"Fuck you, I'm not doing that!" Cliff snarled, tossing the knife into the shadows. "There has to be another way!"

"You know there isn't!"

They were falling apart. These two hunters, my unshakeable captors. Tears glinted in their eyes, brimming with grief and fury. Whatever had turned our attackers into monsters was now coursing through Jon's veins. He would soon be one of them.

The thought of watching Cliff kill Jon should have brought me unbridled joy after what they'd put me through. But now, I'd seen the monstrosities they were after. Jon had saved my life. I couldn't bear to see the light leave his eyes.

I couldn't let it happen.

Unable to sit up any longer, Jon fell back, his chest rising and falling rapidly. I flew toward him, trancelike, until a hand swatted at me. I dodged, whirling to find Cliff's vicious stare.

"You stay the hell away from him!" Cliff put himself between me and Jon.

When he lashed out again, I sent a warning flash of frost his way. He looked like he might tear me to pieces, but I jolted once again out of his reach and held my hands up.

"I can heal him!" My exclamation was met with heavy silence. I drew a deep breath. "I can try, at least. I… I healed my wing, see? Maybe I can cure his infection before it takes hold. If you'll let me."

Desperation clawed through the seething green fire in his eyes. Cliff looked between Jon's prone form and me.

Something gave in his expression. "Do it."

I landed on the floor by Jon's face, sucking in a sharp breath at the sight of his injury up close. The bite on his neck was deep and already bruising. The smell of blood made my stomach churn. I wondered if Cliff could feel the illness the way I could—how his friend's blood was curdling like milk as the unnatural infection crept through his body.

Jon's eyes flicked open and made me freeze. "W-what… what's…" He shifted back, fearful.

"I'm going to help you," I told him softly.

His brow furrowed, and a bleak glaze of resignation crossed his pained features. His eyes fell shut as though he was bracing himself.

I realized with a jolt that he thought I was going to kill him—put him out of his misery since Cliff couldn't.

Jon hadn't turned vicious yet, but my skin crawled with a whisper of the horrible sensation that had warned me of the monsters nearby. In minutes, or hours, or days, he would be a corrupted, savage thing that would make my nerves scream again.

The grotesque image spurred me into action. I stepped into the shadow under Jon's jaw and pressed my palms into his skin to begin the healing spell.

Perhaps he thought I would end his agony quickly with an icicle through his head or relieve him of the fire in his veins until he peacefully froze to death. Whatever he had in mind, he was too far gone to recognize how wrong he was.

Mere seconds passed before the enormity of the task hit me. I'd never healed anything so complex before, but I couldn't back down now.

I chanted the spell over and over. Blood flow slowed, and the toxin pooled together, dribbling out of Jon's wound in a sickly amber color. The puncture marks began stitching back together, but my energy was fading.

It wasn't fast enough. I wasn't strong enough.

With a cold shock, I realized I wasn't going to save him.

Tears welled up in my eyes as I muscled past dizziness. He couldn't die like this, quietly and dutifully sacrificing himself. Tales of warriors never ended this way. He slayed the monsters. He saved me. *He saved me.*

I begged silently—a prayer to the stars, to *anything* to give me the strength to finish this.

I never expected something to answer.

"*You ask a gift of us?*"

A beat of peace and power thrummed through me like a rush of water poured from the crown of my head, trickling slowly down my body. I could feel the active magic in my hands and hear Jon and Cliff's labored breathing. But time felt strange and thick, crawling to a halt.

When I tried to move, I was frozen. Even the dust particles catching the dim light of the floor above had cemented in midair.

Ethereal, disjointed voices whispered softly like the distant echoes of forgotten dreams.

"Look at this. She is a child."

"They both are."

The voices swirled around me, their words fragmentary and elusive, teasing my senses. It was as if the very fabric of reality had been woven into these murmurs, reaching out to touch the depths of my consciousness. I couldn't see anyone, fairy or otherwise. My skin didn't prickle the way it did for spirits or monsters.

"Please," I breathed, fairly certain I was going mad. I wasn't sure if I was thinking the words or if my lips were forming them. "Save him. Let me save him. He's going to die."

"*What will you give us?"* Several voices layered to inquire.

I hesitated. "What do you want?" I asked.

The haunting beauty of the voices turned eerie and harsh. "*What will you give, Sylvia?"*

"A-anything," I stammered, delirious with terror and exhaustion. Jon didn't have time.

I held my breath, searching the basement's darkness for any sort of entity to be staring back at me. Then, it answered.

"*Very good, child,"* the voices rasped.

"*Good."*

"Good, good, good."

Time flew back into motion.

My fatigue vanished, and I snapped upright, gasping as though I had been held underwater. Magic thrashed in my chest like I had never felt. I channeled it all into my spellwork, gritting my teeth in effort. The vigor of the healing that flooded out of my hands burned like a bright light. I heard Cliff lean away behind me, a soft breath of wonder passing his lips.

The impossible task was done in less than a minute—the last of the venom pooled around my feet. Jon's skin stitched together. I watched his face flood with healthy color and his breathing even out.

Finally, I lowered my hands and staggered onto my knees.

Jon's eyelids twitched, his gaze darting about with confusion. He lifted a shaky hand to touch his healed neck. The skin was scarred, but it was sealed and venom-free.

Then, he turned his head slowly and locked eyes with me. His hand pulled away from his neck, and his fingertip brushed my folded knees with a featherlight touch.

"What did you do?" he whispered—not angry or disgusted, but bewildered. Like it was too good to be true. I hadn't noticed the green flecks in his eyes until now.

I couldn't answer. The hair on the back of my neck rose as the strange, shuffling voices spoke in my ear: *"As promised, child. The reward of your sacrifice."* The murmurs faded, tapering off into laughter that I couldn't be sure was real or not.

Even as I turned my head to seek the phantoms, inexplicable pain bloomed over my body—a wash of aches all over my arms and shins. A particularly acute pain cut across my left outer shoulder. I seized the wound, expecting blood and shredded fabric. I frowned at my unblemished fingers, flexing them in disbelief. My sleeve was intact. There was no wound.

The ground shook, banishing my flicker of confusion. I lurched back, dizzy, as Cliff swept Jon into a brutal embrace. More tears streaked down Cliff's face as he spoke in tight punches of words—half proclamations of relief, half reprimands about Jon not dodging the monster's snapping jaws.

His rumbling voice almost faded into the background entirely. My eyelids drooped, but I snapped right up as Cliff released

Jon and turned his attention to me. Against all odds, I managed to heave myself to my feet. I shuffled warily from Cliff's stare, priming my wings. I doubted I could fly for longer than three seconds.

"So," Cliff said. "No magic? Totally harmless, huh?" He jutted his chin toward the ice-riddled monster beside him. His jaw clenched dangerously as he regarded me.

After everything, *everything*, he was still angry about the truth.

He lunged. The wonderful thrum of magic that allowed me to heal Jon had vanished. I was too spent to defend myself. A cry lodged in my throat as he swept me off the ground, and I found myself pressed up against a warm wall of fabric. Registering his rapid heartbeat and heavy breathing, I realized he was holding me to his chest. His grip wasn't painful. After a stunned second, I squirmed madly, wondering what would possess him to kill me through suffocation, of all things.

My struggles slowed when the rumble of his voice surrounded me. "*Thank you. Thank you.*"

I couldn't believe it.

He was embracing me with the same ferocity he'd just shown Jon. I whimpered in relief and allowed myself to relax. When he pulled me away and held me in front of his face, my shoulders slumped.

"Oh, *stars*, I thought you were trying to crush me," I said.

He scoffed. "It's a fucking hug, Sylvia. Don't fairies hug?"

"Sure, but I didn't think hunters did." Catching my breath, I looked from him to Jon and back again. "Now what?"

Cliff gave me a slow nod. "Deal's a deal. You're free to go."

13
JON

I stood there, transfixed by the reflection staring back at me from the murky depths of the mirror.

Cliff and I had made quick work of hiding the monsters' ice-riddled bodies in the basement. After we took Sylvia where she needed to go, we'd come back and burn the corpses in the woods.

Pulling at my collar, I turned my head and gaped uncomprehendingly. Only faint scarring was left as evidence of my scrape with a painful death. The feverish memory of the toxin throbbed in my bloodstream. And then… coolness and light.

A non-human had saved my life. *Sylvia.*

Living as we did, dying was a possibility every day. Granted, Cliff and I were pretty damn good at *not* dying, but I was always keenly aware of the chance.

For a split second, I glimpsed a young boy with circles under his eyes standing in my reflection's place. Frightened. Adrift. Resilient. I wondered if that kid would recognize me now. I was a far cry from the gangly teen I used to be in every way, but for a moment, our wide eyes aligned with the same wonder as I touched the smooth, healed skin on my neck again.

"So, those were werewolves, right?" Sylvia asked, sounding confused. She was still sprawled on her side in Cliff's palm. Even sitting up straight seemed to exert her. "I thought they'd be bigger. And that they only transformed at night."

"Those weren't werewolves," Cliff answered. He paced near me, studying the old photographs hung on the wall. "They were dogs. We've seen this before. Animals bitten by a werewolf don't transform the same ways humans do. They permanently become a gnarly, juiced-up version of whatever they started as."

"*Stars.* All animals? Even squirrels?"

Cliff shuddered. "*Especially* squirrels."

I stole a furtive glance at Sylvia, giving a small start to find she was looking at me. She averted her gaze when Cliff moved her higher and pointed at a gilded frame.

"I think I recognize that head of hair," Cliff said, tapping the glass. I moved beside him to see. A young woman wearing a long-sleeved ballgown with silken tresses splayed over her shoulders stood at the base of a staircase.

I glanced behind me, tensing. *This* staircase.

"Is that Alice?" I asked.

"Yes," Sylvia said. "See, I knew she wasn't the one hurting people."

"Surprised she's stayed out of trouble all these years," Cliff said. "Kid ghosts are usually the biggest dicks."

Sylvia shook her head. "She's got her head in the clouds most of the time, but she's good. All she wants is to see her lover again, but there aren't any other spirits around here. She doesn't even realize how much time has passed. That's a small mercy, I guess."

The genuine fondness in her voice made me falter. I couldn't help but wonder how long Sylvia had been coming to Dottage, innocently befriending a tortured spirit. She could have pinned all of this on Alice from the beginning and saved herself a lot of grief. But she didn't.

"Ghosts stick around for a reason," I said. "Waiting for something. Wanting something."

"Yeah." Cliff raised his eyebrows at Sylvia. "You're lucky she didn't get pissed at you for stealing her jewelry."

Sylvia straightened with a sour look on her face. "I know what I'm doing. The only thing she cares about is her music box."

Cliff and I locked eyes. "Music box, huh?" he said. "I thought I saw one in the attic."

"That's hers," Sylvia said. "It always starts playing right before she shows up."

She offered the information so readily that there was no way she understood what would come next. The chill in the air was unmistakable. Alice was a rare, non-violent ghost, but she certainly wasn't at rest. Given how fully visible she had been earlier, there was no time to sit around on our asses.

After I offered the excuse that we should sweep the house one more time, I broke away from Cliff and Sylvia to search the attic. Sure enough, the music box was sitting on a dusty dresser. It was engraved, *To My Beloved.*

There were signs of Sylvia's rifling. Pieces of jewelry were strewn about, tiny footprints and handprints in the dust. One of the floorboards was pulled up where Cliff had found her stash. Guilt churned through me at the thought of her treasures, though I hadn't been the one to taunt her with them. Now, we'd be taking away her friend, too.

Examining a yellowed photo I found in the uppermost dresser drawer, I glimpsed Alice as she had been in life—at least, toward the end of it. She was frail and bedridden, tucked up to her chest in blankets. Her vacant gaze mirrored my view outside the broken attic window, where evergreens stood as silent witness to her fate.

I set the photo back in the drawer, giving the tree line one last glance.

I considered waiting until Sylvia was gone before going through the necessary routine, but at the very least, she deserved to know the truth about what would happen to Alice. Though I doubted Sylvia would ever want to come near this place again, there was always the chance she would show up and find the mansion no longer haunted.

"Wait, what are you doing with that?" Sylvia asked as soon as I entered the living room with the music box in hand. "Alice won't like that you're touching it. Put it back."

Cliff grimly nodded and set Sylvia on a shelf adjacent to the fireplace. He decidedly ignored her frantic stare as he began fiddling with kindling and a lighter.

"Jon?" Sylvia prompted. "What's happening?"

"We're putting her to rest," I told her gently.

She flinched as flame caught in the fireplace, then looked at the music box in horror. "No. No, you *can't*. She doesn't hurt people. She… She's like me!"

"She isn't." Although I didn't think Sylvia would attack, I regarded her warily. "You may not be human, but you're *alive*. She's not supposed to be here."

"Who are you to decide that?" Sylvia snapped, the crackling flames glowing on her skin.

"You don't know a fraction of what we've seen," I said, heat roiling in my chest. "No matter how friendly and docile a spirit seems, they always turn. *Always*. If we leave her be, one day, someone's gonna walk in here, and she'll be too far gone to do anything except attack. All she'll know is hate and viciousness. It's not a matter of *if* but *when*. People are going to get hurt, Sylvia."

She hugged herself, mouth pressed into a hard line. I hated myself a little for frightening her, even if it was a necessary truth.

"She wouldn't…" But as Sylvia trailed off, her frown deepened. "She… She's normally fine. Except when you scared her. Maybe she was only upset that you couldn't see her."

"What do you mean?" I asked.

"The other night. She got angry. She looked different. Scary." Sylvia shook her head. "Her mouth stretched, and her eyes rolled back. I'd never seen her like that before."

"That's a sure sign that she's on the brink," Cliff said. "Look, sweetheart. This is mercy. Would you rather her stay here, lost and moping around for all eternity? We can end this now and let her move on."

"Where will she go?"

Cliff looked at the floorboards with a heavy sigh.

"She'll be at peace," I assured her, though I wasn't entirely sure myself. Even if the afterlife was an empty, dark *nothing*, that was better than what lost spirits went through. "She'll never be happy here. And sooner or later, it'll make her insane. We can help her."

Sylvia's expression pinched like she wanted to argue again, but soon enough, her shoulders slumped.

She didn't protest when I dropped the music box into the blazing fire.

The chilly air turned downright freezing. I drew my gun as the windows frosted over. Most of the time, furniture would start rattling, or glass would shatter. Instead, Alice simply appeared in the room—melancholy but not violent. She approached Sylvia, and I had to swallow the urge to get between them. Sylvia didn't look frightened, only mournful.

"Sylvia," Alice said softly.

The sound of her own name made Sylvia light up with a teary smile. "You won't have to wait anymore," Sylvia said. "You'll find him."

As the wood of the music box began to crackle, Alice's form grew fuzzy around the edges. "I know I will, my sweet visitor. My friend." At last, she fully dissolved into a mist with a euphoric, grateful expression on her face.

The chill withdrew from the room as sunlight permeated the dirty windows.

"Do you need a minute?" Cliff asked as Sylvia wiped her face.

She shook her head. "No. You were right. She suffered through more than a lifetime in this house."

"Turn right after that tree."

I followed Sylvia's instructions, ducking under a low-hanging branch. After all of her admirable refusals to share anything about where she came from, I was surprised she permitted us to bring her closer to her true home before parting ways. Then again, she needed me to act as a mule since she was too strained to fly very long.

Cliff stayed in step beside me, studying every gnarled root and branch like they might spring to life. I doubted we would find much more substance to inform the entry in his journal. The deal with Sylvia was more than fair, but it was hard to swallow all the unanswered questions about her kind. In nine years of hunting, we'd never seen something like her before. I wondered if we ever would again.

"How long until you can fly again?" I asked.

Sylvia twisted around from her seat in my hand, eyebrows hiked. "Am I that heavy?" She interrupted my stammering with a laugh that was so musical that I didn't mind it being at my expense. "Probably a few more days until I'm fully steady. It takes more than one round of healing to patch a hole like that."

Her eyes moved to Cliff, swimming with shadow.

As I walked, her resting wings caught patches of sunlight between clouds. The semi-translucent appendages shimmered with iridescence that made my breath catch. The bullet wound was still easy to spot, the membrane dull and wispy by comparison. Tiny patches of paint clung to some spots. Her fragile weight seemed to defy the fierce magic she had wielded in the basement. How could someone so small have that kind of power?

She folded her wings when she caught me staring.

"Where will you go after this?" she asked, peeking back at me again. "I get the sense you're not going to take the rest of the day off to drink wine and sit in the sun."

Cliff gave a short laugh. "Really? What makes you so sure?"

"I don't know. Maybe it's the..." She gestured vaguely at us, crinkling her nose. "The *everything* about you."

"Should I take that as an insult?" Cliff asked.

"Try not to think too hard about it." Although she'd spent the past days snapping insults at every turn, her tone had softened significantly. She frowned in thought. "Do you think the werewolf will go back to the house?"

"Chances are, it'll steer clear after mauling that security guard if it wants to stay hidden," I said. "We'll keep an eye on the place, but the dogs might give us a hint of where to start looking next. We'll comb through missing pet reports."

"Poor things," Sylvia murmured. She fell into heavy silence for a few moments, then tugged on my thumb suddenly. "Hang on, you're going the wrong way. I told you to turn right."

Coming to a stop, I glanced around in confusion. "I did."

"No. Look, we've passed this stump three times. It must be the glamour. I've seen it turn animals away, but never—" She waved off my wide-eyed expression hurriedly. "It's not dangerous! This glamour just keeps away things that shouldn't be here."

"*Things*," Cliff said with a snort. "Guess this is where we leave you, huh?"

She nodded. "I can make my way from here."

Digging in his pocket, Cliff withdrew Sylvia's knife and bracelet charm. Her jaw dropped as he held them out to her. She accepted them hesitantly, then clutched her items close like he might decide to snatch them away again.

"Stay away from monster dens in the future," Cliff said, his rough tone at odds with the glimmer in his eyes. "And try to be less of an idiot. Capiche?"

She rolled her eyes and mimicked his deep voice. "Capiche."

As Cliff stepped back and started trekking back the way we came, I knelt and allowed Sylvia to step down to the woodland floor. She turned to face me and shuffled back. Her wings trembled. I could imagine the uncertain relief pulsing through her.

"Thank you," I said, then chuckled bleakly at my words. "I owe you more than that. You saved my life."

"You saved mine, too," she said, glancing away with a shrug.

"You were dragged into this mess. Of course I was going to look out for you in there. But you, what you did…" I brushed my fingers over my neck, lowering my voice so Cliff couldn't hear. "I owe you a favor—big time. Anything, Sylvia. What can I do?"

The astonishment on her face was hard to read. After all, what could a monster-killing maniac offer a fairy?

"No offense, but I never want to see either of you again," Sylvia said. "But a hunter owing me a favor…" She chewed her lip, a glint surfacing in her eyes that rivaled the look of any seasoned gambler. "I'll admit, that's hard to pass up. Not many people can say they've had the pleasure—or lack thereof."

"I can't sell you my soul," I added quickly. "Or bring you any ritual human sacrifices."

"I wasn't going to ask for that!" she gasped, loosing a nervous laugh. As I smirked at her, her expression slowly flattened. "Oh. You were kidding."

"Mostly," I said.

I glanced over my shoulder. Cliff was far behind me. "I'll be back tomorrow to make sure what's dead at that house stays dead," I told her. "If you're in this part of the woods again, you can give me your answer then."

Her expression clouded, wings doing that anxious little flutter. She nodded. "Fair enough. I'll be right here when the sun is at its highest. Okay?"

"Alright."

She didn't move until I stood and started walking away. When I looked back, she was gone. I wondered if there were dozens, maybe hundreds of fairies like her, missing her. She'd been gone for days. I buried the little stab of guilt that surfaced as I imagined her reunion with loved ones. She'd tell them stories of the sick fucks that kept her captive, and Cliff and I would become immortalized in those legends she spoke of that made hunters sound worse than werewolves. Maybe we deserved that much.

I wouldn't blame her if she didn't show up tomorrow, but the least I could do was follow through.

14

SYLVIA

You don't ponder what to truly be grateful for until you're deprived of it. A hot, nourishing dinner. A soft bed your own size.

I pulled my quilt up to my chin, nuzzling against the familiar shape of my mattress. My back ached from sleeping in the box. An awful pain still throbbed in my arm. I must have hurt myself in the battle and forgotten. It all felt like a distant memory—one I tearfully explained as an owl attack to Mother and Hazel as I ate at the foot of my bed that evening. I told them I'd flown too far, been targeted, and hurt my wing trying to escape the vicious swipes of a talon.

One part was true. I was lucky to be alive.

But Mother and Hazel were not the first to see me when I returned to the village. Damian had intercepted me as I dragged my feet under the willow. Exhaustion and inner tremors had settled into my bones.

"Sylvia?" Damian had grabbed my shoulders, trying to embrace me. "Sylvia! Stars—what happened to—"

I'd wrenched myself out of his grasp, brushed past him, ignored him. He'd stopped following before I reached my dwelling.

Eventually, I would need to confront him—and everyone else who noted my absence—with my lies. But that could wait. I was home, safe. Tomorrow, I could have a healer look at my wing. I could perfect my cover story. I could reconsider if I even wanted to take that hunter up on his favor.

Tonight, I'd sleep safely and deeply. I was certain not even the strongest storm could shake me.

Until I heard Mother scream.

Hazel whimpered as I shot out from under the covers and grabbed my dagger off the nightstand, just in case.

Something shattered in the hearth room. Mother shouted, her words indistinct.

My first thought was that the village was under attack. Perhaps Jon and Cliff had been tricking me all along. Perhaps they were clawing into the ground with their monstrous weapons, prepared to impale every last man, woman, and child with iron.

"Who's out there?" Hazel whispered. Her wild red hair stuck out from beneath the blanket.

"Don't worry," I told her. "Mother and I won't let anything hurt you."

My palm was sweaty on the hilt of my dagger as I approached our bedroom door. It couldn't be the hunters, I thought as my head cleared. No, the whole village would be shaking if Jon and Cliff had decided to come back and uproot our home willow in the dead of night. Besides, they hadn't even seen me enter Elysia. I'd made sure of that.

The argument outside tapered off in an explosive shout before the door flew open. A pair of Entry Watch guards—Ayden and Titus—crowded into the bedroom, seizing me by the shoulders before I could so much as flinch in surprise.

"Drop the knife, Sylvia."

I whipped my head up. Ayden gripped my right arm. The lines on his forehead were more pronounced than usual as he stared down at me with a chilling mixture of concern and determination. Reluctantly, I let my dagger drop.

"What's happening?" I breathed.

They dragged me into the hearth room, where Mother stood across from Lireal, one of the Elders of the Elysian council. Those vibrant, cascading clothes were unmistakable, pinned with a gold crest at the collar.

"You have no right!" Mother snarled, her face contorted. A third guard, Solon, waited by the entryway hall and looked fully prepared to restrain her.

"You know that we do, Melanie," the Elder said, her voice velveteen. "This is imperative. It is my joy and my grief to perform my duty."

"I demand more time. Forcing your way into my home at this hour is despicable. You've frightened my children, and for what?"

Ayden and Titus shoved me into a chair by the hearth, and the argument stopped in its tracks. The Elder turned and locked eyes with me.

"Sylvia is twenty-one summers," she said. "More woman than child, no?"

A flicker of recognition sparked within me. Although we had never spoken directly, I knew her. Lireal was a stoic earth affinity and a fixture on the council as long as I could remember. She carried herself with an air of authority and grace that was usually comforting, like a grandmother.

But shards of the clay pot I'd made when I was seven littered the floor.

"What are you doing here?" I demanded.

Her thin lips quirked. *Stars,* I shouldn't have spoken to an Elder like that—much less an esteemed member of the council.

"I see your Mother's fire shining in you," Lireal said. "I apologize for the late-night intrusion, but it was important that we have this conversation discreetly."

My heart beat so loudly that I swore the whole room could hear it.

"Why?" I tried to keep the quiver from my voice. Council members never made house calls. Why did she need guards? Did she think I was dangerous?

I'd never seen Mother look so panicked.

"Others might be... perturbed by the nature of our discussion," Lireal explained with a tilt of her head. She studied me, her rainwater eyes seeming to stare right through to the whirlwind of questions in my mind. There was something dark there, as if she was searching for something wrong in me. "I'd like you to tell me where you were the last day and a half, Sylvia."

My breath hitched. Drenched in silence, the whole room awaited my answer.

"I already told my family," I said carefully. "An owl attacked me. It was awful. I'm so happy to be alive, to be *home*."

Lireal's face did not flood with warmth and sympathy like my family's had. "Is that the truth?"

I scowled, gesturing at my healing wing. "Does this look fake to you? Did you come all the way here to call me a liar?"

I started from my seat the same instant Lireal lifted her hand. She scarcely needed to move her lips to beckon spellwork. Vines emerged from the packed earth floor, snaking around my legs.

Mother gave a cry of outrage, but Solon forced her back. "How dare you!" she snapped. "How *dare* you!"

Lireal paid her no mind, circling me slowly as I struggled against her spell. Perhaps I could freeze the life out of the vines, but then what? She was far more powerful, and the guards would descend upon me before I had a chance to defend myself.

"What a peculiar wound," Lireal said, eyeing my wing before coming to stand in front of me. "Unlike any *owl* attack I've seen in my years. You'll have to forgive me if I'm skeptical about the nature of your absence. If you explain yourself now, I can grant some leniency."

I gritted my teeth. "Should I have told the owl to claw me up in a way that was more *familiar* to you, Elder?"

There was no mistaking the disappointment in her eyes. She sighed and beckoned behind her. "Bring him in, Ayden."

Ayden dutifully strode out the door and returned, pulling the arm of another fairy. All the breath left my lungs at once.

Damian. The moment he set eyes on the state of me, he tried to surge forward, but Ayden yanked him back. "What are you doing to her?" Damian demanded. He looked at me frantically. "Sylvia, I… I didn't mean—"

I dropped my gaze, trembling as Lireal addressed me once more.

"Damian approached me with worry after your arrival," she said. "You were injured, ragged, and barely responsive, as though something terrible had happened. And he says you confided in him shortly before you vanished. You have been stealing away to the human structure. You had a close encounter with *humans.*"

"No," I whispered, seething in Damian's direction. "That isn't true."

Lireal nodded somberly. "We will discover what is true in a moment. While your mother's fire within you is admirable, you must understand our concern about you having your father's less than favorable… *tendencies.*"

The vines strained as I jolted toward her. "Don't you *dare* speak of him that way," I hissed.

Lireal gave me a pitying look. She summoned Titus closer, and together, they performed a spell in tandem that I had never heard before. The effect spilled over me like a splash of freezing water. Their chanting brought a lightness to my chest. A loosening to my jaw. As though words were prepared to leap from my mouth without my say-so.

Although the incantation came to a close, the air still hummed with the enchantment. Lireal drew closer, tucking her cold fingers under my chin and forcing me to meet her hard gaze.

"Where have you been for nearly two days, Sylvia?" she asked.

"Motel room. Injured and captured by—" I clenched my teeth and huffed resistantly. "*Hunters.*"

A gasp rounded the hearth room, but I could hardly hear it.

From there, I answered the Elder's questions readily and without resistance. I had no choice. She needled me with every inquiry about the nature of my captivity and the potential danger raining down on Elysia. Everyone's stares burned into me like iron.

No, I didn't escape. They let me go.

No, the hunters don't know exactly where Elyisa is.

No, they don't appear to have any interest in hunting down fairies. Not in the end.

They only wanted my help in tracking a mactir. They call it a werewolf.

"Dear girl," Lireal said, shaking her head in disbelief. "What did you reveal about our kind? Did you perform magic in front of these brutes?"

"Not at first. Not until today. I kept my magic hidden until I fought alongside them to kill the animals infected by the mactir. And I..." My voice choked, wanting to revolt against the spell, to not reveal the most damning thing of all. But I had no such power to resist. "I healed one of the hunters. Saved him from death."

Amidst the murmurs of disgust from the guards, I heard Mother whisper my name in horror.

Lireal exchanged a harrowed look with Ayden. She waved her hand, and the spellwork that loosened my lips released.

"You vile creature." The coldness in Lireal's voice cut like a blade. "You risked all of Elysia for your foolishness. Every child in the village knows never to make contact outside of our kind. You betrayed us all."

I looked from face to face, tears welling as I found only fear and disappointment gazing back at me. Lireal was right. If anything had happened to Elysia, it would have been my fault.

Hazel peeked out from the bedroom, ashen. Shame flooded me. Her lost innocence was like blood spilled on my hands.

"I didn't mean to," I said weakly, shifting my eyes back to the Elder.

"Sniveling words to proclaim, should they be the ones to bring down an entire people," Lireal sneered.

"She made a mistake. It was just a mistake!" Mother cut in desperately. Solon hissed in pain; his hands singed where her skin had flashed white hot. She broke away to stand in front of me.

Solon surged forward to pull her back. Hazel started crying, calling out for Mother.

"*Stars,* Solon. Keep her still," Lireal said, watching impassively as Mother was restrained. "Ayden. I'm afraid I need you."

I wriggled in my seat as he approached, but the constricting vines held me in place.

"What are you doing?" I breathed as he gripped my hair at the root, forcing my face toward the ceiling. "Stop!"

His other hand lifted, a finger extended.

A spell was whispered, and the digit blossomed with heat like a fiery ember.

From the corner of my eye, I saw Damian bucking madly. Tears choked his voice. "No! Don't touch her!"

More vines slithered from the ceiling, one gagging my friend as he called my name.

The first touch of Ayden's hand to my cheek was *cold* for one instant before turning white-hot. I shrieked in agony. He leaned close to me, his breath rasping against my ear. "You had so much potential."

"Stop it, stop it!" Hazel shrieked. "Leave her alone!"

Ayden's finger was briefly wrenched from my face, and I watched through squinted eyes as Hazel battered at him with her little fists. Lireal herself took hold of my sister, forcing her arms to her sides and gently shushing her. She kept Hazel facing toward me, letting her observe what happened to traitors.

My heels dug uselessly at the earthen ground.

"You don't realize it," Ayden murmured, "but we're saving you."

He kept my hair in a brutal grip, taking my screams impassively as he continued his work. His touch on my cheek was steady, like an artist's.

When he finished, the pain rose exponentially, settling into my skin like millions of iron needles. The vines slackened, and I wrenched myself free of the chair. I swayed, watching them all with bleary vision.

I wanted to shred Ayden's wings to ribbons with icicles. I wanted to inform him that he would experience the wrath of a hunter who'd promised me a favor. Instead, I staggered back until I hit a wall and sank to a pathetic seat, trembling.

"Should you ever put Elysia in jeopardy again," Lireal said, releasing Hazel, "you will be executed."

My stomach twisted dully, my body knowing to react with terror when my mind was still too exhausted.

"*Executed*?" Mother breathed. "You can't be serious. We haven't had to exercise that ruling in decades."

"This is not a *joke*, Melanie!" Lireal's raised voice made several in the room flinch. "Hunters have made contact with one of our own. I will not risk the safety of our entire village for the whims of one foolhardy girl."

As I lowered my head, I was unable to even bury my face in my hands. It hurt too much.

I didn't hear our guests leave.

The next thing I knew, Mother was kneeling before me and reaching for my face. "What were you thinking?" she whispered tremulously. "Healing that man… They forced you, didn't they? Tell me they forced you."

Turning my face away, I pushed her hand aside. "N-no," I croaked. "I offered."

"Why?" Mother breathed heavily, gripping my shoulders and digging her fingers in so I couldn't pull away. "How could you be so *senseless*? Look what they did to your wing! They held you prisoner like some creature! Death for that brute is a kinder fate than he deserved!"

I dropped my head against the wall, tears flowing and stinging my cheek. I couldn't fully open the eye where Ayden's touch had brushed so close.

"He saved me," I choked out. "He thought I was a monster at first, but he let me change his mind. He saved me like a warrior in a story, and I couldn't watch him die. It wasn't fair."

"Wasn't fair?" Mother echoed me like she had never heard a more asinine explanation in her life. I sensed an explosion of anger around the corner, but miraculously, it fizzled out. She shuddered, murmuring, "What have you done?"

Too ashamed to bear the look on her face, I kept my eyes down. I pushed myself to stand and retreated into my bedroom.

As I sank to a seat at the edge of my bed, my tears slowed. The same couldn't be said for Hazel, who crept inside like she was afraid of me or perhaps afraid I would shatter. When she finally closed the distance, she nudged herself under my arm and wept against my side.

"Why did you h-have to go there again?" she whimpered miserably.

Quietly removing myself from her, I found my satchel where I'd discarded it by the door and dug out the bracelet charm. I dropped it on her lap. She clutched the charm in shaking hands and hunched over with an awful cry, making me regret my callous decision.

"I'm sorry!" Hazel's breathing hitched. "I-I shouldn't have said I wanted one! It's my fault!"

"It's not." I finally opened my arms and held her tightly, kissing the top of her head. "I would have gone back anyway."

After ushering Hazel back to bed, I waited until she'd cried herself to sleep before slipping back under my sheets. My face throbbed. No amount of whispered ice or healing spells seemed to bring me any relief.

The pain wasn't isolated. My wing still twitched from the half-finished healing.

And my arm… That phantom ache only became more pronounced through the night. As I desperately tried to fall asleep, a terrible piercing sensation stabbed my upper arm over and over, like a needle was burrowing in and out of my skin. It went on for several minutes.

Delirious tears wet my eyes. I rubbed at the spot, but there was nothing there. Nothing.

15

JON

I couldn't believe I wasted twenty minutes fiddling with that stupid vending machine. The more I dwelled on it, the more ridiculous I felt.

Sylvia had saved me from an excruciating death, and I was offering her a necklace that cost a quarter. Well, technically, more than a quarter. I had to put in several coins to finally get the snowflake necklace that caught my eye when passing the display.

Arriving at our rendezvous empty-handed felt wrong, and the little charm wasn't too different from those she had been pilfering from the valuables at the Dottage mansion. Maybe Sylvia would start a new collection with it.

If she even showed up at all. After everything we put her through, I wouldn't fault her if she had come to her senses and didn't want anything to do with her former captors. Maybe she'd been lying about wanting to meet today, willing to say anything to escape me. Couldn't say I blamed her for that, either.

Still, I clutched the plastic capsule in my jacket pocket as I trod cautiously through the dense forest. A cool wind tousled my hair, bringing with it the crisp freshness of fallen leaves. Verdant oak canopies were beginning to show swathes of golden yellows and burnt reds, hinting at the cooler months soon to come.

I searched the shifting leaves for a glint of iridescent wings and listened for a tiny voice in the rustling branches. I was close to where I'd left Sylvia yesterday, but so far, there was no sign of her.

It was no wonder her species had remained hidden for so long. How the hell was I supposed to track a fairy? It wasn't like she left me a trail of magic icicles to follow like breadcrumbs. Her footprints would be too small to trace if she left any at all. And with the glamour I'd experienced yesterday, I was paranoid that I'd be walking in circles all afternoon.

That harrowing thought pulled me to a halt. I looked back the way I'd come. Had I passed that fallen tree before? Another strong breeze wafted around me, making the forest seem to bend in on itself.

"Jon!"

Her voice made me jolt and look all around. "Sylvia?" I called.

"Shh! This way."

Sylvia fluttered into view, beckoning me. My breath caught at the sight of her. Her flight was steady. I hadn't gotten much of a chance to admire it when we were fighting for our lives yesterday. Looping effortlessly in the air, she darted back out of view.

"Wait!" I staggered after her, trying to keep track of her for several yards. Pushing past a curtain of willow fronds, I stopped short when I found myself nose-to-nose with her. "Hey," I whispered.

"Shhh!" Sylvia put a finger to her lips. "They're on wide patrol today. Step behind here, and don't move. Don't make a sound."

Alarmed, I moved behind the trunk of the tree as directed. I was even more surprised when she alighted on my shoulder. The fluttering of her wings silenced. I held my breath, hearing another approaching buzz less than a dozen feet away.

My eyes widened—another fairy. With the tree and the fronds blocking me from view, all I could do was listen as the sound of the wings grew louder. A faint silhouette drifted down into view, easily mistaken for a hummingbird if not for the faint glimpses of iridescent wings and tiny leather boots I caught behind the drifting curtain of leaves. The figure paused, and for a moment, I was certain they felt the weight of my stare. My heart drummed as I racked my brain for how the hell I would counteract an attack of magic ice—possibly worse. I wasn't sure I could count on Sylvia to save my skin a second time.

After a moment, the fairy flew off in another direction. I let out a soft breath of relief, but Sylvia put a hand on my neck in silent warning. She kept still for another full minute before her voice chirped by my ear.

"Gone. Another patrol sentry won't be around for another hour or so."

She sounded so confident that I couldn't help but chuckle. "You know your way around breaking the law," I said.

"Strict rules inspire clever escape artists. That's what my father always said." Sylvia flew off my shoulder, wheeling to face me. She studied me for a moment. "I half-expected you not to show."

I frowned, trying to get a better look at her. Her chin-length red hair was pulled forward in a style that covered half her face. The raised hood of her green blouse further obscured her features.

"Looks like your wings are back in action," I noted.

"I was able to do another couple rounds of healing. It's far from perfect, but it keeps me from having to meet you on the ground." She grimaced at the thought. "Where's Cliff?"

"Across town, interviewing a potential lead about the lost dogs." I sighed, wishing we had more to go on. "The werewolf's next transformation is due for the full moon. We're running out of time to prevent a slaughter."

"And you're here instead?"

"I said I'd come, didn't I? I passed through Dottage." I hesitated, deciding to spare her the gory details of sweeping for remaining evidence while wiping away any trace that Cliff and I had been at the scene. "Thankfully, it's quiet now."

Her expression clouded. "So, Alice. She's..."

"She's at rest," I assured. "It's just a rickety old house now."

Sylvia's brow pinched, but to my great relief, she didn't start crying. She looked past me through the drifting branches of the willow. "It'll be strange to visit without her there. She wasn't unpleasant company when she was more herself. The house will feel so quiet now."

I couldn't muscle down my shock. "You're not going back already, are you?"

Sylvia stiffened at my forceful tone, arms folding over her chest. "You said it was safe."

"The hunt is still open. I can't say for sure what will happen. You should keep your distance."

"*Stars above.* Are you always this overbearing?"

"I don't want to clean up any more bodies," I told her coolly. "Even yours."

She paused for a beat, posture going rigid. Her chin lifted. "You're trying to intimidate me," she accused.

Begrudgingly, I acknowledged that she was more observant than I had given her credit for. I scoffed. "You're so damn stubborn. What choice do I have?"

"Coming from you, that's a compliment," she said. "And in case you were wondering, it's not working."

"No?"

Sylvia shook her head. "I'm not afraid of you."

A self-assured smile lifted the corner of her lips, but her knuckles were whitening on the hem of her flowy blouse.

"Refreshing to hear." I let my tone soften for her, hoping to strengthen her resolve. I wasn't here to sow terror. Even if the idea of her staying the hell away from Dottage Mansion set me at ease in a way I didn't fully understand.

In our resulting stalemate, Sylvia gave me another once-over. Her smile turned contemplative.

"Anyway, since you came all this way..." Sylvia flew off to one of the nearby branches and returned with a little bag.

When I brought my hand up, she dropped the offering onto my palm. There were about half a dozen blueberries inside. I was too stunned to say anything right away. Even after everything, she was handing out gifts. She must have taken my silence as confusion because she laughed gently.

"It's food," she explained slowly, like I was two. "Straight from the ground. This is what Pop-Tart filling looks like *before* it's put in. Don't eat the leaves, though."

I nodded graciously, fighting a laugh. "Good to know. I've got something for you, too, actually." As I pulled out the capsule, my smile faded. The shadow of her hood made it difficult to see her face, but I somberly tried to meet her gaze. "I can't even begin to apologize for what we did to you, let alone find a way to thank you for saving my life. But I saw this, though, and I thought you might like it."

Her lips parted in the shadow of her hood as I popped open the capsule and held the necklace up. She inched forward and took the charm in both hands, gasping like she'd never seen anything so beautiful in her life. She didn't seem to care in the slightest that it was made of cheap plastic.

"A snowflake!" she exclaimed.

"I know it's too big for you," I said hurriedly. "But you liked those bracelet charms from Dottage."

"It's perfect! It's like an affinity symbol." She tugged the chain out of my fingers and made quick work of wrapping it several times around her waist like a belt. She secured the clasp, wiggling her hips and grinning at how the snowflake rocked side to side.

Twenty minutes and a dozen quarters were more than worth it.

Just as I was about to goad her with a compliment, she dipped her head to admire the charm. I glimpsed the hidden side of her face, and the words died on my tongue. I took a quick step forward for a better look, hoping it was a trick of the light.

"Sylvia, what—" I frowned, noticing how tense she became. "Are you hurt? That's... Is that a burn?"

"Don't worry about it—it's nothing." Her voice went taut, matching the sudden stiffness in her posture. She twisted away from me.

I lashed out my hand and grabbed the snowflake charm to hold her in place. The second I did it, regret coursed through me, certain I'd hit the point of scaring her off for good.

When Sylvia jerked back, her hood fell. She stopped struggling. Her left cheek was badly inflamed with a swirling, dark red mark that stretched from her hairline to jaw. She looked lucky to still have that eye.

"What is that?" I asked quietly. I pinched the snowflake charm tighter, tugging her closer. "Who did this to you?"

Eyes shuttering, Sylvia tucked her hair behind her ears. "My village gives this to those who betray our people." A quiver entered her voice. "It's a... A traitor mark."

She confessed it with the same shameful inflection someone might say *felony*.

"Did they see us?" I asked, wrestling my voice into a soft decibel. If her initial reaction to us was anything to go off of, I could gather the general hateful consensus on humans. "When we brought you here yesterday, were you spotted with us?"

Sylvia shook her head. When I released her, she fluttered over to sit on a branch. Her wings drooped. "They didn't need to. They violated my mind and pulled everything out. My visits to that stupid house. Contact with humans." Her eyes flashed up at me, wet with tears and twinkling with dark humor. "Healing a hunter," she said.

My mouth went dry. I didn't know what to say, but that despairing look on her face was hard to bear.

"Can you heal it?" I asked. "Like you did with your wing?"

Sylvia ran a hand through her reddish hair, pulling down a few locks to conceal her left cheek. "No. It's everlasting magic. Designed to be unhealable, to alert communities of dangerous individuals."

I thought that was fucking harsh, but as one of the people partially responsible, I kept my mouth shut. She'd been so desperate to return home, and this was what had been waiting for her.

"I'm lucky they didn't kill me," she sighed, pulling at her hair again to cover her eye, too.

I gaped at her. "Execution is on the table?"

"Only if they catch us here."

I stole a look around our shaded space under the willow, tensing at the idea that there might be a dozen tiny eyes watching me from the branches. If Sylvia was at ease to speak to me, I supposed she was confident that the guard wouldn't be returning anytime soon. But then again, she'd also been confident about entering a haunted house without consequence. I wasn't exactly sold on the quality of her judgment.

"Well, for what it's worth, it's a good-looking scar," I offered. She lifted her head and scowled at me. "No, really! You can trust my opinion. I've lost count of how many scars I have. It's kind of gross, actually."

Sylvia looked at my collar. Her hands fisted on her lap. "I'm sorry I couldn't save you from one more."

I brushed a few fingers over the raised skin on my neck. "I like this one. It's a souvenir of the first time I met a fairy. Besides, it's hardly the worst I've gotten."

"Doesn't your salve help with that?" she asked.

"It took me years to get it right, and that's *with* all the herbal remedies I knew from my family. Either way, it's not magic. There's no avoiding scars with the deeper cuts."

Latching onto her curious stare, I decided it wouldn't hurt to show her. After what we'd put her through—and the result of our misadventure—a little vulnerability was the least I could give her. Unbuttoning my shirt, I pulled it open and let the sleeves slide halfway down my arms.

Sylvia gave a little gasp, eyes tracing over the faint, ribbed claw marks that sliced across my chest. Those were the worst, but certainly not the only ones. My torso was little more than a connect-the-dots of old scrapes. Her gaze snagged on a long, twisted ridge of flesh along my ribs.

"That must've hurt," Sylvia said. Her eyes went dark like she was imagining the lethal talon that had buried itself in me.

"You should see the other guy," I joked weakly.

Her eyes lifted to mine, studying my face with a furrow between her brows. "Is the other guy… alive?"

I hesitated, weighing what line I might be crossing if I revealed that the ghoul that had caused the scar was now in eight scorched pieces, buried deep beneath the Appalachians.

Sylvia held up her hands, shaking her head with a grimace. "Nevermind. If it takes that long to say it, I already know." She angled her head to the side, spotting the bandages wrapped around my upper arm. "How's that one coming along?"

Wincing, I unwound the white fabric to show her—and to check the wound. "I needed stitches," I explained. "I was hoping I wouldn't, but the gash was too wide. Those dogs probably needed a nail trim even before the werewolf got hold of them. I let Cliff get it over with last night."

"Stitches?" Sylvia's eyes widened upon seeing the threaded slice.

"I guess with your healing, you'd never need something like this. Stitches close the cut with a needle and thread. Not fun." I touched the end of the wound, grimacing at the dull stab of pain.

Gasping, Sylvia clutched her upper arm suddenly. She went pale in the face, gawking at me like I was a ghost.

"Sylvia?" I asked with a frown.

She continued to stare, deep in her sudden bewilderment. Her wings slowed, and for a second, I thought she might fall out of the air.

"Hey!" I said.

She drew in a shaky breath, blinking hard. "I-I'm fine." Her fingers dug into her arm. "That... It must be painful."

I wrapped up the stitched wound, wishing I'd kept it hidden. "Hey, I'm sorry. You didn't need to see this."

"I'm alright." Her voice was shaky—understandable, considering she'd been exposed to scars and cuts longer than she was tall. What was I thinking?

"Listen," I said as I finished buttoning my shirt. Reluctance wrestled within me. She'd saved me and was marked for life because of it. I felt like an asshole, unable to offer anything more than a plastic snowflake. The best thing I could do was get as far away from her as possible. "I should head out before I get you into more trouble."

"No, you can't!" Sylvia surged forward. Catching herself, she stammered for a second before hurriedly adding, "I... I want to come with you. To help you with the werewolf."

A startled laugh escaped me. "You can't be serious."

"Don't look at me like I'm a child. If I hadn't pointed out those creatures to you yesterday, *both* of you might have died!"

"A bit of a stretch," I said under my breath.

"And what happens if you get bitten again? You *know* I can help." Her words spilled out so rapidly, there was no way she was thinking clearly. My hesitation only made her more frantic.

"I have a family," she said. "Even if the rest of my damn village has turned its back on me..." She paused, shaking her head fervently. "This werewolf out there is a danger to us, too. It was at Dottage. Who's to say it wouldn't venture into these woods? And if there's bloodshed from that, it would be on me, wouldn't it?" Steely resolve locked in her gaze as she looked at me, daring me to refuse. "You promised me a favor. Anything I wanted. This is what I want. To help."

I narrowed my eyes, studying her with a mixture of suspicion and curiosity. After everything we had put her through, why would she willingly offer her assistance?

"You'd help *savages?*" I asked cooly, recalling her snarled words in the motel room.

I half expected another smart-ass remark. Sylvia fiddled with her hands instead, looking pensive. "Savage was the wrong word," Sylvia admitted. "You and Cliff are… different. Certainly less disgusting than stories put forth."

"Gee, I'm blushing."

She gave an adorable laugh, folding her arms over her chest. "Well, don't expect me to compose a song for you. Now, do I get my favor or not?"

"Your village hurt you already," I pressed. "What are they going to do to you when they find out you were with humans again voluntarily?"

"Simple. They won't find out this time. I'll make sure of it."

"And you're saying *what,* exactly? You want to come with me right now?"

A fleeting smile touched her lips. "Unless this monster is taking a long holiday in the sun?"

Jesus, she wasn't backing down. I studied a bit of mud on my boots as I mulled it over. We'd never had the advantage of a supernatural ally before, and the small taste of her power at the old mansion had been intoxicating. Her brand was different from witchcraft, and it was hard not to get greedy, thinking of the possible applications. She could pick out a vampire in a lineup.

Sense a werewolf outside of its true form. Hell, she could probably freeze a fucking prowler solid with that ice magic of hers.

I took a deliberate step closer, testing her resolve. Sylvia jumped in the air as the space between us became inches, but she did not back away. The forest held its breath as our gazes locked.

"If this is a trick… If you double-cross us, " I said, my voice low, "I'll have to kill you."

This close, I could see her more clearly—how a flurry of emotions danced over her expression. Her fear of me was unmistakable, but there was more now. She seemed to mirror the morbid curiosity I knew was written all over my face.

"Likewise," she said with a clench of her jaw.

It was hard not to admire her brazenness.

I muttered an agreement and held out my hand to her the way I'd done yesterday to carry her, trying to ignore the fucking strangeness of it all.

"Can your wings take you a mile out, or do you need help?" I asked.

Sylvia gathered her flowy sleeves and fluttered down to land in my palm without hesitation. "*Stars,* I was hoping you would offer," she said, rolling her shoulders with a wince. "My back is killing me like you wouldn't believe."

Fascination gripped me as she settled. Her cerulean wings caught the dappled sunlight and cast prismatic shimmers across my skin and hers. There were so many intricate details in her clothing and the swirling patterns of her wings. Cliff was talented, but he hadn't come close to capturing the ethereal edge of her presence on that journal page. My fingertips twitched from Sylvia's fragile weight, fighting the primal urge to close around her. My mouth went dry as I imagined it—how soft and warm she would feel if I gave a gentle squeeze.

She looked up at me, and when her expression turned to expectation, I realized I was staring abjectly.

As I turned to push past the willow fronds, a tiny rustling among the leaves caught my attention. A tiny winged figure burst into view right in front of me and cried, "*Stop!*"

A guard.

On instinct, I whipped my other hand out and captured the second fairy before it could chant a spell. I held Sylvia close, curling my fingers to shield her. With what her people had done to her face, surely she would be outright attacked for being near me.

But Sylvia was far from comforted by my initiative. She writhed madly until she squeezed her way out of my grip and bolted back into the air. I gave far less leeway to the other fairy, who seemed to be doing far more trembling than fighting.

"Hazel!" Sylvia darted for my other hand, pulling at my fingers. She gave me a vicious look, and I swore the temperature plummeted. "Let her go, now!"

I opened my hand cautiously. Dread washed over me at the sight of a little girl weeping in my palm. Her face was buried in her hands, but the shade of her hair was unmistakable. This had to be Sylvia's little sister, and I'd just scared her to death.

"Sorry," I breathed. "I-I didn't…"

Hazel flinched at the sound of my voice. When she peeked up and spotted Sylvia, she scrambled off my palm and took to the air, throwing herself into her sister's arms.

"Don't go!" Hazel cried. "Don't go with *h-him*! Please, please!"

Hushing Hazel, Sylvia tugged her to a nearby branch. As they landed, Sylvia threw me another wary look, like perhaps I couldn't be trusted around her sister.

"I'm so sorry," I tried in a steadier voice, leaning a hair closer. "Hazel? That's your name, right? I'm not going to hurt you. You just startled me, that's all."

Hazel hugged Sylvia around the waist from behind, huddling under her sister's wings. One blue eye peeked at me. She whispered something to Sylvia, then hid her face entirely.

"She says she doesn't accept your apology," Sylvia said matter-of-factly. "And that she's not going to talk to you because she's scared she'll get marked."

Tapping Sylvia's arm, Hazel whispered to her again.

"Hm. I'm not telling him that," Sylvia murmured back.

Hazel made an insistent noise.

Sylvia sighed. "And she hopes you get eaten by a bear."

I laughed wryly, guilt surfacing with a vengeance. "I guess I can't blame you for hoping that. It's okay, you don't have to forgive me. I get it."

And here I thought Sylvia made me feel like a monster. Hazel couldn't stand to look at me for more than a second or two. No matter how I racked my brain, I couldn't think of a single thing I could say to make her less afraid. Any warmth or charisma I could usually muster meant nothing here. It didn't matter that some of the victims I'd saved might even call me charming on occasion—Sylvia and Hazel would never know it. To them, I was already cemented as this big, blundering thing that lashed out at sudden movements.

Gingerly unlatching Hazel from around her, Sylvia clutched her sister's hands and bent to her level. "I need to go," Sylvia told her. "I know you heard everything. Something's happened. There's a monster—a *mactir*—and I can help the hunters get rid of it."

"But why?" Hazel shook her head insistently. "Why do *you* have to help? Stay here!"

"Hazel." Sylvia leaned closer, gripping her sister's shoulders. "There are things I can't explain to you right now. There's no time."

"You'll get in trouble again!"

"I won't. Not if you help me. Just tell Mother and everyone else that I won't leave our room. Take extra meals. It won't be hard." Although Sylvia spoke lightly, I could see the guilt swimming underneath from asking this of Hazel. "I'll be back before you know it."

She shook her head. "I can't do that. Your friends are gonna ask."

"Yes, you can. They'll believe you, for a short while at least."

"But…" Hazel's fleeting gaze rested on me again. Her voice dropped lower. "What if he hurts you?"

"I won't," I murmured at the same time that Sylvia said, "He won't."

"He'll let you come home?" Hazel asked.

Sylvia turned to me, and I nodded confidently. "Home, safe and sound," I assured. "She saved my life, Hazel. I'll make sure she's alright. I promise."

Although Hazel's face was wet with tears, she finally gave a solemn nod. Sylvia gave her one last hug and kissed the top of her head three times.

When Sylvia retreated back to me, her sister didn't follow.

16

SYLVIA

I could feel the wound on Jon's arm as if it were my own.

What I couldn't make sense of was *why*. Whatever had helped me heal him eluded me like a foggy dream now. There had been voices, an offer, and my dizzy desperation muddling my pleas.

The oldest legends told of Ancients who would prey on desperate fairies. I had never given the stories any merit. At the very least, I'd written them off as thoroughly extinct. Even now, the memory of the voices floated out of my reach. I hadn't heard them since.

Whatever this strange, painful connection to Jon was, I could only hope that the price was considered paid. I healed him, so I was forced to endure the agony of his wounds from the fight.

But I couldn't let him walk away without knowing for sure. I had to figure this out, and if he left the woods without me, I would have no sure way of tracking him down. I had the stars to thank that he bought my blustered front about protecting Elysia from the *mactir*. I wished I was that noble.

A pang of remorse shot through me, knowing that Mother would be the perfect person to seek counsel from about the Ancients, apart from maybe the archivist. Mother had tried to speak with me this morning over a breakfast of nutmeg tarts and peaches that I refused. I had given her only clipped replies until she gave up with a sunken expression and left me alone.

She hadn't done anything wrong, but bitterness stung all the same. After her questioning last night, I had neglected to tell her about the surreal deal I made to save Jon. I couldn't stomach another layer of shame.

Now, I wished I'd said something, even if it resulted in another lecture about meddling with desperate promises.

The ache in my arm faded to the back of my mind as Jon drove. It was hard to focus on *anything* when so many new sights were flying by. The forest vanished behind us, and the human city began to flash through the car windows—towering buildings made of glass and stone, colorful cars racing beside us on the road, and signs that glowed like magic.

I flitted from window to window, determined not to miss a single thing.

"Hey, quit it," Jon grunted when I flew past him for the seventh time. "I need to see the road."

"Uh-huh," I said, gaping at a pair of humans with sparkling wheels under their shoes.

I zipped toward the passenger's side and nearly collided with Jon's nose in my hurry. He gasped, and when I landed by the window, the car swerved. My head thunked against the glass.

Jon looked over at me with a mixture of concern and exasperation. "Can you sit still before you give yourself a concussion?"

Rubbing my head, I settled for a seat on his shoulder.

"It's unfair that humans have vehicles to take them stupidly long distances when they're already so big," I griped to him.

Jon laughed a little, relaxing now that I had selected a perch. "So, if contact with other species is forbidden where you come from—"

"On the threat of death," I reminded him, still stunned at that final revelation myself.

"Right. Does that mean you've never been outside that forest your whole life? I'm not interrogating," Jon added as though he read my mind. "Personal curiosity, I promise."

I eyed his profile skeptically. "The Dottage mansion was as far as I went," I said. "But I still feel like I barely got out from beneath the damn willow."

"You live underground?"

"Mostly, yes."

"How do you get light down there? Is it through a special tunnel system, or...?"

"Okay, how is that *not* interrogating?"

He chuckled. "You have to understand this is all new to me. But fine, I'll lay off."

To my surprise, he did.

"What's that on your wrist?" I asked to fill the resulting silence. "You're always wearing it. Is that charm an *eye*?"

Jon lifted his hand from the wheel, allowing me a better look at the thin gold chain with black and red beads. "Now who's interrogating?"

"What, is it a confidential hunter secret?"

"Could be." After another beat of silence, his tone became more reverent. "It's an azabache bracelet from Puerto Rico. Black glass beads. Red coral. The eye is meant to be protection from *el mal de ojo*. The evil eye. Basically, it's a good luck bracelet."

I winced, thinking about how he didn't have much luck when the dogs came at him. "Does it work?" I asked delicately.

"Normally, I'd say no. I've worn it since I was a kid. Force of habit." Though I couldn't see his face from my perch, his smile was unmistakable. "But... I'd say having a fairy save my life is a stroke of good luck."

I toyed with the edges of the snowflake necklace. For a single second, I considered telling him about the fact that I'd experienced his stitches secondhand. But he was still a hunter—even if he had a warrior's heart.

How would he react to knowing that I called upon a mysterious unknown force to save him and had somehow created a link between us?

It felt fair to assume I would be very, *very* fucked.

I pinched the side of my thigh discreetly, wondering if he could feel my pain, too. As the sting became uncomfortable, he didn't react at all, ruling out that possibility. Unsurprising. After all, he would have felt my face being cooked last night if this was a two-way connection.

Before long, the car slowed outside a neighborhood. Two figures idled several houses down, speaking. I might have been lost in fascination with the human dwellings, but one of the figures was unmistakably *Cliff*. My heart jumped. Although forgetting someone like him was impossible, I hadn't considered his reaction to my decision to join the hunt.

Uneasiness prickled my skin as he nodded goodbye to the other human—a curvy young woman with tousled black hair. Spotting the car, Cliff started toward us.

"What are you doing?" Jon said, bemused, as I flitted down and ducked behind a lever that sat between the two seats.

"Can't I at least brace myself?" I hissed back.

The passenger door opened, and Cliff's voice rumbled as he settled into the car.

"Lily Bailey," he said without preamble. "Dog walker. She's still helping the owners put up missing posters around town. And get this—one of the dogs belonged to the Astles. Went missing a few weeks before they did."

"She knew Rick and Charlie?" Jon asked.

I bit back a yelp as he took hold of the lever and shifted it, setting the car in motion again. A faint smirk tugged on the corner of his lips as though he could sense my unappreciative glare.

"Longtime clients of hers," Cliff answered. "Apparently, Rick was trying to make a name for himself in the real estate business, hoping to flip the Dottage property for a shiny penny. He and his husband drove out there last week to take pictures. Never came back home."

Jon scoffed. "I still can't believe they'd risk going alone. The first bodies were found just down the road from there."

"The things people do for money," Cliff said. "Anything new at the house?"

"All quiet now," Jon answered. Tentatively, I peeked out from behind my hiding spot. "I ended up going off-road after checking it out."

Cliff chose that precise moment to look at Jon in confusion. His eyes, sharp as ever, caught my movement down below and made me freeze.

"You took her again?" Cliff snapped. The concern in his brutal tone might have been a little sweet if it wasn't so terrifying. "I know you're a klepto, but what the hell?"

"He didn't take me," I assured. "It was my idea to come!"

His eyes narrowed. "No offense, sweetheart, but why the fuck would you want that?"

I pouted. "I'm surprised you're not happier to see me, considering I slayed a monster."

"*Helped* slay a monster."

Jon cut in. "I went back to thank her. She wants to help."

Flitting up to Jon's shoulder, I peeked back and was startled by how close Cliff was leaning to get a better look at me. My humiliating flinch was noticeable enough to make Jon's hand dart up to steady me, but the weight of Cliff's stare didn't leave.

"What happened to your face?" Cliff asked.

"What happened to yours?" I muttered, drawing my hood up. Not my finest comeback, considering he was nice to look at when he wasn't being a jerk.

"Her village marked her for helping with the hunt." Jon's fingers tightened on the wheel. "And for saving my life."

"What are you doing here, then?" Cliff demanded of me. "You want them to give you a full sleeve? That looks like it hurts."

"You let me worry about that," I said.

Cliff regarded me for a long moment, unimpressed. "We don't need help. Jon, turn the car around."

"You've been searching for this werewolf all week!" I protested. "You didn't even know what it was until yesterday."

"It's just acting out of the pattern. And what do you know, anyway?" Cliff eyed me sharply. "You live in a fucking tree."

"Let me help you find it," I said. *And figure out what the Ancients pulled on me.* If it *was* the Ancients, anyway.

"What's in it for you?" Cliff asked.

"What do you mean?" My palms went sweaty.

He gave a noncommittal shrug. "I wasn't expecting to make the Christmas card list after the whole…"

"Keeping me in a box like an animal?"

"Yeah. That."

I sucked in a breath and let it out in a puff. It was still hard not to curl in on myself when I thought of that harrowing day in captivity.

"Well, what do *you* get out of it?" I asked. "Don't tell me you're a hunter just because you like the smell of blood."

"You seem pretty damn sure of yourself. Spend a lot of time thinking about me overnight?" His full lips twitched into a smirk, but I couldn't shake the chill that came from his studious gaze. I swore he could see right through me and hear my hammering heart. Maybe he *could.* Legends often claimed that hunters had more pronounced senses than ordinary humans.

Leaning my arms onto my knees, I gave him a pointed once-over. "No one who hugs like you do is *that* vicious. I want to protect my people, same as you."

Cliff scoffed a small laugh again. I liked to think I was surprising him pleasantly, but maybe he was only annoyed.

"I don't get why you'd want to be anywhere near this. No one does. It's ugly," Cliff said, his athletic frame going taut as he considered something. "Wait a second—is this *glamour*? Are you forcing him to do this?"

I looked at his hands. He was reaching under his jacket, and I knew he had weapons there—guns and knives and who knew what else. My blood ran cold. *I'm shit at glamour*, I wanted to say, though I doubted that would be helpful.

"She's telling the truth," Jon said, and *stars*, I'd never been more grateful. Cliff relaxed in his seat marginally. "She wants to make sure her sister doesn't become collateral damage in this case. I saw her today, back in the woods. If you'd seen this kid, you'd get it."

I whipped my head toward him. "Jon!"

Indignance turned my cheeks pink. I'd been under the impression he understood my desire for discretion. There was no need to bring up Hazel in front of the even more intense, trigger-happy monster hunter.

"What?" Jon said. "You already said you had a sister, remember? All it took was a piece of Pop-Tart."

I crossed my arms over my chest, making a mental note to be more reserved. I trusted them not to murder me, but I'd be a fool to underestimate them.

"Do you have any more of those things?" I mumbled, looking around for the Pop-Tart box.

I came to find this was the neighborhood where Rick and Charlie Astle lived before they seemingly vanished into thin air. Cliff had been questioning their neighbors.

Jon circled the block for nearly thirty minutes, giving me the chance to sense any werewolves in human form. After the fourth loop around, we called it for the day. After all, some people might be at work. It was funny to think of a bloodthirsty monster having a day job, but I supposed that was part of the tragedy.

I tried not to dwell on the disappointed clench in Jon's jaw as he drove away.

Seeing the motel room from a higher angle didn't soothe the dread that resurfaced in my gut when we returned. The box I'd been kept inside was still sitting on the round table by the TV. Jon and Cliff hadn't even swept up the little crumbs of cardboard that peppered the table by the hole I'd dug.

Flitting off Jon's shoulder, I hovered over the table and contemplated the box. *My prison.*

Without giving it much thought, I lifted my arms and unleashed every destructive spell I knew. Icicles punctured the cardboard, dense and rapid. Thick frost grew over the edges, increasing pressure until it collapsed into a shredded mess.

The room was silent.

Eventually, Cliff heaved a sigh. "Thanks. That'll be a treat to clean up." Stray flecks of ice crunched under his boots as he crossed the room to grab a drink out of the fridge. "Why didn't you just do that to escape?"

"I'm sure that would've gone over *very* well with the guys who can put a hole in me from across the room." I shook out my hands, breathing heavily from the intense display of magic.

"Fair enough." Cliff took a long drink. "Can't believe we're taking on a fucking fairy for consulting work."

"I'd be able to consult more if I knew exactly what we were up against." I alighted on the edge of the table, allowing my destructive handwork to sit behind me like a backdrop. Ruse or not, I found myself intrigued to piece together the case I'd overheard in fragments the day before. "Your werewolf sounds quite like what my people would call a *mactir*. A wolf person. They're affected by the moon, aren't they?"

Jon nodded. "They transform a few nights a month, connected to lunar phases. With how fresh that attack was at Dottage, it won't be feeding for a few nights. The brighter the moon phase, the more frenzied they are when they turn."

"And the longer they'll be wolfed out," Cliff added. "So that means they're the worst—"

"During the full moon," I said. The chaos yesterday and my lack of sleep made me pause to yawn. "That's just a few nights away."

Cliff raised an eyebrow at me, but he nodded. "Sad part is, many werewolves don't even know what they are. They wake up with shredded clothes and blood and no memory of what happened."

"This one seems more lucid, though." Jon crossed the room and dug through his bag. "Choosing an abandoned house as a feeding ground hardly seems like a coincidence." He pulled out a knife, holding it out to show me. The sight was unsettling, but my skin didn't prickle. "Silver's their weakness. They heal fast under almost every other circumstance. Silver needs to pierce their heart while they're wolfed out."

"Lovely," I said faintly, trying not to dwell on the images of Jon's rageful knife skills in the Dottage basement. "So even if I find your monster, you won't be able to kill them unless they've transformed?"

"It's a little hard for them to transform if they're dismembered," Cliff said with a cryptic quirk of his lips. The blood drained from my face, and he added, "Not that we'd *do* that unless we knew we had our wolf for sure." He gave me a pointed look as though questioning my credibility to point out the correct person.

"Normally, it's easier to trace attacks back to the werewolf," Jon said. "We tail them until the next transformation and take them out before they can kill again."

"And you don't know where else it could be?" I asked.

"We're still sweeping that neighborhood," Cliff said. "Just gotta keep an ear to the ground."

Over a meal of microwaved food that begged for culinary redemption, we dissected the remaining case details. My appetite was lacking long before I tasted the bland, soggy vegetables—pried free of the meat they'd been packaged alongside, thankfully. Jon and Cliff made killing sound so *easy*.

Still, questions bubbled to my lips like a gushing stream. *How many humans total has it killed so far? Does it have heightened senses even when it's not transformed? Does it know when silver is near, like me with iron?*

At my prodding, the hunters recounted the tale about the last werewolf they had taken down. Human authorities in a small Iowa town had been misguided in their pursuit of what they thought to be a serial killer—in reality, the monster was hiding in their very ranks. It had been particularly tricky, Cliff explained, to get close enough to the detective to drive a silver knife through his heart and escape the town without being arrested. He painted a vivid image. It made me ponder the havoc someone like Ayden could do as an Entry Watch leader if he were infected with a malevolent disease like that.

Like the disease that had almost claimed Jon, I thought with a glance at the exposed skin above his shirt.

Though I wasn't exactly rolling in grime, thoughts of a soak in the Elysian hot springs began to dance in my mind. Glancing uncertainly between the hunters, I carefully asked about the adjoining washroom. It had that large basin, if nothing else. To my slight surprise, there was no objection to my request. Jon simply closed his laptop and motioned for me to follow him.

I hovered in the doorway, glancing back at Cliff. A part of me suspected their hospitality might be some sort of trick, but he was engrossed in his phone and nursing a heavy pour of whiskey in his other hand.

"You'll need soap, right?" Jon muttered to himself.

I faced forward, watching him work. Jon turned on the sink and pulled a knob on the faucet to close the drain at the bottom. I watched in delight as it began to fill up with warm water. This wasn't like the elegant hot springs in Elysia, but it was clean and *huge*. My bitter memories of splashing my face with water from this faucet began to ease.

"Not too deep!" I blurted, the words tumbling out as I staggered toward the sink. Jon shot me a quizzical glance, and I once again wondered if my honesty was a grave mistake. "I… I can't swim."

But if I'd handed him ammunition with this, he concealed it well, as Jon simply shut off the water with a subtle nod.

I turned my head toward the frosted window embedded in the far wall of the washroom, where the last straggling rays of daylight pushed inside. Right now, Hazel would be lying to Mother and saying I didn't want to be disturbed, pushing out an empty tray of food from our bedroom. At least, I hoped she was. I'd be pretty fucked otherwise.

A large mirror adorned the space over the sink that I hadn't appreciated before. Catching sight of my reflection, I made a beeline for it. I had been swept away by my own beauty when I glimpsed myself in the Dottage foyer, but this time, my eyes honed in on the ugly mark on my left cheek. My flight slowed, lowering me inch by inch to the counter until my nose was nearly touching the glass.

I turned my face side to side, unable to focus on my pouty lips or my watering green eyes. The traitor mark was a vicious mess of swirling, ancient Fae. The angry redness made that side of my face look swollen. I knew when it fully healed, it would transform into an inky blackness, branding me forever.

A sob welled in my chest. I was horrible to look at now.

I didn't notice the stillness until Jon cleared his throat. Narrowing my eyes up at his reflection, I realized he'd been observing me.

"I don't want your pity," I spat.

His lips quirked. "I wouldn't dare," Jon said, fiddling with a bar of soap. "You know, I've been around a lot of non-humans. Horrible things. Nightmares. And all these years, I've never seen a non-human so…"

"Pathetic?" I scoffed, gingerly touching a swirl above my eyebrow.

"No."

"Small?"

"Pretty."

I froze and met his gaze through the mirror. He was trying to make me feel better about the traitor mark—right of him, too, considering I got it for saving his ass. But it was sweet. And to my surprise, Jon seemed to grow bashful, breaking eye contact.

Incredible. Just yesterday, I had seen him in a rage, stabbing the werewolf-infected beast over and over. Now, he was fastidiously scraping off the exact right amount of soap for me to use in a bath.

"You don't have to lie," I said. "I know it looks awful. One of the Elders decided I was a monster, so she ordered a guard to make me look like one. Poetic, isn't it?"

Jon dropped a little chunk of soap on the edge of the sink. Setting aside the rest of the bar, he fixed his full attention on me. I casually brushed my hair back in front of my left cheek, a lump forming in my throat. But I swore he could see every burnt swirl right through the thin curtain. Something warm glimmered in his gaze—the way he had looked at me this morning in the woods.

He shrugged, wearing a small smile. "I wouldn't worry about what they think. I find that people who don't know shit about monsters throw that word around too much."

"I called you a monster," I pointed out.

"To be fair, *you* don't know shit about monsters." Jon's smile widened. After a beat, his expression clouded. His gaze became flighty, as though battling whether to open his mouth again or not. "Earlier, you said you weren't afraid of me anymore—of us. I hope that's true. I'd like us to start fresh if that's possible."

I cocked my head, regarding Jon skeptically. "I'm surprised you give two shits about what I think." Surprised he didn't desire the *opposite* effect when fear might serve him well.

"I guess you're not as easy to ignore as I'd hoped."

The laughter dancing behind his eyes disarmed me. It was unjust for a killer to have a boyish smile like that. I pushed a hand back through my hair. *Stars,* I think I believed him.

"If you're so concerned, it sounds like it's *your* job not to be scary," I decided.

"That's fair. Okay, scale of one through ten. How scary do you think I am right now?"

He rolled his shoulders and lifted his chin, awaiting my appraisal. Pressing my lips into a thin line to mute my smile, I looked him up and down and gave a small, analytical hum. "Five." I hesitated, and just to see how he'd react, I said, "No. Six."

His brows drew together, but he nodded. "Sounds like I've got some work to do. I'll bring that number down."

"Looking forward to it."

Deciding I'd better make use of the warm water before it cooled, I undressed and dropped my clothes into a pile by the sink. As I slipped into the pond-sized bath, I didn't hesitate to submerge myself fully and enjoy the miraculous heat. Surfacing, I heaved a sigh at the pleasant sensation.

"I forgot to grab the soap," I said. "Can you—" The question died on my lips when I looked up and found that Jon was frozen, absolutely pink in the face. He flinched and looked elsewhere when we made eye contact. "Is something wrong?" I asked.

"What? No. Nothing." Jon plucked the sliver of soap from the edge of the sink and handed it to me clumsily, never looking.

"Is it that strange for you to see a body with wings?" I pressed.

"N-no, you're fine." His deep voice wobbled into a chuckle. "It's just—I thought you would wait for me to leave before you, ah…"

"Oh." I winced, laughing apologetically. "Have you never seen a female before? I'm sorry—"

"It's not that! I've seen plenty of females, trust me."

"Then why does your face look like a strawberry?"

Jon scoffed and palmed his face. "Most people don't strip down in front of a stranger. Humans don't, anyway."

"Are you *shy*?" My jaw dropped in utter delight. "Look at you! Able to rip apart a monster, but terrified of skin. Stars, I hardly know what to say."

He chuckled again, but he didn't make any move to leave just yet. Perhaps he was in too much shock.

I waded closer and folded my arms against the curved wall of the basin. "I don't mind if you look. I won't tell." It was oddly sweet how he continued to stare at the door for a few seconds longer. He reminded me of the late bloomers among my peers who still blushed and giggled breathlessly at the revels.

Jon tentatively set his gaze on me, and I grinned teasingly to diffuse his uncertainty. "You're so human," he said at last, sounding incredulous. "All over."

"Thanks," I said in a tone that should have been reserved for *how dare you.*

"Hey, it's up to you if you want to take it as an insult."

I glanced down at myself and gave Jon a quick once-over—what I could see of him, at least. I wondered suddenly if Jon was built the same way as Damian. I tried to shake the thought, but that was hard to do when Jon was still looking at me.

Our eyes locked, and he pulled back sharply. "I'll leave you to it," he said in a forced, easygoing tone. He glanced over his shoulder as he opened the door. "Thanks, uh… for talking."

"Thanks for staring," I piped back.

It was only meant to be a tease, but it spooked him off so hurriedly that he walked face-first into the doorframe.

I might have laughed until I cried if not for the sudden jolt of pain that lanced through my forehead. I rubbed the spot, breath catching at the awful realization that whatever had tied me to him wasn't finished.

He closed the door to give me privacy, mortified and oblivious.

Heart pounding, I lowered myself in the water. I should have been biting my lip and giggling at Jon's bashfulness. Instead, I berated myself for losing focus. Jon didn't matter. All that mattered was that I was experiencing his pain—and I needed to get to the bottom of it while making sure he didn't inadvertently destroy me on this werewolf hunt.

I swore I heard sinister chuckles at the back of my mind, but they faded further and further the more I tried to listen.

17

JON

"Over my dead body."

"Just a little taste. I'm curious!"

I side-stepped to dodge Sylvia as she chased Cliff across the motel room, wings buzzing in urgent flight. He cupped a hand over his coffee to keep her from sampling it. She was damn quick with her wings fully healed. She flew close, dipping and dodging his fingers like a moth darting around a porch light.

"You're already more wired than the fucking Energizer bunny," Cliff said, twisting away. "And I don't need your grubby little fairy hands in my drink."

Stopping short, Sylvia gasped dramatically. "That's rude."

The coffee maker purred as I brewed my own cup. I had slept restlessly last night, dreaming of my father. I would've thought it was a mare plaguing my dreams over these years, but I slept with a silver knife under my pillow. Most superstitions were bullshit, but admittedly, that trick was effective for those particular Norse nightmare-feeders.

There was no other entity to blame. This dream was all me.

Mom used to say it was best to air out nightmares right away, to talk about them openly so that we didn't give them any more power than they were worth. I wondered if she would still say that today or agree that some visions were better kept locked far away from the light.

While I had my back turned to take my mug, I heard a tiny splash and a "*Hey!*" barked from Cliff. Sylvia had managed to scoop a handful of his coffee as he seated himself at the table.

Sylvia sipped at her handful and immediately spat it back out, spraying droplets on Cliff's open laptop.

"Lovely," Cliff muttered, dabbing at the keyboard.

"That's vile. It's so bitter!" Sylvia wrinkled her nose, looking utterly crestfallen. She wiped the remaining coffee off on her fitted green pants. "You don't have any rose water, do you? Or nectar?"

"Fresh out," I replied dryly, sipping my coffee.

She settled for a capful of room-temperature water as we pulled up the available case information on our respective devices. I tuned the police scanner on the two-seater table, keeping it at a volume that we could catch anything pertinent. More juiced-up dogs mauling civilians, for one thing.

When his laptop was satisfactorily disinfected, Cliff plugged a flash drive into the USB port—which we'd nicked from the security guard's abandoned car the day before. Cliff made quick work of scanning through the video files it held until he found the date that matched the incident. I could see questions bubbling on Sylvia's lips as she stared at the tiny clip of metal and plastic protruding from the laptop. To my surprise, she was reverently quiet when the video filled the screen.

The grainy dash cam footage depicted the guard's arrival at Dottage Mansion that night, the glow of headlights cutting through the gloom of the winding road. Though we knew the grisly end to the man's story, the motel room cloyed with tension as we watched the car pull to a stop in front of the towering Victorian home. The guard got out of the driver's seat and crossed in front of the idling headlights, speaking to someone in his earpiece. The footage flickered, briefly distorting the guard's face into a grotesque mask. The audio clipped and pitched into unsettling tones. Sylvia flinched out of the corner of my eye.

The rest of the video played with minimal glitching. We listened to the crackling audio from a static frame of the Dottage front porch. For long minutes, silence stretched. Then, howls—both human and animal. The noise was short-lived, and the new silence that followed bore a new weight to it.

Cliff's jaw ticked when he scrubbed forward again. Dead of night on screen became day. Cliff and I entered the frame, our figures pixelating as we followed the guard's fated steps into the house.

"What do you think that man was thinking?" Sylvia asked, soft but not meek. "When he walked inside that night?"

I eyed her expression—no judgment or childlike wonder this time. Just a haunted glaze in her eyes.

"I don't know," I said.

It was a bitter truth that our minutes were numbered, but no one expected a painful death. Like every victim before him, the security guard had simply been doing his job, blind to the fragility of his mundane routine.

While we scrubbed back through the footage, Sylvia's attention eventually strayed to my phone—though I wondered if she wasn't purposefully clearing her head. I had propped my phone up against the back of the laptop to watch local news highlights earlier, but the screen had gone dark after being left idle. She knelt in front of the black screen to use it like a mirror.

Just like the bathroom, she seemed magnetically drawn to her reflection. The snowflake charm glinted at her hip. I hadn't seen her take it off except to bathe. She swept her hair this way and that, obsessed with her mirrored countenance as she tried to cover her traitor mark just right. Despite her protests that my salve smelled foul, I'd managed to convince her to sleep with a thin layer of it on her burn last night. It was hard to tell if it had offered much relief.

The phone screen buzzed with a news alert that lit up the screen. Sylvia yelped and lurched back like it might bite her.

"Does it have to be so dramatic?" Sylvia said as I plucked up the phone.

"I could say the same thing," Cliff muttered, fixated on the laptop.

Sylvia threw him a pout, but I drew her attention back before they could start bickering. After confirming that the notification had nothing to do with us, I swiped it away and opened the camera.

"Here, you'll be able to see yourself better this way," I told her.

As I lowered the phone to her level, she frowned. The slight delay between her movement and her reflection seemed to boggle her, but not as much as when I tapped on a filter—something I hadn't used since high school.

Her eyes widened when hearts and sparkles exploded around her image. "*Stars*, how—" She looked over her shoulder, expecting to see the filter manifesting in real life. Instead of looking frightened or overwhelmed, wonder glinted in her gaze. "How can you have these things and not call it magic?"

"Because it's called technology." But I supposed it wouldn't make a difference to someone who'd only been exposed to magic.

Wincing, I lowered the phone and let my arm relax. The stitched wound was healing at a snail's pace. Sylvia eyed my discomfort, her expression mirroring mine. Her wings buzzed to life, and she inched closer to the bandages.

"Would you let me heal that for you?" she asked tightly. "It's hurting you."

I raised my eyebrows. "Can you sense it—like with monsters?"

She glanced away, smiling shyly. "Some healers can sense pain, yes."

Cliff's jaw-clenched glare bore into me from across the table. I understood his hesitation, but *he* wasn't the one gearing up for an all-out hunt with a compromised dominant arm. Besides that, seeing more of what Sylvia could offer wasn't a bad idea.

I rolled up the sleeve of my gray tee, watching her face as I unwound the gauze to reveal the puckered injury. Sylvia's cheeks puffed like she was bracing herself. She lifted her hands and started chanting something so softly that I couldn't make out the words. Soft blue light flooded her palms. She flew forward and touched my arm, and the healing sensation coursed through me.

Her healing prowess was no less surreal the second time around. Surreal and… *breathtaking*. With a clear mind this time, the experience deepened. I wasn't wavering in the haze of a shadowy fever. I could see it all in vivid detail. The intense focus on her face pulled my eye, illuminated by the shimmering magic she wielded. The searing ache of my wound ceased almost at once, and the tightness of my jaw softened. Cliff's careful stitches popped out of my skin as the wound sealed over. Not even a scar was left behind. It was incredible. *She* was incredible.

"That's better, hm?" Sylvia extinguished the magic.

"You have no idea," I said. She looked winded, I noticed with a frown—her cheeks flushed and breathing labored. Odd, considering this wound was nothing compared to the life-saving magic she'd done for me at Dottage. "Are you okay?"

"No adrenaline rush to fuel me this time, but I'll live," she assured, tossing her hair behind her ear. "And you guys are *not* fairies, I hope you remember. More to heal." She gestured widely at me.

I let my fingers trace over my arm one more time before rolling my shirt sleeve back down.

Sylvia turned to Cliff. "What about you? Any injuries?"

Cliff snorted, dodging her attention. "I'll heal the old-fashioned way, thanks."

"Are you still afraid of me?" She quirked a mocking eyebrow.

"I've survived this long without magic. No good can come of going soft with shortcuts." His eyes cut to me, flashing in warning.

"You were singing a different tune when I saved your friend's life," Sylvia said.

"That was life or death," Cliff said, raising the volume on the police scanner as though trying to tune her out. "An exception. I'm flattered you want to put your hands all over me, but I don't need you to heal every damn paper cut."

Sylvia looked over her shoulder at me, rubbing her own arm in sympathy. "I would hardly call *that* a paper cut. But fine, have it your way."

If Cliff hoped that his sour attitude would ward Sylvia off, he was sorely mistaken. Out of all the objects in the room she had grown curiously obsessed with, the laptop had been left alone—until now. As I turned my attention to analyzing the map on my phone, Sylvia hovered over the table.

"What is that called again?" she asked.

"Laptop," he said tersely when he realized she was speaking to him. She flinched as he turned the screen to face her halfway. "It's not gonna bite you if that's what you're scared of."

She rolled her eyes. "It doesn't even have teeth."

Her sharp defensiveness drew a smirk out of Cliff. "Then why don't you check it out for yourself?"

For someone who was insistently *not* scared, she took her time inching toward the screen. She stared at the search engine page and reached a tentative hand out to touch it.

"Is it like the TV?" she asked.

"Kinda."

Cliff moved his finger on the trackpad to make the cursor dart up to her hand. She yelped and snatched herself away, pulling close enough to bump my shoulder. Her face flushed as she glared at the cursor, wary that it might fly off the screen and chase her.

"Did you do that?" she demanded of Cliff, creeping back in front of the laptop. "How?"

He gave her another scare by shooing her away from the screen. "Burning your eyes out by putting your face against it isn't gonna help you figure it out."

She dodged around his hand. "What do you use it for?"

He sighed. "I guess I can give you a crash course while I do some research. Just don't ask a million questions like you do with everything else."

"What if I *really* need to know something?"

"Tough shit if you *really* need to know something."

After giving Sylvia a tour of a local news website, Cliff allowed her free reign of the laptop—as long as she didn't click on an ad or try to buy anything. When she fired off a series of questions about what that meant, he didn't bother explaining.

He nudged my arm and nodded for me to join him on the other side of the room. I should have known a serious conversation was coming. Something uncertain had been swimming in his eyes as he showed Sylvia the laptop.

"I don't feel good about this," Cliff muttered.

"Seriously? You still don't trust her?" I scoffed, tugging at my collar to make the scarring on my neck more visible. "After everything?"

"What, you want me to write her into my will?" He shot me a withering smile. "No, it's more than that. I mean, just… just look at her. She shouldn't be anywhere near this. She's too wide-eyed."

Having been fully prepared to defend her intentions, I was taken aback by his argument. We shared a furtive glance toward the table, where Sylvia was painstakingly pressing letters on the keyboard. There was no doubt that she had limited exposure to the horrors of the world—to *any* part of the world.

"She can lead us straight to the werewolf and skewer it with ice," I retorted. "Nothing wide-eyed about that."

"Magic or not, she's a civilian at best. Since when do we let civilians get involved like this?"

"She's different," I said, scoffing when Cliff arched an eyebrow. "We've never seen a werewolf with this staggered pattern and so many missing bodies. The number of lives we'll save with her help… It could be *dozens*. You can't tell me that doesn't mean anything to you."

"Oh, the ends justify the means now?" Cliff folded his arms over his chest, giving me a once-over that made my skin crawl with guilt.

"I'm not—" I gathered myself. "You saw the damage she dealt those things before. She can handle it. We'll keep her out of the way once we find the fucking thing. She'll be fine."

Cliff paused, some of the tension easing from his shoulders. He shot me the soft, older brother eyes that sent me hurtling right back to high school.

"Take a beat," he said, lowering his voice. "Focus up and stop blaming yourself for what he did."

The smell of smoke and burning flesh made my eyes sting, though the room was empty.

"I'm not," I snapped. "But we save as many innocents as we can, right? Or did that change for you?"

Cliff's nostrils flared. The hum of beating wings caught my ear, and I sucked in the rest of my words.

"What are you talking about?" Sylvia asked, flying over. "Your faces look all brooding and weird again."

"Trying to decide how close you need to get to this case," Cliff told her point-blank.

Her eyes narrowed. "And that doesn't sound like a conversation I should be involved in?"

"Wanted to see whose side Jon would be on first," Cliff said.

I threw him a look. "There's sides now?"

"Why wouldn't you want me to help?" Sylvia frowned between us like an affronted hunter who was told to leave their weapons at the door.

"We don't want you to get hurt," I said.

"We don't want you to get in the way," Cliff answered at the same time. Seeing the flat looks we gave him, he shrugged at me and added, "And that, too."

"I didn't uproot myself for nothing," Sylvia said. "I came all this way to help, and that's what I'm going to do."

"Tracking the wolf is one thing," Cliff said. "Sticking around for the bloodbath is another. We don't need you for that part."

She turned to me, the strident note of desperation in her tone catching me off-guard. "You have to let me be there to end it. I mean, you almost *died*, and no one's questioning whether you should be there!"

"That's a cheap shot," Cliff scoffed on my behalf.

She whirled on him. "So is everything you grumble about me when you think I'm not listening. If you don't want me here, just say so."

He leaned closer to her, unflinching. "I don't want you here."

Her hands jumped up like she had the instinct to throttle him with magic. Cliff could sneer all he wanted, but we'd seen what she'd done to those dogs and her former holding cell. Thankfully, she had the good sense to cross her arms instead of following through with an icy outburst.

"You know what?" Sylvia lowered her voice, matching Cliff's unwavering stare. "I think you're worried about me. I think you *like* me."

"Give me a fucking break." Cliff rolled his eyes. "Your life motto is 'terrible judgment.' I'm just trying to make sure we all survive your decisions."

"So you do care."

"Don't flatter yourself."

"Do you guys need a room, or can we focus?" I said, prompting both of their glares to turn toward me. "Unusual or not, attacks have still been spaced apart. We don't expect another transformation until the full moon."

I eyed Sylvia. From what I could see of her exposed midriff—and based on her casual unclothing in the bathroom—she was certainly fit. But given her size, fitness wouldn't mean much if she didn't know how to use it to her advantage.

"We chose this motel because of the woods behind it," I told her, blinking away when I realized I was staring a bit too hard. "We like having a spot where we can train without drawing attention. If you want to do more than help us track this thing down, show us what you can do out there."

18

SYLVIA

By this time in the afternoon, the denizens of Elysia would have finished their midday meal. Sentry guards would be flying in for their lunch, switching shifts. Ayden would be among them, perhaps bragging about how he had the opportunity to bestow the first traitor mark in generations.

Hazel would be taking extra food to my room with the excuse that I still refused to come out. Maybe later, she'd sneak the scraps to some mice outside the village.

Mother would be training a small group of older adolescents of fire affinities. That was if their parents still allowed them to be instructed by a traitor's mother.

And Damian… I couldn't remember if he had training sessions or a free day today. For all I knew, my absence had been noticed mere hours after I left. My family could be under lockdown and interrogation. I itched to go back and find out, but that wasn't an option right now.

Worst of all, I was no closer to figuring out the bond that tied me to Jon. One thing was clear: I had to stay close to ensure he didn't get torn apart by the *mactir*. His pain was my pain now. If he died… I wasn't sure what that meant for me, but I wasn't keen to find out.

And if that meant playing along with the hunters' insistence that I train with them, so be it.

I tried not to think about the appalled looks my family and friends would give me as I willingly followed Jon and Cliff deep into the unfamiliar woods behind the motel.

My bare arms tingled at the gentle bite of cool air. The forest swallowed us, carrying the scent of rain in the humid breeze. I glanced at the cheerful sky overhead, grateful that the storm had passed overnight. I was going to have a hard enough time focusing as it was.

If I missed a spell out here, I was going to blame Jon's gray tee shirt. It clung to his sculpted frame, emphasizing his well-toned physique as we hiked uphill. In all my revels, I'd only seen a handful of males so fit. His dark eyes, which I knew could be warm as honey, held an intensity that sent my pulse racing. Beautiful. Deadly.

I made a note to focus more on the *deadly* part.

"So, what do you do out here?" I called, hoping Cliff wouldn't snap at me for yet another question. "Wrestle? Throw knives at each other?"

Jon laughed, the sound of it dancing through the trees. He twisted, scanning the air before finding me. "Target practice, mostly. Sorry to disappoint."

We stopped in a clearing bathed in dappled sunlight. It was a stark contrast to the underground caverns I trained in with the other ice affinities, where our only illumination was the fae lights fixed along the ceiling. I fished a ribbon out of my pocket and tied back my short hair out of my face.

"It's not just the full moon we need to be worried about," Cliff explained, facing me. "You've got flight and magic, but that isn't worth shit if you don't know how to use them to your advantage. You can't freeze up—not even once."

I lifted my chin at him. "I've been training for ten years. Since I was just over eleven summers old." I wasn't sure why I felt the need to rise to the challenge in his eyes. This man had shot my wing dead through from across a room.

"They teach you any strategy?" Cliff asked.

They. I stammered, still hesitant to confirm the number of my kind. "There—there is no..."

Cliff gave me potent *don't-bullshit-me* eyes, but he moved on. "Werewolves have supernatural speed. Nothing in your legends will prepare you until you see it in action. They're practically a blur in the heat of a fight. You need to be able to dodge while conserving your energy."

"Dodge?" I snorted. "Do you see who you're talking to? That's easy—"

Before I had finished talking, Cliff had grabbed me out of the air. Faster than I had ever seen him—or any human—move. I tensed in his fist, defensive magic coursing down to my hands while I gaped at him. His lips were cocked in a grim, self-assured smile. The panicked thudding of my heart melted into embarrassment.

"That doesn't count," I said, wriggling against his tight grip. "I wasn't ready, you asshole."

Cliff released me, and I quickly flew out of reach. As the boys paced beneath me, I was still catching my breath and trying desperately not to appear flustered.

"There is no mercy during a hunt," Jon said, his deep voice reaching my perch in the branches. "No second chance. There is only alive and dead. Who walks away, and who is a corpse put in the ground."

Meanwhile, Cliff seemed eager to finish proving me wrong. He draped his brown leather jacket over a mossy stump and stepped toward the center of the clearing. I steeled myself. They weren't going to hurt me. But that didn't quite soothe the primal terror of facing them down.

I recognized the provoking glint in Cliff's face. Karis gave me the same look when my spellwork wasn't up to snuff. *Try again.*

I flew back into the clearing with them, level just above Cliff's eyes. Under the sleeve of his white undershirt, there were twisting tattoos climbing up his right arm. I tried to glimpse what the images were and made a mental note to ask him about them later. One of them looked vaguely similar to the swirls on my cheek.

I unconsciously touched the traitor mark and glanced at Jon, who was leaning against a tree. He was standing here, breathing, because of me. Because of my deal.

Distant whispers drifted in like a mist. The disjointed voices seemed to echo in the forest and scratch at the back of my mind.

"Do you feel noble for saving a life?"

"A hero, aren't you?"

The voices drifted from angelic praise to mocking growls, as tangible as though someone were standing over me. It was the first time since Dottage that I had managed to make out actual words from them.

My chest tightened. I looked around—toward the rolling hills, back toward the motel, straight up through sunlight winking in the branches... There was no one else around. Jon and Cliff didn't react at all. The voices, Ancients, *whatever they were* intended to speak to me alone.

Real. The voices were *real.* And they weren't finished with me yet.

Ancients...

For a moment, horror clouded my vision as I considered their presence again. Those vicious fae spirits that no spell could touch. Mother had warned me, and I had blindly reached out to the ether anyway.

The voices chuckled as though listening to my train of thought.

"We must collect what's ours.

"Must, must, must."

Ancients had found me.

"You look a little green." Cliff's voice pulled my wide eyes back to him. He circled me slowly. "You sure about this, kiddo?"

Ice gathered in my hands. "Don't call me that."

He lunged, no warning this time. I gave a short yelp and dodged backward through the leaves of a nearby tree. A small gale of ice crystals manifested from thin air and shot his way. He outmaneuvered them—which was embarrassing, considering how big of a target he was.

The humiliation didn't end with that exchange. He reached higher than I could have expected and yanked the branch I had alighted on, snapping it. Normally, I considered myself a fairly accurate flier, but the shivering leaves and branches left me disoriented as I tried to get away. I smacked right into his waiting palm.

He pinned my back to the tree with obvious care not to injure me, but I was acutely aware nonetheless that he could grind my wings to tatters with the right amount of pressure. He released after a beat of heavy silence. I couldn't bring myself to look either hunter in the eye as I caught my breath.

"No way you're coming with us," Cliff said, swaggering back toward his jacket. "The last thing I need is your blood on my hands."

My fists clenched. He thought I was weak. If I were human, I could yank him back and face me. Frost bloomed in my palms, crawling up my wrists. Karis would call me childish for allowing emotion to manifest ice.

Before I could think better of it, I darted behind Cliff with my hands raised. Jon tensed; his mouth started to form a warning. I didn't bother with precision—I merely screamed a verse that fired a vicious burst of icy air at Cliff's back.

The surprise and force of the attack sent him sprawling onto his hands and knees in the dirt. He sprang back up in front of me, eyes ablaze. I clutched my hands close and moved back slowly, debating whether I should make a break for one of the higher branches while I still could.

But Cliff sighed and then, remarkably, smiled. "That's a start."

Cliff and I practiced for another ten minutes while Jon shouted advice at me. A lot of my troubles were fixed when I simply stayed high out of reach. The hunters were tall, but they'd have to waste time climbing a tree if they wanted to get a hold of me in the higher branches.

However, if I wanted my ice to be effective in any capacity, I needed to close the distance a dangerous amount and put myself within arm's reach. I created icicles and shards with dulled tips and eased up on the biting cold of my spells—so long as Cliff didn't squeeze too hard whenever he caught me.

Although I wasn't perfect by any means, the rhythm of Cliff's movements was becoming easier to read by the time Jon stepped in to replace him.

I bit back a whine. It wasn't fair that I'd have to analyze an entirely different person in the same training session, but as the hunters were quick to remind me, the werewolf would not be *fair*.

"You look tired," Jon said. The dimple from his smile was a distraction in and of itself. I focused on his hands.

"All part of my evil plan," I countered.

As I parried with Jon, the voices clamored.

"You wish to harm your gift?"

"A shame."

"Wasteful."

Jon seized a low-hanging branch and let it snap back, shaking the leaves around me. I had to veer hard to the right to avoid being smacked out of the air. Scrambling away, I conjured a shower of frost to disorient him.

"What would he do if he knew of your sacrifice?"

"Kill you or kiss you?"

The disjointed voices seemed to be strengthened by my heightening anxiety, growing closer and closer. This last word was all but whispered right into my ear. I swore I felt a pair of invisible hands grasping my shoulders from behind. They felt *hungry*.

What price had I agreed upon?

The archives in Elysia were my best shot at answers. But first, I needed to focus on not making a fool of myself.

Gripping tree bark with one hand, I lashed out with the other and released offensive spellwork. I was still looking around for my invisible stalkers when a cold slice of pain bloomed on my abdomen.

Stars—one of my icicles had been sharp. Jon was peering at a thin line of blood peppering the bottom of his gray tee. Much like Cliff, he looked encouraged that I had been able to draw blood. My sympathetic pain dulled the victory.

After that, I didn't let my attention stray.

"You're pulling your punches," Jon said, ducking easily under a hard line of frost I sent his way. "What, you think I can't take it?"

I forced a smile to lighten the tension rippling from me. "I just healed you. I don't want to do too much damage."

Jon stalked closer, but he didn't test me this time. He seemed to note how fatigued I was—not that he had even broken a sweat. I saw a blur of movement behind him. Before I could warn him, Cliff had stepped in and swept Jon cleanly off his feet with a well-placed kick.

"Asshole," Jon said, grinning as he launched back to his feet.

I landed in the knot of an oak tree, more than happy to catch my breath as the men began to spar with each other. Their synergy was obvious, making me wonder how long they had been hunting and traveling together. They seemed able to predict each other's moves, countering with fluidity. Their roughhousing made the trees shiver, but they appeared to be genuinely enjoying themselves—laughing even.

Most of their contact was light touches, but a few of the blows Cliff landed on Jon sent dull flashes of pain on my skin.

Some of the tightness in my chest eased. I couldn't hear the voices anymore and found myself studying the dance of movement below me. Even without their knives and guns, Jon and Cliff's bodies were well-honed weapons. Jon utilized a grounded, practical approach, using his size and strength to his advantage. Cliff was only a few inches shorter than Jon, but his agility was unmatched. His muscles tensed and released gracefully like a predator.

I was damn glad to be working alongside them this time.

It wasn't more than a few minutes before their spontaneous match drew to a close: Jon had Cliff pinned to a tree. For a moment, at least. I flinched in sympathy as Cliff twisted an arm free and elbowed back and up *hard,* connecting with Jon's chest. My own lungs seized, the wind knocked out of me. Jon staggered back a step. I clutched my chest. Cliff tore free and, with brutal speed, kicked Jon's knees out from under him.

I nearly fell out of the tree.

Shivering, I took to the air. If this went on any longer, I'd be crawling back to the motel room. Desperate to end it, I sent a burst of freezing, crystalline air between them. Both hunters jolted back from the spell, turning to me.

"You're *hurting* him," I shouted and immediately regretted it. My shoulders curled forward from the bewildered looks they gave me. The options were either accept that they assumed I was overly protective of Jon or admit that I'd recklessly created a powerful sympathy bond with a hunter.

The latter simply wasn't feasible.

Cliff scoffed. "Hey, I didn't see you coming to my rescue when he had me pinned."

I folded my arms and diverted the subject at once. "So, are you satisfied?"

Cliff gave me a once-over, catching his breath."Seems like you won't get us torn to shreds in seconds. Stay out of our way, and we won't have an issue."

I should have soured at the comment, but the woods were covered in evidence of my spellwork. Ice shimmered on leaves and branches in a twenty-foot radius—more vast than I had ever been allowed in the affinity caverns. A strange warmth bloomed in my chest at the sight of what I had done—what I was capable of.

Cliff's smile flashed in the sun as he offered a hand to Jon, pulling him to his feet. "Taking her interference as a forfeit. Loser buys drinks."

"*What?*" Jon stood, dusting leaves off his pants. "You're crazy. That doesn't count if you just make it up now."

"That's always been the deal," Cliff said, already heading off.

"Since when has it been the deal? Name *one* time when it's been the deal."

"Don't be mad just 'cause you lost."

I might have been more worried that they were genuinely arguing if I hadn't experienced several of these boyish back-and-forths already. They went on and on until they forgot what they were squabbling about.

As we approached the motel grounds, I settled by Jon's collar to avoid prying human eyes.

"You've been quiet," Jon noted.

I'm fine.

I'm just hungry.

I'm just thinking about the potentially fatal, magical bond I've forged between us.

"I need a favor from you," I said, muscling down my mounting panic. "I need to return to Elysia—just long enough to grab a few things."

Jon's gait slowed, and I registered the weighty caution in his voice. Perhaps he thought their demonstration of force had scared me off. "You want to go back?"

"Not unless you're revoking your favor," I said, more sharply than I intended. "Just for an hour. Two, tops. Will you take me, or do I need to stretch my wings for a long flight?"

"It's not a long drive. I'll take you."

I deflated with relief, having been prepared to plead my case further. I let silence fall between us as he walked onward, considering the pleasant profile of his face. My legs still throbbed from the residual kick Cliff had landed on him. "Are *you* okay? That looked… intense."

He chuckled. "Never better."

I wondered if he was lying or if he simply was so used to getting the shit beaten out of him that he didn't even notice anymore.

"You two are strange," I admitted when I checked to ensure that Cliff was too far away to hear. "You remind me of fairies with different affinities sparring. All fun and games and showing off. I wouldn't have expected that from hunters."

"What, you expected us to be emotionless death machines?"

"Who bathe in the blood of their victims, yes."

"Ouch. Trust me, any blood I've gotten on me has been against my will." Jon hummed thoughtfully. "How am I doing on the scary one-through-ten scale?"

I thought about the juvenile grins on the hunters' faces as they fought and argued with each other. I isolated those thoughts away from the pain I'd been struck with in the midst of it all.

"Terrifying," I said with a shiver. "A nine."

I had a feeling Jon knew I was lying.

19

SYLVIA

"Stay right here."

I gave Jon the firmest look I could manage as I hovered above him. He had parked the car exactly where I'd instructed, but I still anxiously surveyed the distance between us and Elysia. This forest had been home my whole life. My entire world. The traitor mark gnawed at my cheek, making me feel like the once-familiar trees might betray me at any moment.

But this trip was unavoidable, no matter how unwelcome I felt. The archives held the only sources of knowledge I could count on. There were bound journals and tomes that held stories about arcane magic. I had to get to the bottom of this bond before it ruined me.

My excuse to Jon was that my green shirt and soft embroidered leggings were stale from working up a sweat while training yesterday. If I was going to be away for a few days, fresh sets of clothes were in order. And more importantly, I needed to make sure my absence hadn't been noticed.

Jon leaned against the car and studied me curiously, an amused smile crooking his lips. Annoyance rippled in me.

"What are you smirking about?" I said. "If the Entry Watch spots you, they'll glamour you immediately. I won't be able to help you."

"I've been hunting for nine years. I know how to be careful." Jon's expression sobered slightly. "It's just a funny feeling, having someone so… *delicate* be protective of me."

His assessment shouldn't have stung so much; of course that was how he saw me.

I drew my gossamer hood low over my brow. I'd left my snowflake charm back in the motel room. If my traitor mark didn't bring seething eyes, wearing a human's token certainly would. "Just don't draw attention to yourself," I said crisply. "I'll be back in an hour at most. Probably less."

Feeling like a thief, I flew toward Elysia and stuck to the irregular shadows cast by the early morning sunlight. I was glad I hadn't left the village in something more gaudy; my earth-colored clothes blended in with the rustling leaves around me as I approached.

My heart lodged in my throat when the home willow came into view, its swaying leaves bathed in the golden hues of sunlight. A mixture of relief and dread fought in my chest. I didn't dwell on the strange feeling, forcing myself to assess the grounds instead. There were four Entry Watch guards flying around the perimeter, chatting amiably with fairies leaving to forage blackcurrants and herbs for the day.

I chewed my lip. The main entrance set under the looping roots was too trafficked. I'd bump into someone immediately, and I'd be fucked.

Instead, I snuck down into the stables—a small structure constructed of elegantly interlaced tree roots. I squeezed through one of the gaps between the roots, my hips nearly sticking. This had been easier when I was a kid. I landed with a grunt on the feather-strewn dirt in one of the stalls.

The hummingbird beside me chirped in alarm. I ducked low in its stall on instinct, stroking its iridescent, feathered back to hush it before it disturbed the other twelve.

"Shh, shh... Nothing to worry about—" I glanced at the nameplate hung above the tiny riding gear on the back wall. "—*Poppy*. Be a good girl and be quiet. Please?"

Poppy flapped her wings, fussing and jerking her head this way and that. Feathers and dust flew into my face as she struggled. The handlers weren't on duty until midday, but someone was surely going to notice one of their birds having a panic attack. I cursed the stars, wishing once again that I'd been born an animal affinity. It would be easier if I could channel my calming sentiments right into the bird and sense its own thoughts in return.

Wings fluttered from outside the stable—certainly not hummingbird wings. A fairy's shadow darkened the window, peering inside.

I jerked my head around, scanning the saddles, stirrups, and brushes stored on corner shelves.

Yes! My eyes lit up when I finally spotted what I needed hanging from the lattice of the stable structure. A few nectar pods were strung in a neat row. I stayed low, shuffling through the shadows. Snatching a pod, I ripped off the cap and offered it to Poppy. The hummingbird went quiet, plunging her beak into the tube. She guzzled, the stables becoming calm once more.

The shadow at the window retreated.

As Poppy drank, I knelt and peered around the corner of the stall. My grip tightened on a root, the wood dry and warm in my hand. Little carvings of initials and playful couple's runes were etched into the weathered construction, built by earth affinities over fifty summers ago. At the end of the stalls, there was an arched door. This secondary entrance would lead me through the animal affinity ward and into the main hall.

"Enjoy breakfast," I whispered, patting Poppy on the head as I strode past her.

Before long, I was traversing familiar pathways. Light roots crawled along the ceilings and walls, tunnels opening into larger chambers that branched into further pathways.

People were sparse since breakfast had started by now. There were stragglers I couldn't avoid crossing, especially in one of the narrow tunnels. I diligently brushed my hair in front of my traitor mark and dipped my head, heart pounding. Turning away now would only look more suspicious.

Please, Hazel… Tell me no one has noticed I've been gone.

Fairies eyed me in passing. My breath stayed suspended in my throat as I wondered if they could smell the motel room on me. I became conscious of my every step, as though mingling with humans might have affected my gait. To my relief, their whispers were not panicked—but hardly discreet.

"That was her, wasn't it?" one said.

"Did you see her face?" the other questioned.

"No, but did you see her *wing*? You can still see the scar from that owl. I'm never flying at night again."

Relief drummed through me. The gossip about my traitor mark may have spread, but apparently, everyone assumed I really was holed up in my room the past day. With any luck, those two fairies would spread the word that they'd spotted me sulking through the tunnels. It would buy my ruse even more time.

There were even fewer fairies in the eastern dwellings corridor. I avoided eye contact all the way to my family's home. Perhaps I should have gone straight for the archives, but severing this bond would take time—maybe days. Just because I was allied with a pair of brutes didn't mean I had to *smell* like one.

Bracing myself, I entered through the polished wood door. I paused in the entryway, holding my breath. Thankfully, Mother and Hazel had already gone to breakfast. Our home was silent, the air tinged with familiar memories.

I had to resist the urge to throw myself on my bed to enjoy it once more. I could have curled up under my quilt and slept for hours, but there was no time. After hastily packing two more days' worth of clothes into a satchel, I was back out the door again. It was imperative now that no one took a good look at me—I would have difficulty explaining why I was packed like a traveler.

The paths to the archives were quiet. I brushed my hand along the familiar earthen wall, steeling myself for an inevitable return to the motel room's dull white plaster.

As I peered into the canvernous chamber, the archivist was nowhere to be seen, likely in the dining hall with the others. Normally, his absence was a clear message to stay out. This time around, it seemed like a sign that the stars were rooting for me.

Stuffy as the archivist could be, he was meticulous in his organization. There were very few journals that described events involving unusual magic encounters, but I was able to locate them with ease. As I was pulling the third journal from the shelf, a hand dropped onto my shoulder.

Shifting the books to one arm, I whirled and held up my other hand with an icy mist held at the ready.

Damian staggered back, eyes wide. "I thought that was you," he breathed. "I-I saw you, and..." He shook his head, equal parts alarmed and relieved. "Where have you *been*?"

"In my room," I said at once, voice cracking. "I wanted something to read while I mope about being branded for life. Is that alright with you?"

As I turned to grab the last book, another sickeningly familiar voice came from the archives' entrance. "Is that you, Sylvia? You know you're not supposed to be here while the archivist is away. But I suppose doing what you're told isn't your strong suit."

I froze. If Damian hadn't grabbed me by the shoulders and urged me behind the nearest shelf, Ayden would have spotted me as he turned the corner.

"It's just me," Damian said in a voice that shook at the edges.

Ayden scoffed. "You're sure about that? I heard whispers that Sylvia finally left her room. She's always favored the archives—I thought I'd find her here."

"I saw her. She didn't stay out for long. She asked me to bring her some books."

The following pause made my skin crawl. Damian had never been the best liar, but he was halfway decent at the moment. If Ayden kept pushing, however, Damian was bound to stumble. Although Ayden believed I'd been in my room, he would take great interest in the fact that I had packed a bag of clothes if he found me.

"A shame," Ayden said at last. "I wanted to see how her mark was faring."

"You take that much joy in tormenting her?" Damian asked, his voice adopting a razor-sharp edge.

"I'm only doing what I must. You have no idea the danger she poses to Elysia."

"Really? I'm listening," Damian drawled out in a flat voice that made me proud.

Ayden sucked in a breath, considering it. His pause was so pronounced that I was tempted to peer around the shelf to gauge the look on his face. "It's not my place to say," he finally said. "Trust me when I tell you it's better for her to suffer now than to doom the whole village. I'd love to hear from her lips that she accepts she did wrong. But if she wishes to cower away under her sheets like a child, I won't stop her."

"Sylvia never meant any harm," Damian pressed. "She just… wanted to explore. Things got out of hand."

"Careful. You might begin to sound like her."

The sound of footsteps faded away, trailing into the milling fairies in the hallway. I held my breath until I knew Ayden was gone. Shakily, I stood and made my way back around the shelf. Damian gave me a pained look before pulling me into his arms. I allowed it.

"I'm so glad you're alive," he said into my hair.

"I've been in my—"

"You think I was going to let Hazel stop me from seeing you?" Damian pulled me back by my shoulders, his brown eyes ablaze. *Stars help me.* He knew. He cared too much to turn away when Hazel tried to block our empty bedroom.

I stayed startled into silence as he cupped my face in both hands, the hard look on his softening. "She wouldn't share where you've been, but I know it's not been at home. I checked everywhere—the training halls, the kitchen, the herb gardens..."

"Did you tell Mother?" I rasped.

Damian's gaze darkened as though he had been hoping I would laugh and explain he had simply missed me hiding in the tunnels of rosemary and thyme.

"No, I haven't spoken with her more than a few words since that night," he said. "But you should see her. She's sick with worry. For all we know, she's already caught on that you left again."

"Considering she hasn't razed the forest to find me, I'd say she hasn't."

I stepped out of his reach, clutching the journals tighter to my chest. His touch was tender, but he was the reason I had this damn mark permanently marring my face.

"I'm surprised you haven't told her yourself," I said, bitterness seeping into my voice. "You seem to enjoy spreading word about my whereabouts to anyone who will listen."

"I... I didn't want to get you into trouble."

"Didn't stop you last time."

The guilt that crushed Damian's expression nearly made me backpedal my words. He opened and closed his mouth, searching for the right sentiment as his eyes grew wet and distant.

"I'm so sorry, Sylvia," Damian whispered.

I couldn't hold his gaze lest I break down sobbing right there in the archives. He had promised to protect me so many times under our tree.

"It's too late now, isn't it?" I muttered.

"I had no idea they were going to brand you—it's so arcane. How could I have known?" His words were frantic, desperate for me to listen.

"You're a coward," I seethed at him. "And I need to go."

He caught me by the arm, gently pulling me back to face him. "I just wanted things to go back to the way they used to be. I just wanted you to be safe, away from all that dangerous human waste."

"But that's not what I wanted!" I snapped, snatching my arm out of his grasp.

He swallowed, reaching inside his tunic and pulling out a somewhat flattened snowdrop. My favorite flower only grew in the earth affinity training garden, and my heart ached at the thought that Damian must've snuck in to steal one for me. He might've been carrying it around for an entire day, waiting for this chance to present it.

"I still love you. Desperately," he breathed.

I shuttered my eyes away from the offering, though I longed to inhale the delicate, honey-like fragrance. A little flower couldn't fix what had been done.

"Loving someone isn't trapping them where they don't want to be," I said, pretending I didn't notice his flinch. I began stuffing journals into my satchel. He grabbed the last one before I could stop him. *Encounters with the Ancients, A Collection.* I yanked the book away and shoved it into my bag.

"Where are you going?" he asked. "What have you gotten yourself into?"

"I haven't the foggiest idea, but I intend to find out."

"The *Ancients*, Sylvia? Whatever this is, you need to go to the Elders. They can help you."

Huffing, I tucked my hair behind my ear so he could take a good look at the traitor brand. My throat closed when he shrank away ever so slightly, but at least he stopped spouting nonsense.

"They don't want to help," I said. "They think I'm a danger to everyone here."

Damian pulled himself together. "You're not proving them wrong, running off like this, being secretive. If you just try to explain to them—"

"Don't you understand? I can't trust them."

"What about me? You know I didn't mean any harm. I'm on your side. You know you can trust me, right?" His shoulders sagged when I couldn't bring myself to answer. His voice wavered. "I thought we told each other everything."

"I *did* tell you." I swallowed the lump in my throat, blinking the tears away. "I told you where I was going, and I suffered for it. I'm sorry, Damian. I don't have time to argue. He's waiting for me." I brushed past him.

"What? Who?"

As he followed in step behind me, I whirled suddenly and gave him a tight hug. He stood there silently while I whispered, "Thank you for keeping Ayden away."

I tore away from him.

On my way out, I diligently avoided anyone by taking the upper paths, which gave me a vantage point of the dining hall exit on the floor below. A slight commotion in the crowd below made me white-knuckle the railing, thinking I had been spotted. I relaxed when I saw children crowding toward a basket of excess nutmeg tarts that were being carried out of the kitchens.

Ayden stood out amongst the crowd, making me bristle. The children moved aside for him, respectfully allowing him to take his fill first. But instead, Ayden handed out the tarts one by one to keep the children from squabbling amongst themselves. He tossed a few high in the air, encouraging a few laughing boys to fly and catch them mid-air.

Double-braided red hair caught my eye. Hazel joined the others, waiting patiently. The moment she realized who was handing out the tarts, her posture stiffened. I held my breath, certain that Ayden would deny her the sweet.

To my shock, he handed her one without hesitation. He said something to her—and his expression didn't appear snide or cruel. Nonetheless, she hurried back to Mother, who watched with crossed arms.

My throat closed, my heart aching to join my family. I could fly down, say hello, and pacify their worries. But there was no time. Jon was waiting, and Mother would have too many questions about the bag around my shoulder.

For now, I was as much a ghost as Alice had been.

Once I figured out this bond with Jon and did away with it, I could return. My family would forgive me once they understood. For now, I couldn't tangle them in this mess. I'd done enough already.

I slipped into a narrow corridor and wound my way to one of the larger pathways. This one led outside, straight to the fire affinity training grounds. Thankfully, lessons hadn't begun yet. The sandy, charred piece of earth wouldn't stay empty for long. After a cursory glance, I took to the air.

"You're back sooner than I thought," Jon said when I returned to him.

"What's all this?" I said, chuckling with bemusement as I caught my breath. There were no guards pursuing me. I allowed myself to relax.

The car was covered with shrubbery as though it had been sitting for years rather than an hour. An absurd part of me wondered if decorating the car with nature was Jon's way of wooing me.

"I figured camouflage might be a good idea with how worried you were about me." He smiled warmly. "Kept me busy, too. No wandering, I promise."

I pressed my lips together tightly to keep a laugh at bay. His attempt to hide his presence was better than nothing, I supposed. It might have worked on a human from a distance, but even he had to know that there was no way a massive vehicle could go unnoticed if a fairy came close enough.

"Let me give you a hand." He reached for my bag, which I gladly handed off. "You should go easy on your wings—save it for training." Even as he tucked my bag into his pocket, he took notice of my wince at the suggestion. "Come on, you did great yesterday. You need to keep challenging yourself."

"I'm starting to think you just like to see me work up a sweat." I lifted an accusatory eyebrow at him. His charming smile morphed into stammered protests.

"You're the one eager to prove yourself!" he insisted.

Unable to contain my grin, I flitted closer to his face. "Or maybe you're eager to make another grab at me."

He merely scoffed and rolled his eyes.

"*Or*," I pressed, "maybe this has all been some calculated scheme, and you can't wait to get me alone in those woods so you can end me in some barbaric hunter ritual."

Jon gaped. "If you don't want to train, a simple *no* works just fine."

"Boring. What's life without a little conspiracy?"

Out of the corner of my eye, I caught a flicker of movement. I turned, squinting against the blinding rays of sunshine filtering through the foliage.

"Sylvia?" Jon's voice sounded a mile away.

A spot of iridescence glinted between leaves. Panic gripped me like an icy fist in my chest—a fairy was positioned almost directly above me.

Damian, his dark skin blending into the bark of the branch he perched on, looked absolutely horrified as our gazes locked. He had never encountered a human before, and the fear in his eyes turned my stomach. His trembling up there was so intense that I feared he might lose his grip and plummet down.

"Who is that?" Jon's voice was low and dangerous. His leisurely posture vanished, replaced by an aura of coiled tension. It chilled me how quickly Jon spotted Damian, too—a seasoned hunter's instincts in full play. I could practically see him assessing the trees around us, calculating how to evade or attack should the need arise.

And I'd given him *plenty* of practice with subduing a fairy.

I flew in front of Jon's face to put that line of thought to a halt. "No one. We need to get out of here, Jon," I urged. "*Go!*"

"What are you doing with her?" Damian's voice rang out in a snarl.

I couldn't believe my eyes. Damian glided down, stopping short at Jon's eyeline. He could've flown back to Elysia to inform the guards of my newest treason. He could've just stayed up in the branches, pissing himself. The forest held its breath as the two assessed each other.

"You… You're one of those hunters who took her, aren't you?" Damian's breaths trembled, eyes wet with furious tears I knew were meant for me.

Jon eased forward, each step nearly noiseless on the leaf-strewn ground.

Damian skittered back, hands lifting in front of him. The air began to shimmer with defensive magic. "I-If you take another step, I'll kill you."

Jon's jaw ticked. I already knew he didn't respond well to threats, and I was pretty sure the things that antagonized this man typically ended up dead.

"There's not a problem here unless you create one." Jon's voice was calm but firm. I was looking past his right shoulder now, and I realized he had placed himself in front of me. "Sylvia's not a prisoner. She's safe. You don't need to be afraid, I swear."

Damian's gaze darted from Jon to me and back again. The fire in his eyes blazed at the sound of my name on Jon's lips.

"I don't believe you," Damian spat. Before I could find my voice, he had thrust his hands forward with a cry, bending the very air around us to his whim.

Jon jumped for a weapon in his jacket with startling speed. But a knife wouldn't do him any good if he couldn't breathe.

He made a horrible, strangled noise. Clutching his throat, he staggered back.

Suffocating pain hit me at once. I surged past Jon toward Damian. "S-stop!" I gasped, my voice little more than a wheeze. But his eyes were fixed on Jon, blinded by adrenaline and fearful hatred.

Jon managed to get his knife in hand, but it made no difference. Damian was high overhead.

Agony bloomed in my head and chest, vision swimming. With no other choice, I croaked out a spell. Icy shards raced through the air and struck Damian's hands. He jolted, his attack interrupted. My breath returned, but the pain lingered.

"Damian," I forced out, flying close enough to grab his hands before he could begin again.

His furious gaze met mine, but it quickly morphed into confusion and horror when it dawned on him that he'd affected me, too.

"H-How…" He freed his hands and cupped my face tenderly. "I-I didn't… I wasn't trying to—" He looked stuck somewhere between apologizing and demanding answers.

I gave him no time for either. I simply whispered, "If you hurt him, you hurt me too."

With that, I hurried back to Jon and urged him to get into the car. Now that he could breathe again, he looked downright murderous. I had no way to explain to him that Damian wouldn't attack again—not when he knew he would make me suffer in the process.

I threw an icy blast of wind to remove the shrubbery from the windshield. The spell left a spider web of frost on one corner of the glass, but it did the job. I tugged at Jon's collar frantically. He was still glaring up at Damian, who was too shell-shocked to move.

"Let's go!" I insisted. "Before any others come!"

That finally snapped Jon out of it. He never took his eyes off Damian, stepping back and groping for the door handle. As he settled behind the wheel, I braced myself on his shoulder. He drove off, and even as he pulled onto the road, I couldn't shake the image of Damian's horrified, betrayed expression.

I massaged my throat and coughed heavily. "I'm sorry," I croaked. "I didn't think I was followed."

Jon was silent for a few seconds. "Is he the one who marked you?"

"What? No! No. He wouldn't hurt me. He doesn't understand—he thought he was saving me from you."

"He attacked you just now! He hurt you."

The venom in his raised voice was terrifying, softened only by the fact that it was for my sake. A ridiculous part of me wanted to confess everything right then. But I didn't have a clue what I was dealing with. For all I knew, he'd pull over and leave me behind if he realized I'd involved him in an ancient binding. Or worse, he'd change his mind and kill me after all.

"It was an accident," I said. "Damian, he… he was upset. Careless. The spell spread to me. He didn't mean it. He stopped when he realized, didn't he?"

"Are you okay?" Jon demanded rather than address my explanation. His voice was rough.

"I'll be fine. Here—"

I offered a soothing spell to his throat as best I could. Aches and internal injuries had never been my strong suit. The spell exhausted me but alleviated some of my pain. I slumped against Jon's neck, digging my heels in to keep from slipping.

"What does this mean when you go home again?" he asked. "He saw you with me. What'll they do to you?"

"I'm sure you can guess," I said. "But I think—I *hope* he won't say anything."

A heavy pause. "Is he your…" Jon trailed off.

"My what?"

"Never mind."

"My lover?" When he didn't respond, I chuckled humorlessly. "Sometimes. Probably not anymore."

"It's our third time looping around the block," Cliff grumbled at me from the driver's seat. "I'm starting to think you scammed us to get more Pop-Tarts."

Both the dogs and Rick and Charlie Astle had disappeared without a trace from this neighborhood. All signs pointed to the werewolf lurking in these uniform lines of white-shutter houses, but once again, I couldn't sense anything out of the ordinary.

For all I could tell, these humans mowing their lawns, gathering mail, and walking their dogs were just that. Only human.

"Maybe I need to get closer," I said, rubbing the back of my neck.

"*Maybe*?" Cliff glanced at me, his square jaw ticking. "I was hoping for something a little more solid than 'maybe.' I thought you knew what you were doing."

"I never had to sense any monsters before running into you two, so stop being a dick."

Behind me, Jon stifled a laugh.

I flew over to his window, pressing my hand against the warm glass. "I don't have to *do* anything. It's as intuitive as smelling or hearing," I said over my shoulder. "When the werewolf is near us, I'll know. I promise."

"We can't waste our time circling this street all day. A few of these folks look ready to call the cops." Cliff eyed a surly old man standing on the porch of the corner house. When we had first driven through, he'd been sitting inside by the window.

Cliff parked the car in front of Rick and Charlie's neglected two-story home. Although they had vanished about a week ago, I swore I could sense the abandonment of the structure. I stared at the dark upper-floor window, wondering if the victims had been killed in the home, their corpses hidden away. For all I knew, there were spirits staring back at me through the dark panes. Would they be trapped here when the home was inevitably occupied by a new family?

"I already told you," I sighed, frustration and sadness battling as I looked between the hunters. "This house is empty. It's a dead end."

"Hold your horses, sweetheart. It's my turn," Cliff said, studying himself in the rearview mirror. He made small, hasty adjustments to his hair and clothes. My gaze drifted to the house again—then to the neighboring one, where a young housewife was tending her garden.

With a wink, he climbed out of the car.

"What's he doing?" I asked when it became clear that Jon was staying behind with me. I scrunched my face at the sight of

Cliff's easygoing gait and charming smile as he approached the woman. "This is hardly the time for him to pursue a new romantic chapter."

Jon chuckled. "He's just trying to get some last-ditch answers out of her. He's already winning her over."

"Seriously?" I said in a flat voice.

"Seriously. Watch." Jon leaned closer, one hand braced beside me in front of the window. "He's complimenting her dress. He's telling her he never notices stuff like that."

I scoffed, but sure enough, the woman smiled widely and gave a bashful look down at her simple sundress.

"Now, what's he saying?" I asked, too intrigued to stay skeptical.

"He's feeding her our cover story. Rick is an old friend from college, and we had plans to reconnect."

"And you were horrified to hear he disappeared?" I guessed.

"You learn quick."

Cliff's smile was sparkling and loaded with the promise that the woman was the center of his world at the moment. He was tall but not crowding close enough to frighten her. It hadn't occurred to me until then how *much* taller he was; the top of her head just reached his collarbone. There was an unmistakable air of tragedy about him compared to other passing humans—but he wore it wonderfully well.

"Now he's asking if she's noticed anything else unusual lately," Jon said. "He's worried about how safe it is to stay in town."

The woman pursed her lips, looking uncertain.

"She's starting to retreat," I noted.

"Wait for it—he's gonna touch her arm and tell her he knows how hard it must be to talk about this stuff... Yep, there it is."

My jaw dropped. The woman's unsettled expression softened. She talked, and Cliff nodded sympathetically.

"Do you do this, too?" I asked, looking over my shoulder and nearly flinching at how close Jon was. "Do you go around charming answers out of people?"

"When I have to," Jon answered.

My throat tightened as I fixed my gaze out the window again. I imagined him in Cliff's place, giving the woman's bare arm a squeeze and wearing a smile that was impossible not to fall in love with. Ice crawled to my fingertips. When he'd called me pretty in the mirror, had he just been working me like Cliff was doing now?

I supposed it was hardly fair to be upset, seeing as I kept my own motives under lock and key.

I was so lost in thought that I nearly jumped out of my skin when Cliff yanked the driver-side door open.

"You know that dog walker chick I was talking to yesterday? Lily?" Cliff was breathless with excitement at a new lead. "Looks like she might've been holding out on me."

I tried not to pout with envy that he'd been more successful with his method than I was with mine. He was a seasoned hunter, after all.

"Apparently, Lily's got a creepy on-and-off-again boyfriend she failed to mention," Cliff said.

"And?" I prompted.

"*And* little Miss Sunshine over there invited me to come by to ask more questions when her husband's working tomorrow." He looked very pleased by this. Even as the car lurched forward, he glanced back at where the woman was pruning a yellow rose bush. "*Eleanor.* Cute, right? You think she's into roleplay?" He dragged his teeth over his lower lip.

"Cliff," Jon said, pulling his attention back.

"Relax, I'm not walking you through blow by blow."

"Thank fuck for that."

"Anyway, I think we've got all we need," Cliff said. "The ex's name is Nolan. Past couple days, he's been lurking around the neighborhood without Lily. This is weird because he'd usually come around to argue with her right in the middle of the street while she was walking dogs. But it was just him creeping around before he drove off. Nosy neighbors are a godsend, aren't they?"

"So where are we going?" I asked.

"Lily lives nearby," Cliff explained. "Let's see what she has to say about Nolan. Since *he* doesn't live around here, that might explain why you haven't been able to sense jack shit."

I flitted to the dashboard, giving a mockingly wistful sigh. "So I'm not completely broken and useless?"

"We'll see."

20

JON

Lily's house seemed to shy away from the sunlight, tucked away at the end of a long driveway. At first glance, it looked as nice as any of the other houses in this area—just a little more humble in square footage. Cliff parked behind a black Ford Focus.

My breath caught in my chest as I climbed the porch steps. The chipped white paint, the faded red door, the perpetual need for repairs—the similarities to my childhood home were striking. An irrational part of me wondered if we could have stumbled onto the very same property by a sick stroke of chance.

But that was impossible. My home was nothing but charred ash.

Cliff rapped his fist on the door and stepped back.

No answer.

We waited a few minutes before knocking again more forcefully, calling Lily's name. Still, nothing but filtered birdsong answered.

"Looks like she hasn't come out today," I said, nudging a soggy newspaper on the doormat.

My neck tickled as Sylvia came out of hiding from behind my collar and flew freely. Her lips drew into a pout as she looked me and Cliff up and down. "Maybe you're scaring her. I wouldn't open the door to a couple of big, strange men, either."

Cliff scoffed. "Come on, me and her are practically old friends now. She's probably not home."

"Her car's here," I noted.

Sylvia made a lap around the entire property before fluttering back onto the front porch to land gracefully on the doorknob. "The curtains are drawn on every window," she announced. "Impossible to tell if anyone's home unless we—" She stiffened suddenly, voice tapering to a croak. She leaned forward, her fingers brushing over a tiny mark on the doorframe. She looked back at me, eyes wide.

I leaned closer. The spot was so faint that I had to squint to see it. A delicate splatter of crimson stained the faded white wood. On closer inspection, the edge of the wood had been damaged, like it had been hammered brutally and reassembled.

Holding my breath, I traced the edge of the panel and gave a test pull. The wooden panel swung up and off easily, nearly splitting right off the rest of the doorframe. There was more dried blood under the paneling—three fingers smeared across the aged stone beneath.

"Lily… Do you think—" Sylvia's voice tightened. "You think it's hers?"

"The blood's old," Cliff said, leaning over me with a frown. "And I just saw Lily yesterday. She seemed fine."

Letting the panel fall, I turned my full attention to Sylvia. She looked frightened by the evidence facing her, but I pressed her anyway. "Do you feel anything else? Anything at all?"

"I… I don't know," she said, dodging my gaze to stare at the panel. She chewed her lip.

"Come on, *try*." I all but growled.

"Jon," Cliff cut in, giving me a reproachful and fairly surprised look.

But slowly, Sylvia nodded. "The werewolf's not here now, but something's *off*. I feel sick. Like the presence of it is lingering."

"Can you track that feeling?" I asked.

"I'm not a hound," she snapped, turning to me sternly. "It's not like a trail of breadcrumbs. I haven't felt anything since Dottage—not until we got here, to this spot." She swallowed hard and shut her eyes like it was the only way she could stop looking at the blood. "Maybe one of the transformations happened nearby. Every bone in my body is warning me to stay away from this spot."

I squared my jaw, burying the compassion that lurched in me, begging me to urge Sylvia far away from this.

"Sorry, but you're going to have to bear with that for a little while longer," I told her.

I stole a cursory look across the shaded yard to make sure no unwanted observers were around. I reached into my jacket and carefully unraveled my simple lock pick kit. The worn leather case held an assortment of slim metal picks and tension wrenches that had served me on more occasions than I cared to count.

Cliff followed my lead and side-stepped to cover me as I inserted the tension wrench into the keyway. Sylvia flew off the knob, hovering to watch in silence from above. A faint *click* echoed. Gripping a hook pick, I delicately explored the tumblers, searching for that satisfying, familiar resistance that would indicate success.

Standard suburban home locks were typically nothing special, but to my mounting frustration, my tools were noticeably slowed by some kind of obstruction. My jaw tightened, trying to block out the buzz of Sylvia's beating wings and the drone of passing cars as I gently raked the pick over the pins.

A subtle creak sounded behind me, followed by liquid sloshing. The sound was amplified in the focused silence.

"What are you doing?" I asked, tossing an irritated look over my shoulder.

Cliff lifted his eyebrows at me, uncapping his flask. "Pouring myself a drink. We'll be here through dinner at the rate you're going."

He took a leisurely sip.

"Hilarious," I muttered, turning my eyes back to the meticulous task—ignoring Cliff's buried chuckle at my expense. If I applied much more pressure, I risked fracturing my tools and damaging the lock permanently. "Damn thing won't budge."

"It's karma for bragging about getting the last one in twenty seconds," Cliff said.

"Twelve," I corrected.

"Huh?"

I shrugged, my gaze narrowed on the keyhole. "It was twelve seconds."

Cliff laughed low in his throat—though I was right, and he fucking knew it. "Sure it was. Scoot over, MacGyver. I'll try."

I shoved the supplies back in my pocket, shouldering Cliff out of my shadow as I stood. "Don't bother. It's rusted through inside. We'll have to go around back or kick it in."

As I started toward the stairs, Cliff put a hand on my arm. His green eyes raked the porch. "Where's the kid?"

I went rigid, realizing Sylvia was nowhere to be seen. I called her name softly, to no response. Just as a twinge of worry tightened in my chest, the front door lock clicked open. After a second, another metallic scrape came from the other side—the security chain slowly unclasping. Then, silence.

Exchanging a frown with Cliff, I slipped one hand around the knife in my inner jacket pocket as I turned the knob and swung the door open.

Sylvia hovered in the otherwise dark hallway, her red hair noticeably windswept but cheeks flushed with pride.

"The back window was cracked just enough," she said. "No need to kick the door down."

I relaxed my grip on the weapon, stepping inside.

"Killjoy. I was kinda looking forward to kicking something down," Cliff remarked, brushing past her as I shut the door behind us. "Nice work."

I didn't miss how his gruff acknowledgment made her cheeks glow a little brighter. Her posture remained rigid. If the sensation of being near the house was as unsettling as she claimed, I imagined being *inside* wasn't any easier.

She wrinkled her nose. "It smells awful in here."

"Wet dog," I murmured, flicking on the entrance light.

Harnesses of all sizes and several leashes hung by the door. The smear of blood wrapped around part of the doorframe from the outside, though it was clear someone had attempted to scrub away the stain. A few wadded-up sanitizing wipes lay on the ground. Messy. Hurried.

I followed Cliff through the living room, eyeing the disturbed furniture. Dog hair covered the sofa. Chew toys overflowed from a basket beneath the end table.

Amid all the obvious signs of a beloved pet, silence engulfed the house. No barking or whining could be heard from a dog recognizing intruders' scents—just an oppressive quiet that set me on edge. I found myself plagued by the unsettling image that the house itself was holding its breath, watching us through walls as we tread deeper inside.

I exchanged a look with Cliff, noting the unspoken question—if a dog lived here, where the hell was it?

College textbooks were stacked haphazardly over the coffee table, highlighters and pens strewn about. A basket of clothes was piled high by an open laundry room door. From a cursory glance, there were men's and women's clothes. Cliff followed my gaze to a pair of men's sneakers tucked by the door and hummed.

"Either she's quick on the rebound, or Nolan's been making himself comfy here for a while," Cliff said.

The dank mix of odors didn't get any better in the kitchen, where fast food wrappers and delivery receipts littered every available surface and spilled over from the trash can.

Empty as the house was, it felt so lived-in that I half-expected to see someone standing in the doorway every time I peered around. I was so used to only having Cliff by my side, I tensed whenever Sylvia's darting movements caught the corner of my eye. We ventured around the kitchen with care. With so much crap lying around, one wrong step could make our intrusion noticeable.

Sylvia inspected the magnets on the fridge, cocking her head with fascination at a pinned Snoopy birthday card. I rummaged through the kitchen drawers, wondering if her kind even celebrated birthdays. Certainly not with store-bought cake and paper cards. Everything about her—apart from her inclination toward profanity—seemed so ethereal. Her clothes. The way she moved. That glint of animal buried in her eyes. Some kind of otherworldly, celestial celebration under the stars seemed like it would be far more befitting for someone like her.

I doubted much information could be garnered from the magnets, but it was better than having her wander off into another room on her own.

"Hey—check this out," Cliff said, swiping a small object from the kitchen counter. "Definitely prescription grade. There's at least six different ones. Shady stuff." He tossed it to me.

I inspected the unmarked bottle, popping it open to find a dozen little white pills inside.

Pulling away from the fridge, Sylvia hovered over my hands. "What's that?"

"Medicine," I said. "This is in line with a couple other werewolves we've hunted."

"Sometimes, the lucid ones tried to rationalize. Before they knew what they were, they thought they were sick with some freakish disease," Cliff explained, pilfering through the rest of the bottles. "Which, I mean—they are. But popping some pills isn't gonna cure it. One guy tried to sedate himself every night. Didn't work out too well."

After snapping pictures of each type of pill, we filed into the short hallway. In the bedroom, there was no question that two people were living in this house. The unmade bed was a disaster area—sheets and pillows were torn up, and even more clothing was scattered like a tornado had passed through. The ceiling fan spun at a low setting, making the shadows flicker nonstop.

"Stars." Sylvia shuddered and found a perch on my neck. "The transformation happened in here."

"I coulda told you that," Cliff muttered, already beginning to pick his way through the room.

"How much longer do we have to be in here?" Sylvia whispered to me.

"You insisted on coming along," I pointed out.

It was hard to focus with her frightened breathing so close to my ear, but I didn't have the heart to shoo her off. Looking at the room was difficult enough. I couldn't begin to wrap my mind around how *feeling* it might be.

While Cliff looked through the closet, I busied myself with the dresser. The various knickknacks littering the top might have been begging Sylvia to fly down for a closer look, but she didn't leave my shoulder. Half the drawers were haphazardly open, gaps in the clothing that suggested they had been grabbed quickly and at random.

Faint outlines of adhesive and scraps of tape littered the frame of the arched mirror fixed at the back of the dresser. Most of the pictures had been ripped down, but two remained. Lily's tangle of dark hair was unmistakable even at a glance at the hazy Polaroids. In one image, she was seated in a corner booth clutching beers alongside who I assumed to be her good friends. The photo captured a moment of candid laughter. The only other image left dangling by a sliver of tape revealed her with a dark-haired man. Perhaps she and Nolan during easier times—smiling widely at the photographer, his crushing embrace around her.

When I found nothing else of interest, I moved on to the desk that was positioned by the curtained window.

A few more textbooks sat on its surface, along with some composition notebooks. One notebook, however, stood out among the rest. It had a blue hardcover, for one thing, and was tucked beneath the others as though it was meant to be inconspicuous. When I opened it and scanned the shaky handwriting on the most recently penned pages, I could understand why it would be hidden.

It's getting worse. The mood swings. The snapping. He's scaring me—the things he's telling me to do. I have no choice. The dogs ran faster than we expected. I can still hear their yelps. I keep picturing them limping through the woods, finding a place to lie down and die.

I was supposed to take care of them. Nolan says it's better than people dying, right? But it isn't working. I can't take this anymore. I don't know what to do.

I never want to see him again. But I can't leave him now. I can't.

The page was tear-splotched. I knew Sylvia was reading, too, because she seemed to be holding her breath.

"This poor girl," she murmured. "He's forcing her to help him."

I nodded gravely. "She'll be next on the menu."

Movement stirred in front of me through the window. A car was pulling up to the curb in front of the house, parking right behind ours.

"Shit!" I hurriedly tucked the journal back into place.

Hearing the urgency in my voice, Cliff retreated without question. "The back door," he hissed, leading the way to the kitchen.

While I paused for Cliff to unlock the door, Sylvia dropped from my shoulder and hurriedly stowed herself away in my front jacket pocket.

"What the hell are you two doing hanging around there?" a voice barked from the top of the driveway when we tried to make our way around the side of the house.

I hurriedly peeked down to ensure Sylvia was hidden while Cliff answered, "What's it to you? You the owner?"

Fighting a wince, I braced myself. Cliff could charm the pants off most people if he wanted to. He was less pleasant when caught off guard by someone interfering in our case.

A man who looked to be in his mid-fifties came to stand nearly nose-to-nose with Cliff. "I'm Henry Lehman. Vice President of the neighborhood watch."

"Your mom must be so proud," Cliff said. "Couldn't quite snag the top seat, huh?"

I turned and took a sweeping look at Henry as I came to stand by Cliff. Ordinary build. Nice clothes. The man's silver-flecked hair was receding, though he obviously made an effort to conceal that fact. He made no move to shake our hands.

"We're friends of Lily's," I answered calmly. Hopefully, he wouldn't notice the smear of blood—or *Sylvia*, who was squirming to find a comfortable position. "She said she needed help fixing the front door frame, but it looks like it needs to be replaced entirely. She's not answering." I smiled sheepishly, but my unspoken question was clear. *Do you know where she is?*

Henry narrowed his eyes. "Bullshit. I've seen you circling the block. You two are friends with that junkie boyfriend of hers, aren't you?" He started up the steps. "Beat it before I call the cops."

"Just trying to help our friend, *Vice*," Cliff said derisively.

"What are you really doing here?" Henry insisted.

"It's… personal," I said, trying to diffuse the situation. "A little hard to explain. It's more Lily's business than ours."

Henry took a beat, sizing us up. His expression soured into a grimace. "Is this some sex thing?"

While I was still fumbling for a response, Cliff asked, "Why, you want in on the action? Lily's got leashes to spare." There was a roguish twist to his smile, which widened as color rushed to Henry's face.

"You think you're funny," Henry all but spat the words.

Cliff shrugged. "It's easier when you don't have a stick shoved up your ass."

Closing the space between us, Henry shoved Cliff's chest with one hand. "Listen, douchebag. This neighborhood has grieved enough without more weirdos snooping around our doors."

Sylvia would have been pummeled if he'd pushed *me* in that same spot on my chest. I glared at him as we stepped toward the driveway. "Keep your hands off us," I said. "We're heading out."

Henry grabbed my shoulder from behind—and that was my limit.

"I'm serious. If I catch you around here again, I'll—" He choked off in surprise as I fluidly grabbed his arm and turned, shoving him against the side of the house. I kept him pinned with one arm, glowering. The shape of a wallet jutted against my sleeve. The opening of his coat pocket gaped slightly.

"I said, *hands off*," I snarled through my teeth.

I waited for the satisfying glaze of fear to enter Henry's watery eyes. Something cruel in me enjoyed it.

"Okay, okay! Get off me," Henry stammered.

I let him go and carefully smoothed my jacket down. Sylvia had fallen remarkably still.

We made our way to the car without further incident, other than a few choice words from Henry—*"fucking psycho"*—which I pointedly ignored. He stayed at the bottom of the porch steps, glaring knives as Cliff pulled the car out of the driveway. Cliff gave him an all-too-friendly wave before heading down the street.

Sylvia climbed her way out of my pocket, dismissing my offer to help. She flew to perch on the dashboard and gave me a harried pout. "Did you have to get so physical?" She raked her hair down.

I chuckled. "That was nothing. Are you okay?"

"I'm fine. Do you normally go around antagonizing people? No wonder you guys don't have any friends." She pressed a hand to her chest and caught her breath. "If I had more time to look around there, maybe…" Her expression was almost timid as she returned her attention to me. "I'm sorry."

Guilt slithered through me. Maybe I'd been too tough with her. As much as I would have liked a direct path to the werewolf, I smiled reassuringly. "It's fine. We've got a new lead now."

"Nolan and Lily must be who I saw at Dottage," Sylvia said. "It lines up. And if she's been taken… It must be him, right?"

"It's the first theory that makes any goddamn sense in this case," Cliff said, pulling out of the neighborhood and onto the main road. "Creepshow hangs around his girlfriend's street, gets infected somewhere. Accidentally takes out a few residents. Starts going after dogs, but a few get away, mutated. Tells his girl to help him cover it up."

Sylvia shuddered. When we locked eyes, she squared her shoulders, trying to keep it together. I was sure I'd look like that when I first started hunting—trying to look braver than I actually felt.

"So, we're going after him then?" she asked.

I nodded. "We find Nolan, we end this."

She swallowed hard, playing with the edges of her snowflake charm.

I dug through my lower jacket pocket and produced the wallet I'd slipped from Henry's coat pocket. "And hey—Henry getting riled up wasn't a total waste. If he'd just kept his hands to himself…"

Cliff glanced my way and laughed. "I don't know how you do it. Anything good in there?"

I thumbed through the contents. "Hundred bucks, at least. A couple credit cards. *And* his neighborhood watch card."

"Man's gonna be devastated," Cliff said, clicking his tongue.

I pulled out a loyalty punch card, noting the restaurant name imprinted under a striking image of a reuben sandwich. "Oh shit, Cliff—you just won a free sandwich from your favorite spot."

"No way. Fusion Grill?"

I waved the card at him. The car swerved slightly as he shifted his grip on the wheel to snap it out of my hand.

"Fuck yeah!" Cliff grinned like he'd won the lottery. No matter that he could buy fifty sandwiches with the stolen cash. He glanced at Sylvia, who was watching us like we were excited children. "They've got the most incredible cheesesteak sandwich I've ever had, hands-down. They do something with the smokey provolone between layers and these little onion crisps that just..." He sighed, and I swore he was tearing up a little. "I saw one a few miles outside of town. Trust me, it's worth the drive. Almost better than sex."

"Doubt that," Sylvia said.

"I said *almost*."

She cocked her head, smiling impishly. "I've never seen someone so excited about a meal."

"You get used to it," I told her, smirking at Cliff's expense.

"It's cute," she said. "I wish you could see our Solstice Feasts. You'd have your pick of everything from herbed stew to raspberry trifles." Turning back to me, she nodded curiously at the wallet. "What is that, by the way?"

I shut Henry's wallet and turned it for her to see. "People use them to carry their IDs, money, and all that. Almost everyone has one."

"Do you?"

"Of course." I pulled my wallet out of my jeans pocket and held it open. Sylvia scooted forward to look inside, cocking her head in recognition when she saw my driver's license under a film of weathered plastic.

"That's your picture." Pausing, she frowned. "*Jonathan Nowak*. Your name is *Jonathan*? Should I be calling you that?" A little smile lit up her face. "And you thought *I* would have a strange name."

I scoffed and put away my wallet. "Thanks a lot. Jon's just fine, *Sylvia with five y's*."

Giggling, she looked at Cliff in wonder. "What about yours? Do you have a longer name too? Let me see!"

Cliff didn't look away from the road. "Fuck no. Next, you'll be asking for my social security number."

"What's a—"

"Forget it."

21

SYLVIA

"Here. Mac 'n cheese. You'll love it."

As sunset encroached, Cliff pushed a water bottle cap into my hands. The plastic was warm, filled with food smothered in a gooey yellow sauce.

I frowned suspiciously. Most of the things he ordered at Fusion Grill had been packed with roast beef and bacon. "It doesn't have any—"

"No meat." He smiled smugly. "See, I even remembered that you don't eat bugs or grass, either."

"Who knew you had such a soft heart." I dipped my finger into the rich sauce, hesitant to bring it to my lips.

Cliff made an impatient noise. "C'mon. Just trust me."

Eyeing him tentatively, I took a bite. The savory flavor danced over my tongue at once, more powerful than any stew or herbed bread that Elysian kitchens had ever offered. Cliff's smile widened into a grin as I dove in for a second bite.

The humans' lives were so different than at the village. No community dinner served promptly at sunset from a central kitchen. Instead, Jon and Cliff routinely chose individual meals from a seemingly endless number of establishments throughout the city. They could drive to get their food, or another human could bring it to the door. Such a varied selection was incredible but a little overwhelming.

"Do you have any more Pop-Tarts?" I asked thickly.

Bemused, Jon retrieved the box and offered me a small corner of the pastry. I broke off a piece smaller than my palm and, without hesitation, plunged it into the cheese sauce. The savory and sweet were almost overpowering, but the novelty of both tastes… *Amazing.* Unlike anything I'd ever eaten before.

Jon buckled with laughter while Cliff made a noise of disgust.

"Fairies are so weird," Jon muttered.

"Or," I said with a flourish of my pastry. "Am I a genius?"

Jon broke off another piece of Pop-Tart and dipped it into his own bowl of pasta.

"Incredible, right?" I demanded.

"It's… not as bad as I was expecting," he said around the bite.

Cliff waved me off when I turned to him expectantly. "Keep your experiments to yourself," he said. "It's a shame this place doesn't have a kitchenette, though. Jon whips up a decent meal."

"You cook?" I asked, looking at Jon with surprise.

He gave a humble shrug. "My mom taught me some simple dishes when I was growing up. *Arroz con gandules* isn't too tricky to make."

"Next time we have a kitchen, you're making *arepas*," Cliff said.

Jon rolled his eyes. "Just 'cause I cook better than you doesn't make me your personal chef."

"It's called being practical."

The levity in the room emboldened me. I leaned forward to catch Cliff's eye, a wicked smile pulling at my lips. "So, Jon cooks *and* hunts. What exactly do you bring to the table again?"

"Obviously, I'm the handsome one," Cliff said, shooting me his signature *I'm trouble but you're gonna like it* smile without missing a beat. As he watched how I wrestled with another noodle as thick as my arm, he sank his chin into his hand and sighed. "You have it made, kid."

I lifted a finger. "Still not a kid."

"Food must be amazing at your size. I'd kill to take on a burger and fries bigger than I am."

I almost burst out laughing at how sincere he looked. He glowered at his sandwich, suddenly looking disappointed that he could hold it in his hands.

"I was thinking about calling that chick Eleanor," Cliff announced between bites. "Maybe booking an extra room for the night." He faltered, eyes catching over my head and hardening. "Jon, don't make that face at me."

"Of course I have the face," Jon said, his expression indeed lined with annoyance. "It's a terrible idea."

"She was nice," Cliff protested. "And she had legs like Anne Hathaway. All I'm sayin' is, I deserve to let off a little steam."

"You're terrible at one-night stands. You always get too attached."

"Now that's fucking cold, dude. Forgive me for feeling something."

"I think you should go to her," I volunteered, raising my voice to match theirs.

I half expected an admonishment, but Cliff brandished a hand at me, shooting Jon a stern *told you so* with his eyes and an *attagirl* toward me. "See? Girl after my own heart."

Jon sent me a reproachful look. "We're too deep into this hunt to be getting distracted. Don't encourage him."

Cliff chuckled. "Really? You're going to lecture me about getting distracted?"

Jon's jaw feathered.

"Passion is one of the greatest gifts the stars blessed us with," I said. "It feeds our spirit like the air we breathe." Letting the cap of food slide to the table, I ran a hand through my hair, recalling how it felt to be caressed under the willow by starlight. "Memorizing every curve and angle beneath your fingertips. Bodies intertwined, pressing and pulling as one divine force..."

I sighed as memories filled me like wine poured into a cask. I imagined Damian's hands on me. Eva's. Teague's.

Trailing off, I registered that the room had gone silent. Cliff and Jon were staring at me—hard.

"What?" I asked.

Cliff exchanged a look with Jon before offering a nonchalant shrug. "That was kinda hot."

His lips quirked in an innocent smile as our eyes met. I glanced over at Jon, who refused to look up from his plate as he agreed.

"You both *clearly* need a revel," I said, shaking my head as I returned to a cross-legged position before my portion of food.

"A what?" Cliff asked.

"It's… You know, a gathering of passion. Humans don't have them?"

Cliff's jaw went slack for a second. "Fairy orgies," he breathed, then looked at Jon with wide eyes. "She's talking about *fairy orgies.*"

Jon heaved a sigh that suggested he would rather we talk about anything else. I bit back a grin at the flush rising to his face.

"Maybe after this hunt is finished, you should host one. I'm sure you'd be good with a little practice," I said. "You're not horrible to look at; plenty of humans would be glad for an invitation."

Cliff gave a derisive scoff. "Honing skills isn't the issue, sweetheart." He leaned in conspiratorially, voice gravelly. "Your people have any stories and legends about hunters being insatiable in bed? Those ones are true."

He winked, drawing color to my cheeks as I smiled brightly at him. Those high cheekbones and pillowy lips… He would have done *very* well at Elysian revels in another life. Jon rolled his eyes, muttering something in that language I didn't understand. Cliff's smile turned wicked as he watched Jon squirm.

"You know," Cliff said to him. "If you're feeling left out, we could ask Eleanor if she's down for one more…"

"I'm really over capacity at thinking about you having sex today," Jon groaned, reaching for the remote while Cliff snickered softly.

Jon turned on the TV, the familiar bright colors and grating voices of the broadcast disorienting me for a moment.

The humans on-screen were selling things, embracing, running through the woods, laughing, and eating—it was impossible to keep up as Jon flipped through channel after channel. Briefly, he let a black and white film linger where well-dressed humans were singing and dancing in the pouring rain. Cliff made a comment about how old films like that were for people who fell asleep with Kleenex in their arms, but I couldn't help but notice his foot tapped along in perfect time to the music. Eventually, I recognized the news channel click into place.

A part of me felt oddly compelled to be documenting notes on the reality of human life. Even with only the last few days' experience to inform me, I could return and write the most popular, soon-to-be-banned manuscript the archives had seen since Karolyn the Gilded first described using a gemstone to change forms.

But there was too much to think about. I was sitting between two human hunters having dinner, for stars' sake.

And I was really tired—more tired than I should've been.

Some of it could be attributed to feeling Jon's pain, but it was more than that. The thought of conjuring another spell made me sick to my stomach. I shouldn't have been magic-exhausted from fending off Damian's attack. I'd pulled off greater feats while being mentored by Karis. This level of fatigue was concerning.

The dread pooling in my gut was interrupted by news reports' rising volume. The hunters had set down their respective meals, staring raptly at the screen.

"Somber news tonight as the search for Rick and Charlie Astle is still underway. Authorities have widened the search area, but there has been no trace of either man… The community has gathered for a candlelight vigil to pray for their safe return."

The screen cut away from the human at the desk, showing an assembly of people holding candles. They were gathered around a set of the victims' pictures. A group of so many humans should have made my skin crawl with fear, but instead, my heart gave a painful tug. There were tearful faces, people holding onto each other for support.

I hoped we weren't too late. Rick and Charlie looked too young to have met their end already. Deaths in Elysia were rare outside of natural causes. Aside from Father, I'd only known six fairies who had died in my lifetime, each an elderly fairy who had died peacefully in their chambers. Though the bodies were burned, the gatherings were celebrations of life.

"As the search wears on, friends and family continue to hold on to hope," the reporter went on. "I know we can all agree that it's touching to see the community come together in this difficult time."

The hunters must have been unnervingly good at their job of doing away with the bodies of the guard and dogs at Dottage. If those had been found, perhaps the reporters would have recounted that information as well.

I turned to look between the hunters. "They mentioned *authorities*. Are they looking for the werewolf, too?"

Cliff scoffed. "See all those people there? They have no idea that things like werewolves exist outside of scary stories and legends."

"Then… tell them?"

"It's not that simple," Cliff told me. "They'd think we're crazy, and then there's no helping anyone. They'd lock us up and throw away the key." His tone made it clear that this wasn't up for further discussion.

Jon stood suddenly, his expression dark and unreadable. He muttered something about showering off. His startling change in demeanor made me want to apologize, though I didn't know what for. I frowned, tracking his hurried path as he set his bowl on the counter, grabbed a change of clothes, and swung the washroom door mostly closed.

Cliff changed the channel to a show about humans frantically trying to create a meal in a limited amount of time. I struggled to focus on the screen when I could hear Jon undressing in the next room. My insides stirred.

I tried to shove away whatever silly, traitorous thoughts attempted to surface. But then, the shower hissed to life. He'd left the door cracked the slightest bit. I fiddled with a speck of dirt on my pants, imagining what was happening right behind that wall.

I *had* to get a grip. He was human—a *hunter.* I was damn lucky he'd turned out to be reasonable, but when this hunt was over, and I severed the bond between us, I'd never see him again.

But I'd never been that disciplined.

Making sure Cliff's eyes were glued to the TV screen, I quietly took wing and backed away. Something electric surged through me as I peered through the crack in the door, my heart stammering in my chest.

Through the hazy veil of steam, Jon stood beneath the cascading water. His figure looked like the stars themselves chiseled it. Humans were modest—I knew I should've pulled away, but *fucking stars,* I'd never seen anything so beautiful. Beautiful things were meant to be adored. I was merely a curator, admiring living artwork.

The foggy glass shower stall muted my view as he ran his hands through his hair and tilted his face up with a sigh. I imagined the water ribboning down his muscled back and the tapestry of scars across his chest. Hunger rippled within me as I wondered what it would feel like to reach out and grab those strong shoulders to pull him against me. I wanted him on top of me at the revel, under my favorite tree. Equal in stature, not divided by our species. I braced my hands against the wooden doorframe. I *needed* to know what those perfect lips tasted like.

No. Picturing him as one of my own kind wasn't just looking. This was... dangerous. Yet, the want remained like a glowing ember in my belly. I'd never felt like this before with even the most intimate of revel partners. Not even Damian, I realized with a little pang of guilt.

I had the urge to remove the snowflake necklace Jon had given me. Wearing it so loyally—though it had been an innocent gift—suddenly felt like a statement. *I am yours.*

Sobered, I tore myself from my reverie and banished the images of Jon's hands in my hair. I hurried back to the table.

As I landed, Cliff looked over. "You full already?"

I shrugged, stretching my wings to hide the relieved quaver to my voice. He hadn't caught me staring at Jon. "Don't rush me. I'm savoring the experience."

"By all means, eat at a snail's pace," Cliff muttered, shaking his head like I was becoming his favorite joke.

The sound of the shower now seemed to mock me. If the council read my mind again when I returned, they would traitor-brand me head-to-toe.

The TV show switched to something Cliff said was a commercial. Designed to sell people stuff they didn't need, apparently. He muted it.

"What do the cooking people do during the commercial?" I asked thickly around a bite.

"It's a recording." He pursed his lips as though bracing himself for another slew of questions about *recordings*.

And while that was the case, I blurted a different question. "How long have you and Jon known each other?"

"I swear, you've got the attention span of a dragonfly on crack." He toyed with his fork in the bowl. I couldn't help but wonder if he'd ever used cutlery as a weapon. "Almost a decade," he answered. "Since high school. You wouldn't believe what a scrawny sophomore he used to be."

Figuring I had a finite number of questions left before he got too annoyed to answer, I swallowed the instinct to ask what *high school* was. "How did you meet? Did you happen upon the same prey during a hunt?"

"We met before this hunting stuff when we were teenagers." Cliff paused, chuckling softly at the memory. "I hit him with my car."

I almost dropped my bottle cap of food. "Stars! Why would you laugh at that? Was everything okay?"

"There were a few scratches on the hood, but I was able to buff them out."

"I meant *Jon*, you toad."

"He was fine. Shouldn't have been jay-walking." He smirked like my outraged stare was highly entertaining. "My dad was pissed about the car, though. It was a restored 1964 Thunderbird. A premature graduation present. I wasn't allowed to touch it for a month."

Something heavy settled in my chest. I hadn't thought about the hunters having families. The thought of someone like Cliff being punished by a parent didn't seem possible.

"Your father, does he… know what you do?" I thought about how Cliff said the people on the TV didn't know the truth about the werewolf.

His jaw ticked. "How's your wing? Hanging in there?"

When our eyes met, the silent warning was clear. This conversation could continue to be pleasant if I didn't overstep. Although curiosity burned through me like wildfire, I nodded.

"I'll give it another healing session before bed, but it's getting easier to stay in the air for long periods of time," I told him.

"I've noticed," he snorted. His gaze lingered. "What about your mark? Looks a little less gnarly. Does it still hurt?"

Having finished my meal, I set the cap aside and let my hair loose from its tie. "It stings sometimes, but there's not much I can do except wait. The edges are turning black already. It could have been worse. Some ancient marks are meant to torture the recipient for the rest of their life."

His pause was heavy, but his tone was unusually gentle after. "So once it's done healing, you'll be left with a badass tattoo." He waggled his eyebrows at me when I gave him an unconvinced look. "Girls with tattoos are hot. What can I say?"

"You seem to have more than your fair share," I said, eyeing the ink on his arms.

For once, his eyes lit up at my probing. Cliff rolled up the sleeve of his white cotton tee to reveal the interlacing design I had glimpsed earlier. I stepped forward as he leaned his arm on the table. Scars distorted the ink. One looked mottled like something had been hooked deep into his bicep and ripped out. I tried not to wince as I drank it in.

"Like what you see?" It was hard to reconcile that cocky smile with the soldier-like intent when he had leveled a gun at me.

I moistened my lips. "Those… They didn't brand you for betrayal, did they?"

If the masses didn't even acknowledge the hunters, it wasn't far-fetched that their violent lives might have made an enemy or two of other humans. However, it was hard to imagine anyone being able to hold Cliff down as his arm flexed, muscles gleaming in the lamplight.

"Nah, nothing like that," he said. "We don't do that kind of stuff." His gaze flickered toward my left cheek, darkening.

"Is it a sigil?" I asked.

"Hell if I know. I got it just to piss off my folks junior year. I guess I just thought it looked cool."

I couldn't help but giggle at that. Cliff shifted in his seat to face me, showing me the rest of his collection. I got a good look at the hourglass tattooed on his right forearm, specks of sand filtering down a gilded vial. A phoenix emblazoned his upper left arm, and a pair of interlocking triangles disappeared under his shirt. The style of each design was different but drawn with care. He explained that he had more on his back and chest that he couldn't show without giving me a strip tease—which he didn't do for free, apart from a few choice exceptions.

"Why's that one the only tattoo with color?" I asked, flying above his left hand. He turned his hand over, where the delicate bouquet of flowers was inked on his wrist. The petals were so vibrantly blue, they seemed to jump off his skin.

Cliff's mouth twitched in a sad smile. "My kid sister, Anna. She loves forget-me-nots. I designed that one myself."

He'd *shot* me, but I couldn't help but feel a tug of sympathy for the grief flashing behind his impenetrable exterior. For a moment, Cliff didn't look like a hunter. He just looked like a lonely boy.

The washroom door creaked.

"Ask him about his tramp stamp." Jon walked into the room wearing clean clothes, his wet hair pushed back.

Cliff glared at him, pulling his sleeve back down. "When are you gonna stop bringing that up?"

Grinning wickedly, Jon took a seat across from him. "When the ink fades."

The flush on Cliff's face had me terribly curious, though I had no idea what a tramp stamp was. "What is it?" I asked, flying up to look Cliff over. "*Where* is it?"

Cliff's snarl was almost frightening. "Don't—"

"Lower back," Jon said.

I zipped closer, but Cliff hurriedly pushed me away with the back of his hand and repositioned his chair against the wall. Though I relented, I gave him a menacing smirk.

"You can't hide it forever," I said, trying to ignore the flutter in my chest as Jon snickered with me.

"This is the last time you bring home a stray," Cliff huffed at Jon.

My thoroughly insulted scoff seemed to lift Cliff's spirits.

The TV show was all but forgotten as Jon became fixated on his phone, and Cliff pulled his journal closer from across the table. He cleaned his hands meticulously before opening it to a spread of several pages about werewolves. I flew in closer, reaching out to flip to the next sketch.

"*Hey*," he said forcefully enough to make me freeze. "Wipe your hands off, or you'll get grease on the pages."

"Are you kidding me? Isn't that dry blood on the corner?"

"That doesn't mean I want tiny little handprints all over the place."

After I wiped my hands off on my leggings with enough friction to start a fire, he allowed me to approach. I tugged at the page, needing to fly higher just to turn it. Sketches portrayed werewolves in every gruesome phase of their transformation. My stomach churned at the overly detailed visual directions of how to locate and remove the werewolf's heart most efficiently.

"How long have you been working on this journal?" I asked.

"I've gone through a couple. Had this one maybe three years now."

"These are… incredible," I said in earnest. "I want to throw up, but the drawings are incredible."

I paused to glance through his notes. The hunters had already disclosed all the information they knew. But a note on the bottom corner caught my eye—words that looked like they were more freshly-inked than the others.

Also known as a mactir.

Strange to think that my contribution to Cliff's research would be more than his intrusive sketches of me. At that thought, I began picking faster through the pages until I neared the end. I caught a glimpse of a sketchy, damaged wing and my own miserable expression before Cliff suddenly reached over and closed the journal.

"You already know what you look like," he said, avoiding my gaze.

"Very sweet of you to not want me to relive that," I scoffed. When he rolled his eyes, I added, "Next time, draw me in a more flattering light, and I may even smile."

He stood abruptly, making me jump. "You know what? I think I have just the thing to get you off my ass for a while."

A jingling sound came from his bag as he dug through it. My wings burst to life when I saw something glinting in his hands. He returned to the table, brandishing a clear bag that held rusted keys, gemstones, tarnished silver, and stained gold.

"My stash," I whispered.

"It's about time I got this junk back to you." Cliff dropped the bag on the table. It was open from the top, perfectly accessible for me to dive down and reach into. "I was gonna leave it back under the Dottage floorboards before we left town, but then you had to come along and *help*."

I grabbed the first thing I could pick up—a thick ring with a sapphire the size of my fist. My voice wobbled. "I thought you destroyed it."

"Guess those Bambi eyes got to me after all."

"Thank you." Hugging the ring to my chest, I turned to him with a watery smile. While I was still assessing the contents of the bag—freshwater pearls, an ornate skeleton key, fragments of an opal-crusted comb I had once tried to weave through my own hair—I freed one hand to send a harmless burst of frost his way. "You *asshole!* You had it this whole time and didn't tell me?"

Cliff staggered back, brushing ice shards from his shirt. "Hey! I'm getting mixed signals here."

"You had it coming," Jon said with a shrug.

"Yeah, yeah." Cliff gave him a sour look. "No wonder you're soft on her. She's a klepto like you."

Blatantly ignoring him, Jon smiled warmly at me. "Is that one your favorite?"

I considered the sapphire ring and shook my head. "The things I treasure most are under my bed at home. It wouldn't have been worth the strain on my wings to lug such heavy pieces all that way." I rapped my fingertips on the cool, glimmering facets of the sapphire. "This one's not even charged. It's only pretty to look at."

"Charged?" Jon echoed, brow furrowing.

Maybe I was as irrevocably twisted as the Elders thought me to be to find his curiosity endearing rather than threatening now. After my insatiable line of questioning about human oddities, I found myself happy to return the favor for once.

I held out the ring, placing it in Jon's hand. "Some gemstones are seeded with a raw, special kind of fairy magic. With the right spell, that magic can be absorbed and enhance the caster's powers, but…" Father's face flashed through my mind's eye. I shook my head. "That's not allowed in Elysia anymore."

"Good," Cliff said curtly, dropping back into his seat. "I'd rather not have you hitting me with a goddamn blizzard every time you're pissy."

"Charged gemstones are more than just that," I said, feeling a tentative rush of excitement that I could discuss this topic without receiving dirty looks from fellow fairies. The tales were terrifying—my memories even more so. "There's stories about gem magic creating new spells and unlocking old ones. Even arcane transformation spells. Fairies being able to shift into birds or beasts, or even—" I stopped short when I saw Cliff reaching for his journal, ready to start documenting me like a specimen again. I set my hands on my hips and glared at him. "Touch that pen, and I'll freeze your hand to the table."

Cliff pulled away with a little roll of his eyes. "You can be kind of a bitch sometimes, you know that?"

"You, too," I said, my lips curving.

Laughter flickered to life in his eyes, though he clearly fought to hide it from me as he raked me up and down. It was a nice reprieve from the gruff indifference that so often seemed to be his default concerning me. "*You're welcome* for giving you back your shit. Remind me to never do anything nice for you ever again."

I pulled the sapphire ring back into my lap, wishing I could wear it properly on my finger. I stared into the deep blue facets, allowing myself to imagine for the first time in years what I might do with a charged gemstone in my possession.

22
SYLVIA

A delightful bouquet of scents overwhelmed me. Fresh blooms, sugary confections, and expensive fabrics whirled under the same ornate ceiling. The room reminded me of the largest chambers in Elysia, but the walls were not earthen. My heart thrummed with the same anticipation that came before a revel, but I was not outdoors.

No, I found myself in a grand ballroom, bathed in the soft glow of chandeliers that glittered overhead like enormous circlets of diamonds.

Despite a sea of unfamiliar faces, an unmistakable feeling of belonging surged through me. Everyone was so happy I was there. I stood among them like an equal. Like a *human.*

One of the guests, a woman with strawberry blonde hair that framed her face in undulating waves, approached me like an old friend. She placed a string of pearls around my neck, her eyes holding a familiar glint.

"Alice?" I whispered.

Before I could grasp her identity, she was already vanishing toward the dance, arm in arm with her partner. I followed in a daze, noting the color of my midnight blue gown as I descended the staircase. The fabric was reminiscent of the starry sky, the silk adorned with silvery threads mirroring my favorite constellations.

At the base of the staircase, a man waited for me. His eyes sparkled with anticipation as he extended a hand, sweeping me into an effortless waltz. My feet glided as though I'd danced like this a hundred times before—though nothing could be further from the truth. Laughter bubbled from me. Strains of strings and piano encircled us with a haunting beauty, the plucking of violins matching my fluttering heartbeat.

I couldn't quite focus on the details of my partner's face, as though he were swirling as much as the room around us. In his arms, I felt weightless. Incandescent. Desired. I could have danced all night.

As we swayed, my partner's hand brushed gently over my back. I took a small, sharp breath—my wings were nowhere to be found. I should have been panicked, but an unearthly calm settled into my bones instead. It was a worthy trade for this euphoria.

Memories of his warm touch lingered, intoxicating, when I awoke.

I stared at the ceiling of the motel room, shifting on the pillow Cliff had put on the dining table. My wings were folded carefully beneath me, tugging delicate muscles in my back as my weight shifted. A bewildering stab of disappointment pierced my heart. I replayed the shiver of the man's hand on my back over and over, the allure of the lavish ballroom.

What it might feel like to be human.

A soft, pained moan came from behind me, bringing the hairs on my arms to attention. I sat up with a scrambling, jolted motion, recognizing the timbre of Jon's voice.

He was in danger.

23
JON

Every ghost has a fixation. That's why they stick around. And the ones with the most violent fixations are the most desperate to possess the living. Many spirits manifest innocently at first—others start off twisted because they were already twisted as ordinary humans.

Through the faded red door, hang a right at the end of the hall. The last room on the left. I knew this room. I knew what was going to happen. I'd been here over twenty times, but terror paralyzed me like I was a scrawny teenager again.

A kid was crying on the other side of the door.

Despite my fear, I pushed it open.

Blood, both fresh and stale, soaked the floorboards and splattered the abandoned toys strewn across the room.

He sat in a chair in the center of it all, facing me. Although he was slumped entirely to one side, his pale eyes were wide and alert. A broad, vacant smile was frozen on his face.

While I hesitated in the doorway, his breathing became heavier, more frantic through his clenched teeth.

I pleaded, trying to reason with him. Not with the ghost but with *him*. But I knew by then that he couldn't hear me—or maybe he could, but he was too far away to do anything about it.

Tears gathered in my eyes.

He shot into a standing position like a marionette yanked up by its strings. I staggered back from his convulsive approach.

No, no, no, please—

"Jon!" The whisper in my ear was accompanied by a plummeting temperature.

My eyes flew open. I was in the motel bed. He was gone, the old room was gone, the blood, the toys—but there was a glow and a presence in front of my face. I tore my knife out from under my pillow, wielding it defensively.

The glow cried out and jerked away from me.

As my eyes adjusted, I could discern past the light—a frightened face. Hands raised with sparkling frost on the fingertips.

"Sylvia." I lowered my weapon and rubbed my eyes, sighing. "Sorry."

The ice rescinded from her hands as her troubled stare raked me over. "I thought you were a light sleeper," she said. "I've been calling your name for five minutes."

I stuffed the knife back under my pillow. "Usually, I am."

She relaxed a little, but tension still bundled in her shoulders. She looked uncertain like I might change my mind and snap at her. To be fair, I'd been on edge all afternoon, hoping we would have the werewolf in hand before its next transformation.

Using pictures from Nolan's social media accounts, we'd been able to track down his apartment and pry open the back window for a browse inside. Sylvia had looked like a kicked puppy when she couldn't sense anything remotely off. Besides some skin mags and a framed photo of him and Lily that hadn't come down months after the breakup, there was nothing damning at all at Nolan's place. I hadn't exactly offered Sylvia a word of comfort when we left either, too busy planning the next steps.

I wouldn't have been surprised if she wanted space from me for the remainder of the hunt. Yet, to my surprise, she landed right beside me.

"Bad dream?" she asked.

I wrestled the shock off my face as Sylvia plopped into a seated position on my pillow. It was kinda cute how the fabric barely sank under her weight. She was still bathed in that ethereal glow that seemed to come from within her. A voice in the back of my head still howled that there was a *non-human* on my fucking pillow. Another part of me was pleased she wanted to be near me.

"I've had night terrors since I was young," Sylvia explained when I hesitated to answer. She shivered and shook her head in recollection. "I know how damaging it is. It can feel so real, making sleep a place where you're trapped instead of resting at all."

"Any night terrors tonight?" I asked—a thinly veiled attempt to keep the focus off myself.

I swore she blushed. "No dreams at all, actually." A blatant lie, but I didn't press, especially when she leaned closer curiously. "Are you alright, though? What were you dreaming about?"

She was sweet. It was hard to look at her lithe figure and bright, kind eyes and not want to tell her everything she'd ever wanted to hear. I glanced across the dark motel room, ensuring Cliff was asleep.

"It's always the same moment. I was dreaming about my father," I told her. "When a spirit possessed him."

She covered her mouth with a luminescent hand. "It was a memory?"

I nodded. "I wasn't alone, but in the end… I had to be the one to expel the spirit from him. He was killed in the process."

A beat of silence passed. "I… I'm so sorry, Jon. I know what it's like to lose a father," Sylvia said, tears of sympathy shining back at me.

Her admission registered heavily. Sylvia was guarded about sharing information surrounding her village but *vigilant* about her family. And she had willingly divulged it for my sake. I thought of Hazel—how heartbreakingly young she still was. Sylvia mentioned her mother only once or twice.

I wanted to pry more, wanted to offer a word of comfort, but Sylvia's attention was fixed on me, waiting.

"It's best that my father died," I admitted. "He wasn't himself by the time we got to him. Maybe if I had noticed sooner, it would have been different, but… I was just a kid. Barely seventeen." I ground my teeth, fighting angry tears that burned the back of my eyes. "The spirit in him was twisted. It made him do horrible things. Unforgivable."

Sylvia's expression withered in horror—because how the hell else do you react to shit like that—and her gaze dropped to her lap. Whatever terrible fallout she was imagining couldn't be worse than the truth, so I didn't offer a correction. People looked at you differently when they found out your father murdered four children with his bare hands. Some thought that kind of darkness was genetic. Over the years, there had been countless times that I worked my stomach into knots over the same worry.

She climbed to her feet, and I thought she was leaving. I'd crossed a line—frightened her again.

But I should have known better by now to think I could predict Sylvia.

She walked across the pillow toward my face, her steps wobbly where they sank into the plush cushion. I held perfectly still as she knelt at my eye line—so close, I couldn't look at her properly anymore. A tiny hand brushed a rogue lock of hair off my face.

"What are you…" The words died on my tongue.

She pressed her forehead to mine. At first, I thought she was trying to heal me again, as though my grief could be remedied by magic. But no—she wasn't saying the spell I'd heard her dutifully chant at each healing. She was just… sitting with me.

I shuddered slightly as her fingers smoothed over my skin in a petting gesture. Slow and patient, like a mother. She was so fragile, but she touched me with such aching gentleness, like *I* might be the breakable one. I hadn't realized there was a crease between my eyes or the clench in my jaw. I let out a soft breath, coming to terms with the unspoken—the simple kindness of feeling less alone in a mottled world for a moment.

She drew away without a word, returning to her previous spot on the edge of the pillow.

"For a hunter, you're good at being gentle when you want to be," Sylvia said, her voice low like it was a secret shared between us. "Hasn't anyone ever been gentle with you?"

I didn't know what to say.

She had smelled like cinnamon and rain.

In the neighboring bed, Cliff rolled onto his back and continued to breathe evenly. Sylvia watched him for a moment.

"It's good to have someone you can count on in your life. I'm glad you and Cliff have each other's backs, considering he doesn't seem to be in touch with his family, either." Her expression darkened. "He mentioned his father once, but that's all."

"Really? He hasn't said a word about his dad in over a year."

"And the flowers on his wrist—he said they're for his sister." Sylvia pursed her lips, sorrow flooding her expression. "Is she…?"

"She's fine." I glanced at Cliff's sleeping form and took my voice even lower. "His family's still around, but he hasn't spoken to them in years. He helped me get rid of the spirit that possessed my dad. When he tried to tell his parents, they thought he was crazy. But he wouldn't back down. They don't want anything to do with him, and they definitely don't want him anywhere near Anna."

"If it's been years, maybe he should try again."

I couldn't help but be moved by her optimism, misplaced as it was. "The last thing his parents told him was that they'd be better off if he had never been born. You don't come back from that."

"But—"

"It's not my place to talk about this," I said firmly, realizing I'd disclosed more than enough already. I could imagine the betrayed glare Cliff would send me if he found out I'd been loose-lipped about his folks.

"Fine. Then, what about you?" She cocked her head, eyes boring into mine like she could see right through me. "What about your mother?"

I had to look away. "She's alive. She's just… out of reach. Not in the same way as Cliff's family."

Sylvia's voice was whisper-quiet, almost silent. "What do you mean?"

"She saw what happened to my dad. She wasn't the same after that. Probably never will be." I lifted my hand to show her the azabache bracelet forever affixed to my wrist. "She gave this to me. Had it specially made and blessed when I was a kid. She always said it would keep me safe."

The way her shoulders slumped made me think she might crawl over to comfort me again. I silently reeled over how much I wished she would. It dawned on me how easily I was sharing my situation with her—things I would consider carelessly free ammo if she were any other non-human. Then again, I'd had a front-row seat to some of the most traumatic moments she'd ever experienced in her life the past few days. Maybe it was only fair that she could see me at my lowest, too.

"Anyway," I murmured. "Sorry for waking you. And for pulling a knife on you."

She cracked a smile. "You *do* owe me for the knife, but I don't mind being awake. I was hoping to get some more reading done during the night." She nodded at the nightstand that had become her favorite perch. The books she'd stolen were stacked by the alarm clock.

"What are those about, anyway?"

She shrugged. "Theories about improving magic."

"I doubt studying ice from a book is going to do you more good than getting some sleep."

"Oh, and you're the expert?"

Her argument was interrupted by a yawn. When I smirked, she gave me a thoroughly defeated pout. Instead of heading back to her spot on the table, she tipped herself over and sprawled out on my pillow. Again, I couldn't help but gape.

"Sorry about the light," she said. "It'll fade soon."

That may have been the equivalent of her saying *good night,* but I wasn't ready to shut my eyes just yet.

"When you glow," I whispered, "do you have to think about it, or does it just happen?"

She brought one cerulean hand in front of her face, turning it back and forth to make the air shiver with light. "It's a spell—one of the first we learn as children since it's simple and doesn't take much energy."

The light flickered. For a moment, I swore her breathing was a little heavier before her glow resumed its full power.

"Are you okay?" I asked.

"I'm fine. But I suppose I can admit you're right. I *am* tired."

Rather than give in to the urge to tease her, sympathy loosened in my chest. I could still feel the ghost of her touch on my forehead, and I was compelled to offer some sort of comfort in return. She'd had a chaotic day, after all, and I hadn't been much help.

The sheets rustled as I reached for the pillow. Her wings twitched and tensed at the shadowy approach of my hand. I froze. It must have looked like a monster was coming for her through the darkness, invading her light.

"Sorry," I said, drawing back.

"No." Sylvia stretched her little hand in offering. "It's okay."

The stiffness of her wings said otherwise. Even they were lit with blue, highlighting every shattered and healed bit of membrane that made up the bullet wound.

She beckoned again, and I caved, gingerly touching her arm. I tried not to balk at how my finger and thumb could engulf so much of her forearm. Her glowing skin was soft under my touch, pleasantly warm.

"Hazel used to be so scared of the dark." Her calm tone assured me she wasn't uncomfortable. "I'd stay with her through the night, glowing until she drifted off. When I have night terrors, she still does the same for me. She gets a little careless and blinds me when she's too sleepy to control the spell, though."

I chuckled. "You're each other's nightlights." My fingertip grazed the end of her hair. "I used to be afraid of the dark, too."

"And now?"

I cast my gaze away from her, considering the weight of the simple question. "I worked my ass off to become better than anything out there in the shadows. Smarter, stronger."

I felt her staring. After a moment, Sylvia hummed. "Careful. You're starting to sound a little cocky."

"Arrogance is for people who can't follow through on their threats."

Feeling bold, I reached further to touch her wings. They snapped shut instantly, sending a clear message. Hard to blame her, considering the damage that had already been done to them.

Despite that, she didn't run from me.

Letting my hand come to rest behind her, I watched her light grow dimmer with each rise and fall of her steadying breath. Not long after her eyelids fell shut, her glow faded entirely and bathed us both in darkness.

Even as I drifted off, the imprint of her shape continued to glow in my mind's eye.

24
JON

Scant nightmarish imagery lingered when I blinked my eyes open and squinted at the bedside clock. I groaned at the time—*4:05 a.m.*—and cursed my perpetual inability to get a full night's sleep.

Sylvia was still there.

I would've expected her to put distance between us the second I was unconscious, but no—she was sprawled out on my pillow like she owned the place. A beat of embarrassment ran through me when I tried to move, only to find she had the thumb of my hand clutched to her front like a body pillow. She breathed deeply and evenly. I swallowed hard, suddenly alert.

Her traitor mark was pressed to the pillow, all but invisible to my eye. Some of her hair, peculiarly redder at the roots, fell across her cheek, but I could still see the exhaustion written on her face. This poor girl was putting everything she had into this hunt—and *why*? Protecting her village was a noble motive, but I couldn't shake the inkling there was more to it. Her change of heart had been so abrupt—calling us savages, saving my life, now begging to stay rooted at our sides for the duration of the hunt.

Maybe… she wanted to be *here*. To be near *me*.

The thought was ridiculous, traitorous. But she was so beautiful.

In my drowsy state, I wanted nothing more than to close my hand around her fully and tuck her under my chin. I wanted to feel the soft skin hiding under her delicate clothes. I wondered if she would blink her eyes open and smile at me, pleased by my advance. Would she tease me for being so cautious or beg for more? I vividly remembered how she had grinned at me from the sink; her body bared without an ounce of shame. My blood heated as I stared at her like she might be able to read my filthy thoughts while she dreamed.

No. I must've lost my fucking mind. If she were human, that would be one thing. But she wasn't.

I pulled my hand free as delicately as I could. If that woke her, too bad. Sylvia's arms fell limply on the pillow, and she did little more than adjust her legs before falling still again. Absolutely worn to the bone.

I tore my eyes away and got out of bed as discreetly as possible, wrestling with myself. I'd woken up beside many women, but this was different. She'd seen the ugliest side of my life, but she hadn't run for the door. She'd only wanted to offer me a simple kindness. The delicate yearning in my chest was foreign—wanting someone I knew I could never have. Someone I shouldn't want in the first place.

Every day that passed, I felt my shields lowering. I was *letting* them lower—for her.

Cálmate, I told myself. Sylvia would be gone the second the hunt was over, and I would merely be a brief, frightening story she would share by firelight. Nothing more.

The early morning air was brisk as I stepped outside. A walk would help me clear my head. The dark parking lot was emptier than it had been in the last few days. A faint rumble in the air alerted me that an engine was on, but none of the cars had headlights on.

I didn't think anything of it. I'd encountered shadier things in motel parking lots over the years.

After I circled the building once, the ridiculous thoughts I'd woken up with were more distant. The car engine was still rumbling, and as I turned the corner, it abruptly pulled out of its space and turned onto the road.

It was a dark Mustang, but I was too distracted by the faint claw marks near the taillight to note any other identifiers before it was out of sight.

25
JON

Peaceful as Sylvia looked while lying in bed that morning, the same couldn't be said once she awoke. From the moment she rose, she was completely absorbed in her books. She'd flip through a few pages of one, toss it aside, grab another, and cycle through where she left off on each one.

After pinpointing our suspect's workplace, Cliff took a break from scouring through Nolan's social media connections to question why Sylvia hadn't eaten much of her lunch—crumbled-up bits of a baked potato with chives.

"I'll get to it," she'd assured.

That had been hours ago, and she hadn't taken another bite.

She didn't move from the nightstand until the thunder started rumbling outside. Instead of checking in with us about our research on Nolan's potential location—not that we had any updates—she hovered in a tight pattern in the corner. And she was still reading.

"What's her problem?" Cliff asked, frowning in her direction. He didn't bother lowering his voice. That morning, Sylvia didn't seem to hear us unless we called her name multiple times. "You let her down easy last night or something?" Cliff raised his eyebrows when I glared at him. "Or was it the other way around?"

He'd already given me shit for seeing Sylvia curled up on my pillow for a second time. I wasn't about to argue in circles about that again. I pushed out of my chair, muttering for him to shut up.

Sylvia didn't even look up when I approached her where she hovered by the curtained window. One delicate hand was cupping the aged tome while the other pried at the roots of her hair.

"Are spellbooks really that riveting?" I asked, wincing when my voice made her flinch and drop the book as though I'd materialized out of thin air.

I caught her book before it could hit the ground. I turned it over in my hand, flipping through the pages and trying in vain to read the scrawled title across the front. The pages were worn soft and yellow from age. I wondered how old it was. How many generations her village went back.

"You can't read that!" Sylvia barked, flying in to snatch it back. She schooled her expression, sweeping locks of hair behind her ear. "It's… it's in ancient Fae. Spellwork language. Human eyes won't be able to read it."

"You gotta stop saying 'human' like it's an insult," I said.

This drew a smirk out of her. "Why? It's intentional."

"Hurtful."

At my feigned offense, she stifled a laugh behind one hand. It was rare to see her smile so wide, particularly since her encounter with that other fairy outside Elysia—*Damian*.

"You know, you could read it to me," I pointed out. I found a coy smile on my lips, the one I gifted our more timid victims when I was trying to warm them into answering my questions during an open case.

"This old tome wouldn't interest you." She drummed the spine. "It's mostly full of complex theories and pronunciation guides. Dry as dirt."

I would have been content to listen to her talking about fucking *grass*, but I conceded and refocused on the case.

"We dug up information about where Nolan works," I said. "Night shift security at MPT Construction. Cliff and I are going to scout the active sites they're contracted for. If I'm right, one of these sites is where he's playing house with his victims. Lily included."

"Why keep them alive?"

"Werewolves are overwhelmed by their hunger, but they can still be strategic. We've seen more lucid ones prepare for a full moon feeding. They'll gather up to five victims like it's a fucking buffet. It satiates them until the next transformation."

Sylvia's fluttering wings gave a stammer in sync with the disgust that flashed over her face. "I can't believe you can say that without wanting to vomit."

"Practice."

She puffed out her cheeks, frowning. "So, which of these sites is his?"

"Not sure yet," I said. "We need to sweep the areas. We're still pulling the list. I'm going to check the perimeter of the motel here if you want a little fresh air."

She snorted, eyeing the rolling black clouds visible between the curtains. "Yeah, it's a beautiful day for a stroll."

I gave her a conspiratorial smile as I pulled on my leather jacket. "You think monsters wait for the weather to clear up? It's only a sprinkle right now, anyway."

Sylvia brushed off the playful jab, intelligence gleaming in her eyes. "What are you checking for *here*? This isn't one of the security sites."

"Come with me, and I'll show you."

Cliff coughed behind me. He was giving me a reproachful glare over the rim of his mug, eyes flashing: *this joke isn't funny anymore*. Thunder rolled in the distance, making the window rattle. Sylvia winced.

"I can't," she said curtly, flying past me in a burst. I watched her land on the nightstand and sit cross-legged, spellbook opened in her lap again.

Her bizarre behavior left me too shocked to argue. I had to wonder if she was getting cold feet about the hunt and was too proud to admit it—she'd looked chilled to the bone outside of Lily's house.

Leaving Cliff and Sylvia to their respective research, I stepped out into the evening. My worn leather jacket warded off the chill that had crept into the air. Drifting storm clouds concealed the sinking sun, casting the area in a prematurely dark hue and sapping colors from the forest.

The parking lot was stagnant. The same ten cars had been occupying their spots for the majority of the day, likely discouraged by the weather. No sign of the battered gray Mustang that had been idling here in the early hours of the morning. The skid marks remained where it had peeled out of here like a bat out of hell. I had a feeling about it that I couldn't shake.

After all these years, I knew when I was being watched.

When I cleared the parking lot, I turned my attention to the hilly forest that stretched behind the motel. It was a feasible walk for our likely stalker. The woods themselves could hide plenty.

My favorite silver knife was tucked within easy reach inside my jacket, but I left my heavier weapons in the room. Tonight wasn't the full moon, so I could at least rule out running into a fully-transformed werewolf. Small fucking blessings.

The patter of raindrops was softened in the woods. A creek cut through a cropping of rocks overflowing from the storm. My boots sank into the earth, the slick and elevated terrain forcing me to move with particular care. The scent of wet earth and pine filled my nostrils, invigorating me.

Tammy had taught me years ago to notice subtle disturbances in the terrain: broken twigs, displaced leaves, and the occasional snake burrow. She said the foundation of all hunting was to observe, to notice the things that others would overlook. There was always a story in the signs—but this one was likely just a small rodent scurrying to evade a predator.

My gaze caught on a deeper indent in the earth at the plateau of the slight incline. Too big to be a deer. A chill ran down my spine. There, partially concealed beneath a layer of sodden leaves, was a pair of human bootprints. I crouched, brushing leaves aside carefully. The rain was only just beginning to erode the deep prints. Judging by the size and pattern of the shoes, this had to be a man—maybe a size ten.

Looking over my shoulder, my suspicions were confirmed. The motel sat at the bottom of the hill. This was a vantage point. A good one. The foliage provided ideal coverage, but the angle of the position made it easy to survey the windows below without being spotted. Our window was the third one from the right. I could see Cliff's silhouette faintly through the drawn curtains, still hunched over the laptop.

"*Puñeta*," I muttered, pushing to my feet.

I scanned the ground, pushing deeper into the trees. The car had peeled off. I doubted Nolan would be back, but my heart pounded nonetheless. Not only was our monster aware of our presence, but it was stalking us in return. I loathed to admit he was one step ahead of us, turning this hunt into a fatal, fucked-up game of cat and mouse.

Over the drumming of raindrops on leaves, another sound caught my ear. I stopped walking, tension snaking through my body as I searched for the source. Something was moving in the branches with incredible speed, rustling the green and gold leaves. Birds didn't move like that.

Something small burst from the branches above me like a bullet. My knife was in my hand in seconds, blade angled upward. The thing—oh fuck, it was *Sylvia*—gave a shriek of fear as she barely avoided flying right into my weapon.

I glimpsed her hands glowing cerulean a split second before a freezing gale rushed around me. Ice formed rapidly, glinting in the mist. The conjured icicles were like twin blades of her own, flying toward me at her command. I cursed, ducking out of one icicle's way. I reflexively snapped up my free hand to catch the other that whistled by my left ear. A less practiced man might've lost an eye.

"Oh, *stars*, I'm sorry! Are you alright? I didn't mean to… I could have killed you!"

Sylvia's voice was distant as I analyzed the razor-sharp point of the icy shard—easily an inch in circumference. I tried not to imagine the ice buried deep in my chest. Just like in the basement of the Dottage house, she'd conjured it out of *fucking nothing.*

My heart was still hammering as she sank lower in the air, pulling my attention. Her flight was spastic, jumping every time a raindrop plunked onto her wings. I tossed the icicle aside and tucked my knife back into my jacket, pushing off the muddy ground.

"What are you doing here?" I demanded.

Her flight bobbed dangerously again, and I thrust out my cupped hands tentatively beneath her. Sylvia landed between my palms, giving her wings a good flap to rid them of excess water. Some of it sprayed my chin and made me wrinkle my nose.

"I changed my mind," Sylvia offered in a small voice.

A rough laugh escaped me. "Yeah, I see that. What's wrong with your wings?"

"Wing membrane is porous. Water soaks through and makes it impossible to fly. Why do you think I needed your help getting out of the bath?"

Truthfully, I'd thought she'd just been trying to embarrass me again. It took a great deal of effort to steer my thoughts away from the memory of her perfect body—particularly as she was currently making herself comfortable in my grasp once again.

"Kind of a stupid move, then, flying out here." I lifted an eyebrow, unimpressed by the idea of her being flightless and plucked up as an easy dinner for an owl or snake.

"You were the one who extended the invitation." An impish smile crept onto her face, pushing out the shadows lingering in her gaze. She caught her breath, looking up at me and wringing out excess rainwater from her tousled hair. "Is this going to be a regular thing with you? Pulling knives on me?"

I smirked at her. "Don't take it personally. I pull knives on a lot of people."

As my fluttering pulse settled, I glanced around me. The icicle I hadn't caught was buried in the trunk of a hearty pine ten feet away. Shuffling Sylvia to one hand, I walked over to it and wrenched it out of the tree.

"I'm so sorry, Jon. I wasn't thinking straight," Sylvia stammered, looking pale and shaky as she considered her handiwork. "I could have hurt you."

"Not even my top three near-death experiences—and trust me, it's a packed list. Don't worry about it."

The icicle in my hand had a pleasant weight to it, like a frozen blade. I turned it over, observing how the ice caught the light. A faint shimmer rippled in its depths, a mere whisper of its unnatural origins. It was painfully cold but slow to melt.

I weighed the ice, scanning the trees. I picked an oak no more than twenty feet away and hurled it as hard as I could. The icicle flew like a javelin, a sharp whistle sounding through the air. The ice embedded itself into the oak's trunk, making the branches of the oak shiver and shower water. A little smile touched the corners of my mouth as I imagined what a strike like that might do to a monster.

"Whoa. Nice shot," Sylvia said softly. She gave me a fleeting once-over, something akin to admiration gleaming under her long lashes.

"The ice doesn't shatter?" I asked, unable to keep the dumbstruck awe out of my voice.

"Not when I strengthen the spellwork. I was scared, so I didn't think about it. All instinct." Sylvia let out a shaky breath, staring across the trees to where her blade of ice glinted dully in the dusky light. "I didn't know I could conjure anything this big. I've never tried before. Karis would've killed me if I tried this in the training halls."

"Well, there's no one here now. You wanna try again?" I asked. "Shifting your target off me this time."

A conflicted expression came over her. "I should save my energy."

"Come on," I goaded. "How else are you going to defend yourself if I double-cross you in your sleep?"

She snapped her head up. My playful grin only seemed to make her expression sour further. "That's not funny, Jon."

I found a seat on a mossy boulder hugging the creek, where a proud oak offered shelter from the worst of the drizzle.

"What does your village have against you knowing how to defend yourself?" I asked.

"Elysia's been secure for nearly a hundred years. Ever since I found my affinity, I've been told over and over not to overshoot what counts as *reasonable* magic. To make myself smaller." Sylvia's confession came so softly that I had to lean in. "I've always hated that, but… I guess a part of me is a little scared at what I might be able to really do."

Her profile was illuminated as she spoke. The side of her face with the traitor mark was bathed in shadows, but its presence was known all the same. I imagined different ways to kill the fairies who'd hurt her.

"I don't understand why they wouldn't want you to do all that you can," I said.

Sylvia turned over her shoulder, eyes narrowed despite the bemused quirk of her lips. "You're not afraid I'll change my mind and freeze your heart?"

"Just a healthy amount." She tightened her jaw, and I offered a smile. "Your magic isn't witchcraft. I can see that. I think I'm finally getting a read on you."

She studied me, sliding her gaze back across the forest. After another steeling breath, she stood in my palm and flared her wings for balance. Whatever was holding her back was clearly no match for the hunger in her eyes. She wanted *more*, wanted to *do more*. I held my breath as Sylvia focused, flexing her hands open and shut in elegant motions. Frost and light were drawn to her hands like it was as intuitive as breathing. Fractals of ice shimmered in the darkness above her palms, not quite solid.

Thunder rolled above, and the magic vanished.

"Sylvia?"

No reaction. Her entire body was tense, knees touching, and ankles locked. Her wide eyes would not stray from the overcast sky. I remembered how she had flinched away from the window earlier in the evening. Now, it connected.

"Hey. Breathe through it," I said, keeping my voice low and gentle. "The fear."

When Sylvia acknowledged me, she had the fiery gaze of a cornered animal. "What do you know about fear?"

A cold laugh escaped me. "I'm afraid all the time! Every damn day." Gathering myself, I fixed her with a placating look. Fight or flight was etched all over her face. Flight I could handle. But if her spellwork exploded… "Look at me. You're stronger than whatever you're feeling."

"I don't think so," Sylvia muttered.

My frown deepened. "Yes, you are. You're not weak. On the other side of that fear is stillness. Precision. *Breathe*, Sylvia."

Her expression wavered. My nightmare last night couldn't have been far from her mind as she studied me up and down—it certainly wasn't for me. I didn't dodge her searching gaze. I let her see every ounce of brokenness and savagery that poisoned me.

Then, to my surprise, she closed her eyes and breathed deeply. The knot between her slender brows eased. Fractals of luminescent frost blazed over her wrists, blossoming strong within both of her hands. Water from the creek ribboned through the air toward her, collecting raindrops that followed like ants in line. When she opened her eyes, Sylvia gave a shout, and the water transformed, becoming a volley of icicles that shot across the misty forest like knives. Nearly two dozen at once flew at wind speed.

Sylvia looked back at me and beamed.

I was a little speechless at the display. The icicles varied in size and width; some were a spindly two inches, while others were as long as my forearm and nearly as thick. They were sharp enough to puncture on both ends, and I couldn't help but note how quickly a fight with a werewolf would end if Cliff and I were able to throw its body onto a bed of icy knives while we harvested its heart.

"No offense, but your village can go fuck itself." I lifted my eyebrows at Sylvia, who tossed me a musical laugh that was equal parts indignant and delighted. "I'm serious! If this area had been crawling with monsters, they'd all be skewered right now."

"Would that kill them?" she asked.

"For most of them, it would be a solid start, at least."

Her wings gave a little flutter that I was coming to understand meant she was pleased. "I should be horrified, but… Thank you."

"I'm just a little surprised that thunder scares you more than an actual, living monster," I said.

"Can't that be part of my mysterious intrigue?" Sylvia shrugged with equal parts humor and embarrassment. "I know it doesn't make sense. It's an old childhood fear. Normally, I'm underground when it storms."

I hummed thoughtfully. "It's hard to imagine you living in underground tunnels like a rabbit."

"It's not like that," she said rather defensively. "But it's not very much like your motel, either. It's... *home*. Horrifically boring sometimes, but safe and beautiful." She sighed, brow knitted. "It's not all bad. I wish you could see it."

"I'd love to visit, but..."

"One treason at a time." Her eyes drifted back up to the tree canopy. "Thunder is mostly blocked down there. Glamour has something to do with it. Some rumbles are too big to be ignored, though." She shuddered without an ounce of irony.

"I'm starting to think we need a scary scale for *you*." I held my hand at waist level, bringing it higher with each word. "Werewolves. Iron. Thunder."

She hummed and crossed her arms. "I'm not abandoning the hunt, but I have to admit... I'm starting to see why the council is so strict about keeping us in place. There doesn't seem to be an end to the chaos out here."

"Hey, I'm not gonna let anything happen to you. I promised Hazel, didn't I?"

Sylvia raised her hand over her head and gave me a pointed look. "You forget who's at the top of the scary scale. That sweet smile doesn't change who you are. You're a killer."

"Sweet, huh?" Though my grin widened, my insides deflated. She was right. Who was I kidding? She didn't know half of what I'd done, but it was like she could see the aura of brutality clinging to me. She was sunlight, and I was broken beyond repair.

Nonetheless, I prickled instinctively at a non-human hurling an accusation like that at me. "Don't act so innocent," I said.

"Look around—you've got the ability to rip anything apart without even touching it. How's a gun any worse? You're a living weapon."

"You don't know a damn thing," she snapped, playfulness vanishing. "Magic is more than just violence and survival. It's… *everything*."

The rain fell harder, slipping between the leaves more frequently. Sylvia pursed her lips and lifted both hands. An incantation was at her lips. I leaned back, ready to dodge whatever she was about to conjure. My anxiety spiked when I realized she was affecting the raindrops themselves. They were slowing down, shivering in the air.

"Sylvia—" If she decided to make it rain razor-sharp icicles to prove some kind of point, I wouldn't stand much of a chance at dodging.

As the temperature dropped dramatically, I braced myself to stop her. She spread her fingers wide and said the final words of her spell with conviction. Change came gradually, then all at once. The pattering of raindrops slowed around us. The droplets turned white and fluttered gently to the ground while I gaped. Snow stuck to the damp ground, gathering in clumps.

Speechless, I held out a hand to catch a few flakes. Same as her icicles, the snow didn't melt in a hurry. The product of her spell clung to my palm. Her fingers glistened unnaturally, but oddly, that didn't fill me with unease. Unless the snow could somehow be poisoned, I didn't see how this enchantment could be dangerous.

Lure. Angler fish.

But the growing peace on Sylvia's face said otherwise. The spell brought her a simple joy.

Beyond our vicinity, I could see past the influence of her enchantment. Rain still pooled like normal outside the misty bubble. She had created our own personal winter wonderland with a few words and a wave of her hands.

"Some things are just meant to be beautiful," she said as though she could read my mind. She twisted her hands in my direction, sending a little gust my way.

A playful flurry of snow swirled around me. As snowflakes brushed my cheeks, I remembered my mom blowing a handful of snow at me while we waited for the school bus during the first snow of winter. We had battered each other with snowballs, laughing breathlessly by the time the bus turned the corner.

For a moment, I swore I could see that gangly teen standing there with us in the woods, his head tipped back toward the sky with a dumbstruck smile.

If my mom could see Sylvia's magic now, would she assume fairies were benevolent nature spirits or unearthly beasts?

"You learned this from your books?" I asked, blinking away the wetness in my eyes.

Sylvia's expression became more guarded. "My father taught me. He was beside himself with pride when we discovered I had the same affinity as him." An impish smile twitched on her lips. "I know you'll be shocked by this, but I was a vicious little thing as a child. I wanted to know the most powerful spells. He showed me how to channel magic for beauty as well as power. Back when he was still… *him.*"

I know what it's like to lose a father, she'd said last night.

"Sounds like he was a good teacher," I told her gently. When she didn't elect to divulge more, I cleared my throat. "You said magic's everything. What would happen if you didn't do it?"

She lowered her hands. Raindrops began pattering like normal again. "Well, I wouldn't die from it," she said. "Affinity magic manifests one way or another. Going weeks without use can lead to a burst. But even going a few days without ice, I'd feel… empty."

Without warning, her stance wavered, eyelids fluttering. It was like an invisible gust had tried to sweep her off her feet. I lunged to put my other hand around her, offering support. She didn't even protest, holding onto my middle finger to steady herself. I bit back a shudder—her skin was freezing cold.

"Seems like *using* it leaves you empty," I muttered. "Are you okay?"

Her smile was forced. "I've just overworked myself, that's all. Sure, magic takes energy, but it's worth it. Like… working on a masterpiece and being exhausted but accomplished after. Or staying up all night reading a good book." Her gaze dug into me, searching. "So… Am I still just a living weapon to you?"

Out of everything she'd been put through so far, somehow, the realization that I'd hurt her feelings put the biggest lump in my throat. She'd been branded as a traitor by her people, yet here she was, seeking *my* approval.

"I shouldn't have said that," I muttered. "You've convinced me otherwise, I promise."

Sometimes, I could read her like a book. Now, her eyes swam with a mixture of mischief and something deeper, darker that made me want to squirm.

"Say it," she said suddenly.

My eyebrows rose. "Excuse me?"

An impish smile spread across her face as she elaborated, each word dangled like a challenge. "I want to hear you say it. 'Sylvia is *good*. And incredibly talented, sweet, ravishing—'"

A deep laugh caught in my chest. "I'm not saying that!"

"Then I don't believe you." She shrugged, wings fluttering in sync with the movement.

I bit my lip. Something about the way she sat there on her knees, blustering confidence from the palm of my hand… It drove me crazy. If I just curled a fist, I could end her in a second. But she trusted me. *Teased* me.

I lowered my voice, watching her face closely as I murmured, "Sylvia is *inolvidable.*"

Her eyes widened, focused on only me like the frozen forest had vanished.

"What does that mean?" she asked in a reverent hush.

Unforgettable.

"It means," I said, punctuating each velveteen word. "Stop screwing around when we're getting soaking wet."

A moment passed before she blinked, leaning away with a startled giggle. She turned her face up toward the sky.

"Well, looks like we won't have to worry about that much longer," she said.

I followed her gaze. She was right—the storm was beginning to pass, much to the relief of the ice-cold jeans clinging to my skin. Clouds drifted apart to reveal a twilight sky between the dark outlines of the forest. Stars freckled the periwinkle swath of color. Sylvia squeezed my finger, noticing the Waxing Gibbous moon the same instant I did.

"It's lovely," she sighed. "Isn't it terrible that something so beautiful should be dangerous, too?" Then, with a delighted gasp, she scrambled to her feet. "Oh—look! You can see the String of Sapphires!"

I squinted at the sky. "The what?"

Sylvia chuckled, reaching for my right hand, which was still cupped behind her. She guided my index finger to extend, leveling it to point toward a faint cluster of stars.

"I think we call that one the Big Dipper," I said. "Though I'll be honest, I don't know many of the constellations by sight."

She scoffed. "How can you tell direction when you're hunting at night, then?"

"GPS." I bit my lip to keep from laughing when she squinted up as though she expected to see those letters written in the sky. "What other ones do you see?" I asked.

She pointed and named so rapidly, I couldn't hope to keep up. *The Silverwing's Path. The Fox's Harp. The Eternal Chalice. The Whistling Arrows.*

"I think that one's part of Orion's Belt," I cut in, eager to not be completely lost. "But my mom used to call it *Cacibajagua*."

Tearing her eyes away from the stars, she gave me a blank look. "That word..."

"It's Spanish," I said.

Her lips parted with delight. "So you *do* speak another language."

I rubbed the back of my neck, wincing. "Not as well as I used to. Lack of practice over the last decade took a toll. My family would give me an earful if they knew."

"Would your mother be angry?" she asked, glancing down at my bracelet.

My throat closed. "Without a doubt. I got a C in Spanish class once, and she threatened to send me to live with family in Puerto Rico for a year. That's where she was born."

"*Puert-o Ric-o*." Sylvia pursed her lips thoughtfully. "Can you say that constellation again?" When I did, she cleared her throat, and with a great deal of effort, she echoed, "*Caciba-hag-ooha*."

A shiver raced through me at the sound of Spanish on her lips. Unnatural, yet enticing all at once.

"That wasn't terrible," I said too brightly.

"Don't patronize me."

"Just try again. Relax your tongue."

Her next three efforts improved marginally, and her cheeks flushed when I finally couldn't hold back my snickering. She crossed her arms haughtily.

"Stars, I'll have to give you some Fae to pronounce," she muttered.

"You say that a lot," I pointed out, sobering. "*Stars*. Do your people worship them or something?"

"Not exactly. We revere them. Back when fairies roamed freely, the stars helped them navigate from village to village. The old ways have become muddled over time, but we like to believe that our final resting place is up there."

I didn't have the heart to tell her otherwise. Then again, what did I know? The general public was practically blind to the monsters living under their noses. I couldn't begin to have authority on the stars.

"I never thought about humans having different cultures amongst themselves," Sylvia admitted. "If you had any beliefs, I assumed they'd all be the same. Seems like we all like to name the stars, though."

She sat cross-legged in my palm, gaze swimming with memories. Her face was tilted up toward the sky, which was slowly staining deep hues of indigo.

"I used to sit with my father during his Entry Watch shifts some nights," Sylvia murmured. "Even Mother was giddy to join us back in those days. He'd pick the highest branches, and we'd sit there for hours sharing stories about the warriors up in the stars."

I followed her gaze. It had been a long time since I paused to simply take in the beauty of the night.

"Sorry," she tacked on, hastily wiping her eyes with a smile. "It feels like another life now, anyway. He's been gone for nearly a decade now."

She looked so broken by the memory, I found myself wanting to pry more. To comfort her. To know everything about her. She wasn't human, but her grief was as real and vulnerable as anyone's.

"Some losses disrupt our entire world," I said softly. "All that anger and grief simmering inside, taking and taking until you have nothing left to give. Until it feels like that's all you are—a vessel for that rage."

Sylvia went very still in my grasp. I glanced down to find she was already looking at me. She smiled and shook her head, tears still glinting in her eyes.

"That's exactly it," she murmured. "Sometimes… I'm so *angry* at him. But more than anything, it hurts. I'm so tired."

"How did he die?" I asked tentatively.

"He would experiment with magic in ways that became unstable. He bit off more than he could chew, I suppose. One night… he was gone."

He was gone. The words made me have to catch my breath, and she noticed. Her gaze was meaningful, searching far too deeply. I couldn't help but feel like she *saw me.* She understood something dark in me, even though we never should have met.

Her bare shoulders pinched as she chuckled darkly. "Look at me, baring my soul to a *hunter* of all things."

"How do you think I feel?" I muttered.

"I honestly have no idea." Sylvia turned, fixing her full attention on me as though she might try to read my mind.

I lifted my eyebrows in a silent challenge, holding her gaze—though it became more difficult as the seconds dragged. As she studied me, I felt the invisible thread between us manifest again, tugging. I wondered if she felt it, too—wondered if it terrified the shit out of her like it did me.

"You may have a read on me," she said, "but I'm still figuring *you* out. Sometimes, you're terrifying, but other times… you're nothing like what a hunter should be. You're all wrong."

Scoffing, I lifted her a bit closer. "Since you're an expert, tell me what I'm doing wrong."

She leaned forward gamely. "Hunters shouldn't appreciate the beauty of the stars. Hunters shouldn't know how to touch a fairy without crushing their wings into dust." Something softer flickered in her gaze. "You don't strike me as someone who's meant to be so lonely. Why would you choose to live like this?"

I stared hard at her. No one had ever questioned me so gently about this. "Someone has to keep people safe. I have to do this. I *want* to do this."

What else am I good for?

"What about when you don't want to anymore? What will you do after?"

Shaking my head bemusedly, I glanced away. "There's nothing after. Chances are, something's gonna take me out sooner or later."

Sylvia winced, but she cleared her throat and nodded. "A warrior's death is honorable, I suppose." But she sounded so glum about it.

"Hey. It's thanks to you that I can live to fight another day."

"You don't see coming back from the brink of death as an opportunity to stop?" she challenged. "A second chance?"

"I can't just forget what's lying in wait out there." Surprised by how insistent she looked, I added, "It may not make sense to you, but I feel like if I stop saving people, I'm bound to slip up like my dad. Something in him was susceptible to darkness. The same could be in my blood, waiting."

Sylvia appeared strangely heartbroken. "But there's so much light in you," she murmured.

My breath caught, and I swiftly changed the subject. Eyeing her traitor mark, I noted, "The swelling's going down."

She gave a start, cheeks pinkening as she hurriedly brushed her hair in front of her face. I brought my other hand close, pausing her movement with a fingertip.

Turn away. The thought pulsed through me, electric and aching. *Pull away from me. Make this easier.*

Gingerly, I tucked her hair back. When her wide-eyed gaze met mine, I wanted to assure her again that she was still pretty. It felt like such a childish, frivolous assurance, but I wanted to see her shame melt away.

"You're staring again," she said.

"Is that a bad thing?"

She sucked in a shaky breath. "In your case? I think so." The air was charged between us despite the lingering chill. Sylvia broke eye contact first, pushing my touch away and squaring her shoulders. "So, did you find anything out here or not?"

Blinking hard, I straightened.

"Footprints," I said. "Someone's been watching us. Probably Nolan. He's long gone by now. I'm sure I saw him peeling out of the parking lot this morning. We should head back so we can settle on our next move."

She nodded. The rain was gone, but she still gave her wings a pitiful flex and peeked up at me with those wounded kitten eyes Cliff griped about so often. "I created a snowy wonderland for you. I don't suppose a ride back to the motel is too much to ask in return?"

"I'll muster up the strength." I heaved a groan, making her giggle.

As we approached the treeline, she tapped my palm to get my attention. Bringing her higher, I noted that her easy smile had faded into something more contemplative.

"How many werewolves have you killed?" she asked.

"This will be the sixth."

She pursed her lips. "Is there any chance Nolan will go quietly? Maybe he'll see reason, like Alice."

"Sorry, but it won't go down like that." Spotting the argument rise on her face, I added, "We got lucky with Alice. Who knows, maybe since you were around to talk to her, her spirit softened. Most ghosts turn malignant long before she started to."

The quarrel in Sylvia's expression dampened. "She always made me feel uneasy, but it was worse in the end. If her lover's spirit was there, do you think she could have stayed happy?"

"If they were happy, they wouldn't be there at all," I explained. "Spirits stick around because they badly want something they can't have. Love, revenge, closure. It's what drives them crazy. Desire eats at them like poison until they've lost everything else about themselves."

She shuddered as I made my way onto the field that separated the forest from the motel's property. "If you were to die, is there someone your spirit would be waiting around for?" she asked.

"Is that your extremely morbid way of asking if I'm seeing anyone?"

"You lead a morbid life. Expect morbid questions."

I chuckled. "One, if I were to die, Cliff knows what to do to make sure there's no chance for my spirit to manifest. Two, I'm not exactly boyfriend material. If you haven't noticed, I'm a little fucked up."

Sylvia pursed her lips. "That's true."

I shot her a flat look, but she only grinned wider.

"A relationship can only go so far in this line of work. It's not like I could keep hunting in secret forever." I laughed bitterly. "Last girl I tried to come clean to about what I really do, who I really am… She tried to have me locked up in a psych ward."

"What's that?" Sylvia asked.

"It's a place for people who aren't mentally well. It's… complicated. Some of those places help people—others make it worse. But the bottom line is, I'm *not* supposed to be there." The memory pained me: sterile sheets and the echo of heavy doors closing. Before I knew it, I was ranting. "Over my dead body, I'd be dragged back into that place, waiting for Cliff to bail me out. This time, there's no way he'd have the pull to bribe any hospital directors into releasing me."

When I was met with silence, I wished I could take it all back. I chanced a peek at my hands, expecting to find Sylvia looking up at me in horror. Instead, her overwhelming compassion had returned.

"I think I can sympathize." She sighed, kneading the bridge of her nose. "Damian thinks I'm out of my mind, and there isn't much I can do to change that. We used to tell each other everything. Lately, I just feel like I'm too much or not enough. Never the right amount."

One of her fingers idly traced a line in my palm. What would life be like for her when she went home? She claimed that Damian didn't want to see her hurt, but seeing me so close to the village may have pushed him over the edge. A protective pull stirred in my chest as I wondered how her people might punish her further.

Execution.

Telling myself that she was a means to an end was getting harder.

"Isn't there anywhere else you can go?" I asked. "There have to be other fairy villages out there, right?"

"I've always wanted to visit other communities, but I don't know where they are." The desolate look on her face broke my heart. "There's an old map in the archives, but it's decorative by this point. It hasn't been updated since the Elders stopped opening the village to nomads years ago."

"I doubt entire villages are picking up and moving. Maybe you could find one, even if the map's outdated."

She winced and whipped her head to the side. A huff shivered through her. "Right. One look at my face, and they wouldn't want anything to do with me anyway."

Before I could begin to conjure any comfort for that, she suddenly turned her head the other way, eyes wide. She rubbed her ears and hissed, "*Shut up.*"

My muscles tensed as she straightened and searched all around us, squinting like there might be something lurking within the rain. I came to a stop, prepared to draw a weapon.

"The werewolf?" I whispered.

"No, it's…" Her breaths came heavily. "Jon, I need you to be really quiet and *listen*. Can't you hear them, too?"

I frowned at her, but I tried to listen. All I could hear was the distant rush of cars and her little panting. Her mouth tightened into a pleading grimace when I shook my head.

"I'm not crazy," she insisted. Then, she blinked hard and snapped her head to the side as though she was listening again to something I couldn't hear.

"If it's not the werewolf, what is it?" I asked.

Seconds ticked by, stretching into half a minute.

"Nothing," she said finally, her voice less frantic. "I'm sorry. It's just nerves. Can we go inside? And can you fill the sink with the hottest water imaginable?"

I believed her that she hadn't sensed the werewolf. But it certainly hadn't been *nothing*.

Distrust threatened to overshadow the rapport we had built. After everything she had shared with me, she was *still* keeping secrets. But there was no forgetting how she had saved my life. There was a mark on her face to prove it and a hostile home that had turned its back on her.

I cupped my hands closer around her and headed through the parking lot. I would keep her safe—*and* figure out what the hell she was hiding from me.

26

SYLVIA

"I was no more than four summers when illness ravaged me. It was a rare case, awoken when I stumbled onto a witch's cursed ground. The healers decided I was a lost cause. My father refused to give up."

Both hunters were asleep. And this time, Jon's night appeared to be dreamless. I was relieved for him. Sometimes, the look in his eyes scared me. It made me wonder if people could be as haunted as houses.

I huddled behind the alarm clock as I read by the light of my glow, heart pounding with the hope that I had *finally* found an entry that matched my situation.

Encounters with the Ancients, A Collection was the project of several generations of nomadic fairies. The book was an attempt to gather as many interviews and stories as possible regarding the Ancients. None of the tales were firsthand—a realization that came gradually with each entry I read. Each interviewee recounted the tales of families, friends, and rumors.

This particular case had happened in Elysia, perhaps even before Alice graced the halls of the Dottage house in life.

"I was too young, too ill, to understand at the time. But my father invoked the Ancient Ones, pleading for my life. They answered. I was healed, but any pain I experienced was mirrored by my father's own body. My mother said this didn't upset him—I was cured, and he was more than willing to endure my occasional scraped knee in exchange."

My hands trembled as I read faster, terrified that perhaps the father simply lived with the bond for the rest of his life. That wasn't a viable option for me.

"*But the Ancients were not finished with my father. My mother and the healers declared him mad within weeks. He claimed to hear voices—the voices of my saviors. They demanded more. His power. His life. He researched frantically to put an end to the madness, traveling from village to village as he withered. He heard tales that the Ancients' true names would be their downfall.*"

Breath catching, I flipped to the next page, disheartened to find that there was only one paragraph.

"Though he claimed to hear at least three voices, he could only uncover one true name: Laelithar. My uncle, a spell architect, researched arcane magic. He and my father declared that they had recreated a traveling rune that could send one's spirit into the spectral plane to confront the Ancients where they are most vulnerable. The Ancients fully drained my father of his life before he could confront them."

Below the entry, there was a circular rune and an incantation. I lifted my wide eyes to where Jon slept. His lips were slightly parted with peaceful breaths. He was blissfully unaware that he would soon end me simply by being alive.

By all accounts, I should have despised him. This man I barely knew would be all that was left of me—all because of my impulsive decision. But I thought of his face when he reached for the gently falling snow. He carried a world of suffering and violence on his shoulders, yet he found the capacity to be gentle with me.

He didn't deserve to die in that basement. No matter how self-preservation gnawed at me otherwise, I didn't regret saving him.

My attention strayed back to the Ancient's name written neatly on the page.

"Laelithar," I whispered.

Invisible fists closed around my heart and throat.

"*One name*," the voices hissed, overlapping each other. "*It will make no difference, child.*"

Their presence chilled me to the core. But if they were bothering to taunt me, they felt threatened. That should have filled me with hope, but the father in the written encounter had access to resources that I couldn't dream of finding now.

I was alone. Utterly alone.

We had narrowed the hideout location to two possible construction sites that Nolan had access to. "We" being used loosely, of course—I had sat on Cliff's shoulder while he scrawled addresses onto a pad of paper.

The first location was a half-finished parking garage next to a shopping plaza. After a quick inspection, Jon and Cliff decided the area was teeming with too much activity to possibly hide a werewolf. If the situation were less dire, I would have begged for more time to explore each and every one of the stores on the strip, brimming with human oddities.

The atmosphere shifted as we approached option two.

The warehouse was located on an industrious side of the city, where loud trucks and construction machines growled incessantly during the daytime hours. A sign fixed to the chain link fence that surrounded the building informed us that the renovation inside was stalled, offering a phone number to contact for questions. A thick padlock kept intruders at bay—apart from Jon, who made such quick work of picking the lock. I had hardly registered his movement before the chain fell in a heap.

The twist of unease I had felt outside the building strengthened into a vicious chill when the door shut behind us. A phantom weight settled in my stomach, my skin aflame with those terrible, inexplicable goosebumps.

The hunters trod carefully, guns drawn as their boots crunched on the gravel-strewn floor. Dust danced in the blocks of sunlight that filtered through gaps in the roof, creating an ethereal atmosphere. Other than that, there wasn't much light inside. The sounds of the city were muffled. Any screams from within these thick walls would be just as affected the other way around.

"This is it," I said, voice hushed as I flew between them. Even then, I was anxious I'd disturb the silence and provoke something terrible to happen. Every flutter of plastic tarping in the light breeze made me grip my snowflake charm for dear life. "It feels even worse than Lily's house. I think the werewolf transformed fully here."

"But it's not here now?" Cliff eyed me with a mixture of caution and skepticism. "How can you be sure?"

"Sorry, do *you* have a sixth sense for detecting monsters?" I whispered back. "You're a human. You wouldn't understand."

"Try me."

I huffed. "It's the difference between seeing a pile of bullets next to a gun and having a loaded gun pointed at you. I've got goosebumps, but I don't feel like I need to immediately fly for my life."

His mouth thinned, but he didn't press it.

When we had covered the first floor without incident, the hunters relaxed their weapons.

"Stay here," Jon said, jutting his chin at a ladder that led through a walkway covered by plastic tarps. "I'll scope out the floor above."

"I'll go with you," I said too quickly. Although the monster didn't seem to be present, I wasn't eager to let Jon out of my sight in a new location.

"There's plenty to check down here," Jon said, hoisting himself up. "Help Cliff. I'll shout if I need anything."

I opened my mouth to argue, but Cliff's side-eyed stare bored into my skin. Although his expression was unreadable, I could only imagine the analysis whirring behind his sharp gaze. Better to not give him a thread to pull on.

Piles of construction materials remained scattered around—stacks of lumber, concrete bags, and metal beams—all waiting under a blanket of sawdust for their intended use. Plenty of places for a werewolf to stash a body.

While Cliff and I split apart the search for any unfortunate victims, I was drawn to a reflective sheet of metal propped against the wall. My image was more distorted than the clear view in the washroom mirror, but there was no mistaking how weak I looked. My skin was dull, and there were bags under my eyes.

The hunters knew something was off. No matter how I tried to perk myself up in their presence or eat through my nonexistent appetite, I noted the looks they shared. My saving grace was that they cared more about the hunt than anything. I was just the convenient fulfillment to Jon's offered favor. Perhaps they simply wrote off my appearance and behavior as nerves. *I should tell them.*

Even when I tried to tear my eyes from my reflection, the mark on my face demanded to be noticed.

If my own people were disgusted by my actions, what hope did my tentative alliance with the hunters have? They couldn't know what I had done. With any luck, I could ensure Jon made it through the hunt unscathed, and I could search the archives more thoroughly for the other two Ancients' names before he threw himself in harm's way once more.

"Doing okay over there?" Cliff's voice jarred me away from my reflection.

Focus on the hunt. I squared my shoulders and flew to him. "I was just thinking I should make the first strike."

"Oh, really? Can't wait to hear this." Cliff folded his arms over his chest, following my path as I perched on a stack of lumber at his eye level.

"Guns are ear-shattering," I informed him. "What if the werewolf has more animals on its side? You and Jon move quickly for humans. I'll give you that. But there's no way for you to attack from a distance without immediately drawing attention to your location. Spells are better for that. I can strike and be out of sight in a blink."

He nodded all while I talked, clearly only half-listening. "Tell you what," he said the instant I paused for a breath. He pointed to another stack of lumber across from us. "Why don't you hit those with some ice?"

I looked between him and the stack, narrowing my eyes.

"You have my permission," he assured.

Although his insistence was unsettling, I murmured a verse to summon ice and then another to shape it, throwing my hand out. Icy shards lodged deep into the wood with hardly a sound.

"See?" I raised my eyebrows at him. "So much quieter than—"

Cliff moved so quickly that I didn't realize what he had done until there was a faint *thunk* across from us. I turned, jaw dropping. A knife was buried precisely in the center of my ice, and Cliff had another ready in his hand.

"You were saying?" He smirked at me.

My insides became as cold as the lingering ice on my fingertips. Any time I began to relax around these hunters, they were swift to remind me why I should be fearful.

"You don't have infinite knives," I managed.

"Doesn't stop you from carrying one around." He lifted a finger to jab the sheath at my thigh, but I took to the air before he could touch me. "I still don't get why a fairy would bother with a knife fight when you've got magic."

"Life's not all about violence." I pulled out my knife, weighing it in my hand. "It's a tool as much as a weapon. I've used it to cut through heavy underbrush while exploring. I'm useless with earth spells, and I'm not going to kill an entire plant with ice just to get through." Although the hunters had figured out that iron was my weakness, I didn't need to mention that my knife would be my only defense if that toxic metal made contact with my skin.

"You seemed pretty ready to slice me to ribbons back at Dottage. Do you even know how to use that thing?"

"When I was first coming into my affinity, my father taught me to use my knife as a conduit for more precision," I replied, the memory like a sunlit flicker in my mind. "Younger fairies need the control early on."

"Like a scope or some shit." Cliff nodded, taking a slight pause. "Sounds like no one ever taught you how to use a knife like a *knife*. Why don't we give it a go right now?"

I frowned at him. "What's the point? I doubt you and Jon would let me get close enough to the monster to draw a drop of blood."

"Don't worry about the werewolf. Fighting with a knife is good for honing your concentration. And who knows, if you're ever squaring off with a fairy who's got more firepower than you, they'll never see your knife skills coming. Like, what if you and your little boyfriend get into it again?"

"My—what?" My face heated, and I looked past Cliff as though Jon might choose that moment to come back down the ladder. "He told you about Damian?"

"*Damian*," he said, drawing out each syllable. "Sounds hot."

"I don't want to talk about him," I snapped. "Jon should have never—"

"Settle down," Cliff said. "Don't take it personally. We've known each other for nearly a decade—he tells me everything. Now, watch my stance. Mirror me."

He took a fighting position: legs spread and shoulders rolled back, his weapon angled expertly in one hand. I wondered how many monsters had been faced with this very image. Maybe the last thing they had ever seen.

I followed Cliff's lead, certain he looked more impressive when he did it.

"Relax your grip. You're squeezing that thing like it owes you money," Cliff said.

I glanced at my white knuckles. *Damn*, he was right. I adjusted, and Cliff showed me a clean, powerful jab forward. It looked simple enough, but he had no shortage of corrections.

Focus on wrist strength. Power comes from the legs. *Don't swipe that wide. Are you trying to stab something or fucking dance?*

I'd attempted perfect form and failed nine times before he stepped in and offered his hand as a living test target.

"Karis would love you," I panted, lunging toward his thumb with my dagger. I missed by a wide margin.

"Another lover of yours?" Cliff shot me a suggestive grin.

I gave him a flat look in return, but I couldn't hide my breathless chuckle. "She's my affinity mentor. You have her to thank for my ice being focused and not a blizzard every time I wield. She's uncompromising. Doesn't take shit when she knows we have more *control* in us."

"She sounds like a real peach."

Cliff moved his hand from my swipe, but I had accounted for that and lunged right. My dagger made contact, sinking deep into his palm. My triumph lasted for all of two seconds before Cliff gasped in pain. Blood welled from his skin.

I dropped the knife and stumbled back, my shoes scraping on the rough lumber. "I'm so sorry! I didn't mean to… I-I'm sorry."

"Relax, sweetheart," Cliff scoffed. "You think I'm gonna hit back or something?"

I swallowed hard, unable to convey that, *yes,* I thought he may have been minutes away from finding another box for me—maybe iron this time.

Cliff pressed a thumb over the cut, smiling at me even though a flicker of pain crossed his face. "That was a solid hit. For you, anyway. Good work."

"Thanks," I managed, still reeling. "Can I heal it for you, at least?"

"Save your magic for the hunt."

"Suit yourself." I scooped my knife off the floor and paused at the slick crimson staining the blade. For a human, this amount of blood was nothing. If my target had been a fairy, I could've killed them if I hit the correct mark.

"Here," Cliff said, offering me a stained handkerchief that had been stuffed in his jeans pocket. I used the corner to clean off the blood, nearly dropping the knife in my haste. His gaze softened at my shaky movements. "You get used to it. Over time, it's just like any other chore."

I coughed out a little laugh, shaking my head. There was no world where *getting used to it* was a pleasant outcome.

"Tell Jon I've had my fill of training if he asks," I muttered, sheathing the dagger back against my hip.

I thought Cliff was ignoring me, only to stiffen when I looked up and saw quite the opposite. His gaze had turned steely and searching, fixed unwaveringly on me.

"I want you to keep your distance from Jon," he said.

A lump lodged in my throat, blood heating.

"What are you talking about?" I demanded, my voice an octave higher than usual. *Shit,* he had to be the worst person in the world to be a bad liar around.

His shoulders pinched, and he cocked his head at me. "I see the way you look at him. You're still wearing this damn thing all the time." He flicked the snowflake charm at my hip. "Listen, I get it. You took one look in those dreamy brown eyes and started thinking in poetry."

"You think his eyes are dreamy?"

Cliff arched an eyebrow and plowed on as if I'd said nothing. "I don't know what your deal is—whether you're studying him for some kind of spell, or you're just good, old-fashioned hot and bothered—"

"Don't be ridiculous!" My forced laugh sounded quite like I was being strangled.

"Hey, no judgment from me. Well, a little." He squinted. "Would it technically be bestiality if he was into you?"

I glowered. "I should have stabbed you harder."

His gaze glimmered with mischief, but I didn't miss the very real wariness that sat in the curve of his faint smile. "I know you've got another agenda, shadowing us," Cliff said, jaw squaring. "I'm putting up with it—you saved his life. I owe you for that. After that, it's a clean slate."

I stared at him, wondering if there was any shred in him that would sympathize with the bargain I had made. Maybe there was a version of Cliff that would—the one who had grown up to be a horticulturist or a teacher. But he was a killer, just like Jon. Anything beyond a temporary alliance was a fantasy.

"I only want to make sure my home is safe," I said, digging my heels into the wood beneath my feet. "I'm not in a hurry to earn another permanent, agonizing traitor mark, in case you forgot."

"Good," Cliff grunted. "Jon's not my brother by blood, but he's the only family I've got left. If you fuck with him, some lines on your face are going to be the least of your problems."

My bravado faltered, replaced by an uneasy knot in my stomach. I swallowed hard, all notes of defiance silenced by the weight of his words.

"I'm counting down the minutes until this hunt is over," I said, firm and placating. "Believe me. You're both insufferable."

After a lingering consideration, Cliff gave me a nod of acknowledgment. His lips pulled into a smirk, a glint of amusement rekindling in his eyes. "Still one of the nicer things I've been called."

"Well, the day's still young." I folded my arms over my chest and eyed the hand I'd stabbed. "Are you *sure* I can't do a quick healing spell?"

He shook his head. "Keep your magic to yourself. I don't need it."

Although I had been the one to call him insufferable, a lump formed in my throat. He could smirk and inject levity into his voice all he wanted. The distrust in his eyes was unmistakable.

Before I could mask my hurt with snark, Jon's voice rang out from the second floor. "Hey—get up here—*now!*"

My heart slammed in my chest as I flew ahead of Cliff. He was barely halfway up the ladder by the time I reached Jon, my hands swimming in ice to protect him from injury. While no immediate threat was present, there was a rancid stench.

I gagged as I joined Jon in the dingy corner. A thin line of sunlight cut through the darkness, illuminating moss that clung to the haggard brick walls behind him.

That smell…

Cliff nearly barreled right into me in his haste to reach Jon—then promptly stopped short as he clapped eyes on what his friend was crouched beside.

Jon's flashlight was pointed at a cluttered pile of building materials he had ransacked. Beneath it all were several blue plastic tarps that appeared to have been tucked around human remains—and he'd unleashed the rotting scent through the second floor.

"Fuck," Cliff sighed.

I caught a glimpse of sunken flesh, bones, and hair that made me dart backward and clamp a hand over my nose and mouth.

"Is it her?" I croaked. "Lily?"

"I don't think so." Jon pushed to his feet, grimacing. "Wrong hair color. Might be another unreported victim."

Seeing a seasoned hunter affected by the scene sent an odd trickle of relief through me. Maybe I wasn't as pathetic as I thought.

While the hunters spoke to each other in low tones, I gathered myself.

My heart continued to pound from the awful sight. I tried to focus on something else—*anything* else. I needed to get the hell away from the corpse. My fear heightened when I looked down—the floor didn't appear particularly stable, and the last thing my body needed was for Jon to fall through.

The roaring pulse in my head wouldn't slow. The cold wash of terror continued to crash over me in waves. I had the desperate urge to fly far, far away, and I realized with a start that the sensation had nothing to do with the corpse.

"Something's here!" I shouted.

I looked in every direction as the hunters watched me wildly, guns drawn.

The beast wasn't coming up the ladder, that much I knew. I darted to the window in time to hear the roar of an engine. There was another car parked not far from the hunters'. It was leaving as swiftly as it had arrived, accelerating back onto the street like it had been spooked.

"That's the car I saw yesterday," Jon said. "Those marks on the back—"

"Wolf claws if I ever saw 'em," Cliff finished. "Big son of a bitch, too, by the look of it."

The primal fear in my veins eased once the car vanished, yet a new dread soon gnawed at my gut.

There was no doubt about it—the werewolf had been in the vehicle.

It was hunting us, too.

After hours of combing the streets, the hunters accepted that the werewolf was too far away for me to sense. It chilled me to the bone as they agreed that the werewolf had been in the motel parking lot early the other morning—so close to where I had been *sleeping*.

My eyelids were heavy by the time we got back to the room. While Jon and Cliff settled at the table with the laptop to draw a connection between the car and Nolan, I grabbed one of the nomadic journals. With what I had learned last night, I was too desperate about my predicament to pretend to focus on the case.

This journal, while not wholly on Ancients, focused on unusual forms of magic that had sprouted around Elysia the past few centuries. If there were any other recorded encounters with the Ancients who'd latched onto me, it had to be in these pages. While I scanned through lines of text, my attention was divided by the hunters' conversation.

"He's tracking us," Cliff huffed. "He was using Dottage to dump the bodies, but he knew he'd been found. Hell, he had to have seen the car and tracked it back here."

"What's he waiting for, then?" I chimed in. "If he knows where we are, why hasn't he attacked?"

"He's only dangerous when he transforms," Jon explained. He took a pause when he saw me at the edge of the table with an open journal on my lap. Suspicion clouded his gaze, but he made no comment. "Werewolves shift a few nights a month, and he must've picked up on the pattern. He's waiting until his full moon transformation tomorrow."

I nodded distractedly. Three to five transformations per month were typical, according to the hunters. It depended on how sated the werewolf's appetite was. The Waxing Gibbous triggered the first transformation of the cycle, riling up the monster to feed. The full moon inspired the deepest hunger, which would fade as the moon started waning.

My breath caught when I turned the journal page. The word *Ancients* leaped out at me.

"Ancients have also been known to attack humans when they are particularly desperate for vessels—or particularly bored. Humans have been known to mistake these encounters for hauntings or religious experiences. They have confused these entities with demons."

"It's him," Cliff declared, turning the laptop around.

I straightened up at the sudden volume of his voice. The screen showed a street-level view of the apartment building Nolan lived at. Sure enough, one of the several cars parked in the street was the same one that had been stalking us.

"He's keeping an eye on us while skirting away," Cliff said. "Tomorrow night, he won't be running off."

"And he knows we're ready to meet him head-on, too," Jon said.

I frowned. "Not *here*, I hope?"

"Nah." Cliff pulled the laptop back around to him. "This werewolf's been stashing bodies. It's smart enough to be discreet. The motel's too crowded. Dottage is swarming with police tape now that the security guard never came back. It's keeping tabs on us, and it knows we're coming after it. There's only one other place we have in common now."

"The warehouse," I said.

Though the answer seemed obvious, the hunters looked oddly proud of me. I tried not to be too flattered. Either they assumed I would be slow on the uptake of information, or they were pleased that I was truly beginning to think more like *them*.

A little hunter. How perfectly vile. So why did I want to smile back?

I returned my attention to the book in my lap as Jon and Cliff discussed strategy in low voices. The handwritten entries blurred as my aching eyes warred against fatigue. I reached a far more recent record.

"It's mid-winter now, following an abundant harvest. Elysia has never seen such a lively and ornate Solstice gathering. It was under the cover of this event that I attempted to make my discreet exit to venture back to the north cavern. Since my last visit, it has consumed my mind. I can't stop thinking about that perfect blue, the buzz of magic calling within. It's worth risking a traitor's lashing to evade curfew. Tristan thought otherwise. He all but froze my ass to my seat to keep me from leaving that night."

I became acutely aware that I had stopped breathing. *Tristan.* My father.

Suddenly alert, I hunched closer over the book, reading raptly.

"I ventured to call him a hypocrite, considering his own greed for the stones. But Tristan won me over—there will be other gems. Gems without the crooning beckon of unseen voices. If the Ancients seem eager to bless a fairy with such unimaginable power, there must be a catch."

The entry drawled on for another page, elaborating on the writer's theories on the Ancients themselves—whether they were truly ancient beings dwindling in numbers or once-fairies trapped in a spectral realm we can no longer reach.

I was keen to ponder this, but I found myself skimming for my father's name again, flipping pages rapidly.

On the second-to-last page, I stopped short, recognizing the heavy-handed, looping strokes of my father's handwriting. My fingertips trembled as I touched the dried ink and imagined him hunched over the book by flickering fae lights in the dead of night.

"No one reads this damn book anymore, not since Hyram. The Elders, in all their divine arrogance, claim me to be a danger to Elysia. I don't know how much more of their ignorance I can bear. The curfews

grow tighter, and the name of a gem scavenger becomes more spat upon each passing day. Melanie shares their concern, though I hope to pacify her. I see the fear in her eyes when I show her what I can do now with the power of two gemstones feeding my magic. It is a thing of beauty, of innovation—but these fools will never see that.

"There is a village a few weeks' flight from Elysia—Aelthorin. I have it on good word from a nomad who passed through. He described the journey to me in great detail, and it is my hope that I can bring my family there. Melanie protests the idea of leaving—our child is barely two. When Sylvia can fly, the conversation will change."

The hunters may as well have been in another room as I pored over the lines time and again, tears pricking at my eyes. So the long-standing rumor was true—my father had been more than a gem scavenger. He'd wanted to be a *nomad*, too, taking us away from Elysia altogether. I racked my memories but couldn't recall the discussion of leaving the village ever coming up between him and Mother. Not in front of me. Perhaps they'd changed their minds by the time I was of the age of reason.

Or maybe the Elders of the council had threatened to brand *him* as a traitor, too.

Many in Elysia would have been disgusted by the handwritten admission. To them, deserting Elysia was a vulgar and ungrateful longing. But I grieved anew. I was more similar to my father than I had ever known. It had been a long time since I had wished so ardently for a little more time with him. Even an hour. Just one more minute.

I tore the page out of the book and folded it neatly, tucking it into my belt.

I stirred from my racing thoughts as Cliff rose from his seat next to me, crossing the room to the refrigerator. He was taking his time, washing the one set of glasses that the motel provided. I took advantage of the vacancy in front of the laptop. He'd shown me how to search in the little question box.

I could ask it *anything*. Perhaps it was even more efficient than the archivist.

Elysian Elders had withheld truth before. They were willing to brand one of their own. Was it possible they had lied to me about how my father died? I hadn't been there. Mother had though. She had refused to leave with Father. She was more loyal to Elysia than her own family.

Maybe the truth was within reach.

With a firm hand on the trackpad, I moved the little arrow and clicked on the empty box, like Cliff had shown me. After considering the buttons before me, I hovered over the letters. I huffed, envying how the hunters' fingers could fly over the keyboard. I tediously spelled out *"tristan."*

Nothing happened.

"You have to press 'Enter'," Jon said, leaning over to see what I was doing. He frowned at the screen. "Tristan?"

My heart skipped, but I forced an unassuming smile. "An old friend who left the village years ago. I was hoping to find out what happened to him."

Jon chuckled. "It doesn't work like that. The only information you can find on this is put there by humans." He tapped the enter button, bringing forth a list of information and images of men I didn't know. "See? Is there anything else you want to know? I can help."

Smile tightening at the edges, I shook my head. "I'm better at figuring things out on my own. How about I give you a call if I need anything?"

He was well within his rights to stay, considering I had no ownership over the laptop. Nonetheless, he took the hint and pushed out of his seat. "Be careful not to smudge the screen," he said in a whisper. "Cliff's a stickler for that."

I wasn't ready to give up on looking for my father just yet. Even if humans didn't know about the fairy villages in their midst, perhaps they had seen things they couldn't explain. *The power of two gemstones feeding my magic*, my father had claimed.

After a few more clumsy searches, I spotted an item on the list that proclaimed "Ice Devastates Area." But it was nothing more than a rare winter storm that had blown through some years ago. I sighed, falling to a crouch on the trackpad. Of course, humans wouldn't have information about a lone ice fairy in their archives.

Chewing on my lip, I regarded the rows of letters again. The journal *had* mentioned that the Ancients preyed on humans at one time. My first few searches were too broad, but when I included the city name and "demon", I was rewarded with several promising items. The first few seemed irrelevant, sharing news about a local music festival.

I nearly passed the next one—"*Unearthing a Decades-Old Cult*"—before deciding to give it a try.

"*Recent research has uncovered the haunting tale of a cult that was once rooted in the area. The group, known as the Eclipsed, worshiped a malevolent demon under the belief that it would grant them immense power. Historical records and testimonies paint a disturbing picture of the cult's activities in the early 20th century.*"

The article went on to describe how the Eclipsed would offer sacrifices to the demon or make deals. Although the human cultists would be granted their desires, they would soon become sick after, drained of energy until they died.

My throat closed as I searched the article up and down, lightheaded. A name. I needed a *name.* The more the information unraveled, the clearer it became that the article's writer didn't really believe in the historical accounts. It was nothing more than a legend. A scary tale.

For me, it was life or death.

Morbid curiosity took hold of me, and I lifted a hand to conjure a small orb of light to my palm. Was every drop of my magic drawing from a finite tap now? Although the glowing spell itself wasn't powerful by any means, my ice displays at the warehouse and lack of sleep cost me. For a terrifying second, my vision went foggy, and I dropped hard on my knees on the keyboard.

"Hey. What's the matter with you?" Cliff's voice jarred me to alertness.

I hovered up swiftly, blinking hard. "S-sorry. Lost my balance."

He leaned from behind his chair and started to look at the screen, but I quickly returned to the search page.

"What are you looking for, anyway?" he asked. "The hunt's in the bag."

"You're awfully confident, considering you're about to face off against a beast that can rip you apart like a pastry."

"That doesn't stop *you* from running your mouth," he said, lifting a drink to his lips.

I wrinkled my nose, able to smell the alcohol from here. He treated grain alcohol like it was its own food group. "Should you really be drinking this much before a hunt?"

"Yes," he retorted dryly. "You would, too, if you'd seen half the things that I have."

"*If you'd seen half the things that I have,*" I said in a mockingly deep voice. "Is it the same you gave me before? Can I try some more?"

He downed the rest in a single gulp, then raised his eyebrows at me. "Try what?"

If I weren't worried about it killing me—either by hunter or magic-draining Ancients—I would have thrown a blast of ice at him.

27
JON

Before a hunt, the world always looked different to me. Colors were more vibrant, shadows deeper, and even the reluctant purr of the engine took on a sharper quality. Things like the gaudy neon sign for a late-night laundromat looked downright beautiful when I knew it might be the last one I ever saw.

Time warped as we drove through the city streets, seconds drawing out into minutes. The downtown sector brimmed with mundane, late-night activity. Families unloading takeout for dinner, friends chattering and embracing in front of a bar, homeless people sheltering in tents under the bridge by the river. A couple on a date paused in a dog park to admire the full moon adorning the night sky, unaware that it was a harbinger of bloodshed.

I gripped the steering wheel tighter, blazing through a yellow light. Many hunters had rituals before closing in on a creature as powerful as a werewolf. I'd seen some cling to voodoo, lighting green candles and tucking a mojo bag in their pocket before embarking. Others prayed, though, for the life of me, I couldn't understand their confidence. The same god who allowed monsters to roam the earth and murder innocent people surely couldn't be listening to a hunter's plea.

Cliff erred more on the side of those who drowned their anxieties in liquid courage the night before. To be fair, Cliff drank like a sailor, even between hunts. I was a little envious, in a way.

I'd never seen anyone be able to pound four manhattans and still have impeccable marksmanship.

I didn't need a ritual. I'd trained for the better part of a decade to become something that monsters feared when I drew my weapon. Still, my heart hammered in my chest, equal parts fear and bloodlust warring within me and sharpening my focus.

In an hour, this would be over. No more innocent blood would be spilled at Nolan's hands.

I looked at Sylvia, trying to keep my expression neutral as I took in the contours of her profile from where she sat on the middle console. She was the knockout punch in our corner—if her nerves held up. Her tense expression flickered in the passing streetlight. She'd changed into the heaviest top she had, but it still had a weightless, ethereal quality to it. The teal fabric shimmered like ocean waves every time the moon hit it. Like everything Sylvia owned, it seemed to be tailored specifically to accentuate her form. The back was cut low to accommodate her wings. A delicate v-neck traced the contours of her collarbones, while intricate cutouts at her shoulders and navel drew my eye.

In the back of my mind, a protective urgency screamed that she was too delicate to be anywhere near what was about to happen. I chewed my lip to keep from asking what was on her mind, worried she might agree with me and back out. She hadn't spoken much since this morning.

Her obsession with the laptop last night had been bizarre. A brief peek at the screen told me that her search had little to do with werewolves. She had smiled tightly when I asked again.

"*I'm checking if fairy legends overlap with human ones. How much longer will I have access to this knowledge, after all?*"

Though, she was mostly quiet while she carefully typed and scrolled through page after page. She finally broke the silence when she said something incomprehensible out loud: *Daeharice*. Her find appeared to satisfy her obsession for the night. The only reason I remembered the name was because I checked the search history after she went to wash up for the night.

Daeharice. A supposed demon that was connected to a cult back in the early 1900s.

If it weren't so vital to stay focused on the hunt, Cliff and I would be grilling her. She was still so feverishly adamant about participating that it was almost too easy to relegate her odd behavior to the background for the time being.

The warehouse blended in with the night sky as we pulled into the vacant lot, gravel crunching under the tires. As Cliff got out of the passenger seat to pull weapons from the trunk, Sylvia made to follow. I reached out, gently stopping her and guiding her hover back toward me.

"What is it?" she asked.

Last night, she was snappish. Now, exhaustion dripped from each syllable. Her eyes were alert, though, flicking toward the darkened windows of the warehouse behind me.

"Hey, look at me." I tipped her chin up with a finger. She was pale. The swirling strokes of the traitor mark were black now in stark contrast.

I hesitated. Losing such a powerful ally in this fight pained me, but—

"You don't have to do this," I said softly.

Sylvia touched the side of my finger and gripped it like a lifeline. Her voice was fragile and raw when she finally spoke. "I can't let you get hurt."

"You don't need to worry about me, Sylvia."

"Yes, I do." Something complex crossed her face—frustration, fear, affection, resentment.

My frown deepened. I wanted to hold her. "This is going to be ugly," I reminded her, letting my voice roughen. "Worse than the dogs. There are no words or journal entries that can prepare you for being near a full-moon werewolf."

"You don't understand." She wrenched away, shaking her head. "I put myself in danger to see this through. I left everything I've ever known to make sure this threat is dealt with in no uncertain terms. To try to convince me to sit this out after all I've done is just cruel."

With Cliff's car door shut already, there was no way for her to get out until I allowed it. When she came to that realization herself, she fixed me with a glare so severe that she would have fit in among a line-up of hunters based on expression alone.

Small. Delicate. Determined as hell.

I breathed out through my nose, giving her a nod. "Stay close to me in there. And if I say run, you *run.* Got it?"

The bags under her eyes were a little less pronounced when she smirked, teeth teasing her lower lip.

"So bossy."

"Sylvia—"

"Got it, got it. *Capiche.*"

I could only hope she meant it.

She vacated the car, wheeling around the back to look at the contents of the trunk. Our firepower was normally well-hidden, but tonight, every box and hidden compartment had been ransacked to make sure every silver bullet was at our disposal.

"Stars," she murmured when I joined her. Her face was turned toward me, but her eyes were locked on the small supply of iron we had tucked behind a bundle of sharpened pine stakes. She then regarded the multiple handguns we were tucking into our jackets and holsters, along with the shotgun I gripped at my side. "I thought we were only going after one werewolf," she said.

Cliff handed me an extra box of shotgun shells and raised his eyebrows at her. "Not like we can summon silver to our fingertips."

The padlock was still hooked on the chain link fence surrounding the warehouse, but as we neared, I realized I had no need to pick it this time. It was unlocked. It was hard to tell if this fucker was toying with us or just sloppy.

Metal hinges groaned as we pushed open the fence, sticking to the generous shadows cast by the pallets of plywood. There was a mobile floodlight on-site, but it was inactive. The only light cast was from the cloudless night sky.

A muffled sound floated across the darkness. Cliff and I exchanged a tense look as the strangled bark petered into a whimper. My finger fluttered over the trigger of my shotgun. Every muscle in my body prepared for another infected dog to tear around the corner of the building.

Sylvia flew ahead, and I had half a mind to yank her back. She perched on a brick that jutted out at the edge of the wall, peeking around the corner.

"That's his," she said in a thready voice.

Nolan's beat-up Mustang was parked by the back fence, where the property ended and the untamed woods began. The vehicle juddered as the distorted barking started up again. Something was locked in the trunk.

I didn't lower my gun until it became obvious that the creature was trapped. The whimpering launched back into nightmarish snarling as though it could sense the fresh meat standing right outside.

"Appetizer before the full meal?" Sylvia asked.

"Or maybe he was trying to contain his latest mistake," I muttered. "Carnage from a monster-infected dog isn't what I'd call lying low."

Cliff tucked his .375 caliber into the thigh holster strapped to his right leg. His gaze darkened as the car gave another violent lurch.

"Now I'm pissed. Monster or not, anyone who fucks with dogs needs to die," Cliff growled. He brushed a hand over the trunk as the distorted barking quieted back to whimpers. His expression twisted with anguish. "Sorry, sweetheart. We'll come back for you. You won't hurt much longer."

Cliff stepped around the side of the car, shining a flashlight into the tinted windows. Sylvia ignited a soft cerulean glow on her skin, lending an ethereal illumination as she pressed her hand to the glass.

"He was living in here?" The pity in Sylvia's voice was unmistakable.

A garbage bag of clothes was shoved in the backseat. I raised my eyebrows at a bra stuffed in between the driver's seat and the middle console. A bottle of body wash sat in the cup holder. Fast food wrappers covered everything.

"Someone really took advantage of that buy fifty, get one free deal," Cliff drawled under his breath.

The sheer volume was revolting. Dozens upon dozens of cheeseburger wrappers were piled in there. Shoved in between the seats and the doors, under the seats, spilling out of the paper bags they'd come in. My stomach turned as I noticed some were half-eaten and discarded, mold blooming on the greasy buns.

"He was trying to stave off the bloodlust," I said, catching Sylvia's bewildered gaze.

A pointless endeavor, but most people at least tried to avoid being flesh-eating monsters.

Sylvia's glow flickered. She whipped her head toward the warehouse, shuddering an exhale as she edged closer to Cliff.

"It's happening soon." Her thin voice sent a chill up my spine.

"How do you know?" I asked as calmly as I could.

"There's this scream at the back of my head begging me to fly in the other direction. It's worse than being near the dogs. Much worse."

I followed her rapt gaze to the second floor of the building. The unmistakable prickle of being watched washed over me, even though nothing but empty darkness occupied the window panes.

As Cliff and I approached the building, I half-expected Sylvia to stay frozen where she was, heeding that scream at the back of her mind. But the buzz of her wings trailed loyally behind me.

What moonlight we had was swallowed up as we entered through the side door to the warehouse. The gaping windows thirty feet above our heads framed glimpses of the starry sky and cast eerie shadows on the floor. I was keenly aware of every door and exit as we crept forward. An emergency light in the corner of the first floor cast a red glow across the half-constructed floor. The aging bulb buzzed erratically in protest like a dying bug.

Faint voices drifted across the floor, male and female. Muffled pleas whimpered in the background of the conversation. Sticking to the shadows, we advanced slowly and found the source of the distressed noises first.

"Fuck," Cliff breathed, stopping short and urging me to do the same.

Three people were restrained to a forklift, gagged and squirming. Rick and Charlie Astle, along with another woman. Visceral fear twisted in my stomach as two unbound people came storming around from behind the forklift, arguing.

"I don't want to do this anymore!" the woman wailed—Lily. I recognized her curly black hair, pulled back from her face in a simple ponytail with unkempt strands framing her face. "I didn't ask for any of this!"

"I know, baby." Nolan stepped in front of her, putting his hands out to stop her. He gripped her shoulders and pulled her closer. "I know it's not easy, but we have to—"

"No." She sobbed and twisted herself away. "You don't have a damn clue what I'm going through! How hard it is seeing those lifeless eyes when I wake up."

The sound of their voices, low and frantic, caught oddly in the immense space.

We were no more than twenty feet away when Lily turned her head sharply at our approach. She gasped, clutching Nolan's arm.

"Oh fuck," she hissed. The whites of her eyes gleamed with fear.

The captives surged with hope, shouting at us through the dirty cloths stuffed in their mouths. I could practically smell their fear. Nolan kicked the closest one in the knee, warning the others to shut up. Lily kept her eyes low as the muffled pleas quieted to whimpers. She stayed rooted in place like her ratty Converse were glued to the floor.

Sylvia burrowed against my neck, her body coiled with tension. From what she'd described of her sixth sense, I could only imagine what she was feeling right now, facing a werewolf in its guise on the night of a full moon.

"You really came." Nolan studied us, expression twisting into disdain."You're the fuckers who were looking for Lily."

He angled his body in front of Lily. The past weeks had obviously not been kind to Nolan. His eyes were sunken and bloodshot, jaw unshaven. He'd lost weight from the photos we'd found online—his faded Blink-182 tee and jeans seemed to hang off his frame.

But he hadn't transformed yet. Despite the full moon watching above, his mind was still somewhat his own.

"You've been messy," I called over. "You had to know this was coming, Nolan."

The twin silver knives lining the front of my jacket sang to me, begging to taste blood. I kept my gun level, fixated on every muscle twitch Nolan made.

"Look at that," Cliff said, jutting his chin toward two piles of chains and ropes that waited beside the struggling captives.

"Saving room for dessert? I'm flattered, but I'm more of a main course."

"I know what you are," Nolan said, somewhat breathless. "Knew you'd catch up with us sooner or later. Did my research when I saw that arsenal you brought to the old house. Hunters." He sneered at the word. "People die everywhere you go."

Those people die at the hands of evil fuckers like you, I wanted to shout.

"Then you know what comes next," I said. Despite everything, the sound of Sylvia's panicked breathing by my ear made me pause and remember her innocent question about Nolan going down quietly. "We can make it quick," I told him. "You'll barely feel a thing."

A sickening chill ran through me as I looked between him and Lily, who was trembling behind him. Nolan had been keeping her alive. My mind swam with images of him keeping her locked up somewhere, putting distance between them during transformations so he wouldn't kill her.

Nolan caught my gaze, eyes narrowing when he saw me looking at his girlfriend. He growled—actually growled—and pulled a gun on us. "If you lay a hand on her, I'll kill you!" he screamed in a hoarse voice. "Do you understand me? I will fucking kill you."

Cliff fired a warning shot that grazed Nolan's shoulder and made him stagger back. The victims flinched.

"Be a good boy and heel," Cliff said. "We're not after your girl."

Lily leaped in front of Nolan. "Don't hurt him!"

"Get the hell back, baby," Nolan snarled, wrenching her behind him again.

I frowned deeply, mind racing as I eyed the compact pistol in Nolan's shaking hands. What werewolf relied on a gun when their body was a perfect, lethal weapon?

"Leave. Us. Alone," Nolan said through his teeth. "You can't have her."

I readied my finger on the trigger. Cliff and I shared a nod. One look and I knew we were on the same page.

But Sylvia was not. "No, wait!"

The shotgun's metal suddenly became unbearably cold. I didn't drop it, but I flinched in tandem with Cliff, who clearly got the same treatment.

"What the fuck, Sylvia!" He shook out one hand. The sensation was fading now that she had our attention. Cliff was still poised to shoot, but he threw a glare over his shoulder at her.

"Don't kill him," she said slowly, uncertainly. She took to the air and fixed me with a pleading stare.

This was hardly the time for her to go soft. I didn't look at her, saying, "We have to—"

"It's not him," Sylvia said sharply, realization laced with horror.

A gunshot went off, but not from us. Nolan missed by a wide margin, trying to take advantage of our distraction. We blocked Sylvia from view, so he must have assumed we were arguing amongst ourselves. Before Nolan could fire off another round, Cliff shot Nolan's right hand. Nolan's gun clattered to the ground while he yowled in pain.

"No!" Lily shrieked. She rushed to Nolan's side, gingerly taking his arm. Tears rolled down her face. She turned to us, panting. "You hurt him," she gasped. "You hurt him!" She gritted her teeth and leaned her forehead onto Nolan's shoulder, her chest heaving.

"Baby…" Nolan huffed in pain. "Let go."

Sylvia's words throbbed in my mind like a racing heart. *It's not him.* How could it not be—

"Jon, it's *her*!" Sylvia shouted.

Lily lifted her head, an unnatural fury contorting her features. Her mouth stretched beyond what should have been possible, a snarl ripping through.

The restrained prisoners screamed through their gags, writhing furiously.

Lunging forward with unnatural speed, Lily pounced toward me. I yanked the shotgun up with lightning speed, muscles reacting on pure instinct. The cold metal barrel met my shoulder in an instant. Before I could pull the trigger, a blast of ice exploded behind me, slamming the half-transformed humanoid against the wall.

"Lily!" Nolan choked out, but he was too locked in pain to do more than kneel and search the ground for his gun. And then he froze, abject horror draining the color from his face as his girlfriend contorted on the ground.

Lily's bones cracked wetly as they reshaped beneath her skin, elongating. She turned her head toward Nolan, eyes flayed with tears. Her clothing shredded like paper as her spine arched. Vertebrae stretched her mottled skin, and she loosed a guttural howl that made hairs rise on the back of my neck. Her brown eyes squeezed shut, becoming predatory black pools flecked with gold.

Sylvia made a strangled noise behind me. I stole a quick glance—she looked like she was going to be sick. "Fucking stars," she said softly.

The line between human and monster blurred until there was nothing left of Lily before us. The werewolf turned its snout toward the bound hostages, baring a mouth of dagger-like teeth as it sniffed the air. Nolan scrambled back against the forklift, cowering in its shadow. One of the men—Rick—shut his eyes and started to pray out loud, words muffled through the cloth.

"Hey! Us first, bitch," Cliff barked, drawing those glossy eyes onto him.

Adrenaline surged in me, taking hold. The world narrowed to a pinpoint—a single, living target. Cliff and I took aim and buried shot after shot into the werewolf's matted hide. It staggered, eyes flashing malevolently even as it retreated to lick its wounds. Long nails scrabbled against the floor as it galloped out of range, darting into the shadows with a low, rumbling snarl.

I ejected the spent shell with a practiced flick and forced my fingers to steady as I slid a fresh one into the magazine. I closed the shotgun's action, sending a satisfying *snick* echoing across the first floor.

"Get them out of here!" I shouted, hardly needing to turn my head to see that Cliff was already breaking away toward the victims.

Wings and icy air sped behind me as I bolted toward the shadows.

The hunt was on.

28

SYLVIA

Cliff was an excellent artist—one of the best I'd ever encountered—but charcoal strokes couldn't have prepared me for seeing a fully-transformed *mactir* in person. Even when it retreated into the shadows, the awful image stuck in my mind.

Lily. There was no sane way to reconcile this beast with the trembling human who had been standing in its place mere moments before.

Silence washed over the warehouse, crackling with tension. It was a silence I could drown in.

Unlike me, the hunters weren't reeling. They moved with dizzying precision. Cliff cleared the distance to the victims and knelt, removing the cloth muzzling Rick Astle.

"Where did it go?" Rick asked, deep voice quavering. His wide eyes darted around the shadows before settling on Cliff, who was diligently sawing through the rope binding Rick's hands together.

A faint, unsettling rustle echoed. A shiver of fear rippled through the hostages, gazes darting about wildly. My heart pounded in time with their terror, threatening to deafen me.

I tracked my flight as close to Jon as I could while he made a wide, slow circle of the area. He kept his gun pressed to his shoulder, his fingers tensed on the trigger.

"Can you sense where it went?" Jon asked, eyes cutting toward me.

I shook my head, stammering, "Not exactly."

"There's an exit twenty feet behind me." Cliff's voice was a commander's growl as he addressed the hostages. "Get the hell out of here, don't look back. No matter what you hear, don't stop. Got it?"

Nolan stirred at the end of the line, making to follow Jon as he crept toward the back wall. Blood soaked Nolan's front. He was using the balled-up edge of his shirt to stifle the bleeding on his wound. Cliff snapped his head up.

"Not you, asshole," Cliff snarled. "Don't move a fucking inch unless you want a hole in your other hand."

Nolan didn't budge.

When Rick was freed, Cliff passed his knife to him and pulled another blade from his seemingly endless arsenal. "Work on him," he said, nodding at Charlie. Cliff moved onto the unknown woman, removing her gag and assuring her that everything was going to be alright.

"Who are you guys?" the woman asked.

Cliff glanced up at her as he sawed at her bindings, a glimmer of mischief buried behind the intensity in his green eyes. "We just watch a lot of horror movies."

Something creaked behind us. I whipped my head around in time to see a wrench topple off a tower of pallets and clatter on the ground.

"What was that?" Charlie's face was ashen.

Cliff sawed faster.

It seemed impossible that a creature twice the size of either hunter could move with such stealth. I gazed intently at the corners of the warehouse, eaten by darkness where the stark crimson glow of the emergency light didn't reach.

What was it waiting for?

The certainty of being watched made me feel like I was going to toss up the early supper I'd forced down. Fresh dread sank into me like an icy hand was reaching into my chest and gripping my heart.

Realization stole my breath. Perhaps the werewolf shared the same awareness as me. Its mind screamed at the presence of my magic the way I sensed its malevolent form.

"Jon, it knows I'm here," I whispered.

A low, resonant growl cut through the tense stillness.

Throttled by the desperate urge to flee, I drifted closer to Jon. There was no option for self-preservation. Staying would draw the werewolf's attention. Retreating would leave Jon vulnerable to an attack.

As Jon drew a slow breath and aimed in the direction of the growl, manic hope thrummed through me. Maybe one good, ear-shattering blow could bring an end to this.

"D-don't!" Nolan cried, his throat raw as he staggered toward Jon. "She'll change back by morning! Help us figure something out so she doesn't have to—" Nolan froze, his eyes locking on me and widening. "W-what the *fuck* is that?"

Jon stepped forward to block me from view, casting a murderous glare at Nolan. Although my skin prickled from the sensation of having another human look at me, I could almost laugh at how unafraid I was of him. Between werewolves and Ancients, a mere injured human was hardly a threat.

A snarl ripped through the darkness. The monster burst into the open. My mouth went dry at the horrid sight of its long limbs scrambling toward us. Those viciously blank eyes were aimed at *me.*

"Don't!" Nolan lunged into Jon, knocking his aim off.

Despite that idiotic move, Jon's instinct to protect didn't falter as he grabbed Nolan's shirt and pulled him against the wall. The werewolf's raking claws would have cut them both to ribbons otherwise.

A scream tore out of me—and so did my magic. From above, I thrust my hands out and unleashed a torrent of ice. I'd never had to fight while this terrified, and my aim was shoddy at best. Still, four of the icicles sliced into the werewolf's back. A few were thick enough to pierce the skin.

Jon fired off a round as the werewolf staggered. It might have yelped—my ears rang painfully from the gunshot. The monster reared back, slamming into the forklift with a vicious *thud.* The huge machine rocked from the impact.

My limbs grew heavy as I banked closer to assess Jon. He wasn't hurt—I would know it—but I had the instinct to check all the same. Despite my exhaustion, a sense of triumph fueled me when I confirmed he was unscathed.

"*What the fuck,*" I saw Nolan mouth. As my hearing returned, I realized he was saying it out loud. "*What the fuck, what the fuck…*" He looked from me to the shadows and back to Jon as though he couldn't decide what was more fucked up.

"You've been helping Lily kill for weeks," Jon growled. "You never got a look at what she really is?"

"S-she always told me to stay behind. She said it was better if I didn't see her like this."

"Maybe she knew you'd come to your senses if you did," I snapped.

Nolan leaned away like I might be more horrific than his flesh-eating girlfriend.

A blood-curdling scream cut across the room. The forklift, already rattled by the werewolf's impact, was overturned as the beast leaped off its side. The sheer power defied belief.

My next heartbeats felt stretched into agonizing minutes.

Shedding their severed binds, Rick and Charlie scrambled out from underneath the forklift, racing toward the exit. But the unnamed woman was paralyzed with terror. Cliff cursed and dove for her, sweeping her into his arms as the machine fell toward them. He curled his body around hers.

Another gunshot thundered. Jon's shot missed the monster by a narrow margin. A strangled shout escaped me as the werewolf pounced and sent Jon sprawling—pain laced through my back that threatened to numb my wings as he hit the ground. His shotgun was knocked from his grasp. Jon clamped his hands on the creature's jaws, desperately fighting to keep it at bay.

But Cliff—

Breathing heavily, I whipped out my dagger and gasped out a spell, willing the magic to channel along the blade. My ice connected to the ground and bloomed upward, forming a wall beneath the forklift door. Delicate, swirling patterns were buried as I pushed past the pang of magic exhaustion and layered more, *more.* The ice refracted the emergency bulb's light, creating a dance of crimson and cerulean hues across the dusty floor.

I sagged, seeing white spots in my vision. It had been enough—barely. The forklift was suspended at an angle.

Cliff seized the seconds I'd given him, pulling the woman to safety as cracks rippled through my ice, quivering ominously beneath the immense weight it supported. He scooped the hostage into his arms, shooting an unreadable glance back at me as he swiftly bore her toward the exit. He wasn't halfway to the door before my ice shattered, and the machine collapsed onto the floor in a deafening impact of crushed metal and a spray of shattered glass.

Softly at first, the Ancients chuckled at the back of my mind. Some felt like fingers caressing my mind. Others felt like claws.

"Perhaps another bargain, dear child?"

"Have you anything left to offer?"

The pain in my back throbbed. Jon. Was he—

I could smell the hot, rancid breath of the creature from here as I hovered six feet overhead. He was still wrestling beneath it, muzzling the werewolf with his bare hands as it writhed and bucked.

Jon shot out an arm, straining for his shotgun. His fingers redirected, closing around a bag of cement instead. He hoisted it upward over his head like a makeshift shield. The werewolf sank its fangs into the bag instead of his throat—though I flinched at the sound of its teeth tearing through the sturdy material. The creature snarled, gravelly bits of cement flying as it violently shook its head, flinging the bag across the floor with a jerk of its head.

My stomach twisted. I begged ice to my hands, but exhaustion rushed in at the very flicker of magic. We were both going to die because I wasn't strong enough.

For a horrifying moment, the werewolf's jaws closed in, inches from Jon's neck. With an astonishing display of strength and resolve, he regained his grip. His muscles strained, sweat beading on his brow. That savage gleam in Jon's eyes resurfaced, making him appear monstrous himself. Something creaked under his hands—bones, I quickly realized—eliciting a haunting groan from the beast. *Bones*. But that should have been impossible.

Fucking stars, he was strong.

The werewolf jerked free, head turned toward the hostages vanishing out the side door. Hunger shone in those golden eyes. Its meal was getting away. If it chased now, it would catch them—I knew that much with sickening certainty. No human was a match for a perfect predator.

Jon twisted, freed enough to pull a knife from his inside jacket. I saw the silver flash for only a second as he slashed wide with a shout. His grip was unfaltering even as dark blood sprayed down on his hand and face. The werewolf bucked off him, teeth bared.

Lupine muscles rippled as it recovered and assessed its surroundings. Jon hurried to his feet. I cringed when his fiery gaze found me amidst the chaos.

"Sylvia, run!" Jon shouted.

I held his stare, unmoving. My shallow breaths anchored me like a leaden weight, even if I'd meant my promise to him in the car. His eyes blazed, narrowing at me. But there was no time for him to ensure my compliance. The werewolf had fixed its sights on Nolan, who was six feet to Jon's right, cowering under the scaffolding that led to the second landing.

As a human, Lily had been a somewhat petite woman next to Nolan. Transformed, she towered, even when prowling forward on all fours.

Jon drew a matching knife to the one in his other hand that was dripping with blood.

"No, don't hurt her!" Nolan cried.

Jon shot him a wild look. "Are you insane?"

"She knows me! She'll—she'll know."

Tears shined in Nolan's eyes. His sneakers caught on rubble as he stepped closer to the wall.

"You know it's me, Lily." His voice trembled, though there was something undeniably tender in the way he addressed her, even now. Her nose paused just short of his chest, scenting. He squeezed his eyes shut and swallowed. "We're gonna find a way to fix you. Find a cabin in the Smokies. Remember?"

The low growl tapered off. The warehouse became deathly quiet once more. Shaking, Nolan lifted his uninjured hand toward her large head. His palm brushed over the space between her eyes.

The werewolf snapped forward quicker than I'd ever seen anything move. One moment, she was hunched before Nolan. The next, she was wrenching out a mouthful of his throat with her teeth.

I wanted to scream, but my voice was far away. Nolan didn't make a sound, either. His eyes were wide and unseeing by the time he dropped lifelessly. And all I could do was stare, frozen, as

Lily ripped into his abdomen and started feasting zealously like she hadn't eaten in days.

A gunshot rang out, a bullet finding its mark directly beneath the werewolf's skull. A perfect shot—but not Jon's. I whipped my head around toward the other side of the warehouse where Cliff was bolting across the room.

With seamless rhythm, Jon lunged the second the werewolf registered the attack. He sank both blades into its back, a blood-curdling snarl filling the air. The monster spun around so quickly, Jon could only retrieve one of his knives before leaping out of range—but not quickly enough. A powerful, clawed swipe sent Jon hurtling into a nearby column.

CRACK.

His impressive frame crumpled at the base, stirring slowly. The shout that tore out of me was raw, animal. I didn't see how the impact had shattered Jon's left arm—I *felt* it.

Agony crashed through me. All-encompassing. Blinding. Every nerve in my wings was set ablaze, rendering flight all but impossible. Tears blurred my vision as I spiraled toward the ground. With concentrated effort, I managed to veer onto a pallet of lumber stacked five feet off the ground, where I landed with a jolt on my hands and skinned knees.

Panic mingled with the weight of my failure. Cliff was too far—Jon was going to die, and I would follow suit.

Through a sob, I desperately beckoned ice to my hands. Mere wisps of magic flickered, forced through the roiling cloud of magic exhaustion and pain. It felt like I was trapped in a thunderstorm—the crippling fear beating over me like roaring gales. In the midst of it all, I remembered what it felt like to hear Jon's gentle voice wash over me in the woods.

Breathe.

There's stillness on the other side.

On the floor, Jon pushed himself up with his uninjured arm. He wasn't done fighting, even now. I sucked in a shuddering breath, and then another. Amid the pain, a point of rage solidified in my chest like an ember.

No. This monster would not have him. It would not have me.

My target fixed, I lifted my trembling hands out before me and focused my rage into points of magic.

A volley of ice exploded from my palms, mist sharpening into icy blades. A few of the sizable pieces hit their mark in the werewolf's hide. It looked like it fucking *hurt* when one of them embedded itself near the open knife wound on its back.

Before the beast could turn on me, Jon seized one of my missed icicles, brandishing it like a lethal shard of cold steel.

"Jon!" Cliff's booming voice was right behind me now.

Jon plunged the ice into the werewolf's eye with a sickening squelch. It roared, fangs bared toward the sky. Static crept into my vision, reducing the world to hazy forms. A Cliff-shaped blur lunged at the monster with a serrated knife, plunging it into its heart.

The werewolf spasmed, jerking on the blade, but Cliff was immovable. The monster collapsed on its side.

That horrible aura faded.

They'd done it.

I sagged, my body leaden. What little magic the Ancients had not yet harvested from me felt like it had been drained to mere droplets, reducing me to an emptied vessel.

The pallet shook from the hunters' movements. Jon moved with audible effort, protecting his broken arm while Cliff knelt and sawed the werewolf's heart free from the chest cavity. The smell of blood cloyed the air.

The wooden crate felt cool against my feverish skin. I couldn't stay awake any longer.

"Let go," something whispered in my ear. "*You've played hero long enough. It's time to let go."*

I knew what it was. The Ancients were trying to bring our contract to a close, and I had half a mind to let them. Jon was alive—and I was so tired. My eyelids dropped shut.

"Be at peace. You never stood a chance, child."

29

SYLVIA

Death was reluctant to claim me—much to my chagrin.

I wept as I came to. Acute, shooting pain enveloped me. It was paralyzing, radiating from my left arm. The limb was perfectly intact beneath my shimmering gossamer sleeve, but the bone felt shattered. Flexing my wings weakly, I confirmed that those were still intact, at least.

Blinking tears away, I tried to clear my vision to make sense of where I was. Soft fabric cradled me, but the hunters were nowhere to be seen. Whatever I was lying on was big enough to block out the immediate vicinity. Above me, jagged branches were silhouetted against the night sky. The smell of fallen leaves and pine needles was a comforting whisper of home. But there was something else—*smoke*. Something was burning nearby.

Something was moving out there, too, sending faint tremors through the forest floor. I couldn't stay sprawled out here like an owl's snack on a platter.

I closed my fists around the sea of fabric. It was scarlet cotton.

"You pushed her too far, and now look what happened." Cliff's voice was a distant rumble. My heavy eyes flickered open wider.

"I didn't mean—I lost sight of myself."

"Lot of good that's doing her now."

"Jon?" My voice was a frog's croak. Gritting my teeth, I stifled a groan as I attempted to sit up using only my right arm. Even that sent dizziness crashing through me.

All at once, the faint stirring in the ground became an earthquake. And then, Jon was there, replacing my view of the forest as he knelt over me.

"You're awake," he breathed. "I thought you were—that you might be…" His wide eyes said the rest.

Cliff knelt beside Jon, crowding in for a look at me. Jon wore only a dark tee flecked with dirt. His well-built physique stretched the fabric, arms shivering with exertion—the right one was caked with blood, the short sleeve in tatters, while the left one was in a makeshift sling fashioned from the button-up shirt he'd been wearing earlier. His tousled hair was dampened by sweat, a few locks hanging in front of his forehead.

Intimidating. Beautiful. Staring at me like the liability I was.

"What the hell happened to you?" Cliff asked, his brows pulled together. Blood speckled his lower face—though I couldn't tell if it was his own. His toned arms gleamed under the thin veil of his undershirt, the swirling ink of his many tattoos almost animated in the firelight. I realized it was his scarlet button-up I was sitting on.

"I'm fine," I said.

Extremely premature. The Ancients had a truly cruel sense of humor to allow me to wake at all. I could feel it in the very core of my being with the same certainty that I knew that winter would follow autumn or that flowers turned toward sunlight when they grew.

I was dying.

"I need to heal your arm," I said, looking up at Jon urgently.

He recoiled slightly. "Fuck no. Sylv, you just fainted."

"Jon, please—"

"You need rest. It's over—you're safe now. I never should've—"

"Shut up!" My frantic plea tapered into a shout. He drew further back, frowning deeper. I breathed heavily, silently begging Jon

to trust me. "You're in pain! You're in so much pain—how are you not *screaming*?"

"I... I mean, yeah, it fucking hurts, but..." He was simply far more used to pain than I was. "You don't have to worry about me. I'm—"

"You don't understand." I was sobbing by then, the pain spiking sharper with each second I was awake. Clutching my left arm close, I scooted myself in his direction. "You have to let me heal it. I just need to touch your skin. *Please.*"

Though he exchanged a perturbed look with Cliff, Jon seemed shaken by my manic request. I was going to fight tooth and nail to reach him—he realized that much and caved into my desperation.

With visible reluctance, he unwound his sling—stifling a groan as his shattered arm was jostled—and lowered himself closer. I crawled to him until I could stretch my arm out and press my clammy fingertips to his forearm. The connection sent shivers down my spine. I let my eyes flutter shut, blocking out the weight of their stares as I whispered the spell. Jon and I breathed in mutual relief as the magic surged from me to him, stitching bones back together, mending pulverized tissue.

"Sylvia."

I straightened at the sound of Jon's voice, not even realizing I had slumped against him.

He was right. The effort nearly knocked me out again. I clung to consciousness by a thread as I finished the spell and crashed onto my knees. I could have sung from relief as the agony was replaced with the faint tingle of residual magic.

Jon sagged with a sigh, too. I caught gratitude glinting alongside questions in his eyes as he pulled back, flexing his left hand with dumbstruck wonder.

"What the hell was that?" Cliff asked. He didn't miss the way I had flexed my left hand, too.

Leaning my hands on my knees, I tried in vain to see past them. With the pain clearing, I could think more clearly.

"What's that smell?" I rasped.

Cliff's profile caught the fiery glow when he glanced over his shoulder to observe the blaze. "Nolan and Lily."

He said it like I had asked for the time of day. Of course. No trace could be left lest humankind discover a truth it wasn't ready for. I grimaced but nodded.

I wanted to pass out again. Even with Jon's shattered bone healed, everything hurt so much.

"You've been out for the better part of an hour," Jon told me. "And you've been running a fever for the last half."

He reached down and brushed the hair off my face, and I forgot what else I was going to say. His thumb lingered over my pallid skin with such gentle precision that I almost forgot this was the same hand that had kept a fucking *mactir* at bay.

I leaned into his touch and shuddered. What I wouldn't give to relax into his warmth forever. But desperation for the impossible was what had landed me in this mess in the first place. Though it hurt my heart, I pushed against his thumb as swiftly as I had embraced it.

Now that the hunt was over, I could part ways with Jon knowing that he wouldn't be in immediate danger. Hopefully, I could survive long enough to find the third name. With my other resources exhausted, a closer look through the village archives was my only hope before I withered to nothing at the Ancients' hands. There was still a chance I could break the bond tonight. Everything could return to the way it should be.

"It's time for me to go home," I said.

Jon looked taken off guard by my simple statement—even a little hurt.

Cliff shook his head. "Last thing you need is to waltz in there like this. Even *you're* not that stupid."

I clenched my jaw, unable to disclose that I had every reason to believe I would die the next time I fell unconscious. "I did what I came to do," I said, harsher. "I'm ready to go home now. You promised you'd let me go."

The hunters exchanged looks which said quite plainly that wasn't happening. Fear snaked inside of me as I considered that maybe they never planned to let me go. In all the turmoil that had befallen me, I hadn't given much thought to the idea that the hunters would go back on their word and try to keep me for my abilities in the end.

"You're hurt," Jon said quietly.

His expression was innocent enough, but with how they crowded me, I still couldn't decide if I was saved or cornered.

Gesturing at myself, I shook my head. "Look at me—I'm fine. Only a skinned knee."

"No," Jon insisted. "There's something wrong with you. Don't bullshit us."

"What do you know?" I snapped. "I'm the first fairy you ever saw. You're hardly an expert."

"You practically brought Jon back from the dead," Cliff said in that dangerous, wary tone of his. "But a few ice spells are doing you in? We're not idiots, Sylvia. Your aim and instincts may have gotten better with practice, but the spells have been taking more out of you every time."

I shivered. Just like a hunter to notice such things, assessing my skills like I was still an enemy.

Or an ally, I pondered faintly.

The thought tumbled in my head before I shoved it aside. "I need to go home," I repeated, bordering on delirious.

As I attempted to stand, Jon's hand cupped beside me. I flinched, but he wasn't restraining me. He was helping me stay steady on the soft fabric. His eyes continued to bore into me like he could leech my secrets if he stared hard enough.

"Why were you looking up local demons?" Jon asked plainly. "Who's *Daeharice*?"

There was a hiss at the back of my mind as though the Ancients hated that filthy human lips were speaking one of their names for the first time since the cult.

"How do you know about that?" I asked.

Cliff scoffed. "Search history, babe. Those little books of yours were too dense to get a full read on while you were sleeping the other night, though."

They'd tracked my research. I looked between them, breathing harder. Any hope I'd had of slipping away without their suspicion was an illusion. They weren't going to let me go, I accepted bleakly. I couldn't fight them off—not like this. The thought of summoning ice to my fingertips made me want to vomit.

Tears spilled onto my cheeks as I looked down in shame. Maybe the hunters would give me the mercy of a quick death. Or maybe I could convince them to simply abandon me where I stood.

Alone.

When I opened my mouth, a thick sob came out instead of words.

"Sylvia." Jon's hushed voice was gentle in a way I'd never heard. His thumb brushed my arm up and down. "You're not okay. Please. You have to tell us what's going on."

"I-I'm sorry," I managed. "I'm so sorry. When you were dying, I couldn't save you by myself. I was fading. I cried out for help, and… and something answered. Something we can't see. It let me save you, but it cursed me."

His stroking paused.

I kept my head down, unable to bear the look of shock that must have been on their faces. I thought of Mother's crushing disappointment. Damian's sorrow. Ayden's eagerness to punish me. Lireal's disgust.

You vile creature. I could have sworn the Ancient's voices were echoing Lireal's words.

"It tied me to you, Jon," I went on. "We're bound. Any pain or injury you feel, I experience it, too." Hearing him draw a sharp breath, I swiftly added, "But you aren't affected by this. In those journals, I found a case just like mine. The person saved isn't in danger, I promise you."

Cliff cursed under his breath.

"My arm," Jon whispered. "You felt all of that?"

I nodded miserably. "These beings, the Ancients—they don't exist on this plane. They have been feeding off of me. They're draining my life, my magic. Every spell gets harder. But I found a way to destroy their hold on me, I think. The true names of all three Ancients will grant me power over them. I found one in the journal and another from your laptop. Your people thought it was a demon." I braced myself and looked up, pleading with everything I had. "Let me go home. My only hope is to find the third name in the archives."

The hunters' stunned silence was cavernous. The fire crackled in the woods behind them, flames eating away at the bodies. Jon's dark eyes cut away from me, a hard clench to his jaw. I could see his thoughts swirling, unstitching the web of my lies over these past days.

"You thought we couldn't handle the truth," he muttered, a flicker of frustration shadowing his face.

I watched every twitch of his hands, fear knotting my stomach. Killing me would solve any issue this presented to him. With my current state, it would be easy for him. Scarcely a flick of the wrist. I wouldn't stop him. Maybe it would even be painless—a reprieve from this slow agony.

"How much time do you have?" he asked.

"Not much," I answered carefully. "I can feel it."

When Jon's gaze locked with mine again, a steely resolve burned in his eyes. I could practically feel the heat of it piercing my core. "You can barely stand. We're coming with you. We'll see this through to the end."

I blinked, recoiling. I had anticipated anger, abandonment, even death—but this?

"Why would you do that?" My voice rose as I felt seconds slipping away, desperation gripping my lungs like cold hands. "I can't offer you anything in return this time."

Cliff snorted, shaking his head. "Just when I thought you couldn't think any less of us. After everything, you really expect us to dump you on the side of the road and keep driving?"

"I did this to myself. I should be the one to unravel it."

"Maybe you can do it alone, but that doesn't mean you have to. Or *should,"* Cliff said. "So, tough shit, we're not gonna let you die."

Until now, I'd never taken comfort in the way he saw through me—instead of taking advantage of my weakness, Cliff could see my inner war to accept help when I was at my lowest. My heart soared and clenched.

"Does this mean we're friends now?" I asked wryly, rubbing my eyes.

"Don't get carried away."

Cliff stood, surveying the smoldering pit in the ground. The warm hues of gold and orange dancing over his profile had weakened, though I could still hear the snap of bones charring. If not for the stomach-churning smell that accompanied it, I could have pretended the sound was merely twigs snapping.

Cliff walked over, picking up a shovel leaning up against a tree. "They're nearly crisped. Let's cover these and get going."

Tentatively, I tried to fly, only to have my body punish me. Pain shot through my spine and down my limbs. I cried out, keeling into Jon's supporting hand. His palm turned to face me, scooping me up.

"I've got you," Jon said.

He stood. The night air clashed with my feverish skin, a contrast that left me dizzy. I struggled to focus on details of the forest, my vision blurring in sync with my throbbing head.

Suddenly, Jon pulled me close to him—embracing me. He held me against his neck, and though he smelled of sweat and violence, I swore I had never felt more secure in my life. Pleasant heat rose to my cheeks that rivaled the fever. I would have let him hold me like that for hours.

"You're going to be fine, Sylvia." Pulling away, he gave me a look that said I didn't have a choice. It was spoken softly, both a promise and a plea.

30

SYLVIA

Every time my eyes fluttered shut, Jon nudged me awake. Cliff's frantic driving should have been more than enough to make me fear for my life and stay alert, but my nerves had already reached their threshold.

While Jon held me securely to keep from being knocked out, he asked questions to keep me from slumping back to sleep. "Okay, we'll get you to the village. Then what? How do we take out these Ancients?"

"Iron through the heart?" Cliff proposed. "Beheading?"

I scoffed a weak laugh. "You don't know the first thing about Ancients, do you?" How could they? Even Elysians scarcely brought up the entities—and most seemed to think the Ancients had faded into nothing.

"They've got to have a weakness," Cliff said. "Just like any other evil bastard we've taken out."

"Your iron can't reach them," I said. "But their names are their weakness. I'm not sure what these beings really are, but invoking their true names should render them powerless. They amalgamate in groups of three to protect themselves. A number strong enough to make it difficult to find each name, but small enough to lower the risk of being betrayed by each other. That's what one entry claimed."

The car banked hard onto one of the bumpier roads of the journey, making me nauseous. I held tight to Jon's finger, and he didn't hesitate to curl his hand reassuringly around my body.

"So, all you have to do is say their names?" One of Jon's fingertips rubbed my shoulder as he spoke. "That's it?"

"Not quite. The names must be spoken in their realm. I have what I need—I have the rune and spell to get me there."

Even after the car came to a halt, my body felt like it was moving. The trees looked more familiar through the windows, but the branches appeared to be swimming. I blinked hard and didn't dare try to fly again—spreading my wings could be the difference between life and death at this point. Jon was hasty yet gentle in his exit from the car.

"Here." Cliff circled around to the car's trunk and pulled out iron bars. He held one out to Jon. "Kind of like walking into a minefield out here."

My lips curled, skin prickling at the presence of the iron. At least it would be enough to disrupt the glamour and prevent them from walking in circles—hopefully. Jon was kind enough to hold me away from his body until he tucked the bar into his jacket, where it couldn't hurt me.

The hunters began their trek. Jon pressed ahead with me as their guide. Cliff fell back by several steps, keeping an eye out for any attackers who might try to sneak up on us. No matter how I insisted that the hunters would be in grave danger if they were spotted, they wouldn't hear of it. All I could hope was that the guards wouldn't kill me on sight—that they would hear out my desperate situation and have mercy.

My mind was too addled to rehearse what I could say to them. But Jon was *here*. All around me. Pushing forward despite everything.

I cleared my throat and tried one more time: "If you see the guards, just leave me—"

"Nope." Jon looked down at me in his cupped hands, appearing thoroughly puzzled that I was still trying to shoo him off. "I'm not going anywhere, and you can't change my mind."

I chewed my lip, guilt surfacing as I regarded him. "Jon, I wanted to tell you. I really did."

He was quiet for a while, jaw tightening. "You were afraid. I get it."

I studied him as he walked—the shame swimming in his eyes. It was astonishing, really. Jon looked like he would prefer another werewolf hunt to me being fearful of him.

Trying to inject some levity, I propped myself up onto my elbows and drawled, "Saving my life does lower your number on the scary scale. In case you were wondering."

His lips quirked. "I'm honored."

"You should be."

Jon chuckled, and the sound of it stirred butterflies in my stomach. It was the kind of laugh that turned heads in a room—a gift I didn't deserve.

The passing forest began to flood with familiar sights—the oak that I knew had the best sap in winter, the abandoned owl's nest, the bushes nearly picked clean of blackberries.

A cold possibility dawned on me that this could be my last look at all of it. I might never see Hazel grow up. She didn't even know her affinity yet, and the thought of missing such a crucial moment in her life made grief lodge like a stone in my chest.

I didn't want to say goodbye to any of the faces I knew so well. I didn't want to say goodbye to solstice festivals with dazzling fae lights beneath the willow, long flights in the warm summer air, or watching the sun set over the lake with Damian and Kyra.

"I used to get so bored foraging for berries," I said quietly, marveling at my own life like I was inspecting someone else's. I shook my head. "I'd kill for a casual flight and a blackberry right now."

A sigh cut above me. "I feel like I should apologize again. For everything." Jon stopped walking for a moment and pinned me with a searching stare. "I was so wrong about you."

My heart thrummed in my chest, and I realized I didn't want to say goodbye to him, either.

"Do you remember Alice's music box?" I asked.

"Yes," Jon said—cautiously, like the fever might be making me delirious. Maybe it was. Loss was bitter, but falling for him was painless.

I smiled at him. "I wish we could have danced like that together. Just once." My palm brushed against his calloused one. "Our hands fitting together."

A dozen emotions flash over his face—surprise, pity, and *desire*. Understanding reflected back at me. And suddenly, the unfocused image of the man from my dream became clear. I wanted Jon there, waiting for me at the bottom of the gilded staircase.

"I'd be a terrible dance partner," Jon murmured.

"Still," I said. "It would've been nice."

His eyes softened. "Yeah, it would have." Jon moistened his lips, struggling to string together his words. "Just so you know, if things were different…"

I smiled sadly, looking at my hand against his. "Yeah. Me, too. Even though you're a bloodthirsty hunter."

That drew another chuckle out of him. I wished I could bottle the sound.

Jon held me closer as he pressed forward. My thoughts swam with the impossible admission that had passed between us. I had been so skeptical about Mother's description of love. What it felt like to fall for someone. I never understood how Alice could pine over someone for over a century.

Now, it made sense.

My soul ached for his. To belong to him, to have him.

Every time he peeked down to check on me, I understood that I'd been waiting—*hoping*—for Damian to give me an equally tender look under our favorite tree. Jon saw the mess I'd made and my reckless desires, and he still refused to leave my side.

How I longed to entwine my fingers with his.

If only. Perhaps the two saddest words that could be strung together.

But he wasn't all tenderness. I couldn't forget that the hands cradling me could kill just as easily. My throat closed at the thought of the hunt. Lily had been living in fear of a brutal death, too. And I had helped deliver it.

"I feel bad for her," I admitted. "Lily didn't want to be that way. I wish we could have helped her. Is that awful?"

"Of course it isn't," Jon said, voice lower and rougher.

"I know it had to be done. But how can you stomach going through with something like this, over and over?"

Jon was quiet for a time, and I worried I had disappointed him by having sympathy for a monster. Then, his answer came softly. "She didn't deserve the hand that was dealt to her, but neither did the people who were tied up. I stomach it by knowing that there was nothing we could do for someone who's been turned. But we *can* save more innocent people like her from dying or becoming monsters themselves." He peered down at me. "You understand it better than you think. When there's an opportunity to save someone's life, you take it."

He really is a warrior, I thought faintly.

It felt like no more than a few seconds passed before Jon was prodding my side like the sky was falling.

"Sylvia! Wake up! Open your eyes!"

I didn't even realize I'd closed them. Jolting, I blinked hard and caught my breath shallowly. My vision blurred as I looked between Jon's worried expression and the familiar trees. My head dipped forward. I wanted nothing more than to succumb to my weakness.

We weren't close enough to the village.

"Jon." My sluggish mind grappled to formulate something, *anything*, to keep me from simply laying down and dying. "Put me on the ground so I can carve the rune. I have to confront the Ancients now before they kill me."

"What? No—no, we're almost—"

"We're not. I-I won't make it."

His stubborn steps refused to slow. "We're so close, just hang on."

I drew my dagger out and jabbed the base of his thumb. The resounding bond between us made me feel it, but the pain was barely a pinprick in the ocean of exhaustion coursing through me. Jon looked at me in alarm, finally stopping.

"Put me down." I pointed the blade up at him. "Either I carve the rune into the ground or your hand."

The seriousness on my face must have been impossible to argue with. Reluctantly, he found a smooth patch of ground. When I instructed him to push the leaves out of the way, he complied.

"What the hell's going on?" Cliff asked, closing the distance.

"She's going through with it now," Jon said, his voice tight. "She says she won't survive long enough to get home."

While I gathered my bearings on the ground, I pulled a torn piece of paper from my belt. The other page—the one with my father's writing—was tucked away among my things in the motel room. This excerpt contained the rune and the chant. I'd carried it everywhere since finding it, just in case.

My blade sank into the soft earth without resistance, but I practically had to drag myself along. The circumference of the rune was nearly as tall as I was. "Anyone who makes contact with the rune or its caster when it's active will enter the spectral plane. So keep your distance."

"But don't you need the third name?" Cliff asked.

I couldn't bring myself to meet their gazes as they knelt over me. The sour taste of fear consumed my world like a vicious fog, quietly blanketing everything in its reach.

"It's too late," I said. "I've never read anything about someone trying to meet the Ancients with two names… but I never heard about anyone making friends with hunters before, either." Drawing a shaky breath, I forced a smile up at them. The worry on their faces floored me. "Whatever you do, don't touch me once the spell is active. My body will be a conduit, and the spectral realm might never let you go. I'm on my own from here. But thanks for staying with me."

Sinking to my knees in the middle of the rune, paper clutched in shaking hands, I recited the chant.

From one blink to the next, the forest was gone.

31

JON

A fairy entering the spectral plane was eerily reminiscent of a human becoming possessed. Her body was no longer her own—she jolted sharply before collapsing onto her back in the dirt.

Sylvia's eyes were rolled back, the whites visible beneath fluttering lashes like she was dreaming restlessly. She was alone in there. Scared and facing any number of visceral nightmares. My hand flexed with a trembling motion. I wanted to reach out and offer a comforting touch, even if she couldn't feel it. But her warning had been clear. I couldn't help her if I was pulled into the spectral plane with her or died in the process.

But I couldn't just sit here and wait for her to die.

"I recognize where we are," I said to Cliff, surveying the trees with renewed focus. I pushed to my feet. The full moon cast generous swathes of light through the otherwise impenetrable darkness. "I met her in that grove last time. The village itself can't be much further. Her wing had barely been healed. I can find her mother or sister—they'll help her."

Hopefully.

"They'll see you coming a mile out. What's the plan to keep the others from killing you on sight?" Cliff asked.

"I'm working on that."

Pausing, I looked back down at Sylvia like gravity centered on her. My boots refused to budge. She looked smaller than ever. So terribly still. Her elegant teal top fluttered like one of the fallen leaves around her in each sweep of the breeze.

"I'll watch over her," Cliff said as though my thought of *if I leave her and something happens to her, it's my fault* was on blast for the entire forest to hear.

I nodded, prying my eyes up and setting off. My landmark willow passed, and I entered unknown territory. The surrounding trees were excruciatingly ordinary. Owls crooned in the distance, crickets chirruped. There was no sign of fairy inhabitance anywhere, and with the village apparently being underground, I realized there might not be any outward evidence to spot. My chest felt tightened as seconds dragged into minutes.

I should turn back.

The thought gnawed at me with each step I took. The wind in the trees suddenly seemed to be whispers. Despite the leather jacket I'd donned during the drive over, chills crept over my skin. Leaves shifted and swayed, laughing at my disorientation. I could hear them saying my name. That I didn't belong here. Maybe this was all for nothing.

I should turn back.

I stopped in my tracks, breath catching in a short burst.

That thought wasn't my own.

Fighting the urge to turn on my heel and obediently march back to the car, I noted the air had become charged with energy. It raised hairs on the back of my neck and made my mouth taste coppery. Last time I had been glamoured, Sylvia had pointed it out. Even as I racked my brain, I struggled to identify the experience. She had guided me where to go until the glamour passed.

Slipping my hand into my jacket, I grabbed hold of the iron bar. With direct contact of my skin on the cold metal, the drug-like haze over my vision cleared. The trees became still—too still. All the wind had stopped as though a celestial switch had been toggled.

The still surface of a lake glinted between the trees. Steeling myself for an ambush, I moved in that direction. I was so ready for a fight, in fact, that the idea that the other fairies might refuse to make contact hadn't dawned on me until this moment. An awful image struck me—my shouts for help ignored. All of their kind holed up far beneath the surface, silent until it was too late to save her. I pictured returning to Cliff, and his head hung low as he held out Sylvia's pallid, limp form—

"You!" A female voice cut through the stillness.

My hand was still tight around the iron rod when something small flew into the moonlight, silhouetted. Tiny gossamer wings beat urgently, glinting in a hover. I tensed, looking all around, but the fairy was alone.

"You! It's you! Damian was right." She didn't fly as quickly as Sylvia, so it was easier to track her when she zipped up to my face. She whispered a little spell, calling forth a gentle amber glow from her skin. Her features became visible, and my jaw went slack.

"Hazel," I breathed, scarcely able to believe my eyes. "What are you doing out here alone?"

Sylvia had made her village's curfew very clear, but it was the trigger-happy enforcement of these regulations that concerned me. Hazel was risking a lot to be here. Fire blazed in my chest as I wondered if these Elders would brand a child for disobedience the way they had to Sylvia.

"Where is my sister?" Though her words were choked with terror at the sight of me, her little fists balled at her sides like she was ready for a fight.

"She needs your help," I told her hurriedly. "Something's happened to her—something with the Ancients." Hazel's hands leaped to stifle a gasp, but I pressed on. "We need a name, and I think it may be in your village somewhere."

She frowned, considering this while she still looked me up and down like I was a rabid, snapping dog. Suddenly, she lifted her head and looked over her shoulder. A squeak of fear escaped her, and without another word, she extinguished the glow on her skin and flew past me in a burst.

"Hazel!" I barked, whirling on empty air. It was impossible to see where she had flown in the darkness. Frustration burned—until I faced forward again.

Five fairies emerged from the gloom, approaching me.

Instinct nearly made me draw the iron. Instead, I bit my lip and kept a hold on it, hidden. Any sign of aggression could make all the difference in what was about to unfold.

There was no time to lose. "Sylvia's in danger," I said. "I'm not here to hurt anyone—I won't get any closer to your village. I just came looking for someone to help her."

As I spoke, I observed each fairy in turn, trying to get a read. Damian was the only one I recognized. My insides bristled vengefully. He'd hurt Sylvia—except that must have been the work of the bond. Still, I stayed sour at the image of Sylvia gasping for breath.

There were two women—an older one with pale hair and long robes, and a fiery redhead who had to be Sylvia and Hazel's mother.

The other two men were dressed similarly in earthen-colored uniforms, like guards. When the robed woman made a gesture with her hand, one of the guards wasted no time making the first strike. All at once, searing light burst from him, and I narrowly dodged a ball of fire that sizzled out against a large rock at the base of a tree.

"Listen to me!" I shouted, having no choice but to pull out the iron.

All the fairies drew back, wide-eyed.

"Lireal." Sylvia's mother darted closer to the older woman, grabbing her arm. "He has my daughter! You can't kill him until we know where she is!"

It was hardly the vote of confidence I'd hoped for, but her plea bought me another second to speak. I lowered the iron, ready to raise it again at a moment's notice. "Please—she's alone with the Ancients right now. I swear, I'll never come near this place again. I only want to help her."

Feathered wings flapped and settled overhead. I glanced up and found the beady eyes of several crows staring at the scene. They huddled together on branches, their deep, resonant caws growing swiftly in number. My skin crawled at the sight, but the fairies didn't seem frightened by the potential threat the birds posed.

One of the guards was murmuring something—it had to be a spell, summoning the birds. The message was clear. I was one wrong move away from having beaks and talons tearing into my flesh.

Not a single fairy had addressed me directly. They all kept staring at me like I was a force of nature beyond reason—a monster that needed every brand of magic to be taken down.

"You're just going to let her die?" I demanded, making eye contact with Sylvia's mother and Damian—perhaps the only two fairies here who might give a shit about her fate.

Lireal sneered. "Death by Ancients is a fitting end for a stupid girl who led a predator to our threshold."

The ground erupted like a series of small landmines had been buried underneath. Roots hit my hand with enough force to nearly shatter it. The iron bar went flying from my grip and fell among scattered leaves. I lunged for it, but the roots surged for me like snakes. Thorny tendrils wrapped around my arms and legs, dragging me to the ground.

"Stop!" I choked out.

The earth roiled beneath me like a living creature that was hellbent on swallowing me alive. I clawed for the iron, but it was buried among the chaos of the sinewy roots, lost forever.

I managed to rip myself free from a few of the bindings, only to have fresh, sharper ones replace them. A flurry of feathers swooped over me, claws swiping at my attempts to struggle. Before long, I couldn't tell the difference between the thorns and talons digging into my skin.

At the back of my mind, I finally understood why Sylvia feared we would end her simply for being a fairy.

From the corner of my eye, I saw Lireal give me a disgusted glare before turning to the guard who had summoned the crows. I could barely hear her voice over the crackling of the earth and guttural bird croaks. "Perhaps you can calm him, like the rabid coyote you willed to drown itself last season."

The fire guard scoffed. "No. Let him suffer."

While I choked on dirt, there was another burst of fire—but from a different source. Lireal and the guard broke apart from each other in alarm.

A molten glow came from Sylvia's mother as she ignited another spell. Rippling flames idled in both hands. "If you won't help Sylvia, then I suggest you either stand aside or kill me yourself," she spat at Lireal.

What I thought was chaos before paled in comparison to what followed.

Lireal was forced to redirect her magic. The roots slackened enough on my limbs to let me pull free. I shoved away the crows—half of them were distracted already, swooping toward Sylvia's mother like they were preparing to tear her to shreds.

"Melanie!" Damian called to Sylvia's mother.

They came together—fire and air magic combining into an explosion that pushed the other fairies back. The animal guard was knocked into a branch, incapacitated at once. The crows faltered, confused, before flying off with frantic caws.

Earth, fire, and air collided before me. I struggled to keep up with the onslaught of spells while I searched the ground for the iron bar, but it was buried too deep. I had little time to look before fire grazed my shoulder. I let loose a roar of pain, wondering if Sylvia could feel it too in the spectral realm.

Panting, the fire guard hovered before me, just out of reach. I started to attack again—faltering mid-stride when the guard's chanted spell cut off with a strangled shout. He clutched his throat and threw a half-finished flame toward Damian, who pulled back to dodge it, the air pulsing around him.

I took the opportunity to lunge forward and close the distance, snatching the guard out of the air and pinning him to the ground. He squirmed madly, searing heat burning at my palm.

Damian flew down and continued his spell, not stopping until the guard was wholly unconscious and limp under my hand. I pulled back slowly. Having been on the receiving end of the spell just the other day, I couldn't help but feel a touch of sympathy.

Gasping for breath like he was feeling the effects of his own spell, Damian took noticed of my expression. "Don't feel too bad for Ayden. He's the one who put the mark on Sylvia's face."

Eyes widening, I stared back down at the fallen fairy and briefly entertained the idea of crushing him.

When the sound of Damian's wings retreated, I pushed the thought aside and turned my attention to Melanie and Lireal. They squared off viciously. Melanie directed her flames expertly at the vines and thorns that Lireal attempted to skewer her with. As Damian joined in, it made no difference that Lireal's magic appeared more practiced.

Lireal coughed on her spells, aim beginning to waver. As she attempted to recover from Damian's attack, Melanie closed the distance. There was no more fire in her hands. She simply reeled back and punched Lireal across the face, making her slump unconsciously onto the branch she'd perched on.

"That's for my daughter, you bitch."

Damian landed next to Melanie, kneeling to check Lireal's pulse with far more care than he had the others. He tucked the wide, flowing sleeves of her robe over her body. Melanie glided down to me, and Damian followed. I pried the remaining vines off me, pushing to my feet.

"You have ten seconds to explain before I burn you alive, hunter," Melanie said, each word bitten off at the end. The flame summoned to her hand was a soft smolder, illuminating the tears shining in her eyes. When she spoke again, her voice was a wobbling whisper. "Is it true? Sylvia is at the mercy of the Ancients?"

"Yes. She's in the spectral plane now, but she's…" My throat closed around the words. "She's *dying*."

"Oh stars, we're out of time," Damian said softly.

"No, we can still make it back," I insisted. "She saved my life. I'm not giving up now."

Damian rubbed his eyes with his palms, then threw a bitter glare at me. "Why would she save *you*?"

"That doesn't matter. The answer to saving her has to be in your village, written down somewhere." I surprised myself with the desperation inching into my voice, each syllable becoming more rushed and tight. "She said she needs the Ancients' names—"

"I know that!" Damian snapped. "When I saw her running off with journals about Ancients, I scoured everything else I could find in the archives. The records were incomplete, and the Elders have been methodically weeding out these texts for years."

Steam simmered the air around Melanie. "I risked my own curfew to get those books for you, Damian. You said you found answers!"

"There wasn't enough time." Shame darkened Damian's face, his brows drawing together. "I could only find one name."

My heart skipped a beat. "Which was it?" I asked.

"Caerthynna. I'm sorry."

For a moment, the world spun. I mouthed the words Sylvia had been reciting while she lay half-conscious in my hand during the drive here. *Laelithar, Daeharice…*

And *Caerthynna.*

A sharp breeze hissed around us as the name formed on my mouth.

"That's it," I breathed. "That's the third name."

Distant voices carried from the same direction that Melanie and the others had come. Movement surged between the crooked branches. Dim lights glowed around every figure, illuminating the approach of over a dozen winged figures. *Fuck.*

"We can still reach her," I murmured.

I turned and bolted back the way I came, Melanie and Damian not far behind me. Low hanging branches whipped against my skin, but I barely noticed the stings as I focused on the path littered by knotted tree roots. I shot glances over my shoulder. The fairy guards flew easily between tree limbs I had to dodge altogether.

Cliff was on his feet when I reached him, iron clutched at his side and eyes wide.

"We don't have much time," I panted, looking over my shoulder. The guards were still visible, closing in. It was easy for them to follow. We had maybe two minutes, optimistically. "Is she—"

"She's still fighting." Cliff jutted his chin to the ground.

I looked at Sylvia, and I felt like I was falling. I blinked, and I was on my knees beside her. All I could hear was my heart pounding in my ears, while Sylvia's was beating a finite amount. I was utterly aware of how pristine she was and how I was caked in dirt and dried blood.

"Sylvia," I said, leaning over her. "Caerthynna. The last name is *Caerthynna.*"

The wind hissed again, cutting at my back. Sylvia was unresponsive. Damian and Melanie landed on her right side, folding their wings.

"Sylvia!" My fingers dug into the earth.

Melanie muscled down a sob at the answering silence.

"She can't hear us," Damian murmured. He extended a hand like he wanted to cup her face but hesitated and dropped his hand to his lap instead. "We can't follow her in there. She has to do this alone."

"No!" I growled so severely that Damian and Melanie looked prepared to defend themselves. "I'm not leaving her to fucking die."

"Do you have any idea the power this connection holds?" Damian's voice rose, hoarse, and choked with fear. "If we touch her, we get pulled in with her. We don't know what will happen after that."

"I know. She told me," I ground out.

"Then you know to stand the fuck back and give her peace. That may be the best thing we can give her now." Damian gave me a pointed glare, the weight of his emotion enough to make me pause. Tears snaked down his face as he regarded Sylvia's fluttering eyes and limp wings. He was grieving her before she was gone.

Anger flashed through me. She had seen the light in me—even for a moment. "No. Not like this. She'll have peace when she's free of this bond, back here with us."

Even if it meant a life for a life. Maybe I had seen too many living nightmares, but the thought of leaving Sylvia to fight on her own was more terrifying than anything that could kill me.

As I extended a hand toward Sylvia, a thin line of fire cut across my path, forcing me to recoil.

"Don't be an idiot, hunter," Melanie said, the air still shimmering with heat around her. "A human couldn't hope to survive."

"You don't know that for sure," I countered despite the tendrils of fear rooting deeper.

The wind tore strands of her fiery hair from its braid, whipping around her face. "You could *both* die. I'll go—"

"Hazel can't lose both of you." I returned her challenging glare in full. "I've faced worse odds than these. Sylvia saved me, and I didn't deserve it. I owe her this."

My stomach churned as I considered what might await me on the other side. Instant death. Vicious nightmares. An eternity in darkness.

Or Sylvia.

I turned over my shoulder, meeting Cliff's wild stare. I cemented the image of him in my memory—just in case.

"No," Cliff breathed. "No!"

He jolted forward to stop me. I didn't give him the opportunity—without another thought, I plunged my hand toward Sylvia and made contact with her body.

When I opened my eyes, I could only understand my surroundings in bits and pieces. Having spent years honing my ability to analyze the world around me, this world made me feel robbed of my senses.

It appeared empty and endless at first, cementing my fears about an eternal abyss. The ground mirrored the sky so seamlessly that I couldn't distinguish the horizon. Constellations, both strange and familiar, were painted above and below. I couldn't feel where I stood. I should have been falling through empty air.

Breathe through the fear. Breathe.

I collapsed, disoriented. I was breathing, yet suffocating. Freezing, yet burning. Living, yet dead. I braced myself and forced another look around.

The laws of nature didn't seem to apply here. Every time I blinked, I swore the landscape changed in color and shape as if stitched together from fragments of dreams and nightmares.

A humming noise came from behind—the first sign that I wasn't alone.

I turned. Although there was no clear source of light, elusive shadows moved. How far were they? Feet, miles, or in a different level of reality altogether? My mind wanted to unravel at the sight of them. Three figures huddled together, vaguely humanoid in shape. They were fully covered in tattered cloth that didn't behave like fabric at all. There was no breeze, but the frayed ends rippled like liquid.

A scream caught in my throat.

I needed to be as far from them as possible. Their presence struck a primal terror into my soul that I didn't believe I would ever experience again—as though they were the reason behind fear itself.

But I caught a faint light in the middle of their obsessive gathering. And I was drawn to it like there was a rope attached to my chest pulling me in its direction.

I crawled at first, then pushed myself to stand when I caught a glimpse of auburn hair and dark swirls across a face twisted in pain.

"Sylvia!"

My voice echoed tinnily in my ears. I closed the distance, ignoring my fear. The Ancients were all over her, stroking her face with gnarled hands, plucking wisps of cerulean light from her skin. As I forced myself between them, they reeled back slightly. The overlapping hum of their voices was maddening.

"*You have put her sacrifice to waste by coming here.*"

"*She will die for nothing.*"

"*The child will fade knowing that her death was meaningless.*"

"Shut the fuck up!" I roared.

I pulled Sylvia onto my lap and curled my body around her. It only occurred to me then that we were the same size. She still felt so delicate, but her hand fit in mine as I entwined my fingers with hers. I couldn't quite feel the contact, as though all physical sensations were numbed in this place.

Still, I held her close and squeezed, desperate to let her know she wasn't alone. Her face, beautiful and streaked with tears, was buried halfway against me.

Her pale lips moved faintly. "*Laelithar, Daeharice. Laelithar, Daeharice.*" Again and again. She shivered and whimpered with each breath. "Make it stop, make it stop, *make it stop. Laelithar, Daeharice. Laelithar, Daeharice.*"

"Sylvia." I leaned in closer. I should have felt her breath on my skin. "The last name," I whispered in her ear. "I've got it. *Caerthynna.*"

Nothing happened, and I knew that she had to be the one to say it.

Her eyes fluttered open, unfocused.

"You're here," she croaked. Sylvia frowned and, with some effort, said, "Caerthynna."

The Ancients howled.

I clutched Sylvia protectively as they swirled like a storm around us, knobby hands clawing at our bodies. Sylvia ducked her head against my chest as their overlapped voices became a hurricane's scream, promising to claw our eyes out of their sockets thread by thread. The ethereal light of the plane dimmed as they circled faster and faster.

Gripping my shirt, Sylvia shouted above it all. The agony on her face was mixed with a mythic rage. "Laelithar. Daeharice. Caerthynna!"

Stillness cracked across the plane.

We clung to each other for a solid thirty seconds after silence set in. Breathing heavily, we slowly unfolded, assessing each other for fresh wounds and—*thankfully*—finding none.

The Ancients were on their knees in front of us in a perfect line. Their heads were hung low, their fluttering cloaks scarcely dancing at the edges that pooled on the ground. After their constant maddening whispers, their silence was unsettling—like they were unable to speak.

"I'm free." Sylvia's voice pulled my gaze right back to her. As she said this, she flung her arms around my neck, burying a sob of relief into my shoulder. "I'm *free*."

I helped her stand. After such an ordeal, I was prepared to support her, but Sylvia was steady on her feet. Color was returning readily to her face, light to her eyes. We regarded the statuesque figures kneeling before us.

"Now what?" I asked as she stepped forward toward the Ancients. I muscled down the instinct to seize her arm and pull her away from any lingering danger.

"I think they're mine to command," Sylvia answered as though she could hardly wrap her mind around it. She held out her hands, flexing her fingers tentatively. They were trembling. "I have power over them. I can feel it."

I heard her breathing quicken as she faced one nearly nose-to-nose—the voices she had been carrying around in her head for days. I pondered how she might plan to attack them, if such a thing was even possible in this place. None of my weapons had come with me here, and I assumed the same for Sylvia. Was she going to strangle them with her bare hands?

She stood before the Ancients, looking at her tormentors head-on.

"You will not have me," Sylvia declared, venom dripping from every word. "You will *never* have me. Or my magic—or that of any being, fairy or human. You will stay here in silence. Never again will you feed."

A chill ran down my spine. Sylvia's verdict was harsh and resolute. *Good.* The Ancients did not speak, but an almost imperceptible shiver of protest ran through each of them.

I stepped beside her, taking a closer look. The Ancients were truly unfathomable, even inches away. Part of me wanted to see what lay beneath the delicate exterior—rotting flesh or pristine, humanoid faces or nothing at all. I reeled at the thought that they had likely thrived for centuries on both fairies and humans, arrogance growing as the bodies mounted.

But everything bled, eventually.

I reached out toward the center Ancient where its face should have been. I gripped a sunken jaw and wrenched its head up to meet my gaze.

"You're going to starve," I said, letting my voice drop to an icy purr. "You'll die slowly, painfully. Forgotten."

If there were eyes peering up at me beneath, I couldn't be sure. Hatred and resistance rolled off the creature in waves, rooting a sick satisfaction in me.

As I let the creature sag on its knees, Sylvia's hand readily found mine. She tugged me away while the Ancients gave whimpering howls. Although it felt like we only walked a short distance, the sounds all but faded to nothing. When I looked over my shoulder, the Ancients were little more than a speck on the horizon. It was hard not to stare slack-jawed at the otherworldly landscape around us. With the dark power tethered, what served as a sky seemed brighter already. Vibrant beams of pink and white pulsed delicately like clouds, the air golden in their light. It felt less like a surreal hellscape now and more like *Sylvia.*

She pulled to a stop and wheeled to stand in front of me. She gaped at me, gripping my arms.

"You came for me," Sylvia whispered. "I can't believe you're *here.* That you survived."

"Unfortunately, I think I'm as stubborn as you are," I said, arching an eyebrow.

Though it was playful, some of the excitement drained from Sylvia's eyes as she registered the uncertainty cloying the air between us. My throat tightened, remembering that our bodies were currently husks on the forest floor. I still had to make it back *out* in one piece.

Giving a small, resolute nod, she shuddered out another breath and assessed me again. Her hands ran up and down my sleeves, squeezing me like I might be a mirage.

"It's been hours," she whispered. "What happened out there? How did you get the name? Is my family—"

"Wait—*hours*? Sylvia, it's been less than thirty minutes."

"No, no. I was… They were…" She glanced toward the Ancients, and I gingerly cupped her face, bringing her back to me. Although they could no longer hurt her, the torture she'd endured swam in her eyes. "It felt like ages."

They'd been playing with their food. My insides burned at the awful question of how long she would have suffered before her magic and life were snuffed out for good.

"The time difference is on our side now," I assured her. "Cliff's holding off the guards with Damian and your mother."

She breathed in sharply. "Forget surviving the spectral realm—Mother didn't burn you alive?"

"It might still be on her to-do list."

Sylvia laughed, breaking out in a full smile that made my knees weak. It was overwhelming, taking in every inch of her at this scale. Bright green eyes. Soft hair. Freckles I had never noticed before. My fingertips brushed the mark on her cheek. Despite its dark origins, she'd gotten this mark in part because of me. It was a permanent reminder that our fates had intertwined, even briefly.

A twisted attraction surfaced amid the queasiness of knowing she'd been injured. As I traced the swirls on her skin, a beast in my chest purred possessively.

Mine.

Her grin morphed into a smirk. "Still think I'm pretty for a non-human?"

"That depends. Still think I'm too scary to reach a one?"

Her hand jumped to grip my wrist. At first, I thought she was pulling me away, but she was holding my touch in place. My other arm found its way around her back and pulled her against me, leaving no space in between. A soft breath escaped her, emboldening me. My thumb wandered across Sylvia's cheek and brushed over her lips.

All at once, she surged onto tiptoes and pressed her mouth against mine. My eyes fell shut. The sensation was muted, but a thrill soared in my chest all the same. Tasting her made all other kisses I'd ever known fade from memory. She was sweet, like sun-soaked strawberries in the peak of summer.

I deepened the kiss, gripping her tighter. I might never get to kiss her like this again, and I wanted her to wake up thinking about me for weeks following.

When she broke away, she wrapped her arms around my ribs and buried her cheek against my chest. "If only there were music," she said. "Then you could show me what a bad dance partner you are."

I tucked her hair behind her ear, wondering if she could feel how thunderously my heart was beating.

"I wish I could hold you like this a little longer," I said.

I wanted hours, allowing me to explore unhurried and without restraint. But we couldn't stay.

"If I don't make it back—" I started.

"You will," Sylvia said, leaning back in my firm embrace so she could shoot me a hard look, eyebrows hiked. I did my best to memorize every detail.

"I want you to know what *inolvidable* means," I told her.

"A Spanish lesson? Now?"

I moved one hand from the small of her back to her face. I traced along the delicate curve of her jaw, catching her chin—pleased by the response it drew out of her when her eyes shuttered as though savoring my touch.

"It means *unforgettable*," I whispered.

Her eyes opened, blazing with a determination that cut through a veil of tears. Eyes I could get lost in.

Sylvia drew a deep breath, securing her stance. "Don't let go of me."

She began to chant—the same foreign words that she had spoken to enter the spectral plane. I squeezed her tighter as though it might prevent her from disappearing from my arms.

In a blink, Sylvia had vanished, and I found myself surrounded by chaos.

32

SYLVIA

I felt like I was slammed back into my body. After days of feeling weak, I almost didn't know how to handle my full capacity. Scrambling to my feet, I gasped for air as though I'd been held underwater.

Jon stirred, his hand dragging away from me. I flinched at how startlingly huge he was again. But that was overshadowed by crippling relief—he was *alive*. He winced as he sat up. Blood trickled from one nostril, and I worried that he had been hurt while he was out.

Shouts came from overhead. I burst into flight. Hours had worn on in my mind, but the battle seemed to have only begun. Mother and Damian wielded bursts of wind and flame in an attempt to hold off a squadron of Entry Watch guards.

One guard—Titus—had dared to get close to Cliff and was paying dearly for it. Cliff had him pinned against a tree with one hand, holding the iron bar a breath away from the guard's protruding arm to threaten away any attempts of magic.

"Cliff!" I shouted as another guard, Aksel, swooped in from behind him.

With a mere glance over his shoulder, Cliff released Titus and ducked to avoid a jolt of lightning. He gritted his teeth, using the iron rod to bat away the subsequent attacks that rained on him. His reflexes were impeccable, but singes and blood adorned his skin and clothes. When he tired, the lightning affinities would reduce that pretty face to something for the crows to pick at.

Heart in my throat, I nearly flew to defend him, but Damian cried in pain from the branch above me. Judging by the fresh vines snaking around Damian's ankles like vipers, this attacker amidst the chaos was an earth affinity.

Frost blossomed at my fingertips before the spell had formed on my lips. I sent a sharp cut of ice to sever the vines. I waved my hand in an arc, conjuring a concave shield around Damian as he landed on hands and knees with a grunt of surprise. The glistening ice froze in a dynamic shape, separating him from the muscular fairy on the other side.

Jon weaved through the trees toward Cliff, making himself a target. I watched in horror as a streak of white flames clipped Jon's shoulder. Only advanced affinities could conjure fire that hot.

I heard Jon utter a curse as he ducked behind a tree for cover, swatting the tongue of fire on his jacket. Blood and skin were visible through the hole in the leather. I flinched, touching my own shoulder automatically.

But I didn't feel his pain this time.

I flew forward, whispering another spell. Glistening frost slammed into the armored chest of the fire affinity that attacked Jon.

"Traitor!" the guard shouted, locking eyes on me. Kalem—he and Mother had trained together as children.

He lifted his hands, still aglow at the center of each palm. I was quicker, targeting his wings and casting a layer of frost over them. Thin enough that he could thaw them out before he hit the ground. Thick enough that he would panic as his flight locked up and he dropped like a stone.

"Jon?" I cried out, starting toward him to assess the damage.

"To your right!" he shouted back.

I whipped my head around. A fairy was tearing out of Cliff's fist, a frosty mist blooming around her. Another ice affinity—Priya. She seemed to enjoy Cliff's hiss of pain when one of her jagged icicles connected successfully into his leg. I should have been used to blood by now, but the crimson staining the stone-washed denim still made my stomach twist.

Before I could spur my wings into motion, Mother dropped into view. With scarcely a flick of her wrist, she set Priya's armor ablaze. Priya shrieked, redirecting her magic to oust the flames. Mother pointedly ignored the grunt of gratitude from Cliff.

As Priya recovered with a snarl and circled in the air, I conjured a wider shield of ice encircling both hunters and Mother. I gave all I had into the spellwork, making the ice thick and frosted like it had been there for years.

"Enough!" I screamed.

The fighting had gradually slowed at my intrusion as guards took notice of the Elysian traitor, but now it came to a halt. All eyes moved to me. My chest heaved as I looked all around, ice charged and shimmering up to my shoulders. The air around me was spiked with energy.

"I'm the traitor, not them. Are you really all so riddled with bloodlust?" I looked around at the Entry Watch members with disgust. I recognized every face; some had been my childhood friends, and some were closer to Mother's age or older. Perhaps they were just following orders.

"If you want blood, come to me." My voice had an authoritative pitch I didn't recognize. "But this doesn't have to end in violence."

The guards looked to each other uncertainly, like they couldn't be sure what to make of me. I must have looked crazy. With any luck, they wouldn't want to cross a fairy who'd made it back from the spectral plane alive.

My hope was extinguished as a burst of flames cut through the clearing and melted a gaping hole in the ice shield in front of Jon. Lireal and Ayden were fast approaching, and I couldn't patch the hole fast enough while maintaining the rest of the shield. In a matter of seconds, Ayden had reduced my shield to a ragged line of icy stumps. I flew in front of the hunters, tendrils of frost charged at my fingertips.

"Don't come any closer!" I shouted as Lireal pulled to a stop across from in front of the guards' staggered alignment. "I must warn you—I've just returned from my engagement with the Ancients. I broke their claim on me. You have no idea what I'm capable of." I watched with a twist of satisfaction as this sent a shiver of shock through many of the Entry Watch guards. I kept my chin high, determined to fuel their frenzied image of me. "I don't want to hurt anyone—but I'll freeze this forest solid if I have to."

Lireal scrutinized me. "You don't have that kind of magic in you."

"Try me," I bit out.

The Elder stared at me for a long moment. My palms began to sweat as I wondered what in the stars' names I would do if she pressed my bluff. I was practically shaking with exhaustion.

Lireal motioned at the guards, who obediently ousted any spellwork. Someone conjured fae lights, sending them at fixed points in the canopy overhead to provide a soft wash of illumination. I swallowed a sigh of relief, even as her gaze became downright venomous.

"What now? You expect to return to your chambers peacefully after everything you have done, girl?" Lireal asked. "The damage you've dealt us... Do you know half the village is terrified to leave their homes from fear of imminent attack?"

I muscled down a flinch. I hadn't considered how vicious the rumors would be in my absence—not to the point of hurting anyone else. I looked from face to face in the line of fairies, each lined with a grim resolve. My heart began to pound.

"But hasn't all of this proven we were wrong?" I demanded. "These hunters saved lives—they killed a *mactir* that could have preyed on even more of us. Jon risked his life to save mine from the Ancients. They're no threat to our people."

I cast a helpless glance back at Cliff and Jon. For the first time since I'd met them, they looked like they didn't know what to do.

A cold smile twitched at the corners of Lireal's mouth. "You really believe that, don't you?"

"It's true!"

"The fact that you say such things," Lireal hissed, "is exactly why you cannot return to Elysia."

The words were serrated, a blade to my lungs. *Banishment.* I didn't understand why the forest blurred until hot tears ran down my cheeks. The weariness in my bones doubled as though my body knew it would not get to rest in my bed tonight.

"Please… I take full responsibility," I said, hating how my voice had lost its power.

"That's not enough."

"This is my home. All I've ever known! My family… I won't hurt anyone—*please*. You don't have to do this, I swear!"

Lireal drifted closer to me in the air. Ayden trailed close to her side as though I might change my mind and lash out. "I've known you since you were but a thought in your Mother's mind, Sylvia," Lireal said quietly. "This brings me no pleasure. Elysia's safety is fragile. You have strayed where you cannot come back."

"No!" Mother howled. "You can't do this."

Lireal snapped her head up, eyes cutting behind me. "Melanie, if you lift another finger, I swear on the stars I will have it severed."

Numbness crept through me. I rubbed at my eyes, refusing to meet the Elder's searing gaze. I wouldn't admit it, but there was a thread of truth to her words that resonated. After entering Jon and Cliff's lives so intimately, taking down a *mactir*, defeating the very Ancients themselves… Something in me felt different. The world was vast now, and to some extent, so was I. It was as simple and terrible as that—my life in Elysia was over.

"I do, however, share your concern for bloodshed." Lireal pressed in my silence. "Do you agree to leave these woods peacefully?"

I nodded my head like it was leaden. Considering I had been threatened with execution, perhaps I should have been grateful. "I swear on my life and magic that I will never return."

"Wait," Jon blurted, incredulous. "Sylvia..."

"What choice do I have?" I asked, whirling to face him.

He had no answer.

I caught a glimpse of Mother hovering near him, along with Cliff's wide-eyed expression. Damian's frozen stare. Pity and grief and outrage everywhere I looked.

Ayden scoffed. "Banishment is too kind. She should be executed before another word falls out of her traitorous mouth."

Jon gave a seething, sharp breath behind me. "If you touch her—" He stopped short at the firm look I gave him.

"You can try to kill me," I told Ayden, injecting new strength into my voice. "But I can assure you that won't end well. Besides, this isn't your call, is it?" I turned my eyes to Lireal, mustering a smirk. "You're outranked."

I looked back to Jon again, a lump swelling in my throat. I could see the faint scar on his neck from the dog bite I had healed in the Dottage mansion basement. I wouldn't apologize for saving him. For learning to trust them both.

Silence hung heavily. Lireal glared like she couldn't imagine a more shameful creature than me.

"A blood oath," she said, raising her eyebrows as though this might reveal that my intentions weren't pure.

A murmur went through the guards, and I could already hear Mother protesting.

I nodded and closed the distance between us, drawing my blade. "I will state the terms," I said, trying to remember the proper way to phrase such a formal oath. "No more violence will be exchanged in these woods tonight. Neither I nor these hunters will enter Elysian territory after we leave." Pulling a deep breath, I carved a line across my palm with a wince.

Still looking skeptical, Lireal held out her hand. It wasn't until I drew the oath rune on her palm with my blood that she seemed to realize this wasn't a hoax. But someone of her stature was well aware that blood oaths ran both ways. I held out the dagger to her. She accepted it cautiously.

"What is your wish in return for this offering?" she asked.

I felt Mother's gaze boring into me, and a sob welled in my chest again. I was losing her. Losing Hazel.

"My family will not be punished for my transgressions, directly or indirectly. They can continue to live in Elysia safely. And… you will give me time to say goodbye to them before I go." Every word felt like poison crawling up my throat.

The Elder waited as though I might add more. When I remained silent, she drew the tip of the blade across her weathered palm. "It is done," she said after she had traced the rune onto my palm.

Although blood oaths came without fanfare, I could feel its promises settle in my bones.

Lireal withdrew the moment the blood faded into our palms. She tucked the long sleeves of her opaline garment around herself like a shawl. To my surprise, sadness flickered behind her wizened eyes as she appraised me.

"Such a pity," she said, too softly for anyone else to hear. Then, she averted her gaze sharply. "You have half an hour. Ayden, I want the Watch doubled for the next month. Assemble a squad to stay between this location and the village until the brutes have left."

"Of course. I'll direct messengers to send word to the other Elders this very evening," Ayden replied self-importantly.

After a final look at me, Lireal flew back toward the village for good, several guards accompanying her in tight formation.

There were so many eyes on me—the remaining guards, the hunters, Mother, Damian. I had half an hour to square away everything I had ever known.

The moment my eyes locked with Damian's, he rushed to my side. His embrace nearly knocked the breath out of me. We landed on a mossy boulder, and all I could do was let myself melt into his arms again. Exhaustion tempted me to close my eyes and fall asleep against his chest like I'd done so many times before.

"You're alive," he breathed, voice thick. "I was out of my mind with worry since you left with that hunter. You can't imagine."

"I'm getting the idea," I teased, pointedly squirming in his fierce grip.

His arms loosened. I leaned my forehead against his. There was a scrape on the side of his head and obvious swelling in his ankles where the vines had cut into his flesh. Guilt rose in me.

Past him, I could see Jon and Cliff assessing their own injuries and eyeing the remaining guards warily. I made eye contact with both of them in turn, hoping they could read my expression: *You can go.* But they didn't move, standing like sentries watching over me while I said my goodbyes.

I was torn away from Damian as Mother landed beside me. We embraced so fiercely that I couldn't breathe. Even if she would release me, my throat was too tight to draw any air. While I was still soaking in the familiarity of her touch, a slight rustle came from above. Hazel dropped from the branches and made a beeline in between us.

"Oh! Where did you come from?" I asked against her frizzy hair.

I looked up at her hiding spot in horror, wondering how long she had been idling by in the midst of the onslaught—one wrong move from possibly being hit by an errant flame or blast of ice. Mother looked equally alarmed, but seeing as our minutes together were dwindling, her scolding was halfhearted.

"Don't leave again," Hazel whimpered into my shoulder.

"I have to," I said, fighting emotion in my voice for her sake.

Mother kissed our heads, hushing us both. "Don't worry, my loves. No one will separate us."

"Don't spin a comforting lie, Melanie," Ayden drawled. His coarse voice came close behind me, raising the hairs on the back of my neck. I hugged Hazel in my lap as Mother rose to her feet. Ayden's hover moved back pointedly as she rounded to face him.

"I don't care what the oath says," Mother said. "I'm not being separated from my daughter."

"And leave your little one behind? You aren't foolish enough to believe she can survive outside the safety of Elysia, even with your protection." He sneered at me. "With Sylvia's penchant for murderous entities, you'd all be dead within a week. Stars, she's as misled as Tristan was."

If the oath weren't binding my sudden thirst for violence, I would have struck him through the heart with ice.

"Watch your tongue," Mother hissed through her teeth. The air felt molten.

"You should be on your knees thanking the stars that we didn't put an end to your accursed bloodline tonight," Ayden said. The promise in his voice would have made any other full-grown fairy turn meek. Mother didn't flinch.

"You and Hazel have to stay here," I cut in, touching Mother's arm.

She turned to me, eyes wild.

"You know it's true," I insisted. "The oath protects you. I made sure of that. I've done enough damage without dragging you and

Hazel outside the safety of the glamour barriers. I don't know what life is waiting out there. Please, Mother." My throat closed again. If I dared speak another word, I might cave and beg them to come with me.

"Where are you supposed to go?" she hissed at me, one hand threading into her hair and tugging. "There are no villages for over a week's flight from here."

"She had her chance," Ayden said. "If she's lucky, an owl will make a quick death for her. Or... other nocturnal beasts." He eyed Jon and Cliff, clearly uncertain if I was their ally or prey.

Mother looked five seconds away from initiating the fire affinity fight of the decade with Ayden. Her cheeks were nearly the same shade as her scarlet hair. Instead, she squared her shoulders and gave me a bizarrely distracted look. "I'll be right back. If you're leaving, you will need supplies."

She stopped short, doubling back to look from Hazel to the hunters. I tightened my grip on Hazel's shoulders, giving Mother a slight nod of reassurance. Though it did little to quell the smoldering distrust in Mother's eyes, she flew off.

Clearly worried that she would try to pull off something nefarious, Ayden followed her. On the way, he barked orders for several of the remaining guards to stay in formation at a distance and ensure that neither the hunters nor I dared to come any closer to the village.

The air was particularly freezing on my skin as I imagined the cozy space of my shared bedroom. I stroked Hazel's hair. I would never see my hand-stitched quilt again or the box of human treasures under my bed. She would discover her affinity, and I wouldn't be there to celebrate her joy.

Damian shuffled closer, putting his hand on my shoulder. "I don't want to lose you again, Sylvia," he said. "If your family can't go with you, then I... I'll do it. You don't have to be alone. We can leave together. Make a life for ourselves." He cupped my face, eyes ablaze as he glanced at my lips. After a beat of hesitation, he leaned in.

I turned my head before our lips could brush. "You don't mean that."

"Yes, I do," Damian said like he was blind to everything else but me. "You're what I want most, and I didn't act on it before. Not the way you needed. I'm so sorry."

Betrayal still burned in my chest. But taking in the state of his clothes, I softened. He had fought for me, too. He was warm and earnest. If I asked, he would leave Elysia for me, but there was fear gleaming in his gaze. It wouldn't be an adventure for him by any means. It would be a sacrifice, a nightmare. Any love he felt for me would fester into resentment in a matter of weeks.

"You'd be miserable," I said, sighing. "There's still a chance for you to make a life here—one you can be proud of."

Damian opened his mouth to argue, but he paused when he saw how I was checking on the hunters again—checking on Jon. He dropped his hand from my shoulder, his crestfallen expression mixed with faint horror.

"Him?" he breathed.

I tore my eyes from Jon's soft, searching gaze. I shook my head at my tattered shoes. "I know it's crazy. I know I shouldn't—"

"But even still, it's *him*, isn't it?" Damian said, voice wooden. "You care about him."

I nodded slowly.

Damian's jaw clenched hard. His gaze was dulled as he lowered his voice further—so the hunters couldn't hear. "Do you love him?"

"I don't know what to call it. If I survive to fall in love, I should be very lucky." I took Damian's hand in mine, extending a tentative thread of reparation between us. "And I have known a great deal of love already."

Damian stood there in silence for an uncomfortable amount of time.

"Was there anything I could have done differently?" he asked. "Would it have changed anything?"

I remembered being children together, mounting our hummingbirds for the very first time. His rich laughter and his hands on my skin during revels, dragging colors over the most sensitive places on my wings. The look of horror he'd given me when I'd begged him to venture to Dottage. The rejection stung, even now.

"Our paths used to intertwine, but things have changed. Take care of yourself," I said. "Be safe."

The resigned look Damian gave me would haunt me for the rest of my life. "You too, Sylvia."

His hand slipped from mine. His gaze flickered to Jon—who was trying very hard not to look like he was watching us as closely as I knew he was.

"If I catch word something's happened to her," Damian called over. "You'll hear from me again. She won't save you this time."

Jon lifted a brow. "I think you're more likely to hear of any threats to Sylvia impaled by ice," he said, eyes gleaming as he glanced at me. My cheeks glowed.

Damian sighed through his nose, assenting. "You may be right about that." His deep brown eyes rested on me once more, like he was memorizing me, mark and all. He spread his wings, mumbling something about checking if my mother needed help with the supplies. And then, he was gone, too.

The fae lights overhead were dimmer than they'd been ten minutes ago, casting deeper shadows across the forest. Only two Entry Watch fairies remained, too noble to leave a ten-year-old alone with a traitor and two human hunters covered in werewolf blood. Though they hovered nearby, they didn't protest when Jon and Cliff closed the remaining distance to kneel beside the moss-covered rock I was perched on. Hazel swiftly flew to my arms, fingers digging in at the back of my neck.

"Are you okay?" Jon asked like it was a breath he'd been holding since the chaos had stopped.

There was no fighting it anymore—the way my heart ached at the resonant timbre of his voice. My soul felt stretched, pulling toward him while still clinging to the home I was losing. It was impossible to pluck an answer out of the churning exhaustion and grief in my chest.

"I fared better than you two," I replied, injecting exasperation into my voice. "I swear, it's like you enjoy being covered in blood."

Both men gave a wry smile at this. The hunters glistened with sweat, their complexions speckled with grime, and their eyes dulled with exhaustion.

Cliff glanced between Jon and me, furrowing his brow. "And… the bond?"

"Gone," I said. "The Ancients are as good as dead."

I swelled at the look Jon gave me—like I was something incredible. I hoped he never looked at anyone else like that.

Cliff nodded, then angled his head to acknowledge the bundle of nerves in my arms—which whimpered as his eyes set on her. "You must be Hazel."

Hazel went rigid against me. "Yes," she admitted, whisper-quiet.

The corners of Cliff's mouth lifted. His voice was a soft decibel I'd never heard him use. "Sylv's told us about you. Do you like sugar as much as your sister?"

Eyes like saucers, Hazel kept looking to me for reassurance, which I readily provided. I could sympathize—having a hunter address you directly was undeniably a piss-your-pants kind of terrifying. I smiled wider, nodding for her to answer.

"I like peach tarts with walnuts," she told him shyly.

Cliff rewarded her with one of those charm-loaded smiles of his. To my surprise, it seemed to work.

"Sophisticated taste. I don't have any tarts on me, but I do have something..."

Hazel leaned forward, her eyes bright with anticipation as Cliff dug around in his pocket. He sorted through some loose change and a butterfly knife before he withdrew a canary-yellow candy wrapped in plastic and offered it to my sister.

"It's just butterscotch. It doesn't bite," he said. "I promise."

At a snail's pace, Hazel peeled herself off me to approach his hand. She stole suspicious looks upward before she accepted the candy. After a beat, she put the candy under one arm and touched Cliff's index finger. Innocent curiosity washed over the abject terror. She felt along his knuckle and lines on his calloused palm. I stole a peek at Cliff's face. The moment she had touched him, he'd gone stock-still like he was afraid to move. The gentleness in his eyes was disarming. Small blue flowers inked on his wrist protruded under his jacket sleeve—the tattoo for his own sister.

"Will you make sure owls don't eat her?" Hazel asked, looking up at him. "Or hawks?"

My lips parted, uncertainty spooling in my gut. Cliff hadn't wanted me here in the first place. Plastering on a weak smile, I pushed to my feet. "Hazel, that wouldn't be right. I don't need them to—"

"We'll look out for her," Cliff laid over me. "As long as she needs."

His resolute gaze moved from Hazel to me, and a beat of understanding passed between us. His jaw feathered, promising the same ferocious protection he provided to any human. I looked to Jon, who mirrored the assurance.

"Hazel! Get away from him!" Mother's voice cut across the clearing as she reappeared in a fury.

She dropped the bulging canvas bags she was carrying, leaving several of their contents to spill out on the surface of the rock we perched on. Sweeping Hazel onto her hip, she leveled a glare at Cliff. "If you harmed a hair on her head, I will roast you where you stand," she hissed, eyes flashing daggers.

Cliff, unaware that his charm would have no effect on my mother, tried to laugh off her threat. "Come on, I bet your bark is worse than your burn."

"She isn't joking," Hazel said. "I saw her do it to a raccoon once. The smell was awful." She wriggled one arm free to show Mother the candy. "It's alright, Mother, he gave me a gift. And he says they're going to look after Sylvia."

"Thank you again, by the way," Cliff said, clearing his throat. "For saving my skin back there. You've got some killer moves."

"I hardly had a choice, did I?" Mother said without meeting his gaze. "You were floundering like a drunken fish."

Cliff's smile dropped into a surly pout.

Mother folded her wings primly to her back before turning toward me. She paused briefly to eye Jon, who was delicately picking up the supplies she had dropped—bits of clothing, jars of jam, a few books, parchment. She didn't seem to know what to make of his unrequested assistance.

"You're really leaving with them?" Mother asked.

"For tonight. I'll have somewhere safe to sleep, at least," I offered. Looking for any shred of positivity in such a bleak ruling only made me feel more hysterical. I muscled it down.

Mother pursed her lips and set Hazel beside me, murmuring for her to *stay put* this time. She approached Jon and snatched a piece of parchment from his palm, not lingering for a single moment more than necessary.

"A map?" I frowned at the aged paper she unrolled between us. It outlined supposedly safe pathways through the wilderness. Human roads and territories deemed unsafe were easily spotted in burnt umber strokes. Villages and nomadic compounds were neatly labeled. "What good is this? This hasn't been updated since before I was born."

"Be that as it may, there are villages marked here that are still active," Mother said.

I wrenched away from her, giving her a confused look. "How would you know? You've never left Elysia in your entire life."

Mother's hand shook feverishly as she traced over the mountains and rivers immortalized in faded ink like she was flying along the route in her mind's eye. "Here. *Aelthorin.*" She tapped a ten-pointed star that rested on a western forest. My heart lodged in my throat; Elysia was marked with a sunbeam on the opposite side of the map. "Find Aelthorin. They will treat you well, even with—" Mother bit off her next words, emerald eyes jumping to my traitor mark.

A pit of betrayal rooted in my stomach, though I couldn't entirely understand *why*. "Mother, what are you talking about? How do you know for certain?"

Mother glanced behind us at the Entry Watch guards—at Ayden. "I can't say," she said. Tears flooded her wide eyes, and she gripped my shoulder. "I'm sorry. I'm so sorry for this and more… But promise me you'll go, Sylvia. I will find you there."

"I… I promise," I answered—because what else could I say?

Mother produced a palm-sized object wrapped in cloth. Her fingers trembled as she pressed it into my hands. "One last thing. This used to be your Father's. I hope you don't need it, but if you do…" She breathed out hard. She was trying to be strong for me. "If something happens, there should be enough power left in this one to get you out of any danger."

My eyes ballooned. I pushed at the fabric to reveal a shard of amethyst glinting up at me. The mere sight of the gem sent shivers down my spine, sent me hurtling back to childhood—the last time I had laid eyes on a charged gemstone. The magic at its core pulsated, beckoning to me like a distant song.

"I don't want it," I blurted, pushing it back toward her. I tried to muscle the emotion out of my voice, mindful of the remaining guards nearby. Again, I reeled at the very presence of what she offered me. Mother could have been penalized for even holding onto a gem after the decree had been issued.

"Don't be foolish," Mother said, slipping into an urgent growl. "You need every aid you can get." I didn't miss the way her gaze cut over to Jon and Cliff.

"I don't want any more external magic. Not after…" I shook my head, still queasy when I thought of the Ancients. Their voices still echoed in the darkest crevices of my mind. I wondered if I would ever fully be rid of them. My gaze lowered, hardening on the amethyst in my hands. "Gem magic killed Father. What, you want me to share his fate?"

Mother's eyes flashed. "His *arrogance* killed him. Nonetheless, this should be used as a last resort. Am I clear?"

She looked at me with such desperate, aching urgency… It knitted my stomach, and I felt compelled to obediently agree. As I closed my fingers around the cool weight of the stone, I heaved a long, slow breath.

"Nine years… He's been gone for nine years," I rasped out, "and you've held onto it all this time? Why?"

Fresh tears wet her emerald eyes, though she fought to keep them from falling. "Because I loved him. Perhaps too much." She pressed a kiss to my forehead. "And I love you, too. Your father would want you to have it—to *survive*."

Throat tight, I wrapped the gem shard and tucked it into my pocket. I swore it pulsed like a heartbeat against my leg.

Mother lifted her chin, the hardness in her face flickering into pleading as she looked between Jon and Cliff. "Please, don't let her get hurt again."

I had never heard Mother's voice drop to such a pitiful croak. She demanded, snapped, reproached—*never* begged. She sounded like she might cry. It was hard to stomach.

"Anything that comes for Sylvia comes for me, too," Jon said.

Mother clenched her jaw, giving a small nod. I knew nothing would satisfy the nightmare facing her, but his words were balm enough.

She cupped my face, her wariness softening for a moment—for *me*. "There is a place out there for us, my love. A home." She brought her voice to a shaky whisper. "We will find each other again. All will be well."

How?

How could *anything* ever feel okay again after this?

Any hope of getting an answer from her was dashed as one of the guards approached and announced that our time was up.

Hazel clung to me immediately as though she could single-handedly root me in place on the rock. Mother wrapped us both in a tight hug before pulling my sister away with some difficulty. Hazel was sobbing by then—no amount of assurances or candy could fix that. Mother had to hold her in her arms as they flew off, prodded forward by the guards.

Her face a mask of tears, Hazel looked over Mother's shoulder and waved goodbye fiercely. I watched until their glows vanished into the foliage, leaving the woods utterly ordinary. The fae lights above had dwindled to mere wisps of magic. The emptiness threatened to consume me.

I didn't move other than to start trembling against my will. I nearly collapsed to my knees, but Jon—hunter reflexes on full display—brought a hand to my side before I could fall.

Cliff's voice provided another anchor: "Let's get some rest." It wasn't a question. When I turned, the look he gave me was almost as warm as the one reserved for Hazel. I surrendered to that warmth.

Swallowing the lump in my throat, I nodded. Despite Jon's gentle insistence, I declined the offer to be carried.

When I crossed the threshold of the forest and initiated my banishment, I would be on my own wings.

33

SYLVIA

The evening passed numbly. I blinked, and we were in the car. I blinked again, and we were in the motel room.

The hunters gave me space while I organized and reorganized my belongings aimlessly. As Jon and Cliff dressed their wounds, their gazes rested heavily upon me. Whenever I glanced in their direction, they stiffened as though they expected me to either burst into tears or rip them to shreds.

I should have been bawling my eyes out, but my cheeks remained dry. There was a void in my chest, all-consuming. It felt like it would slowly turn me into ice.

After running out of clothing, books, and jars to pack, I stood by the nightstand lamp, fully intending to do something. But for the life of me, I couldn't figure out what to do.

Spotting my inability to proceed, Jon was kind enough to remind me what one should do before bed. He led me to the washroom, where he drew a warm bath in the sink. He poked carefully through my belongings until he plucked out clothes he thought would be comfortable for me to sleep in. When I emerged from the washroom, dried and dressed, he offered food that I couldn't remember the taste of. I might have slept on the unforgiving wood of the nightstand if he hadn't directed me to his spare pillow.

It was pure relief to surrender to his simple instructions. Less than a week ago, I would have been mortified by my pathetic vulnerability around a pair of hunters.

As I curled up on the pillow, their voices rumbled distantly. Jon described to Cliff what he had seen in the spectral realm. Apparently, Jon had been frightened out of his mind when confronting the Ancients. I couldn't fathom that. He'd been so solid, so ferociously brave as he held me in his arms.

At some point, the erratic crackle of their police scanner laid over their conversation. Cliff bristled at something that was said on the line—a tip provided by a local neighborhood watch member.

"Dispatcher, I've got a description of a couple drifters linked to a possible crime spree. Two males, mid-to-late twenties, approximately six-foot-one and six-foot-three in height. Caucasian. Driving a silver Pontiac—older model. Witness didn't get a clear look at the plates."

Cliff sighed. "I guess that's our cue."

I was too exhausted to ask what that meant. I trusted them—surely, they knew what to do. Feeling heavy as a stone, I drifted into a deep, dreamless sleep.

My eyes ached the next morning as though I had slept for minutes instead of hours. Jon and Cliff packed up all they owned, leaving the motel room bare and dark. I cast one last look at its papered walls before the hunters checked out of the motel for good.

They made uprooting themselves seem so uncomplicated.

Claiming I needed more sleep, I huddled in the backseat. In reality, I needed to avoid the windows. My miserable heart couldn't bear witnessing how quickly we were leaving behind the only world I'd ever known. Regardless of my lack of view, I could *feel* how every second pulled me away from Elysia.

Isn't this what you wanted? My own admonishment filled the silence that the Ancients' hissing voices left behind.

Yes, I'd wanted to explore. But in my daydreams, I still had a home to return to.

Time forgot reality, passing strangely as morning swept into midday. The monotonous hum of the car's engine was a constant companion to my wandering thoughts, making it easier to lay there quietly. The snowflake charm dug uncomfortably into my hip. I couldn't recall putting it on. Jon and Cliff talked in low tones occasionally, debating on whether they should have the car checked out at a shop.

Jon's phone buzzed. "Hello?" His voice rose after a moment. "Tammy?"

Cliff breathed in sharply while I half-heartedly listened to Jon's end of the conversation. It didn't last long.

"Yeah… Yeah, a werewolf was churning out the body count. We're heading out of town. Thanks for checking up." A pause. He glanced my way so quickly, I might've imagined it. He cleared his throat. "About that… We took care of it. Don't worry." He hung up shortly after.

I nearly fell asleep minutes later, but Jon's voice took on an urgent edge when he spoke again—this time to Cliff.

"Hey—your arm."

I sat up, peering at Cliff in the front passenger seat. A small but persistent red stain spread through the bandages across his upper arm—the one that had been wounded during the werewolf fight. A pang of concern shot through me and broke the apathetic fog.

The men exchanged a few words. Jon guided the car to the side of the road. I followed them outside, then halted in midair like I'd flown into a wall, struck by the beauty that backdropped our unexpected stop.

The car was parked on gravel at the base of a weathered human bridge that spanned across a river. The rushing water sparkled in the sun, disrupting the reflection of towering trees that lined the opposing bank. The air was sweet with pine and juniper.

With the trunk popped open, the hunters rummaged for medical supplies and water. Jon looked up from the car at the distant call of a bird, scanning branches like he hoped to glimpse it. I recalled his quiet, gentle look at the woods outside of Dottage, and I wondered if he had chosen this very spot because of its beauty. It still seemed impossible that someone like him could appreciate the artistry of nature. I had been wrong about him in nearly every way—both of them.

Supplies in hand, Cliff and Jon hiked the short path that led down to the river. They found a spot drenched in the bridge's shade, sitting to refresh and change bandages.

I hovered over the water lapping against the rocks and grass. The current was too turbulent to discern my reflection, but perhaps that was a blessing. I doubted I would recognize the person staring back at me.

After splashing water on my face, I turned to see Cliff carefully peeling off the final layer of bandage to reveal red, inflamed skin. He cleaned the wound, grimacing. Even with Jon's homemade balm, I knew he wouldn't find the immediate relief he deserved.

I flew over to Cliff without a second thought. "Let me heal it." My tone took an abrasive edge at the memory of his instant rejection of my help. "The guards made it worse. They're trained to target weak spots."

Although Cliff didn't look disgusted or angered by my offer, he shook his head at once. "It's fine. I've had worse."

"Why does that mean you have to shoulder the pain?" Searching his worried face, I realized where his uncertainty came from. "Healing you won't hurt me," I assured. "I'm not being drained anymore."

After a beat of hesitation, Cliff nodded. "Just promise you won't make any deals with fairy demons on my account."

Before he could change his mind, I hovered by his wound. His phoenix tattoo had been lacerated through its inked plumage. As I began the healing incantation, part of me awaited the gut-punch sensation of weakness. But my magic was my own again, and Cliff's gash wasn't life-threatening like Jon's dog bite.

A scar remained when I completed the spell. Cliff looked from me to the closed wound with a frown. "So that's how it feels," he murmured.

Turning my attention to his other bandages, I thought of the burns and cuts he had received while defending me from the Entry Watch guards. Ancients or not, I was spent from healing a gash as tall as me. I desperately wanted to try anyway. It was unfair that the hunters should suffer while I had the ability to take their pain away.

My flight faltered, and Cliff brought his palm under my feet. "You okay?" he asked.

"I'm fine, but..." I looked down shamefully. "I don't think I have the strength to heal the rest right now. I'm sorry."

"Give yourself a break." Lifting me closer, he brushed a kiss over the top of my head. I had to wonder if blood loss had made him delusional, but the warmth in his gaze was unmistakable. "Banishment *and* three mystical Ancient beings in one night. Not a bad record, kiddo."

"And a werewolf," I noted.

His smile widened, crinkling the corners of his eyes. "Don't let it go to your head."

My laugh might have been a sob.

Cliff's gaze softened, a gentle furrow in his brow. "I know it hurts like hell. Your own people turning on you. I'm not going to tell you that time heals all wounds because that's bullshit. There are some hurts that *never* fucking heal. You can't drink it off, pray it away, or kill it. That ache doesn't go."

Tears stung my eyes. I wanted to comfort him for whatever his family had done to make him believe what he was telling me. I wanted to be held myself, cradled and coddled and loved.

Most of all, I wanted Mother.

"So, I'm just gonna feel shitty forever?" I asked coarsely.

Cliff's lips parted—I could imagine the placating lies he wanted to tell me, but it wasn't in his nature. "Maybe. But the important thing is, you find a good person or two who won't give up on you. Make room for the good with the bad. That'll make you feel a lot less shitty, I promise."

His gaze cut meaningfully to Jon, a measure of gratitude brimming that I couldn't begin to unpack.

"You ever had single malt Scotch?" Cliff asked, raising his eyebrows at me.

I snorted. "Should I know what that is?"

"You will tonight."

"I could use a stiff drink after that shit," Jon agreed. "Or three."

"What happened to 'you can't drink it away'?" I asked, fighting a laugh.

"You can't." Cliff smirked wickedly. "But you can't fault a guy for trying."

The smile he coaxed from me felt traitorous. I rose in the air, still a little wobbly from the healing. I landed on Jon's bent knee and let my wings relax.

"This place looks pretty different from your home, huh?" Jon asked delicately. "Different—but beautiful."

"After everything last night, it's hard to believe how *anything* can be beautiful." I threw both hunters a somber look. They saved lives last night—mine included. In another life, they could be paraded through the streets like heroes. Yet here they were, alone and tending to their wounds. They hadn't even stuck around long enough for the freed victims to thank them.

"Hunting's a nasty world," Cliff said. Stories danced behind his eyes. Savagery and grief. "Thankless and filthy and a straight shot to a brutal death. True freedom can be fucking lonely. But I never felt alive until I hit the road. Made a difference to a few people along the way. That's worth something."

Freedom. The word blossomed slowly in my chest. Suddenly, the smell of the flowers and pine was stronger. A familiar thrum of curiosity sped up my heart as I looked about me. We were mere hours from Elysia, and I was confronted by varieties of trees I had never seen before. Wildflowers bloomed along the bank in periwinkle and cardinal red, nothing like the varieties at home. The petals fluttered in the breeze, tempting me to fly over for a closer look.

No more curfew. No more boundaries. Everything and everywhere awaited.

And if Mother's instructions were to be believed, I wouldn't be giving up my family in exchange for my freedom.

We will find each other again. All will be well.

A tentative seed of hope rooted in my chest.

Shifting, I drew out the rolled-up map from my belt. The curled edges of the yellowed paper fluttered in the light breeze. I held my breath, tracing a finger over the same path Mother had shown me.

"Do you really think you can get me to Aelthorin?" I asked. My mind and heart may have been distant last night, but I had allowed the hunters to study the map. The details were difficult to reconcile with their own maps, but my destination was clearly westward.

"We pinpointed a region in the Rocky Mountains that looks promising," Jon said. "We can start there."

I had only read about mountains and seen the inked images in nomadic journals. The thought of seeing them in person was dizzying.

"Might be taking the scenic route, though," Cliff said. "I've been tracking some activity in Tennessee. People are going missing around Cherokee National Forest. Survivors claim to have heard loved ones' voices in the wilderness just before an attack."

"Ghouls," Jon murmured, his eyes darkening.

"Probably. Not too many things can perfectly imitate human voices. Local legends agree." Cliff quirked an eyebrow at me. "You up for a pit stop or two?"

Though I felt like I would still need several steaming baths before I had fully scrubbed the filth from the werewolf hunt off me, I straightened. People were in danger, and I was not a naive girl collecting trinkets anymore. I was a force to be reckoned with.

"Well, clearly, you need my help," I said with a grand sigh. "I should probably stick around to make sure you don't batter yourself any worse on the next hunt."

Jon's eyebrows lifted, dimple flashing as he laughed. I forced myself not to stare when our eyes caught.

"Who knows, maybe even Aelthorin would be grateful for some protection from monsters," I said, my hopeful tone coming easier.

Cliff snorted. "Listen to that. You may have a little hunter in you, Sylv."

I made a face. "I'll *never* be a hunter. A warrior, though..."I sobered, giving Jon and Cliff a sincere smile. "I think that suits us better."

Warmth thrummed in my chest. *Us*.

"I don't mind the sound of that," Cliff said. "Does a ballad come with the title?"

"Not from me. Get over yourself."

He rolled his eyes, but the crooked grin on his lips stayed. He stood, rubbing the spot on his arm I had healed. Announcing that he was going to stretch his legs and head back to the car, he ambled off.

Cliff's departure left Jon and me in silence for a minute or so. I busied myself by carefully folding up the map and tucking it away. The fragile warmth within me faltered as I stared down the complicated situation that sat between the two of us. We couldn't simply ignore it, not after what we'd been through. Not after I'd kissed him. Any words that I attempted to form felt frail and insufficient.

Jon was the one who cleared his throat and spoke first. "Sylvia, I..." He paused as quickly as he started, sighing heavily. "I understand if you don't want to talk about it yet, but I'm sorry about how things ended with Elysia last night. If I hadn't—"

"Stop," I said sharply enough to make him obey. "This was my doing."

"I'm still sorry," he murmured.

I pursed my lips, trying to pull something coherent from the churning emotions that sat like a lead weight in my stomach. "I'm not. I'm just... afraid for what happens next."

Jon nodded, pensive. "I'm relieved you don't have to figure that out entirely on your own—even if it's for purely selfish reasons."

"Oh?"

"I'd be worried about you if you flew off into the wilderness without so much as a compass. I wouldn't be able to stop wondering if something happened to you the moment we drove off."

"You don't think I could take care of myself?" I teased.

Jon eyed me with unbridled fondness that made me feel like I was incandescent. "I know that anything unlucky enough to cross you will have a very cold and painful end. But I'd prefer to be the one to end the things that threaten you if you'd let me."

My stomach flipped. That was not an empty promise.

He cocked his head, smile turning sheepish and *adorable* in a way that should have been incompatible with someone capable of bruising a werewolf's bones with his bare hands.

"And... I'd miss you," Jon said.

My heart pounded like I was sprinting, but my wings drooped. It was impossible not to fall in love with a smile like that—a smile that would ruin me, I was sure of it.

"What am I supposed to do with that?" I sighed. "With any of… whatever *this* is between us? We're too different."

"I don't know." Jon dragged a hand through his hair, puffing out a breath. "I've tried to fight it. I just know I want to be near you. Even if I shouldn't. Even if it doesn't make sense."

"Really?"

"All the damn time."

The ache in my chest felt like a star collapsing in on itself. Was this what ghosts felt in their eternal wandering? Wanting something so badly you knew could never fully be yours?

"The stars really cursed us together, didn't they?" I muttered, giving him a sad smile. "You had to go and be born a human."

Jon chuckled softly. "Yeah, sorry about that." After a beat, his gaze lifted, smoldering on me. "Sylvia, nearly all my life, I've thought every corner of the world was only filled with darkness. And then… there was you. Full of light and possibility and *good*. And me…" He sighed, his deep voice turning ragged. "I'm so broken."

"What's so wrong with that?" I asked gently.

"You shouldn't want anything to do with me."

"Well, I do."

His lips parted. There was that molten thread that tugged in me when Jon looked at me like that. Seeing me. Letting me see him. He brushed his thumb over my cheek, where the dark Fae markings swirled over my freckled skin. I couldn't draw a full breath.

"I still remember what it felt like to hold you in my arms," Jon whispered like it was a treasured secret. The bittersweet longing in his voice brought a lump to my throat. I bobbed my head ardently—*I remember, too*.

"I was so worried you wouldn't wake up with me," I said.

"I guess humans don't tend to make it back because they don't have someone to help them leave."

"Then... We can go back there," I said, perhaps too eagerly. "We have the rune. My magic isn't finite anymore. We could return to the spectral plane. Both of us."

Jon sucked in a breath. His eyes lit up so readily, I wondered if he hadn't been hoping for this answer. Still, he searched my face carefully. "Without the Ancients... It's safe?"

"Yes." I let my breathless expression mirror his. "We could be together there, even just for a while."

"I'd like that," he said, wearing that crooked grin that drove me crazy. It didn't meet his eyes. He was looking at me like he was already learning to let me go.

I averted my gaze, picking at a line of stubborn dirt beneath my fingernails. I didn't want to lose him so soon. "I've had dreams lately—living life as a human."

His brow knitted. "Not night terrors?"

"No, good ones. *Beautiful.*" I blinked hard, surprised to feel tears gather as I dwelled on a memory that had never been mine to mourn. If I closed my eyes, I could still feel the stars stitched into that midnight blue gown.

My hand slipped into my pocket, fingers closing around the amethyst shard. It hummed at my touch.

"Those stories I told you about gemstones," I said. "Fairies harnessing that raw magic for centuries to do incredible feats. Impossible things."

A heavy pause. "Like your father?"

I nodded. "He fell victim to their allure."

"What was he trying to do?" Jon asked, frowning. "I mean, why was he after so much magic if Elysia has no known enemies?"

"I don't know. I was barely more than a child. I only know the power became seductive. He let himself become obsessed, and after seeing that... I used to be terrified to be anything like a gem scavenger. Most of them lose themselves eventually. But that raw power might be worth the risk. If I could do better, be more careful than Father was…"

There was a chance, however slim, that I could bring down that wall that separated Jon and me. I shuddered out a breath. I braced myself, forcing the words out. "Mother gave me a sliver of a gem. It's not much, but I can *feel* its power. If I found a full-sized gemstone, maybe I could become human."

Jon's eyes widened. "Permanently?"

"I'm not entirely sure, but… I want to know. Even just for a day."

"What about Aelthorin?" he pressed.

I met Jon's gaze, catching the delicate flicker of uncertainty there. Ripples of bittersweet emotion set through me. I felt the same—torn between desire and what might be the better thing to do.

I smiled shyly, pinching my shoulders in a shrug. "Like Cliff said, it's a long journey. Maybe we can figure out a few things as we go. Fairies have a finite number of places we can exist safely, but humans… you've got the whole world. It's tempting, I can't lie."

Any fairy would have gaped at me like I was mad, but Jon's expression warmed like I'd spoken poetry. "I'll back your play," he said. "Whatever you choose."

His words set my heart on fire. I tugged on a lock of my hair, injecting levity into my voice. "Do you think I'd be bad at it? Being human?"

Jon raked me up and down. "It's hard to picture, but I'm sure you'd be a better member of society than most of the humans I know. We'd need to get you some new clothes, though." He tugged on the billowing sleeve of my gossamer top.

"What's wrong with my clothes?" I demanded in mock offense.

"You wouldn't exactly blend in," he said.

"Who says I want to?"

Jon snickered softly before his gaze lifted and fixed on me again. My dream was becoming *his*, too. The longer he looked, the more exhilarated he seemed at the image of me being one of his own kind. Shocked as he was, he hadn't pulled away. His yearning surrounded me like a sweet cloud. I could see his mind at work, trying to piece together the puzzle laid before us. I would not be searching alone.

"What are you thinking right now?" I smirked. "You hunters are so hard to read."

He glanced at the water, then back at me, swallowing hard. "I wish I could kiss you."

Before I could think better of it, I rose on my wings and flew to his face to kiss him on the cheek. "Promise to tell me everything else you want to do to me, too," I whispered.

As I backed away to meet this gaze, his eyes blazed appreciatively. "If we make it back to the spectral plane, I'll show you."

His tone may have been honeyed, but his cheeks were flushed. My stomach flipped happily, shooing away my anxieties and unanswered questions for the moment.

A sportive little smile tugged his lips as he stood and dusted himself off. "Before we head back—where am I on the scary scale now? Final answer." He brushed his fingers over the spot I had kissed. "It *has* to be a zero now."

I scoffed. "*Ten*, actually. You threw yourself into another realm, stood up to the Ancients, and spoke directly to my mother. You are a sight to behold, Jonathan."

We were still grinning by the time we reached the car. Cliff gave us an odd look, but he kept his comments at bay.

Despite my initial flinch at the roar of the engine, delight quickly thrummed in my chest. Music played softly from the radio—having been kept quiet during the somber drive. Subtle was hardly fitting now.

I flitted to the volume knob and gave it an enthusiastic twist to the right before darting aside to choose the music station. Riotous, exhilarating sounds filled my ears, unlike anything I'd ever heard before.

The car set into motion, and I settled on the dashboard. Colors seemed brighter as the bumpy path was replaced by the paved road. It seemed to stretch on forever, winding into the horizon.

I glanced back, breathless. "So. Where to next?"

Hazel

Every night, I woke up to find Sylvia's untouched bed. I made myself pretend she was off breaking the rules, exploring where she shouldn't. But then, I'd wonder. Was she seeing all the places she always wanted to see? Were the hunters treating her nicely?

Was she still alive?

I knew better than to ask Mother any of this. She hardly spoke a word for an entire week after Sylvia left.

Then, something changed. I heard her whispering at night sometimes—talking to herself. During the day, she seemed less sad, but she acted stranger than ever. Almost the way Sylvia did when she was hiding something.

An entire moon cycle dragged along before Mother's strange shift made any sense.

"Hazel." A hand took my shoulder and shook me awake. Wide green eyes drifted into focus over me. "*Hazel.*"

For a wonderful moment, I thought Sylvia was home.

Mother was seated at my side. The room was still dark, but the air was charged in a way I couldn't explain.

"What's going on?" I asked, sitting up.

My bedroom door was open, spilling warm light from the hearth room. Canvas bags were stacked in a line by the stove, brimming with our belongings. Mother smoothed down my messy braid, winding it over my shoulder.

"We're leaving Elysia tonight," she said, a slight wobble in her soft voice. I saw her smile twitch as she continued to stroke my hair comfortingly. "We're going somewhere else. Somewhere safer, where we can find your sister."

A hummingbird felt trapped in my stomach.

"How long will we be gone?" I asked.

Mother's lips pressed into a thin line. "We won't be coming back."

"What about my clothes?" I asked, thinking about my embroidered green trousers and the new boots I had only just grown into properly.

"I've already packed some for you," Mother said.

"But… but…" Even as I tried to come up with something to say, she led me out of bed. This had to be a dream—a *nightmare*. "I have lessons tomorrow morning. My friends…"

They weren't really my friends anymore. They called me names—*traitor* and *human-lover*—since Sylvia left. They cast spells to muddy the ground when I walked by, dirtying my favorite shoes and making me trip. The adults nearby didn't do anything to stop them.

Mother pressed a canvas bag into my arms as tears brimmed in my eyes. "Believe me, Hazel. I wish there were another option, but sometimes, life unfolds in a way that tests our courage. We are forced to make difficult decisions for love."

"I don't understand." I didn't mean to whine, but the thought of stepping through the front door and never coming back seemed impossible.

"My darling," Mother sighed. "We will never see Sylvia again if we don't leave tonight. That is all you need to understand right now."

The promise made me obedient.

"We must move swiftly and silently," Mother said as we crept down the hall. "Do exactly as I tell you. Understand?"

"Yes, Mother." My eyes skated the path before us. Even with the light roots overhead, the winding tunnel looked scarier than usual. I had never left our dwelling at this hour. "Aren't the guards gonna see us?"

Curfew had been strictly enforced with twice as many Entry Watch Guards since Sylvia left. Even they gave me dirty looks when I went about my day.

"They won't see a thing if you follow me."

Mother hurried me through turn after turn until I had no clue where we were. The tunnels became more unkempt. Even though I never snuck out like Sylvia, I thought I knew every passageway in Elysia. Mother found a narrow opening that I didn't even notice. She ushered me in first, but I couldn't walk very far before tangles of roots blocked the path.

Whispering an incantation, she sent a stream of controlled flames ahead to clear the way. Bugs skittered away with fright. I would have begged her to be more careful not to singe the sweet beetles, but she took my shoulder and urged me to keep moving. The scent of burnt roots tickled my nose. Mother sent orb lights ahead to guide our steps.

"What is this place?" I asked. "Is this how Sylvia snuck out?"

"No," Mother said, but she didn't elaborate.

We walked for ages before the passageway opened up to a small room. A few bookshelves were propped against the walls. One had fallen apart completely, spilling books across the floor. The unloved armchairs looked like they might have been cozy once.

Before I could reach for one of the books at my feet, Mother tugged me through an old doorway on the other side of the room.

Fresh air. The tunnel turned steeply upward until we emerged on the forest floor. I squinted around, realizing I could even see the home willow from here. My heart pounded. How could Sylvia stand to break the rules every other night?

"Where are we?" I asked.

"Outside the patrol perimeter," Mother said distractedly. "Can you carry that and still fly, darling?"

Tugging at me once again, Mother brought us to the branches of a nearby tree. After all her hurrying, the world seemed to come to a standstill as she ordered me to wait. I stared into the woods, breaths pooling with anticipation in the cold air. It was the middle of autumn—the nights would soon be unforgiving.

"What are we waiting for?" I asked, wondering if Mother had packed my favorite quilt.

"An old friend." Mother squeezed my hand. "I need you to be as brave as I know you are."

My throat closed. What could be more frightening than sneaking out of Elysia while it was under strict watch? With my mind racing with possibilities, I nearly screamed when I saw something dark move between the trees. I huddled closer to Mother.

"Nothing will harm you," she whispered.

I wanted to cry as the figure moved closer—footsteps beating out a steady rhythm.

"Mother…" I whimpered. "A h-human. We need to hide!"

She didn't answer, squeezing my hand as tightly as I clung to hers. She couldn't be afraid. She was one of the strongest fire affinities in the village. Probably better than Ayden, though I bet he would never admit it.

So why was she shivering?

The approaching figure was a man, but he wasn't Jon or Cliff. My heart sank into my growing pool of fear. Mother's promise to see Sylvia wasn't going to happen right now.

Going against every lesson about avoiding humans, Mother sent out a red orb light to get the man's attention. He turned and headed straight for us. When he was finally close enough for the light to illuminate his features, I buried myself against Mother's arm. I peeked with one eye.

The lower right part of his face and jaw was covered by a scar—a healed burn, maybe. A strange feeling surged through me when I looked at him, but I couldn't make myself look for long. He seemed to carefully measure the space left between us and him. I stared down at the ground as his boots shifted on the dead leaves.

"You came," Mother said. Her tone was crisp, but she sounded relieved, too.

"You still don't trust me? I told you, Mel." The man's voice was low—quieter than the hunters', but still scary. "I'd always come back for you."

There was a heavy pause. When I peeked up, I found him staring right at *me*. I breathed in sharply, fingers digging into my canvas bag.

Be as brave as I know you are.

"Y-you're Mother's friend?" I breathed.

The man's blue eyes flickered, fixing on Mother instead. "Follow me. I'll get you somewhere safe."

ACKNOWLEDGEMENTS

This book has been over ten years in the making. Don't get us wrong—we weren't working on the manuscript itself for a solid decade, but after writing the original *Shot in the Dark* story at the beginning of our friendship, we never stopped thinking about these characters. When we decided it was high time to give Sylvia, Jon, and Cliff a proper shot (haha) at reaching a wider audience, we were only able to accomplish this because of the people at our side.

Our marvelous beta readers: Melanie Bateman and Fabian Moore. Our fabulous editor, Tabitha Chandler | www.tabithadoesediting.com

Our brilliant Stabby Fairy street team and our enthusiastic ARC team. Our spectacular long-time cheerleaders: Indie, Ashley, Fae, Stacy, and Vicki (amongst others!) Our loving friends and family, especially: Peter, Monica, OJ, Avery, Stephanie, Yannel, and the skate group. And, of course, we must thank our sources of inspiration! Eric Kripke for creating Supernatural, and The Basement Yard podcast, who gave us much-needed laugh-out-loud moments during the writing process and whose banter inspired great dialogue for Jon and Cliff.

Finally, thank you dear reader for taking a chance on this book! We sincerely hope you enjoyed the adventure. There are few greater joys than escaping reality collectively through the pages of a good book, and we're honored to share that with you.

ALSO BY

THE RESTORATION PROGRAM

(PUB. 2023)

THE HEART BETWEEN KINGDOMS

(PUB. 2017)

ABOUT THE AUTHORS

Mary Dublin and Anne Kendsley are a best friend and co-author duo that have been writing and adventuring together for over ten years.

Anne Kendsley is a writer from South Texas with a passion for weaving stories that explore the fantastical and surreal.

Growing up, she developed a deep appreciation for the power of storytelling and started writing her own tales at a young age. Her love for fantasy and sci-fi has carried into her writing today, blending with darker, grittier themes.

Ultimately, she loves to explore complex characters who stand resilient against societal breakdown while finding beauty in a harsh and unforgiving world. When she's not devouring one book after another or daydreaming about her next story, she's taking a walk in the woods or cozying up with a video game.

Mary Dublin was born and raised in the heart of Florida and has had a passion for storytelling since childhood. Her love for words began at a young age, where she found solace in books that transported her to fantastical worlds and inspired her to begin dreaming of her own stories.

Apart from writing, Mary is a passionate traveler, and her experiences in different parts of the world inspire elements in her novels. When she's not writing, she can be found practicing yoga, trying new hiking trails, or curled up with a good book on a rainy day.

CONNECT

https://authorsdublinkendsley.com

Sign up for our newsletter on our website for updates, giveaways, and bonus materials— including a playlist for the book you're holding now!

Facebook – facebook.com/marydublinauthor
Tiktok - @authors.dublin.kendsley
Instagram - @authors.dublin.kendsley
Goodreads | Amazon

If you enjoyed our book, please consider leaving a review on Amazon and Goodreads!